THE PERFECT HUSBAND

DANIELLE RAMSAY

First published in Great Britain in 2023 by Boldwood Books Ltd.

Copyright © Danielle Ramsay, 2023

Cover Design by 12 Orchards Ltd

Cover Photography: Shutterstock

The moral right of Danielle Ramsay to be identified as the author of this work has been asserted in accordance with the Copyright, Designs and Patents Act 1988.

All rights reserved. No part of this book may be reproduced in any form or by any electronic or mechanical means, including information storage and retrieval systems, without written permission from the author, except for the use of brief quotations in a book review.

This book is a work of fiction and, except in the case of historical fact, any resemblance to actual persons, living or dead, is purely coincidental.

Every effort has been made to obtain the necessary permissions with reference to copyright material, both illustrative and quoted. We apologise for any omissions in this respect and will be pleased to make the appropriate acknowledgements in any future edition.

A CIP catalogue record for this book is available from the British Library.

Paperback ISBN 978-1-83751-098-6

Large Print ISBN 978-1-83751-099-3

Hardback ISBN 978-1-83751-097-9

Ebook ISBN 978-1-83751-100-6

Kindle ISBN 978-1-83751-101-3

Audio CD ISBN 978-1-83751-092-4

MP3 CD ISBN 978-1-83751-093-1

Digital audio download ISBN 978-1-83751-094-8

Boldwood Books Ltd
23 Bowerdean Street
London SW6 3TN
www.boldwoodbooks.com

To all those who have experienced domestic violence.

'The most dangerous thing of any society is the man who has nothing to lose.'

— JAMES BALDWIN

'There's daggers in men's smiles. The near in blood, The nearer bloody.'

— *MACBETH*: DONALBAIN (ACT II, SCENE III)

'A man attaches himself to woman – not to enjoy her, but to enjoy himself.'

— SIMONE DE BEAUVOIR

'All things are subject to interpretation; whichever interpretation prevails at a given time is a function of power and not truth.'

— FRIEDRICH NIETZSCHE

PROLOGUE

In a disinterested voice, the receptionist asked again: who was I?

But the muffled chaos surrounding me in the A&E at Treliske Hospital in Truro – not a place to be on a Friday night, let alone my wedding night – drowned her out.

I looked at the clock on the wall behind her. Friday 24 June: 10.33 p.m.

Our wedding reception would still be in full swing. I wasn't supposed to be here, not tonight. This day wasn't supposed to end this way.

It's your wedding night... An hour ago, you were living your dream. And now...

I shifted my focus back to her. I tried to speak. But I couldn't find the words, silenced by the trauma of what had happened.

'Your name?' the woman behind the desk repeated, raising her voice.

Desperate, I stared into her dispassionate eyes. But my muted cry for help was lost on her.

Frustrated, she glanced at her watch, then at the gathering, disorderly queue to alert me that time was ticking. Other people needed her attention.

Tears spilled over. Hot, desperate, salty trails of confusion escaped down my cheeks. I wanted to tell her. But—

'Sophie? Just answer her, will you!'

Jay's exasperated tone startled me, waking me up from my shocked state.

He didn't want to be here. He'd made that clear on the way. He'd berated me for wasting time – his time – and spoiling *his* night.

We should still be enjoying our wedding reception. But...

More tears followed as reality kicked in.

Unable to stifle it, I cried out with pain as I looked down at my wrist.

'For Christ's sake, Soph! It's just a sprain!' Jay hissed in a low voice, irritated with me. At the whole situation.

I swallowed back the hurt. There was no point in arguing any more as he refused to believe I was injured.

'Look around you,' he continued as he yanked irritably at his pale pink tie to loosen it off so he could undo the top button of his white shirt. 'These people need medical attention. If it wasn't for you being such a bloody drama queen, we'd still be enjoying ourselves! Some wedding night this has turned out to be!'

I looked behind us and caught the questioning, surprised eyes of an exhausted, young mother, standing, rocking her screaming, scarlet-faced toddler.

I turned my numb gaze to a seated elderly couple as one mumbled something incoherent to the other before they both stared back at me in confusion.

They're gawping at us. Oh God...

Of course, they are: you're in an ivory bodice wedding dress, and Jay's in a sand-coloured linen three-piece suit with leather flip-flops for your perfect beach wedding.

I realised Jay was right. I was making a spectacle of myself. I should never have made a fuss. If I had iced it as he'd suggested, maybe everything would have been all right. We could have continued enjoying our evening instead of me ruining it.

Ruining everything...

Humiliated, I turned back to the receptionist, who was still waiting to register me, accepting I was guilty of wasting her time. But before I managed to apologise and leave, Jay intervened on my behalf.

'Her name is Sophie Bradley.'

'*Mrs* Sophie Bradley,' he added.

It wasn't his disquietingly unfamiliar tone that caught me off guard: it was the surname. His surname – Bradley – threw me. I had planned on keeping my double-barrelled name, preferring it to his.

You're his wife now...

Numb, I listened as he matter-of-factly reeled off my date of birth, and my address, followed by my GP. My life was literally in his hands.

'So, how did your wife injure her wrist?' the receptionist asked him, giving me a sideways glance.

I watched him flash that charismatic smile of his and shrug apologetically.

I waited, my heart accelerating, unsure of what he would say. About me. About how...

I stopped myself from plunging back into the dangerous, dark watery depths. Now wasn't the time or place to evaluate what had happened. I doubted I would ever be able to make sense of it. It was as if I was looking through a mirror at myself in another multiverse reality; for this wasn't my life. I didn't recognise it. It jarred with me, and no matter how I dissected it, I couldn't piece it back together the way it was before. Maybe this was what it was like to lose your mind.

Or maybe I was Alice Through the Looking Glass, and logic didn't exist any more? Because what was happening to me didn't make sense, not tonight of all nights.

'Champagne went to her head,' confided Jay, leaning in towards her.

The receptionist nodded. 'And how much alcohol has your wife consumed?'

Jay shrugged. But at the same time, he raised his eyebrows. Without a word, he damned me.

'Can you give an estimate?' she asked.

'Enough for her to fall over and...'

How could he say that to her? As if it was all my fault...

'Ah, I see.'

I felt the tell-tale beads of sweat on my forehead and the blood draining from my face. I couldn't tell whether I would pass out or throw up from the shock. Maybe both.

The reality of why I was here on my wedding night, missing my wedding reception, hit me.

The woman behind the desk turned in my direction. 'Do you need to sit down?' she suddenly asked, concerned.

I shook my head, mumbling, 'The bathroom?'

'There's a unisex toilet down the corridor to your left,' she advised.

Don't be sick! Oh God... Not here.

I noted Jay give her a look of vindication before I turned away. My dress swished in protest at the sudden movement as my flip-flops slapped against the harsh, sterile, tiled floor. I felt eyes, fascinated, curious and judgemental, scrutinising me as I rustled my way through the unforgiving, brightly lit waiting room.

I paused and turned for Jay, but he was conspiratorially talking with the receptionist. Hurt cut through me. I unintentionally locked eyes with the young mother, whose knowing expression made me feel ashamed and embarrassed that my husband didn't care enough to follow me.

I found the unisex toilet and forced the heavy door open with my bare shoulder as I cradled my left arm under my chest. I could see the misplaced bone bulging through the unbroken, now darkly mottled skin, accounting for the relentless throbbing. But their words drowned out the pain:

'And how much alcohol has your wife consumed?'

'Enough for her to fall over and...'

How could you say that to her, Jay? How could you lie?

I felt the acidic bile rising from the back of my throat. I locked the door behind me and headed over to the toilet before collapsing on the floor, not caring about my dress.

I bent my head over the toilet bowl, spitting out what was in my mouth, and waited for the nauseous feeling to pass. I then leaned my head back against the wall and shallowly breathed out. I could feel my body trembling as I sat there, eyes closed, tears threatening to spoil my perfectly applied make-up. Frustration, fear and panic pummelled through my veins, reverberating in my ears.

How did you end up here at Treliske Hospital in your wedding dress with a broken wrist, Sophie? How?

But I knew how. As did Jay.

Contrary to Jay's opinion, I wasn't drunk. I had never felt soberer in my life.

The pain escalated, forcing me to look at my wrist again, but my left hand caught my attention.

'Oh God,' I muttered.

Why didn't I think about removing them when it happened?

I tugged and tugged, gouging at the swollen flesh until the rings finally came off.

I stared at the bespoke silver engagement ring with three opening flower petals, each with a large diamond embedded in the centre. Jay had bought it from Silver Origins Jewellery Boutique in St Ives, surprising me with the unusual ring after proposing on Porthtowan Beach. I knew he was the one and ecstatically said yes.

The same jewellers had also designed our matching silver wedding rings with the eight sparkling diamonds circling the wedding ring. Each diamond represented the months we had been together before we married. Jay spent those eight months adoring me, blinding me with his love. I was everything to him. And much more... Or so he said.

And he was to me. He was my soulmate. My best friend. My person.

So how could he do this to you?

I suddenly felt as if I couldn't breathe. Struggling, I gasped for air as I choked on strangled sobs. Mascara-stained tears started to trail down, threatening to discolour my ivory silk dress. Not that I cared. Not now.

This wasn't how it was supposed to be... Not on your wedding night.

I clasped the silver and diamond rings tightly in my right hand as tears cascaded down my cheeks.

Why aren't you checking on me, Jay? Why have you left me alone when I am hurt? And when you did this to me...

More tears slipped down my face as I tormented myself with that question.

He had my phone. He had taken it for safekeeping earlier, so he knew I couldn't contact anyone. He was all I had and he knew that.

* * *

I didn't know how long I sat there until there was a discreet rap at the door.

It stung that it had taken him this long to see if I was all right.

'Mrs Bradley?' a female voice inquisitively called out.

A wave of disappointment coursed through me.

'Sophie? Sophie Bradley?'

I hesitated. 'Yes?'

'Can you unlock the door?'

I somehow managed to get to my feet and walked over to the door. Releasing the lock, I stepped back out of the way.

A short, dark-haired nurse in blue scrubs with a lanyard around her neck peeked her head around the door.

'Sophie?' she gently asked, smiling. 'I'm Zara, one of the A&E nurses.'

I nodded.

'You must be in a lot of pain. Let's get that wrist X-rayed, shall we?'

'Where's my husband?'

I hoped she would say he was frantic with worry and had sent her to look for me.

Instead, her reply confirmed my suspicions.

'I believe he's outside the hospital grounds having a cigarette. At least, that's what the receptionist told me.'

I could hear the embarrassment in her voice. After all, shouldn't he be looking after me?

I felt a knot of panic at the thought that perhaps he had left me here. I refrained from telling her that Jay didn't smoke as I didn't want her to pity me more than she already did.

'Poor you! What a day for this to happen, eh?' she gently sympathised. She smiled at me as she looked at my dress. 'It's a beautiful wedding dress.'

I turned and looked at my reflection in the mirror above the sink. I didn't recognise myself. My face was blotchy, and my eyes were red-rimmed, puffy and smudged with eyeshadow and black mascara. My curly, long blonde hair was coming loose from its intricate pinned knot and was hanging in disarray in frizzy spirals. The red rosebuds that the hairdresser had painstakingly attached to my hair were now limp and precariously dangling. I stared at the dress, hating what it now embodied. When I had first tried it on, it was so perfect. So beautiful. It had made me feel desirable and sophisticated. Yet, now... I felt the air catch at the back of my throat at the realisation that I had never looked so bewildered. So shocked. So...

How could this have possibly happened?

'You're the first bride we've ever had here at Treliske,' the nurse said, in an attempt to cheer me up.

It didn't work. More tears trailed down my face.

All that I could think about was my new husband's lack of concern. I wondered whether it surprised her, but she was too embarrassed to say anything.

His wedding vow echoed in my head:

'I, Jay Donald Bradley, take you, Sophie Blair Kennedy, to be my wife, to have and to hold, from this day forward, for better for worse, for richer, for poorer, in sickness and in health, to love and cherish always.'

How could he break those promises?

The part I didn't understand was how could he have radically changed seven hours after the ceremony?

What happened to you, Jay? What happened to the man I fell in love with and married?

'Hey, come on. It's unlucky to cry on your wedding night. It will all be all right.'

I wanted to yell at her: *I am injured in the hospital, missing my wedding reception. I will never get that back. Never! So how can it possibly ever be all right? And worse, my husband has left me alone and in pain. And he...*

'How about we get that wrist X-rayed?' she urged.

I broke away from my reflection, turning to her. 'Can you take these for me? To keep them safe until...' My voice faltered as I opened my palm to show her my rings.

'Of course,' she replied. 'I'll put them somewhere safe until you're ready to be discharged.'

I nodded.

'Once we confirm it's broken, the doctor will sort out pain relief and put it in a cast. And a hot tea with two sugars will make all the difference. Trust me,' she assured. 'I'll make you one in a proper mug, not that lukewarm insipid stuff out of the vending machines. Okay?' she said, holding the door open for me.

I gave her a forced smile of appreciation. 'Thank you,' I somehow mumbled.

'Least I can do given what's happened, my love.'

* * *

I waited for Jay to say something – anything – but he continued scrolling through his phone, ignoring me.

'Can you pass me mine, please?' I asked.

No reaction.

'Jay?' I urged.

He hadn't talked to me since joining me in the small room after my X-ray while I waited for a doctor to assess the injury. Nor had he apologised for leaving me alone.

I looked around the shadowy room at the other empty chairs.

'Jay?' I repeated.

'What?' he snapped.

'My phone?'

He looked at me as if he had no idea what I was talking about.

'You took my phone earlier. You put it in your jacket. Remember?' I reminded him.

He shook his head.

'Jay? Seriously? Give me my phone? My mother will be worried.'

'I don't have your bloody phone, all right?'

'I saw you put it in your jacket,' I argued, starting to panic.

He blanked me.

'Jay? You promised me you would look after it?'

'I can't trust a word that comes out of your mouth.'

'What?' I spluttered. 'How can you even say that?'

'Because you're a fucking drunken, old trollop! That's how.'

His words took my breath away. I stared in disbelief.

'What did you call me?'

'A FUCKING DRUNKEN, OLD TROLLOP!' he yelled.

Shocked, tears pricked my eyes. I had never heard Jay use such language before. How could he have said such unrecognisable, hateful words?

To me. About me. *Me.* His new wife.

And would he have said that in front of other people?

His best man, Tom's ominous words last night came back to me: *'Are you certain you want to marry him?'*

What did Tom know about Jay to ask me such a question?

'Your best man warned me about you,' I fired back without thinking.

'He what? You better be lying!' growled Jay.

I looked up, embarrassed, as Zara, the nurse who had taken me for my X-ray, entered the room.

'Sophie? I've got your results back.'

'About time. Can we go home now?' demanded Jay.

'Actually, Mr Bradley, if you can come over here, please?'

instructed the nurse as she placed the X-ray against the screen. She switched the light on, illuminating the bones in my left hand and arm.

I noted the icy tone in her voice.

Not that Jay was bothered. He was above caring what other people thought of him.

He sighed with irritation as he stood up. I noted his puffy, bloodshot eyes, the half-unbuttoned waistcoat, lopsided loose tie and creased jacket under one arm. I realised from his dishevelled appearance he must be feeling hungover, considering the countless shots he had knocked back earlier at the bar.

'I said it wasn't broken. Bloody waste of time and a wedding!' he stated.

'Actually, there are two serious fractures in Sophie's wrist. Here and here,' she pointedly said.

He didn't say a word. But the flash of annoyance in his eyes said it all.

I waited for an apology, or at least a recognition of my injury. Nothing.

You did this to me... On our wedding night. How could you not have any remorse?

He folded his arms as he looked at the nurse. 'So, what now?'

'We need to reset the bone and fit a cast,' Zara explained. She then turned to me. 'But first, the doctor will need to anaesthetise your wrist in order to do this. Okay?'

I nodded.

'I can stay with you, if you want?'

'Thank you,' I said, avoiding Jay's glare.

I wasn't scared. Not here. Not now. But I was terrified of what would happen when we went to the bridal suite we had booked. For I would be returning married to a man I didn't recognise. To a man who hours earlier had vowed to love and adore me forever.

To protect me.

I felt as if I was barely clinging to my sanity. Jay had convinced everyone he was the perfect partner. And up until a few hours ago, he had had me truly convinced as well.

How could you have ended up in Treliske Hospital with a double fracture to your left wrist on your wedding night? How was that possible? How could your husband of literally eight hours have done this to you?

Shocked, I stared at the X-ray with one question on my mind: who had I married?

PART ONE

'We live in a fantasy world, a world of illusion. The great task in life is to find reality.'

— IRIS MURDOCH

1

THE EVE OF THE WEDDING

'I'm no good at making speeches, so I'll make this brief,' Jay began as he scraped his chair back.

I looked at him as he stood up. He had never looked more at ease with himself, basking in the attention as he glanced around the small gathering. We had chosen not to have a stag or hen party, preferring this intimate dinner on the eve of our wedding.

We sat outside Blue Bar down by Porthtowan Beach under the bejewelled night sky as the candles on our table danced for us in the warm breeze, adding a dreamy, contented glow to everyone's faces. The bubbling, happy chatter of other people enjoying the balmy evening floated on the air around us.

I let my eyes drift to the idyllic view of the expansive beach and the Atlantic Ocean, combined with the backdrop noise of the waves lazily lapping against the golden, shimmering sand under what was the breathtakingly brightest and lowest-hanging full moon I had ever seen.

It was perfect.

Too perfect maybe?

I discounted the unease I felt, dismissing it as pre-wedding nerves. I was terrified that something was going to go wrong.

I looked around our small collection of guests. We didn't need lots of people or a lavish venue. We had the sublime, rugged and dramatic North Cornish coastline and azure blue ocean as our wedding backdrop and the people dearest to us to witness it. My two best friends from my university days, Anna and Grace, had driven together from London for my wedding, and my mother and sister, Liv, had flown in to Newquay from Edinburgh to be with me this weekend. The four of them were all staying at the atmospheric and historic Driftwood Spars by Trevaunance Cove, where Jay and I had booked the bridal suite for the following evening. We were unsure as to when completion contracts would exchange on our new property and had booked the rooms as our rental flat overlooking the play park by the beach in Porthtowan only had one bedroom.

I knew that the Driftwood Spars would be as much of a hit with our guests as it was with us. The impressive beams, or spars, hence the name, were salvaged from shipwrecks along the coast and formed the construction of the Driftwood in the 1650s. It had been a tin mining warehouse, amongst other uses, before being converted into a pub and hotel in the early 1900s. Filled with character, it was one of our favourite haunts to enjoy a few drinks and listen to live local music surrounded by centuries-aged wood and walls steeped in history. It was a magical, evocative, otherworldly place; especially when the sea mist rolled up from the cove while the wood-burning stove roared and hissed inside the Driftwood, warming stray guests from the wet and cold unfurling fingers of the sneaking, suffocating fog or the driving rain and howling wind. At times like that, as the windows rattled and the beams groaned, I could imagine the lost souls caught in the eye of a storm, eventually shipwrecked against the harsh rocky Cornish coastline and washed, bloated, ashore or forever restless on the ocean's bed.

It had been a difficult decision choosing the wedding venue, Porthtowan, like St Agnes, was a North coast Cornish beach, a popular destination for surfers, with its fine golden sand, imposing dunes and impressive cliffs. Jay had proposed to me on the beach. Blue Bar, with its adjacent Boardroom with a bar and seating for up to 100 guests, was an ideal wedding venue with the beach and ocean on its doorstep. We had also just bought a house overlooking the breathtaking valley below with the beach that stretched for nearly 1.5 miles at low tide. But it was the Driftwood Spars, with its beautiful high garden with a wooden-style altar overlooking the stunning Trevaunance Cove, St Agnes' main beach, that had won us over. Instead of being married at the registry office in Truro, the registrar would officiate the wedding in the garden of the Driftwood Spars, which was part of the hotel's wedding package. Given the short notice of the wedding, we were fortunate they could fit us in tomorrow due to a cancellation, unlike Blue Bar, whose bookings ran through the entire summer and the following one.

My wedding to Jay was the antithesis of the wedding Ben, my ex, and I had planned. My mother was involved in its organisation, unlike this one. Jay had insisted that he take charge of ours, giving me the much-needed time to work on my latest romance novel, which was due in to my editor. Jay was a musician and currently out of work and so had the time to organise everything, even down to the photographer, wedding breakfast, cake and the live music. If left to my mother, my wedding would have been a much more extravagant affair. Our small budget was a significant factor in restricting the size of the occasion and forgoing a honeymoon. Much to my mother and Liv's disappointment, I refused to postpone it to save for a more lavish event.

Jay was happy that our wedding bore no resemblance to the

expensive and excessive day my ex and I had booked and had made a point of making ours as minimalistic as possible. I repeatedly worried about Jay not involving my mother and sister in the wedding plans, only to be persuaded by him that this was about us and not them. He also pointed out that I was worried about nothing, as they would understand. I looked up at him, about to make a speech and couldn't help smiling. We were here because of Jay and his efforts to bring all of us together the night before our wedding.

'Firstly, I want to say thank you to Tom, for agreeing to be my best man, tomorrow,' Jay said, standing up. 'You're like a brother to me.'

'A much younger brother, I'm assuming?' Tom asked with a cheeky grin.

Jay laughed, as did the rest of the table.

However, I noted a subtle flash of annoyance in Jay's eyes. He was sensitive when it came to his age. He spent time with his appearance, priding himself on not looking his years. He also dressed and acted more youthful than his age.

'Anyway,' Jay continued, 'thanks, Tom. I owe you, mate!'

Tom raised his pint to Jay. 'Any time, bro!'

Jay turned his smile on my mother and sister.

'And to you, Joanna and Liv, as you will have noticed, I have no family present, so thank you for letting me be a part of yours. I lost my mother last year, which devastated me. But now I have you, Joanna,' he said, putting his hands together and nodding to her in gratitude.

I turned my attention to my mother, who politely smiled in return. However, I could see from her restrained expression that she didn't receive his words warmly. Jay was nine years my mother's junior and much closer to her in age than he and I, so his words failed to either compliment or impress.

Picking up on her coolness, he added, 'Not that you look old enough to be Sophie or even Liv's mother, can I add! You're far too beautiful and young to be my mother-in-law.'

I felt a sudden wave of jealousy take hold at the realisation that he was flirting with her. I could see it in his eyes and infectious smile.

Oh my God...

However, my mother's expression remained impassive, making me doubt the thought.

Not that he noticed my disquiet.

I conceded that Jay was trying to seduce my mother with flattery into liking him. I had noted from the moment we met that he was flirtatious. Jay had repeatedly assured me that it was harmless as he was devoted to me.

I had seen photographs of him as a lead guitarist in his twenties, and he had been a striking-looking young man who I imagined attracted a lot of attention. He still desired that adulation despite age robbing him of his coveted chiselled attractiveness.

'And now to dear Liv,' Jay began, as he beamed at her. 'I was an only child and always wished for a sister. Now I have you, and I couldn't be happier to be a big brother. If anyone bothers you, you let me know, all right? And that includes my best man. I'm watching you, Tom!' Jay laughed in Tom's direction, who was halfway through taking a mouthful of beer and ended up coughing in reaction.

Jay suddenly turned his focus from Tom to me.

He waited for a beat before speaking, holding my expectant gaze.

'Sophie,' he gently began, 'I knew the moment that we locked eyes in The Slaughtered Lamb in Clerkenwell eight months ago that we were meant to be together. My mother and father married in their mid-thirties and had me in their late thirties. I was such a shock to them that they never dared risk having another child,' he shared, laughing. 'They were the most amazing parents, and they showed me the meaning of love every minute of every day. My father adored my mother and she equally adored him. They were lost without each other, so much so, when my father died three years ago, my mother was never the same. She had lost her soulmate. Her person. I never understood what that was until I met you,' Jay stated, gazing intently down at me. 'They waited until they found each other, and that's what I did, I waited... But I never expected to find what they had. Never. Until you walked into my life and changed it forever.'

I tried to swallow back the tears threatening to come as his heartfelt words overwhelmed me.

He reached out for my hand and, taking hold of it, continued, 'You are my soulmate. You are my person, Sophie Blair Kennedy. Without you, I am nothing. To my future wife, tomorrow can't come soon enough.'

Overcome, I wiped at the tears that slid down my face.

'I love you,' I mouthed as I raised my glass to him.

Grace and Anna cheered and applauded before raising their glasses of champagne to us. I noted my mother politely smile as she raised her glass. Liv watched me, seemingly surprised at my reaction. I nodded at her glass which was still on the table, for her to raise it, which she did. She struggled with the idea that I was marrying Jay, someone she barely knew or liked, and not my ex-fiancé, Ben. My decision had devastated her as no one could compare to Ben in her eyes. My ex had been in Liv's life for eleven years. At the age of twenty-five, most of her teen years involved him as part of our family. We had met at uni in London and had become friends first for a few years, before becoming romantically involved. When Ben and I split up, it wasn't just me he was leaving behind; it was also Liv, who he had equally doted on as if she were his sibling.

'Soph?' Grace prompted me.

'Jay summed it up all perfectly. I can't follow that?' I answered, knowing that she expected me to follow suit.

'Come on, Sophie! You're good with words?'

Jay looked at me as he sat down and squeezed my hand.

I could feel Liv's doubting eyes on me, scrutinising my every move for a sign that I had lost my mind. After all, Jay and I had only known each other for eight months and were now getting married. This short time confirmed for her it was rebound, not love, that influenced my decision. Even at this eleventh hour, she waited, ever hopeful, for me to cancel the wedding.

I raised my glass of champagne to our guests and then turned to Jay. I stared for a moment into his glistening, adoring eyes before speaking, 'Love is composed of a single soul inhabiting two bodies.'

'Babes, you are so special,' Jay murmured as he leaned in and slowly kissed me.

'Ahh, Sophie!' Grace cried out.

'That's so beautiful,' murmured Anna.

I pulled back and smiled at Grace and Anna. 'Thank Aristotle!'

Neither Grace nor Anna really knew Jay. They had met him a couple of times when we were still in London, but hadn't seen us since we'd moved to Cornwall. But I could tell that they both liked him, despite his obvious differences to Ben. Unlike Liv, they were more accepting of my new choice of husband.

'Thanks for coming,' I said to them. 'It wouldn't have been the same without the two of you,' I added.

Anna raised an eyebrow at me. 'You mean you wouldn't have anyone to help you with your make-up and fitting into your dress?'

I smiled at her. 'I just want my two best friends to be there with me on what will be one of the happiest days of my life.'

'And we will be,' Anna assured me. 'But, sticking with tradition, don't you think you should stay at the hotel with us tonight?'

Anna quickly glanced at Grace. It was obvious they must have discussed it before Jay had picked them up.

'There is only one person I want to spend my last night as an unmarried woman with, and he's sat right next to me,' I answered, turning and lightly kissing Jay on his cheek.

He responded by gently squeezing my hand. We'd discussed it and decided we couldn't bear to be separated, even for one night.

'You know it's bad luck for the groom to see the bride before the wedding?' my mother teased.

'I'm sure we'll be just fine,' I reassured her.

The plan was for Jay to take me to the Driftwood Spars in the morning. Our wedding ceremony began at 4 p.m., allowing me to spend the day with them. I had booked us a spa and beauty treatment for the morning and a champagne lunch.

I could feel the excitement building at the prospect that tomorrow evening, at this time, we would be married.

It didn't seem real.

* * *

An hour later, everyone was tired and ready to call it a night. I noted that Tom had drunk a considerable amount, which wasn't like him. Not that I knew him that well. He had met Jay in Blue Bar the first week we had moved here. Tom was a guitarist and played in a local band and so Jay had immediately hit it off with him.

'What's wrong with Tom?' I whispered, leaning into Jay.

He looked at me, not sure what I meant.

'He looks really down,' I answered.

'He's just had too much to drink, that's all.'

'Are you sure?'

Jay shrugged. 'I don't know? Maybe he's got girlfriend trouble.'

'I didn't know he was seeing anyone,' I replied. 'Otherwise, I would have invited her tomorrow.'

'No, it's fine. He hasn't mentioned anyone in particular. I'm just surmising, Soph. Don't worry about it. He's cool.'

I looked across at Tom's slumped figure sat on the bottom stone step leading up to the bar. He was staring into the blackness of the shapeshifting dunes ahead.

'Look, I'm going to round everyone up and get them back to the hotel. If you're that worried about Tom, ask if he wants dropping off? Tell him the taxi is arriving soon. I'm sure we could fit him in as I booked an eight-seater minibus.'

'Sure,' I replied.

I stood up and headed towards the steps.

'Hey, Tom?' I called out as I walked down and sat next to him.

'Soph,' he slurred.

'You, okay?' I found myself asking.

'I don't know,' he replied.

'You want to talk about it?'

'I dunno.'

'You know I'm here if you need someone to talk to,' I offered.

He nodded.

'Jay said if you want a lift home, we're leaving now.'

He morosely shook his head. 'Nah, I need some air and time on my own.'

'Sure,' I replied, about to stand up.

Before I did, he grabbed my arm. 'Are you certain you want to marry him?'

'Who? Jay?' I asked, shocked.

His question came out of nowhere.

Tom intensely stared at me and waited.

'Of course, I do,' I replied, feeling very uncomfortable. 'Why?'

He shook his head and looked across at the blackness of the

imposing dunes that seemed to inch ever closer. A storm had deposited the disruptive, changeable hills of sand the other day, hiding the beauty of the beach beyond.

I sat in silence next to him.

'What do you really know about him?' he asked, turning to me.

Once I had gathered my thoughts, I defensively answered, 'Enough.'

He didn't look convinced.

'What the hell, Tom? You're his best man?' I questioned.

'I know,' he thickly muttered.

'He thinks a great deal of you, even though you've only known each other for four months,' I stated.

Tom shook his head. 'No, he's been coming to Porthtowan during the summer now for some years. Not that we were mates back then or anything.'

'He has?' I questioned, unable to keep the surprise out of my voice.

I felt the perfection of the night slipping away.

My mind went into overdrive as waspish voices hurtled questions from every direction.

How could that be possible?

Jay had never mentioned coming here to me before. As far as I knew, he had never visited Cornwall until I'd surprised him with a long weekend in St Ives for his birthday. He then fell in love with the Cornwall I had known from childhood. We had come across Porthtowan during our stay, and Jay had surprised me by suddenly proposing to me on the beach. Cornwall, and Porthtowan in particular, had so seduced him that we were now living here.

We found this place together.

'You're a good person, Soph. Way too good for him. I felt duty-bound to ask you. I know stuff about him that you don't know. He's not who you think he—'

'Hey, bro,' Jay suddenly called out from the top of the steps, cutting Tom off. 'You coming or what?'

Tom dragged himself up and, ignoring Jay, staggered off down the road.

'Tom?' Jay shouted out after him.

Tom continued walking away.

'What did you say?' Jay asked when he reached me.

'Nothing,' I answered. 'Tom said he wanted to be on his own.'

'The walk home might help sober him up,' Jay suggested.

'He was really weird,' I confided.

'How so?'

'I don't know...' I faltered, shrugging, trying to shake off the feeling of disquiet that had settled around me. 'He asked me how well I knew you,' I finally admitted.

'That's a crazy question.'

'I know, I'm worried about him,' I admitted. 'He said you've been coming to Porthtowan during the summer months for years?'

Jay laughed at this revelation. 'That's what he said?'

I nodded.

'Oh babes, he's drunk. You can't trust a word coming out of his mouth. You know everything there is to know about me. Don't you think I would have mentioned to you if I had already visited Cornwall when you surprised me with that birthday weekend here? He's mistaken me with someone else, that's all.' Smiling, he cupped my face in his hands. 'You're stunning, Sophie Blair Kennedy. You know that?'

I shook my head.

'You are, which is why Tom's so upset that he missed out with you. He's jealous of the fact that I'm so much older than him, and yet, I'm the one who is getting married to you. You're beautiful, clever and successful. Haven't you seen the way Tom looks at you? He's obsessed with you.'

'No, he's not,' I argued, feeling embarrassed.

'I promise you that he is and right now he's very drunk and feeling a tad sorry for himself.'

I didn't reply.

'I love you, Sophie. God, I love you with such an intensity that I know my heart would stop beating if anything happened to you.'

Edgar Allan Poe's haunting words echoed through my mind: 'We loved with a love that was more than love.'

For I equally loved Jay with such a force that it terrified me. Fear of something – or someone – destroying what we had instilled me with absolute terror.

Tom's drunken conversation awakened in me a sense of dread. An acknowledgement that what I had with Jay could easily be destroyed. I could feel the darkness that absorbed Tom, edging ever closer.

Jay suddenly leaned in and passionately kissed me as Tom's surprising question replayed in my head: *'Are you certain you want to marry him?'*

His words made no sense.

What did Tom know about Jay that I didn't know?

2

THE DAY AFTER THE WEDDING

'Come on. It's here,' Jay informed me, checking his phone.

Bleary-eyed, I looked at him as he drained his coffee and then stood up. We were waiting in the emergency room in A&E for a taxi.

I felt dreadful. The shock of my injury and the events leading up to it had taken their toll. It was also now 6 a.m., and I was sleep-deprived. It had taken longer than the nurse had anticipated for an available doctor to reset the fractures and put a cast on my arm and hand. Friday night at Treliske Hospital had turned out to be busy, and other patients with more pressing injuries had taken precedence.

I accepted that I no doubt looked as horrific as I felt. Not that I cared. Not any more. I was in survival mode now. All I wanted were painkillers and sleep, in that order.

Jay impatiently looked at me. 'Are you coming or what?'

'Do you have my rings?' I asked, resisting the urge to tell him that I would rather gouge my eyes out than go anywhere with him. But desperation forced me to accept that, without my phone or money, I had no other choice but to leave with him.

I watched as he felt inside his jacket.

'Yup. Now hurry up. I don't want the taxi to leave without us,' he instructed.

I watched him head out of the hospital exit without me, wondering whether my marriage was over before it had even started.

The thought of what I would tell people made my cheeks flush. It was insane. No one would believe me. Even I was struggling to make sense of it all. Jay had told the hospital staff I'd tripped over my wedding dress train, falling backwards, breaking my fall with my left wrist and consequently fracturing it in two places.

He didn't tell them that hours after marrying him, he snapped your wrist, breaking the bone, Sophie. Then you stumbled backwards, shocked, horrified and in pain. That's why you tripped and fell. But your wrist was already broken – by him. By the man everyone assumed was the perfect husband.

I suddenly felt ridiculous sitting alone wearing a fitted boned bodice wedding dress with a long, ivory silk train. I gathered the excess material with my one good hand and stood up. I slowly breathed out, trying to regulate my shallow breathing and rapid heart rate.

I knew the source of my sudden anxiety; I had no idea what had happened to the man I fell in love with and married. His personality had radically changed hours after exchanging our vows. There was no forewarning, no red flags in the months, let alone days, leading up to yesterday. Nothing precipitated him calling me such vile, hurtful names. Misogynistic slurs that I couldn't bring myself to repeat.

Tears stung my eyes as an acknowledgement of his hatred of me cut another inch deeper. I was so ashamed that he had called me something so extreme that I knew I couldn't tell anyone. My humiliation would be my gaoler.

Not that anyone would believe me, anyway. Jay went out of his way to make people like him. And it worked. No one had a bad word to say about him. And why would they? Until last night, Jay had been the perfect partner and my best friend. He was the person I had come to trust, to confide in, and I was reeling from that loss.

He was my person...

I stepped out of the hospital, blinking in the bright, intrusive sunlight as I tried to get my bearings. Everything looked so different from last night.

I spotted a taxi idling in the emergency bay and headed towards it. Jay was already sat in the front with the driver. He buzzed his window down.

'Come on! What took you so long?' he complained.

I opened the back door and somehow managed to get in, dragging the silk train, one-handed, behind me.

'Well, I've never picked up a bride and groom from Treliske Hospital. This is a first!' the taxi driver commented, surprised. 'Do you need help, my lover?' he then asked, seeing me struggle with one arm in a plaster cast as I tried to fasten my seat belt.

'She's fine,' answered Jay on my behalf, ignoring my struggle.

Eventually, it clicked in place.

'Can I ask what happened?' the driver questioned.

Before I had a chance to reply, Jay cut in. 'She tripped over the wedding dress. Too much champagne, eh, Sophie? Lucky for you we were on the beach. It could have been worse.'

I stared at the back of his head, unable to articulate the words raging through my mind: *Lucky for who? You? Because there was no one there to witness you breaking my wrist?*

'Do you know Eastcliff in Porthtowan?' Jay asked the taxi driver.

The driver nodded. 'Yeah, picked up some holidaymakers from

Truro train station to that holiday let up there the other week,' he shared, pulling away.

'Aren't we going to the Driftwood Spars in St Agnes?' I asked, confused.

'Eastcliff Cottage is on the same road further up from the holiday let,' Jay stated, ignoring me.

'Jay? Why aren't we going to the hotel?'

'Because we'll only have a few hours before we check out,' he replied without looking at me.

'But I wanted to see my mum and sister. And Grace and Anna. They'll all be worried about me. I thought we could at least have breakfast with them,' I reasoned.

'The last thing I want to do is sit in a hotel dining room watching everyone eating breakfast while they interrogate us. I'm exhausted, Sophie!'

'But—'

He cut me off. 'We're going home!'

A heavy, protracted silence followed.

I turned and looked back at where I'd spent my wedding night because of him: Treliske Hospital, located on the outskirts of Truro city.

The grand stature of Truro's iconic three spires in the distance caught my wistful eye. They belonged to the impressive and beautiful architecture of Truro's majestic cathedral, which reached out of the steep valley surrounding the city. Internally, the cathedral was equally visually breathtaking; vaulted throughout with an awe-inspiring gothic arch that pulled your attention away from the long aisle when you entered and immediately up to the roof. My mother would have preferred our wedding to have taken place in the imposing cathedral rather than the more bohemian setting of the Driftwood Spars. However, the gothic revival architecture of the cathedral didn't appeal to Jay, unlike the natural beauty of St Agnes beach, dominated by dramatic high cliffs to the north and the reminders of its mining heritage.

'Beautiful views of Porthtowan Beach and the cliffs up that way!' the taxi driver cheerily commented, filling in the stifling stillness.

'Yeah. We fell in love with the views first, didn't we, babes? Blew us away!'

His happy-go-lucky banter shocked me. It was as if nothing had happened.

Maybe he genuinely believes you broke your wrist when you fell?
No... He knows what he did, Sophie.

I swallowed back the tears, remembering the snapping, brittle sound of a twig underfoot as he twisted my wrist too hard, too far.

'You're not from here?' the taxi driver questioned.

'Nope. Manchester, and my wife's from the east coast of Scotland.'

'What made you move here? Not that anyone needs a reason. The place is magical.'

'Yeah, Cornwall definitely worked its magic on us,' Jay said, laughing. 'But my wife is a writer, aren't you, Sophie?'

I don't respond. The last thing I wanted to do was talk about my writing.

Jay looked back at me for confirmation.

I felt forced to respond. 'Yes,' I mumbled.

He smiled at me, his eyes filled with pride, catching me off guard.

The driver looked in the rear-view mirror at me. 'Are you famous, then?'

I shook my head. 'Nope. Sorry.'

'Come on, babes! She's being really modest! She's a well-known romance writer. She wrote that bestseller just out called *Winter's Child*. You must know the one? Its film rights have just been sold.'

I didn't correct Jay that my agent was still negotiating the film rights. There was a world of difference. Jay knew that, but he liked to big things up. I had found his optimistic spin endearing. Now, I saw it for what it was – grandiose lies.

'Nah. Not into romance, me. The wife is though. What's your name, and I'll ask her if she knows you?'

'Sophie B. Kennedy. I bet your wife's read her books,' Jay assured him.

The taxi driver nodded. 'I'm sure she will have done. She reads two books a week. I keep saying to her, "I don't know where you find the time." I certainly don't have enough hours in the day to work as it is, never mind to read.'

'Same, mate. I'm not a reader. Too bloody busy! In fact, I've never read a book.'

'And your wife's an author?'

I watched as Jay shrugged, unembarrassed. 'Don't have the time. Not that she minds. Do you, Soph? I mean, she runs all her plots by me anyway. So, when you've helped write the book, why would you bother reading it?'

I felt my breath catch at the back of my throat at his casual statement. It couldn't have been further from the truth. I resisted the urge to contradict him.

'So, what do you do, if you don't mind me asking?' the taxi driver continued.

I waited in the back for Jay's response. Cynicism coursed through me like poison. I realised that the wound Jay had opened in me was dangerous. It had the potential to destroy my faith in him. Or maybe the harsh morning sun caused me to see things differently, to see him in a new, unflattering light?

'Well, I'm a guitarist. I was in a band in Manchester. We got signed and moved to London. That's when I met my beautiful bride. Eh, Sophie?' He turned round to me, beaming.

I attempted a smile but failed to make it reach my eyes.

Not that Jay noticed, too caught up in the moment.

'Meeting Sophie was the best part,' he said, turning back to face the driver. 'But as for the band, I had a falling out with the lead singer. He was an arrogant bastard. I had written all our songs, and he claimed the rights. Not that I had any evidence. You know, we were mates? I didn't think I would have to protect myself. But he had other ideas. He took everything from me. I objected and ended up kicked out with nothing. And I mean fucking nothing. How can mates do that to you?'

I watched as the driver shook his head in sympathy.

'Worst part is they're doing really well. They're touring in the States. The bastards! Playing my songs!'

I could feel the rage radiating from him as he fell silent.

I had heard this story many times. It was his go-to tale of a missed opportunity, his nearly made it famous moment.

'So now? What are you doing?' the driver asked.

I waited for Jay's response.

He shrugged. 'We relocated here for Sophie so she could write. She fell in love with this place as a child when her parents holidayed here. That's when she discovered her favourite author, Daphne du Maurier, who was the reason she became a writer. And, well, it's Cornwall, man! The perfect writer's retreat. Who could ask for more inspiration than the landscape and coastline here? When I get the time, I'll get back into surfing. I'm just busy looking after my wife so she can write.'

I listened to his account of my life. The choices I'd made before I met him. I noted that he hadn't answered the question. Instead, he'd claimed I took up his time, which was a blatant lie. I had no idea how Jay filled his days. He made a point of going out so I could write without interruptions. Whenever I asked him, he always digressed, just as he was doing now with the taxi driver. It was impossible to get a straight answer out of Jay. I put it down to his age; he was forty-eight, thirteen years older than me, and never married or had children. He was used to calling the shots and not being answerable to anyone. He had said he was waiting for the one and, until he met me, didn't believe it would ever happen. Allegedly, I was the exception to the rule, as he had vowed he would never marry.

'He's a keeper, this one! You hold onto him, my lover! Not many like him nowadays,' the driver warmly advised as he smiled at me in the rear-view mirror.

He was in his early sixties, overweight, with a kind, jowly grandfatherly disposition. I wondered what Jay had said to compel him to make such an assertion, lost in my thoughts. I faintly returned his smile, despite feeling like screaming. Last night was becoming a blur and what scared me was that Jay was already starting to alter the facts in a way that made me doubt myself. I wondered whether he had always done this, and I had never noticed: too blinded by his love for me. Or was this, like shouting and swearing at me, another new personality trait?

I looked back out the window at the disinterested summer's morning as we sped along the A390 back to Porthtowan. The driver slowed down at Chiverton Cross, joining the B3277 and heading for Towan Road. We would be turning off for Eastcliff and our new property in less than fifteen minutes.

I stared at The Chiverton Arms wooden sign stationary in the breezeless air as we continued past the flat green fields on either side of the road, broken up by clumps of trees, tall, white-painted metal windmills and buzzing pylons. We passed the turning for the old copper mining village of Mount Hawke where we had registered at the GP surgery. We continued, leaving behind the gnarled windswept trees bent at odd angles like stooped, ancient men before the open flat fields disappeared, swallowed by thickets of lush vegetation and trees lining the roads, blocking the surrounding countryside and sunshine. In the blink of an eye, the trees were gone, replaced by a ceaseless blanket of undulating green. I smiled when I saw the independent Sevenmilestone Garage on my right and, to the left, the turning for Porthtowan, which was now only 2.5 miles away.

The driver turned off, and we headed for the junction, then continued straight over. Trees, fields and stone cottages lined the way before we came upon our local, The Victory Inn, and the turning for Towan Road leading to Eastcliff, the third and highest road on the cliff overlooking Porthtowan Beach.

The panoramic view always took my breath away: vibrant green fields flanked me on each side, while the horizon was a sweeping, shimmering azure blue ocean beneath plummeting cliffs. This breathtaking vista, unique to the North Cornish coastline, had seduced me as a child. It called out to me as if beckoning me home from foreign lands.

But what stranger had I picked up on my travels?

My arm was beginning to throb now that the anaesthetic was starting to wear off. The young A&E doctor had put my bone back in place without requiring surgery. He'd explained it was a procedure called closed reduction. The orthopaedic surgeon would see me on Monday, where he would assess the fractures.

Seconds faded into minutes as the scenery blurred past me before we pulled up outside our new property. It took me a moment to remember that I was in the back of a taxi dressed in a crumpled, mascara-stained wedding dress. I opened the door, and pulled my wedding train behind me with my good hand.

'Mind, you take good care of her!' the taxi driver called out to Jay through the open passenger window.

'I intend to never let her out of my sight,' Jay assured him, coming over to me and protectively kissing me on my bare shoulder.

I shivered inwardly at the touch of his lingering lips.

The taxi driver beamed at us, newly married and very much in love.

I looked up at the centuries-old stone-built cottage. Behind it, the cliffs dramatically plummeted to the ocean below as the waves crashed against the rocks. But the repetitive lull failed to soothe my fears.

Eastcliff Cottage was supposed to be the beginning of something magical. But...

But the truth was I was scared of the man I'd married.

* * *

'Jay?' I hesitantly called out.

I could hear him in the kitchen below. I had no idea what he was doing. I'd immediately headed upstairs to the bedroom to try to take my wedding dress off. But with one arm in a cast, which also covered my hand, I needed help.

'Jay?' I repeated, this time with more urgency.

I could hear him mumbling something to himself as he walked to the bottom of the stairs.

'I can't undo my dress,' I apologised.

'Can't I just make myself a bloody coffee first before I start running around after you?'

I found myself stepping backwards as if he had slapped me.

He thudded up the stairs towards me and pushed past me into the bedroom.

'I haven't got all fucking day!' he snapped.

I followed him. He had his back to me, staring out of the large window at the seductive blue sea and Porthtowan Beach below.

'I'm the one who should be feeling annoyed. After all, I'm the one with the broken wrist. In two places, may I add?'

'I know! Christ, don't I know!'

'What's that supposed to mean?'

'Have you never considered that it wasn't just your wedding day that you ruined, that you also destroyed mine?'

'I what?' I spluttered in disbelief. 'You can't be serious?'

He swung around to face me.

I could see the anger flash across his tanned, lined face, surprised at how old he looked. I didn't recognise the hatred in his small blue eyes as he narrowed them at me.

I could feel a knot lodge itself at the back of my throat. It was fear. I had no idea why Jay was acting like this. It had crossed my mind whether he had taken drugs last night to account for his drastic personality change. At this point, it seemed the only logical explanation for his behaviour. People didn't just radically change after you married them. At least, not to my knowledge.

'Jay? I don't understand?'

'I'm sure you fucking don't!'

I shook my head. 'Why have you suddenly started swearing so much?'

He looked at me with disgust. 'Maybe because I woke up to what I'd married!'

Stunned, I stared at him.

He came behind me and spun me round to face the large antique mirror that rested against the wall. 'Look for yourself! This is what I married!'

I let out a startled gasp at his sudden aggression.

He then started tugging at the corset at the back of my dress.

'You're hurting me,' I protested.

'Make your mind up! Do you want me to help you or not?'

I didn't say a word. He took my silence as affirmation.

I barely breathed as he yanked and pulled at the back of the dress to release me. All the time, I kept my gaze lowered as he undid the intricate ties, not wanting to catch his eye in the mirror. I could feel the burning resentment in every aggressive movement without needing to see it in his face.

Finally, the dress came free and collapsed around my feet. I found myself instinctively covering my breasts with my arms.

'Don't flatter yourself!' he replied in response.

I couldn't understand his behaviour or what I had done to deserve such cruel treatment.

'What's going on? Why are you behaving like this?' I asked, forcing myself to meet his cold gaze in the mirror.

'Maybe because I found out what a lying, cheating whore you are!' he spat.

Shocked at his outburst, I turned around to face him.

'Jay?' I mumbled, lost, as he stared at me with such hatred.

'Don't fucking Jay, me! I don't take kindly to being made a fool of, nor do I appreciate finding out that the woman I just married is fucking her ex-fiancé.'

'What?' I spluttered.

'Don't act all doe-eyed and innocent with me!'

Before I had a chance to even react, he stormed out.

I felt winded. I didn't move, not quite believing what had just happened.

I heard him thunder down the stairs, then the front door slamming, followed by the screeching of tyres as he drove off in our new black California 6.1 VW Transporter.

It was then it hit me.

Oh God... My phone.

I had given Jay my phone. I had messages from Ben, questioning my decision to marry so quickly, that I hadn't deleted. I hadn't told Jay about them as it would only have caused an argument, especially if he knew that Ben regretted ending our engagement and wanted a second chance.

Had Ben sent me a new message?

But why would Jay have gone through my phone?

3

THE WEDDING

'Sophie,' my mother carefully began.

I knew from her hesitation that I wouldn't like what was to follow.

'You don't have to go through with this, you know that?'

'Please... don't,' I muttered under my breath.

I turned away from her so she couldn't see my expression and looked out the door at the wooden terrace leading to the garden, where my wedding guests were waiting. I felt my breath catch at the back of my throat when I saw Jay at the wooden altar talking to the registrar with Tom beside him. My heart soared with happiness at the sight of him. I hadn't seen him since he'd dropped me off at the Driftwood this morning. Nor had I seen Tom so I could question our conversation last night. It was odd. I couldn't shake his concerning words about the man I loved.

I pushed the thought from my mind, reminding myself that I was about to get married. We had booked the king-size room with a beautiful wooden four-poster bed with stunning sea views as our bridal suite for the evening. The hotel had excelled itself. The bedroom was fabulous, and the wedding garden was breathtakingly magical. As was the sunroom we were waiting in, leading out to the terrace, set up for the wedding breakfast with ivory wedding bunting, sash-covered chairs and extravagant flower displays.

My mother was responsible for the decadent flowers decorating the wedding breakfast room and the terrace and the garden beyond; despite Jay's objections, he had finally conceded to allow her this contribution, and so, she had made the most of it. My mother wasn't getting what she had planned for my wedding with Ben: a Scottish castle, a traditional Scottish piper and a ceilidh for the evening reception. Having a piper play was a centuries-old Scottish custom; the superstition connotated that if the bagpiper met the bride first, she was guaranteed a happy marriage. This couldn't have been further from the wedding she had envisioned for me with a groom dressed in a sand-coloured three-piece suit and flip-flops instead of a kilt. It may have been different, but it was still beautiful. So why would my mother want to spoil it?

'Mum, this isn't the time. The ceremony is about to start,' I said, turning back to her.

'Not for another five minutes,' my mother corrected me.

'Do I look all right?' I asked, trying to change the subject.

'You look beautiful. I just wish your father was here to see you.'

'So do I,' I mumbled, willing myself not to let my eyes tear up and spoil the make-up that Anna had so painstakingly applied.

'You know that Daddy adored Ben?' my mother suddenly questioned.

'Seriously?' I replied, unable to hide my incredulity.

'Well, he did,' she continued, unabated.

I sighed. I wished that Grace and Anna had waited with me, but my mother had ushered them to the garden to be seated with the other guests. I realised now that she had intended to try to dissuade me from going ahead with the ceremony.

'I love Jay,' I simply stated.

'You loved Ben not that long ago,' she pointed out, fussing over the red rosebuds in my hair.

'Mum!' I chastised. 'You'll pull them out if you're not careful!'

'Really, Sophie! I'm just securing this one back in place.'

I bit down on my annoyance and tried to focus on what was about to happen. Whether my mother liked it or not, I was about to marry Jay.

'As I was saying, it wasn't that long ago you were about to marry Ben,' she persisted.

'Until he left me,' I pointed out.

My mother cleared her throat. 'You know he regrets that decision?'

I shrugged.

'Eleven years, Sophie. That's a long time to throw away.'

'He threw it away,' I counterargued.

'Yes, but he has admitted he was a fool and is desperate to make it right. He still wants to be with you. To marry you,' she reasoned. 'Oh, Sophie, the two of you were so perfect together,' she said, sighing.

'How can you say all this just before I get married to Jay?'

'Because if Daddy were here, he would be doing exactly the same.'

'No, he wouldn't,' I fired back. 'Daddy would respect my choice.'

'Choice? Choice? For goodness' sake, Sophie! This is a classic rebound scenario!'

'It's not, Mum,' I said in a low voice. 'I love him.'

She didn't reply.

I didn't say anything else either. There was nothing I could say that would convince her otherwise.

I thought of Ben. We had been together for eleven years and I knew everything about him, or at least I thought I did. But, in reality, I didn't, because when he asked to break off our engagement, he had completely blindsided me. I hadn't read the signs, for there were none. It was as if he woke up one morning and decided he didn't want our life together. He wanted to try something, or someone, new.

But he was the one who had lost out. Jay had unexpectedly come into my life and radically changed it. I had rejected him initially, too hurt and still in love with Ben. But Jay had persisted.

Some would say he even stalked you.

There was an element of truth in it. We had met that first night at a gig he was playing in The Slaughtered Lamb in Clerkenwell. Tipsy and high on rejection, I basked in his attention. He followed – *stalked* – me on Instagram and started messaging me that night, eventually wearing me down and persuading me to let him take me out on a date.

A fourth date later, I invited him back to my flat for a coffee, where one thing inevitably led to another. The build-up to sex was incredible, unlike the act, which was bitterly disappointing for me, not for him. Not that I said anything. By then, he had managed to get under my skin. The following morning, after he left, a large bouquet arrived for me, accompanied by a card declaring the depths of feeling that he felt for me.

I was flattered by his continuous gifts and cards and he moved into my flat two weeks later, forced by circumstances and not wanting to move back home to Manchester and be apart from me. Our relationship was intense and all-consuming and had continued as it began, with Jay adoring and loving me more than I did him. Obsessed with me, Jay was unable to eat or sleep, something I had found both intoxicating and empowering. I had never had this effect on anyone before, and I doubted I ever would again.

My mother had once told me that if there was to be an inequality where love was concerned, make sure that you are loved more by the person you love. Jay had had more invested in me – us

– than I did at the beginning. But eventually I had fallen hard for him, and there was no going back. I felt scared by that acknowledgement, for it meant that I had given some of my power away to him.

I watched as my mother looked out to the wedding garden. Cascading flowers, chair sashes, and balloons adorned the setting. The altar was spectacular, covered in billowing silk sashes and flowers.

'I know why you ran away to Cornwall, but why did Jay?' she asked, breaking our silence.

'What do you mean I ran away here?'

'You ran from Ben and all the memories you had together in that lovely flat of yours in Kensington,' she replied. 'You ran from all the friends you shared and the plans you had for the future.'

'I didn't,' I argued. 'I came here because Jay and I wanted to start somewhere new where neither of us had any connection.'

'So, what was Jay running from?' she persisted.

I followed her gaze and watched him. 'Nothing,' I answered as I thought back to Tom's drunken words.

How well did I know him?

'Are you sure?' she quizzed.

I realised my expression betrayed me.

'Of course, I'm sure,' I replied, irritated.

'So where are his friends? His family?'

I sighed. 'Seriously? You know his parents died and he was an only child. And as for his friends, well...' I shrugged, 'they're out there with him.'

'All of four months,' she quickly replied. 'I mean friends from his past?'

'I've already explained this to you. Jay's ex-partner sabotaged his friendships.'

'Mm,' my mother murmured, unconvinced.

I accepted that it was difficult for her to understand. Initially, I had questioned why Jay's ex would go to such lengths to destroy his life in Manchester when she was the cause of their breakup. But he explained that it was no surprise that she had lied about him to his friends, given her vindictive and unpredictable nature. She wanted control of the narrative and to portray herself as the victim, which she had done to his detriment.

'I thought you liked Jay?' I questioned.

'I don't know him to like him,' she flatly answered.

'Well, I know him, and that's all that matters. He adores me and treats me like a queen. He does everything so I can focus on my work,' I explained. 'From cooking and cleaning to bringing me breakfast in bed.'

She didn't say anything.

'He couldn't be more different from Ben if he tried,' I continued. 'In a good way,' I added, not giving her the opportunity to misconstrue my words. 'Jay makes me feel alive, loved and appreciated. Whereas Ben had become so complacent that he didn't even know I existed most of the time. Ben would never have done half of what Jay does for me,' I reasoned.

'Ben was real, darling.'

'What is that supposed to mean?'

'Exactly what I say. I'm concerned that my future forty-eight-year-old son-in-law suffers from Peter Pan syndrome. Without a job, how does he expect to support a wife? Or children, come to that?'

'I can support myself!'

She didn't persist. Instead, we waited in silence.

Seconds dragged into minutes until I heard my cue: the cellist had started to play 'Edelweiss'. Jay had organised every detail of the wedding, aside from the wedding flowers, the cellist and the choice of music as I walked down the aisle, lined with hurricane lamps, to the wooden altar and the spectacular views of Trevaunance Cove below and the shimmering Atlantic beyond. Initially, he'd rejected the idea outright, but the cellist playing 'Edelweiss' was my only caveat at our wedding.

My mother suddenly took hold of me and hugged me tight.

The song meant as much to her as to me. My father, who had an incredible voice, would sing it to Liv and me when we were children.

'Daddy is with you in spirit,' she whispered into my hair. Pulling back, she looked at me. 'I wish you all the happiness that your father and I had. If he were here, he would be so proud of you. You're beautiful, Sophie. Truly beautiful.' Smiling, she added, 'All Daddy would want is your happiness. So, if Jay is the one who makes you happy, then let's get you married.'

'Thank you, Mum,' I whispered, choking back the tears. I took hold of her hand and squeezed it. 'I promise that Jay will take care of me the way Daddy looked after you. No one has ever loved me the way Jay loves me.'

My mother looked at me, her eyes glistening. 'I hope so, Sophie. You're so isolated here. It's just you and him.'

'That's what we wanted,' I assured her. 'And Jay will take good care of me. I'm so lucky to be marrying him. The night I met Jay, my world changed.' I faltered, willing the tears not to fall.

* * *

I couldn't stop the tears. No matter how much I tried, they slid down my cheeks.

I held Jay's adoring gaze.

I could drown in his love for me.

My love for him was equally so overwhelming that I couldn't breathe.

I could hear the registrar pronouncing us married.

Jay beamed, then leaned in and kissed me, to the delight of the witnesses.

He let me go to a round of applause.

After countless photographs in the garden at the altar and down on the beach, Jay was now behind me with his arms wrapped around my waist as we stood on a rock staring out at the dazzling turquoise ocean as it lapped lazily against the shore. The brilliance of the late-day sun kissed my skin with her gentle caress while I luxuriated in the heat from Jay's body as he held onto me tightly. I felt so protected and loved. Nothing could happen to me now. I wanted this moment to last forever, never wanting him to let me go.

It was perfect. He was perfect.

'I'll never let you go,' murmured Jay as he squeezed me even tighter as if reading my mind. 'Never,' he repeated. 'You're mine now till death do us part.'

4

THE DAY AFTER THE WEDDING

I couldn't believe Jay had left.

Where has he gone at this time of the morning?

Numb, I stared at the unpacked boxes of clothes and bedroom paraphernalia stacked against the bare white walls. We had moved in three days ago, which was crazy timing. However, we had no choice as the vendors had repeatedly postponed the exchange date. We were so nervous that the purchase of Eastcliff Cottage would fall through at any moment that we accepted whatever date the vendors' solicitor finally proposed.

Against my mother's advice, I used the proceeds from my London flat and all of my savings and took out a mortgage. Jay was currently in between jobs and had been for some time. So, what money he had was mine. Jay had quit his day job right after meeting me to follow his dream as a lead guitarist. He was certain the band he was in was going somewhere, and they had, unfortunately, without him. My mother had insisted on a prenuptial agreement when I had foolishly confided in her about our financial situation. She was troubled that Jay's contribution to the purchase of the property, the majority of what inheritance his mother had left him, was still significantly less than mine. To her dismay, I had immediately rejected the idea and blocked her attempts to persuade me otherwise. I trusted and knew Jay, and I was the one marrying him.

We had rented a one-bedroomed property for the past four months overlooking Porthtowan's play park and beach while we had waited to purchase the cottage. In that time, Jay had managed to get to know most regulars who frequented Blue Bar and the Driftwood in St Agnes. Music was his means of connecting with people, and there was a vibrant music scene in Cornwall. He may have told the taxi driver that I was the reason we left the city, but the truth was, Jay was desperate to put some distance between him and his music friends in Manchester. He made the case that this was a fresh start for him and us.

Jay and I had arranged to meet my mother and sister for a late lunch and a post-wedding catch-up at the hotel where we were all supposed to be staying.

That was before Jay broke your wrist...

Not that I had my phone to check to see whether the plans had altered. I still had no idea of its whereabouts. I swore that Jay had it. I remembered asking him to put it in his wedding jacket's inner pocket. I suddenly thought about my laptop and tablet. I could have used them if we had broadband. But it wasn't due to be installed until Monday afternoon.

I needed codeine, water and a few hours of sleep. Then I would tackle showering with an arm in plaster covered in a plastic bag and try to make myself presentable. If Jay hadn't returned by then, I didn't know what I would do. St Agnes was over three miles away. It was a short eight-minute drive by the back roads through Mingoose and onto St Agnes, but without the Transporter or the means to call a taxi, I would have to walk. Ordinarily, as it was a glorious morning, the clifftop coastal walk connecting Porthtowan to St Agnes via Chapel Porth Beach and the iconic historical landmark Wheal Coates would have been ideal. But I wasn't in the mood for seeing tourists and other walkers enjoying the old tin mine's imposing ruins set on the heather- and gorse-covered clifftop against the blinding backdrop of the Atlantic.

It had seemed fitting to return to the hotel the following day for lunch, but the knot in my stomach twisted and tightened at the thought of going back without the groom.

I headed downstairs for the strip of codeine the A&E doctor had given me. I looked around the spacious, contemporary open-plan kitchen-dining-living space and the two walls of glass bi-folding doors that opened onto the secluded, mature back garden. It felt odd. Different. Unfamiliar. I checked the unpacked boxes and furniture. Nothing had altered in the past twenty-four hours. It was me that had changed.

And Jay.

I suddenly wondered where Sebastian, my five-year-old long-haired ginger cat, was hiding. He was a housecat and had never been outdoors.

'Sebastian?' I called out.

Nothing.

For a moment, I wondered whether Jay had let him out when he'd left.

I knew he didn't like Sebastian. He pretended he did, for my sake, but I was aware he was a constant reminder of my ex, Ben, who had bought him for me as a kitten one Christmas.

Would he really be that callous?

Then I heard the reassuring thud of his portly body above me as he padded out of the guest room towards the top of the exposed wooden stairs.

I turned to the kitchen island for the codeine I had thrown down when I came in. I picked up the packet, took one tablet and washed it down with chilled water from the fridge.

'Hey, Sebastian,' I greeted when he leisurely turned up, rubbing his body against my ankles.

He started meowing in protest at my abandonment of him.

I pulled out a tray of his favourite gourmet pâté and dished it up with difficulty. My wrist was now pulsating with pain. A reminder of how my wedding night had ended. Not that Sebastian cared; all he wanted was to eat, followed by more sleep. I bent down and stroked him while he ravenously ate, despite the fact he had devoured most of the kibble I had left out for him overnight.

I stood up, and as I looked around the open minimalist space, I spotted Jay's wedding jacket thrown over one of the dining room chairs. I walked over and picked it up. I could tell immediately by the weight that something heavy was in the inner pocket. It was either my phone or Jay's. I doubted it was the latter as he never went anywhere without his phone.

Relief quickly dissipated when I realised it was my phone, replaced firstly by anger.

Why would Jay lie to me?

He had distinctly denied ever having my phone.

I felt sick when I saw the countless missed calls and frantic texts from wedding guests. In particular, my mother, who had repeatedly called me. I scrolled through the list of unanswered calls and concerned messages.

Oh God...

There was a missed call and a voicemail from Ben.

I felt a sliver of ice trail down my back when I realised it had been listened to, unlike all the other messages. The voicemail had been left at 1.03 a.m.

Jay...

That was when I was still in the hospital toilet and he was nowhere to be found.

Why would he listen to my voicemail?

But I knew the reason.

I scrolled through the texts not ready to hear Ben's voice, or his message.

It was then that I saw Ben's text, sent at 10.22 p.m., shortly before it had happened. The only one that had been read.

> I saw your photos on Insta. I can't believe you actually went through with it! After what you told me! When you come to your senses, I'll be here. You know I still love you. Always will xx

I felt light-headed as I stared at those words.

Words intended only for me. But Jay had read them.

I could feel my cheeks burning with guilt as if I was a little girl caught in a tangled web of lies.

I waited a moment, bracing myself before clicking on Ben's voicemail.

I could feel hot, frustrated tears pricking my eyes. I didn't want to cry. I had made my choice.

Oh God, Sophie. What have you done?

Shakily breathing out, I clicked play: 'Sophie, are you okay? Liv called me. She's really worried about you. She said you had gone to hospital because you hurt your wrist and she hasn't heard from you. No one has. And...' I listened as he took a deep breath, 'Liv told me something... about him. Something he did. Call me when you get this. Liv's not the only one who's worried about you.'

With that, the message ended.

I swallowed, trying to dislodge the tight ball of anxiety at the back of my throat.

Oh God... Jay listened to this...
I felt a wave of nausea course through me.
All that was going through my head was one question: had Liv witnessed what happened?

5

THE WEDDING

Tom spun me around, making me giddy.

The acoustic duo, a singer and guitarist that Jay had hired were incredible, and the wooden floor between their set-up and the tables and chairs in the intimate rustic wheel room with its high wooden beams and low-hanging lanterns was full of our guests dancing.

I understood why Jay had chosen the male duo. The first song for our wedding dance was mesmerisingly haunting as James, the singer, had sung Tom McRae's 'My Vampire Heart' with Gerren's delicate and subtle acoustic guitar accompaniment. It had the desired result; I was blown away by Jay's choice, which he had kept as a surprise.

'No more,' I pleaded now with Tom, laughing as the acoustic duo continued their cover of The Waterboys' 'The Whole of the Moon'. 'You'll make me regret drinking so much champagne!'

He grinned at me. 'You're a lightweight!'

I caught Jay's eye. It was enough to sober me up.

He was standing at the bar. He seemed to be the only person at the wedding reception not enjoying himself.

I watched as he knocked back yet another shot. I had no idea what was up with him. He hadn't spent any time with me since the ceremony. Instead, he had drunk with his recently acquired friends, refusing my pleas for him to dance with me. It was odd. He had even ignored Anna and Grace, who were dancing, unlike my mother and sister, who, I noted, were still sitting at their table, deep in conversation.

He was acting so differently.

Tom grabbed me again, and swung me round, making me feel light-headed.

The music and lights surrounding me seemed to fade in and out as I spun round and round. All that I could think about was Tom's dizzying question: how well did I know Jay?

But now wasn't the time or place to question why he would ask that.

'Hey, you okay, Sophie?' Tom asked.

I suddenly stumbled backwards.

He grabbed me and pulled me into him. 'Hey?'

I looked up into his deep, dark-brown concerned eyes.

Ben?

It hit me that this was wrong. So wrong. It should have been my new husband's eyes I was staring into, not the best man.

'Sophie?' Tom gently questioned, holding me close.

Oh God, Tom. You look so much like Ben...

I swallowed back the overwhelming thought as I stepped away from him. But it was too late.

I turned in time to see Jay watching me. His expression was hard and his eyes were filled with enmity. I had never experienced him look at me this way before.

Something distracted him and he broke away from my startled gaze. I watched as he checked his phone. He scowled at whatever he read, then raised his head and looked straight at me.

That look. The contempt...
I felt sick.

'Oh God,' I mumbled, not knowing what was wrong. A sense of dread consumed me, its chilling iciness slithering down my spine. I shivered as a coldness I had never felt before took up residency in my body, as Jay gave me a look of disgust as he knocked back another shot, his narrowed, cold eyes never leaving mine.

Horrified, I stepped back from Tom.

Had I spent too much time with Tom?

I watched as Jay slammed the shot glass down and then left.

'Are you all right?' Tom questioned. His brow was furrowed with concern.

I shook my head. 'Something's wrong with Jay.'

Tom looked up and around for him.

'He's just left.'

'He's left?' Tom repeated.

Numb, I nodded.

Why has he left you?

'Maybe he's gone out to get some air?' Tom suggested.

'Maybe,' I mumbled.

I knew it wasn't that.

The way he looked at you! Oh God, Sophie...

I left Tom and made my way outside to find Jay.

'Jay?' I called out.

Nothing.

Gloomy shadows and the roar of the ocean lay ahead. Behind me, laughter and music filled the air as the warm glow of lights from the bar fenced off the night.

'Jay?' I called out.

Again, nothing. I looked around the buildings and car park, but Jay was gone.

I realised where he might have gone to clear his head. I ran down the road towards the beach, carrying my silk train, grateful I had opted for flip-flops instead of the heels my mother had wanted me to wear.

'Jay?' But my voice was drowned out by the crash of the waves.

I continued running, righting myself when I stumbled.

'Jay? Please?'

Then I saw his figure.

He stopped and turned.

'Jay?'

I ran over to him, careful of the rocks.

'What's wrong?' I asked. 'You were looking at something on your phone and then suddenly left?'

'Leave me the fuck alone!' he growled.

Startled, I stared at him. He had never spoken to me in this way before.

'Not until you tell me what's wrong,' I insisted.

'You want to know what's wrong, do you?' he raged, grabbing my left wrist.

'Ow! You're hurting me, Jay?' I protested.

'See this!' he hissed as he raised my left hand up. 'That ring means something to me. But clearly it doesn't to you.'

'What?' I questioned, confused. 'Jay, what's wrong with you?'

'You! You're just like my fucking whore of an ex! That's what! You're all the fucking same!'

I gasped as his grip intensified. 'Jay, please? I don't know what's got into you?'

'Watching you flirting with my best man, that's what! You made a fool of me in front of everyone. It was embarrassing to watch you throw yourself at him like some fucking cheap slut!'

I was stunned into silence. I struggled to believe that Jay could think that about me.

'You're being ridiculous,' I finally replied. 'You refused to dance with me. So, Tom stepped in as your best man. That's all. He just wanted to make me happy.'

'I'm sure he did. And I'm sure that just dancing wasn't on his mind or yours.'

'You're drunk!' I accused.

'Yeah? Not too drunk to notice that Tom looks like your ex!'

'He doesn't,' I weakly argued, knowing that Jay was right. Tom was the same build as Ben, with the same colouring: brown eyes and blond, thick unruly hair. Then there was his age; Tom was thirty-five – mine and Ben's ages – and, much to Jay's obsessive jealousy about our age gap, considerably younger than him.

I felt him twist my wrist back.

'Ow! Jay, please?' I begged as the pain intensified.

'How long have you been talking to him?'

'Who?' I cried out. 'Tom?'

'Don't play the fucking innocent with me!' he hissed in my face.

'Jay, please? I don't know who you're talking about?'

'You're a fucking lying bitch,' he growled as he exerted even more pressure on my wrist, twisting it further back.

'No! Jay, please? You're hurting me,' I begged.

He ignored me, jerking it even harder.

I heard a sickening snapping sound like a dry branch cracking underfoot.

I screamed out in agony as the pain followed, swift and cruel.

Jay looked at me, his face contorted with hatred.

'My wrist?' I screamed at him as he squeezed even harder. 'Oh my God! My wrist! I think you've broken my wrist?'

'Sophie?' yelled out a voice. 'Sophie? Are you all right?'

Liv…

Jay suddenly let me go. I felt myself stagger backwards. Catching my flip-flop on the silk train of my wedding dress, I lost my balance.

'AHH!' I screamed as I landed on the same arm that Jay had restrained.

Twisted. Snapped back. Broken...

I felt overwhelmed with nausea.

'I think I'm going to pass out,' I mumbled.

Jay was crouched down beside me now.

'Sophie? What's happened? Are you all right?' yelled Liv, running towards me.

I saw the worried expression on Jay's face.

Tears fell down my face as I tried to sit up.

'No, babes. Wait, just a minute. Yeah?' He had his arms protectively wrapped around me. 'Shh... I'm here. You're all right,' he assured me, holding me tight.

'Soph?' cried out Liv, collapsing down onto her knees beside me. 'What happened?' she asked as she looked from my ashen face to Jay's.

'She stumbled backwards and fell. I think she's sprained her wrist,' Jay explained, leaning in to kiss my clammy cheek.

I pulled my head away from him, but it was lost on Jay.

But not on my sister.

'Sophie?' she suspiciously questioned.

But I was too shocked to speak.

Liv asked me something else, but her words were muffled, drowned out by the pummelling sound of water in my ears.

I watched as a flicker of fear crossed her eyes. I realised she was doubting Jay's version of events.

'Come on,' she said, trying to get me up.

Between Liv and Jay helping me, I managed to stand up.

'Let me have a look,' she said.

I weakly raised my arm, not wanting to look at the injury.

'Ohh, Sophie, I think it's broken,' she cried out.

'It's just a sprain. Ice will take the swelling down,' Jay reasoned.

'No! She needs to go to hospital. Now!'

'Oh, come on! Don't you think you're being a tad dramatic?'

I watched as she shot him a look which silenced him.

Jay wasn't the sort of person to back down. Nor did he like being told he was wrong.

Liv put her arm around me and started to help me off the beach. I looked back at Jay as he watched us walk away.

'What were you thinking?' she asked.

I shook my head. 'I was looking for Jay.'

'Why?'

'He stormed off,' I answered. I didn't add why.

Liv looked at me. 'I need to talk to you, Sophie. There's something you need to know—'

'I'll take her from here, Liv,' Jay cut in. 'She is my wife.'

'No—' I began, but my words were drowned out as people came running towards us.

'Oh my God! What's happened?' cried Anna, running towards me.

She was followed by Tom and Grace.

'Oh, Sophie! Are you all right?' Grace exclaimed. She looked at my cradled arm and then at Jay. 'What happened?' she demanded.

Jay ignored her.

'Shit!' exclaimed Tom. 'Sophie?' he questioned, searching my face. He turned to Jay. 'What the hell, bro?'

'She fell,' Jay answered matter-of-factly. 'Tripped over her wedding dress and landed hard on her left hand. I think she's sprained her wrist from the impact. Lucky it was sand and not a rock.'

'Nah, bro. That's not a sprain. She's broken her wrist. You see that?' Tom said, pointing at my wrist. 'I have my first aid certificate as a lifeguard and that's bone bulging through the skin.'

I forced myself to look. 'Oh God,' I mumbled. I felt as if I was going to be sick.

Jay caught my eye. 'You're going to be fine, babes. I promise,' he assured me.

I didn't trust him.

'Liv?' I questioned, but I couldn't see her.

I didn't want to be with Jay. I wanted my sister.

I tried to move away from him, but Jay had his arm firmly around me.

I could see Liv ahead, talking to a taxi driver in the Driftwood car park. I assumed they must have either dropped someone off or were booked for a collection.

'Sophie? Oh God, darling...What happened? One minute you were on the dance floor, the next you had disappeared?' my mother asked.

I couldn't bring myself to speak.

She expectantly turned to Jay. He ignored her.

'This taxi will take you to hospital, Sophie,' Liv called out.

'Come on, babes,' Jay said, not bothering to answer my mother as he guided me to the taxi.

'Mum?' I mumbled, but my voice became smothered by everyone else's words. I wanted her to come with me. I didn't want to be on my own with Jay.

Liv held the back of the taxi door open for me. 'We're really lucky as he's just dropped someone off and is heading back to Truro.'

'Liv? You're coming with me? Yeah?'

'Of course,' she answered before Jay cut in.

'I need to help her with her seat belt,' he said, forcing Liv out the way.

'I need my phone,' I said.

'I have your phone. Remember, you gave it to me,' he replied.

'Come on, we need to go,' Jay insisted, shoving my long wedding train in after me.

'Wait! Let me get my bag. I'm coming as well,' my mother said, joining Liv as Jay slammed the taxi door in my face.

'It doesn't need all three of us, Joanna,' Jay pointedly answered.

Without giving my mother or Liv a chance to respond, he jumped in the front passenger seat.

'Just drive, mate,' he instructed.

Horrified, I stared at my mother, standing there with Liv, shocked and equally outraged as the taxi pulled away.

Tears cascaded down my cheeks as I stared out, helpless, until they disappeared from view.

Did you see what happened on the beach, Liv? Did you? Did you see Jay twist my wrist back until the bones snapped?

The question played over and over in my mind.

Numb, I gazed at my reflection in the window.

I didn't recognise the pale, traumatised face staring back.

Hot, salty tears trailed down over my lips as I stared at Jay's silent figure in the front.

Oh my God, Sophie... who have you just married?

6

THE DAY AFTER THE WEDDING

I felt hot and bothered. My cheeks were flushed, and my skin felt prickly and clammy. The high temperature, coupled with the unbearable itchiness and burning inside my plaster cast was driving me insane. I imagined tiny red ants scurrying all over my hidden flesh.

I slowly breathed out, trying to steady my nerves as I walked up the steps to the Driftwood Spars high garden. I could feel my mother's and sister's expectant eyes watching me as I approached their table. They had typically sat outside to enjoy the azure blue sea and beach. I wished they were sitting inside. I was already irritated with the heat. I had a feeling that this meeting was going to make me feel even more uncomfortable.

'Hey,' I breezily greeted with a white-toothed smile. 'Sorry, I'm late. I was waiting for Jay.'

He had returned hours later with no apology or explanation of his whereabouts. He had showered and changed and then insisted that I, in turn, get ready to meet my mother and Liv for lunch as planned. I had argued that I didn't feel up to it, but he was adamant that we come to assure them I was fine, which couldn't have been further from the truth. He refused to speak to me on the short drive to St Agnes, instead turning the music up to drown out my questions about where he had disappeared and why he had ignored my frantic calls and texts.

I sat down, avoiding their gazes, and picked up the opened bottle. I poured myself a glass of white wine and took a much-needed mouthful. I didn't want to be here. Not now. Not ever.

'You do know you're not supposed to mix alcohol and codeine, Sophie?' my mother chided. Her voice was concerned yet, razor-sharp.

Something was wrong.

Of course, something's wrong!

'It's fine,' I assured her. 'One glass won't kill me.'

I could see from my mother's expression that it failed to appease her.

'Where's Anna and Grace?' I asked, surprised not to see them. Nor were there any wine glasses for them on the table.

They had both messaged me, worried about my broken wrist and how I was bearing up, wanting to hear all about it at lunch. Even Tom had texted, checking I was okay and letting me know he would see me at the Driftwood with the others.

'And Tom? He messaged that he would be here for 1.30?'

It was now 2 p.m., which made their absences even stranger.

'Well...' My mother faltered, cleared her throat. 'I wanted to talk to you in private first, and so, Tom offered to show Anna and Grace around St Agnes.'

'Ohh,' I mumbled, feeling uneasy.

My younger sister's large dark brown eyes burned me with their intensity.

'I'm fine. All right?' I snapped in her direction, unable to hold back my irritation at her for calling Ben and telling him what had happened. It was my wedding and my accident. And Ben was my ex-fiancé. Not hers.

Liv suddenly pushed her chair back and stood up. 'I'm going to the toilet,' she asserted, shooting me a look which implied she wanted me to join her.

I ignored the invitation. I wasn't ready to talk to Liv.

Or my mother.

She waited a moment and, realising I wasn't coming, glanced at our mother. Something unspoken passed between them. She then left.

'Jay?' my mother began, turning her attention away from Liv's retreating figure to me. 'I see, he didn't want to come and see us?' my mother questioned.

I knew she was annoyed by her tone. She typically spoke in a light, lilting, soft Scottish accent. This was heavier, swifter and harsher, more Dundonian than her usual refined, gentler Broughty Ferry inflexion.

'He's busy loading all the wedding gifts and our overnight bags into the Transporter. He'll be joining us soon,' I assured her, keeping my voice light.

'Good,' she replied. 'Otherwise, one might suspect he was avoiding us. Which wouldn't surprise me after stopping Liv and I from going to the hospital with you.'

I remained silent.

I watched as she played with her thick, long, sleek black hair, pulling it back from her attractive face. I was always surprised that she never seemed to age, despite now being in her mid-fifties. Whether her secret was botox and fillers, or a portrait hidden in the attic, like Oscar Wilde's Dorian Gray, I couldn't say. She would never share with me, nor would I ever offend her by asking. It was easier to accept that her genes and privileged life had played a part in preserving her youthfulness. She had married my father, fifteen years her senior, when she was barely nineteen and had me when she was twenty, something that I found unimaginable. And, remarkably, she looked the same as I always remembered her – breathtakingly beautiful.

In contrast to my mother's sleek black hair, I had tight, coiled springs for hair, which, when left to their own devices, shot out in every direction. Despite the admiring comments my unruly, naturally curly, platinum blonde hair elicited, I had always felt cheated, coveting my mother's dark, exquisite looks, inherited from her African-Scottish grandfather, who was abandoned by his unmarried mother who left him for a new life in Johannesburg at the turn of the last century. His Ghanaian father, an international actor and musician, paid a white couple in Broughty Ferry to raise him with their children.

'Sophie?' my mother prompted, dragging me back to our conversation.

Her conversation.

I knew my mother was furious, and I accepted she had every right to be. She had no idea what had happened to me from when I left in the taxi at 10 p.m. last night until my text this morning. She had endured hours of not knowing whether her eldest daughter was all right. She had called the hospital twice, and no one could update her.

She still hadn't called me out on my earlier text. Her reply to my message had been terse. I felt bad for not calling her, but I knew if I had, my voice would have betrayed me, and I would have broken down as soon as she questioned me. I was still struggling to process what had happened and why. Jay's atypical behaviour had hurt me to the core, and I couldn't let my mother or Liv know because I was too chagrined. I knew they preferred my ex, Ben, to Jay. Ben had been a part of my family for so long. He had spent Christmases and birthdays with us and had been there to support the three of us when my father had passed. Grief had somehow distanced me from him, and we ended up taking a break from one another at his request. But I knew that was a convenient excuse for him having found someone else. I had struggled without him or my father, and the dark days and nights that followed were interminable as deep depression held me captive. Jay had stormed into my life then, much to my surprise and my mother's dismay, and changed my destiny.

Our destiny.

Ben's abandonment of me had allowed Jay in.

I took another sip of wine to stop myself from thinking about Ben and his kind, dark brown, almond-shaped eyes and gentle smile. He would never have talked to me or behaved as Jay had done. I could feel the pricking, burning sensation of threatening tears. I swallowed back the wine in a bid to drown my emotions. I didn't want to cry, not here, but I couldn't silence the regret that I had taken a chance on Jay.

Ben would never have disrespected my mother the way Jay had.

Or me.

'He definitely has no children?' my mother suddenly queried.

'No!' I spluttered, taken aback by her left-field question. 'That's an odd thing to ask.'

'Is it, considering his age?'

I ignored my mother's raised eyebrow.

She looked behind me and smiled as Liv returned.

'Sophie was just saying that Jay will be joining us after all. It means he can explain himself why he didn't return any of our calls, or texts.'

I took a sip of wine, looking at my sister over the glass. She had inherited not only my mother's looks, her deep olive skin, perfect features and willowy figure, but also her temperament.

'Ben texted me,' I stated as she sat down.

I noted that she didn't seem shocked to hear that he had been in touch. But then, why would she be when she had called him later in the evening? I resisted the urge to question why she would call my ex-fiancé. But I knew why.

'Jay read Ben's text and... Well, that's why he stormed off.'

Liv frowned at this information. 'That's the reason he gave you?'

I stared at her, not understanding her meaning. 'Yes. Why? What other reason would there be?'

I waited for an answer, but Liv didn't respond. Instead, she glanced at our mother.

'What? What aren't you telling me?'

'First, I think you should tell us what's wrong,' my mother suggested. 'I can read you like a book.'

I looked at her, but I couldn't speak. Shame silenced me.

Don't protect him. Not now. Not because he's suddenly acting as if nothing has happened. HE HURT YOU. YOU NEED TO TELL HER!

'I'm serious, you can tell me anything,' she insisted.

But I couldn't bring myself to admit that he'd hurt me. I had willingly jumped blindly and madly into love with Jay without thinking about the consequences. How could I tell her what he had done to me? The names he had called me?

'Sophie? Please, darling? I know you? I can tell something's wrong. Did something happen last night on the beach?'

I found myself muttering the words: 'Jay. He—'

7

I jumped as I felt heavy hands suddenly dig into my bare shoulders.

'What were you about to say?' Jay lightly questioned as his fingers pinched my flesh.

I shook my head, then tilted it up to meet his gaze, smiling. 'Nothing.'

'Now I'm intrigued. You were about to say something about me. Good, I hope!' he said, laughing.

'There's only good to tell,' I lied. 'You scared me then!' I said in an attempt to change the subject.

Jay laughed. 'Yeah. I really surprised you, didn't I? I'm sorry.'

I was struggling to keep up. I felt as if I was going insane.

I nodded, smiling at him while willing my body to stop quaking.

'Are you okay?' Jay asked, crouching down to me. 'You're shaking? Did I scare you that badly?'

'No... Just the shock of last night catching up with me,' I mumbled.

I avoided my mother's gaze. She could always tell when I was lying.

'Another bottle of wine?' Jay asked us.

'Not for me, thank you,' answered my mother tightly.

I noted Liv's stony silence at Jay's sudden appearance.

'Sophie shouldn't be drinking alcohol while taking codeine,' my mother interrupted as he poured the rest of the wine bottle into my glass.

'If anything, the alcohol will help her sleep,' Jay reasoned. 'She's had a horrendous night and didn't get any sleep this morning because of the pain.'

'None of us have had any sleep,' my mother replied.

Jay straightened up.

I felt myself squirm inside. I looked up at him. For a brief moment, his relaxed, confident composure slipped.

'Of course. And I'm sorry that I didn't get back to you, Joanna. My phone died and, to be honest, I was a bit preoccupied with looking after my wife,' he said, resting a hand on my shoulder.

I saw a dangerous flicker of anger cross my mother's dark eyes. I could imagine her holding back from an old Scottish saying she often used with Liv and me as children to silence our irritable whining: Haud yer wheesht, ye wee scunner!

'And this morning? You couldn't contact me when you returned home from the hospital?'

'Ahh... I thought Sophie had contacted you this morning?' Jay asked, acting confused.

My mother simply looked at him.

'You did, didn't you, Soph?' he asked, turning to me.

I mutely nodded.

Satisfied, Jay relaxed. 'Right, I need a drink. It's been a long night! And not the kind of long one I had intended on my wedding night!' He laughed.

I could see from my mother's expression she found the reference indecorous.

I felt embarrassed by him.

For him.

For me.

'I think I've earned that pint after carrying all those wedding gifts down to the car park,' he shared as he stretched his arms above his head.

As he left for the bar, I couldn't help but note Liv's startled look of repulsion at Jay's belly bulging out from under his tight-fitting black T-shirt, accentuated by his otherwise thin body. I knew she was comparing Jay's short, middle-aged body to Ben's thirty-five-year-old, tall, athletic build. I was aware Jay's height was his Achilles heel, not that it bothered me, but I was sensitive to how much it bothered him, especially since my ex, Ben, was his antithesis at six foot three. I resisted the urge to jump to Jay's defence and explain that I had chosen him for his personality, not his looks. After what had happened with Ben, I doubted I could trust someone as attractive as him again. I had genuinely believed that choosing someone I thought was my best friend, my soulmate, far outweighed physical attraction. I had allowed my brain to rule my heart. But, recently, Jay's arrogance had made me realise he believed he was as physically attractive as Ben, or anyone else, come to that.

I couldn't silence the voice in my head. It kept repeating the same question, intent on driving me insane: how could I have got it so wrong?

'I don't like the fact that you are so far away, Sophie,' my mother said once Jay had left. 'It worries me you being here,' she continued.

'I'm fine, Mum. Honestly. Remember, I wanted to move here?'

'I just wish you'd never sold your flat in Kensington. You know how much Daddy loved it. And how much he loved...' She stopped herself from saying Ben's name. Even she realised that it wasn't appropriate.

At that moment, I wished my father was here. Between Liv and me, I was his favourite, perhaps because I had inherited his rare Scandinavian platinum blonde hair and his piercing blue eyes. Narcissism had equally won Liv my mother's favour.

I watched out the corner of my eye as Liv took a drink of wine. I followed suit as I waited for the onslaught. I could feel it in the claustrophobic, sultry air.

'It worries me that you've lost so much weight, darling?'

It took me a second to realise she was talking to me. There was a time when my mother would worry over me weighing too much. Now I had lost weight, she still wasn't happy.

'What bride doesn't lose weight?' I lightly replied, trying to keep the annoyance out of my voice.

'I mean, it's good that you've lost some weight,' she backtracked, as if reading my mind. 'But, darling, you can lose too much.'

'It wasn't intentional.'

She gave me one of her sceptical looks.

'I've just been so busy these past months,' I found myself explaining.

I refrained from mentioning that Jay barely ate, seemingly surviving on coffee and alcohol and that he would shoot me questioning looks when I ate, as if it were abnormal.

'It makes you look exhausted and pinched,' my mother continued.

But the issue wasn't my weight. We both knew that.

'I broke my wrist in two places on my wedding night. I haven't slept and I am in constant pain. No surprise then that I look so "exhausted and pinched"?' I argued.

'Oh Sophie, you're taking this all the wrong way. I'm not

attacking you. It's just that you've never been this thin. I mean...' She turned to my sister for support.

Liv remained silent. But the look in her eyes was enough for me to know that she agreed.

'To be perfectly frank, you just look ill, darling.'

'I disagree, Joanna,' decisively interrupted Jay.

The verbal tennis match had been so intense that no one had seen him return.

'Sophie looks the best she has ever looked. I'm surprised you can't see that?' Jay questioned.

My mother narrowed her eyes at his assertion.

Jay placed his pint of lager on the table and then sat down next to me. He took hold of my right hand and tightly squeezed it.

I noticed my mother tapping the side of her wine glass with her wedding and engagement rings. It was a tic of hers: a sign something was troubling her. Or worse, that she was annoyed.

What isn't she saying?

'Why don't the two of you move up to Broughty Ferry or somewhere in Scotland at least, so we can be closer?' she suggested.

Before I had a chance to reply, Jay responded.

'Cornwall has everything we need. And we've just bought Eastcliff Cottage.'

'We?' Liv muttered thickly.

'Yes, we. I put all of my inheritance money into that purchase.'

I shot Liv a 'How could you?' look.

'We've got too much invested here. Sophie has the perfect study for her writing, and I'm making headway with some of the local musicians.'

'Making headway? Is that your reason for not getting a job?'

'Liv?' I said, surprised.

Jay took a gulp of his pint.

'Anyway,' he continued, ignoring her attack, 'I have open mic sessions set up with this singer for the next few months. Who knows where that will lead?'

'Open mic sessions? I thought you were a professional guitarist, not an amateur?'

Jay smiled at Liv. 'I am, but I am finding my feet here.'

'What? With the woman I saw you with last night?'

'What?' The question had thrown him.

And me.

What woman?

Liv held his eye. The tension between them was palpable. I had no idea what this was about.

'Liv, what is going on?' I interrupted.

'She's my potential new singer. We were discussing a playlist for an open mic session we're doing in a few weeks,' Jay explained. Gone was the indulgent smile.

'At your wedding reception?'

'Rachael was our guest.'

I stared at him, resisting the urge to contradict him, adding to the already tense atmosphere. Rachael was *his* guest. Not mine. The first time I'd met her was last night when he'd introduced us.

'Ask Sophie, artists are always working, regardless. What is that quote you said to me the other day?' he asked me.

I didn't react, caught up in questioning why Liv was so fixated on this Rachael woman.

Why Jay was so fixated on her…

'Sophie?' Jay prompted.

'"There is a splinter of ice in the heart of a writer." It was Graham Greene, in his autobiography, *A Sort of Life,* who said that,' I flatly answered.

'Yeah, that's it,' Jay said. He turned back to Liv, smiling. 'Same applies to songwriters. So, last night, I was talking to Rachael about a song I suddenly felt inspired to write. About Sophie, actually. I wanted it to be a surprise when I played it for her at my first open mic session.'

Liv turned her searing attention from Jay to me. Her eyes burned into mine as she waited for me to say something. Anything. It was evident she didn't believe a word Jay had just said.

What did you see, Liv?

My skin suddenly felt cold despite the scorching mid-afternoon temperature.

I shakily breathed out.

Jay must have felt my body tremble. He turned to me, his voice full of concern. 'Are you okay, babes?'

I shook my head. My mouth felt unbearably dry and my head felt as if it was going to explode.

It was all too much: the heated conversation, Liv's unspoken suspicions, the intrusive sun, the carefree background noise. I wanted to lie down in a cool, dark room and pretend that the past twenty-four hours had never happened.

Jay tenderly stroked my cheek, his eyes filled with concern. 'Come on. Painkillers and bed for you. When the others arrive, tell them Sophie doesn't feel well and that we'll see them later at dinner,' Jay instructed, standing up. 'Come on you,' he tenderly said before kissing my head.

I didn't react.

Couldn't.

I had no idea who I would be going home with, whether it would be the Jay I had encountered last night or the one who had just publicly acted as if he loved me more than life itself. It was alarmingly Jekyll and Hyde behaviour. Whether it would continue or if it was a one-off remained to be seen.

After he had stormed out this morning, I'd called and texted him, but he'd declined my calls and ignored my messages. I had no idea whether our marriage, which was less than twenty-four hours old, was over. I had curled up in a foetal ball of fear in our bed, going over Ben's text which had sent Jay into a furious rage. Then Ben's voicemail.

Maybe that was Jay's justification for the names he had called me?

When he did return home, he walked back in as if the past ten hours had never happened. If anything, he returned as the Jay I knew and had fallen in love with eight months ago. I lay in bed listening to him whistling to himself in the shower. It was a trait of his that I had always found endearing. After sex, Jay would walk around absentmindedly whistling, not even realising he was doing it. This time, I knew it had nothing to do with me. Jay hadn't touched me, bar to greet me with a kiss, which had barely brushed against my lips before he'd headed straight for a shower.

Had he been to see this Rachael woman? This singer he kept raving about?

Tom's words about Jay came back to haunt me: what did I really know about him?

8

I yawned, not quite believing I still felt groggy. It was odd. I had slept for an entire day and night.

It's Sunday, early evening, Sophie. How did yesterday evening and most of today eclipse you?

Part of me questioned whether Jay had put something in the chamomile tea he had encouraged me to drink before I went to bed yesterday afternoon, assuring me it would help me sleep.

For eighteen hours!

Did he drug you with crushed sleeping pills or some other drug?

I discounted the paranoid thought. It was crazy.

You had wine and codeine, and hadn't slept the night before. No wonder you slept for so long!

He had no reason to want me to miss being with my family and best friends. Let alone me not seeing them off when they left to return home.

How could I possibly have slept through the missed phone calls and texts this morning from Grace and Anna? But somehow, I had. I noted that neither my mother nor Liv had messaged or called me, which was odd.

I had tried calling Anna and Grace back, but their phones had gone to voicemail. I assumed they were still travelling home, no doubt dissecting the wedding.

Wedding night...

I had also called Mum and Liv, to be diverted to their voicemails. I had left messages asking them to call me when they got home. I had omitted the fact I was hurt and angry that I hadn't seen them to say goodbye. They would have known how much that would mean to me.

Jay would also know – surely?

So why did he leave you sleeping and go to dinner with them? Why didn't he wake you?

And this morning? How could he leave to say goodbye to them without you? They're your family...Your friends.

And why hadn't Mum or Liv explained to you their sudden departure? Why would they leave it to Jay to tell you?

The shock of my wedding night, raw and visceral, had now dissipated, replaced by numbness as Jay acted as if nothing had occurred. I was struggling with how to talk to him about what had happened.

About breaking my wrist...

Jay had seamlessly returned to being the man I had fallen so madly in love with, who adored and loved me more than I could ever have imagined. No one, apart from my father and Ben, had ever loved me so unconditionally. It was intoxicating and seductive, and I found myself clinging to it as if it were a raft in the middle of a vast ocean.

But what about those cruel words he said to you in the hospital? Then when you came home, calling you a whore? Ask yourself why were you at Treliske Hospital on your wedding night? Why?

'Did you hear what I just said?' Jay called over. 'Maybe I shouldn't be giving you this glass of champagne?'

I reluctantly dragged my attention away from the white-framed bi-folding doors ahead of me and the unadulterated, glorious views of the heather- and gorse-covered cliffs beyond our garden, dramatically plummeting down to Porthtowan Beach and the ocean. Sunday surfers dotted the waves, while clusters of people appeared sprinkled across the sand, basking in the Mediterranean-style weather.

I watched Jay as he walked over to me in the living-room space from the kitchen island carrying two glasses of champagne.

I reached up and took mine.

Sebastian, who was trying to sleep on my lap, glared at me because of the sudden movement.

'To us,' he said, smiling as he clinked my glass.

'To us,' I replied, unsure of him. Unsure of who he was any more.

Tom's words came back to me: '*What do you really know about him?*'

I needed to talk to Tom about what he meant. Crucially without Jay, which might prove difficult as we'd planned to spend the next week at home together as we couldn't afford a honeymoon.

Jay crouched down in front of me and gently kissed me. His lips delicately lingered on mine. 'I love you,' he said as he pulled back and gazed adoringly into my eyes.

I remained silent, unable to return the sentiment.

'Are you okay?'

I stiffly nodded, unable to say what was on my mind. Or vent the rage I felt at him. At my mother and sister and best friends for not being here with me.

For leaving me...

'You are taking the codeine I'm giving you? Not hiding them under your tongue and spitting them out when I'm not looking?' he questioned, assuming my sullenness was pain related.

Pain caused by him.

I nodded.

I watched as Jay leaned back and stretched out on the floor rather than sitting on the other couch.

When I had finally awoken and come downstairs, he had insisted that I lie down on the couch, covering my bare legs in a lightweight grey wool blanket and layering countless cushions to support the weight of my plaster cast.

'I know Liv and your mother think I'm not pulling my weight,' Jay began, surprising me. 'But I'll prove them both wrong. I'm serious when I said I would take care of you,' he stated. 'You know I lost everything because of my ex. Then I gave up my job with the civil service because of the band, and you know how that worked out. No one is more aware than me that I'm starting over again. Here, with you. But I promise you, Soph, I'll make it work out,' he assured me. His eyes were filled with sincerity.

But could I trust what I was seeing? What I was hearing?

'Once I get established here through the open mic sessions, who knows what will happen. I have a really good feeling about Rachael. I never thought it possible, but playing acoustic guitar with a female singer might be it for me. We could be Cornwall's equivalent to The Civil Wars duo.'

'Seriously?' I asked, taken aback.

When I'd met him, the band had just dumped him. He had never really talked about why they had kicked him out, and I had never felt I could ask. But I had assumed that he would end up in another band playing electric guitar, not as an acoustic guitarist with a female singer, which felt very intimate.

Or maybe you're being paranoid?

If I was honest, I didn't think he was a skilled enough guitarist to be part of an acoustic duo. I had watched him play and could see his talent lay in showmanship. It was all an act for him. But it would be harder to hide when it was just him and a singer.

'Rachael has this haunting, unique voice, Soph. With my songwriting and her singing, we could really be onto something. I mean, I don't want to get too carried away, but this could be it.'

'That's great,' I enthused, despite feeling anything but the contrary.

A coiled snake of poisonous jealousy awakened inside me. Its venomous bite filled me with dread about the future and losing Jay.

'Anyway, what I wanted to say was thank you. Without your support, I wouldn't be here now. I don't know where I'd be, but I guarantee it would be some shitty job somewhere, struggling to make ends meet and hating my very existence.'

'I doubt that. I imagine you would be fine without me,' I replied, trying to keep the edge out of my voice.

'Nope, I wouldn't and you know it. I need you, Soph.' He suddenly sat up. 'All of this,' he gestured at the impressive open-plan living space, 'wouldn't be possible if it wasn't for you. The VW Transporter outside is because of you. You traded in your Audi TT convertible, so we had something more suitable for transporting my amps and guitars.'

'And surfboards,' I added. Not that I had ever seen him surf.

The boards and all his music equipment were in the guest bedroom until we could figure out where to store everything.

He smiled. 'Yeah, and those. But the point is, you believe in me, babes. You get me in a way that no one else has ever done. You understand what it is to be an artist and the sacrifices you need to make.'

However, the sacrifice was mine, not Jay's.

He'd persuaded me that my car wouldn't be suitable for the winter country roads and that a VW Transporter would be perfect. He didn't have the funds after he'd invested all his inheritance into the purchase of Eastcliff Cottage, so I'd traded my new Audi in and took out a loan. We were now asset-rich but cash-poor, which explained the small wedding and a honeymoon spent at home.

'Anyway,' he raised his glass, 'to my amazing, beautiful wife without whom I'd be sleeping in my Transporter.'

'Thank you,' I mouthed before taking another sip of champagne.

I didn't correct him with the fact that the Transporter was ours, not solely his, despite the fact he was the registered keeper. However, without me, or my loan with the bank, it wouldn't have existed. Jay had reasoned that he should be the legal owner as he did all the driving and would eventually buy me a new Audi TT for giving up my car.

My independence...

I was now reliant on Jay to drive me everywhere. He had promised he would put me on the insurance but made repeated excuses for not doing so that in the end, I gave up asking. With the wedding and a looming book deadline, I had other things to concern me than Jay's possessiveness over the VW Transporter I had bought him. *Us.*

Such as typing with a broken wrist. I had only managed 40,000 words of my manuscript, distracted by a whirlwind romance that had led me to Cornwall, swiftly followed by a wedding. The word count was supposed to be 90,000, and I had already extended my first of July deadline by a month. I doubted I could write 50,000 words within a month with my hand in a plaster cast.

How did you get so behind, Sophie?

But I knew that events beyond my control had somehow taken precedence.

'You don't mind if I store a few personal things in the attic, do you? I want to try to clear the guest bedroom.'

I realised a flicker of surprise must have crossed my face

because Jay hurriedly added: 'Nothing interesting. Just my parents' belongings and some childhood memorabilia. You're not planning on using the attic, are you?'

I shook my head. 'No.'

I found it odd that he wanted to use the attic, but I had no reason to object.

'Great! I'll get on with that this week.'

As I took another sip of champagne, Jay jumped up and brought the bottle back from the fridge to top me up. I couldn't fault his attentiveness. Whatever I wanted, he would bring it to me. Maybe his behaviour on our wedding night was an anomaly: a combination of alcohol, stress and extreme jealousy?

'Thank you,' I said as he poured.

Jay's phone pinged. I watched as he took it out of his pocket and checked it.

I resisted asking who had texted him.

He looked back up at me, and smiled. 'Well, ma'am, I'm afraid that I'm off duty shortly. I'm heading out for a bit, so you'll have to cope by yourself.'

It took me a moment to realise that he was being serious.

'Where are you going?'

He took a step back. 'I arranged to meet Rachael in The Victory to go over this song I've written.'

I stared at him in disbelief. I felt the waspish, insecure voice inside my head stir.

'It's for you,' he added as if that made a difference.

'You're seriously going out? We're supposed to be spending the week together at home because we couldn't afford a big honeymoon?'

'It's only tonight. We have all week. I don't want Rachael to lose interest, and I'm excited about what we could have together.'

I bet you are!

'Come on, Sophie! You have your writing. I never complain when you lock yourself away for days on end. Do I?' he demanded.

'It's not the same,' I countered.

'Isn't it? What do you think I do when you're working twenty-four seven?'

I shrugged. It wasn't comparable.

But Jay took my silence as evidence that he was right. 'Precisely. So don't begrudge me finding something that could lead to work. Okay?'

Unable to look him in the eye, I took another drink.

I didn't remind him that he had promised faithfully that he would find a paying job, regardless of what it was, when we moved to Cornwall. Chasing dreams with some random singer he had just met wasn't my idea of something that could lead to a lucrative income.

'Anyway, I'm sure your mother or Grace will call tonight to catch up with you.'

'Why didn't you wake me this morning so I could come with you?' I asked, annoyance loosening my tongue. 'I didn't know that Grace and the others intended to leave so early. I would have liked to have said goodbye to them.'

Grace had driven with Anna to Cornwall and agreed to give my sister and mother a lift to Newquay airport for their return flight to Edinburgh airport, where my mother had left her car to drive back to Broughty Ferry. Grace and Anna had always planned on leaving Sunday morning. But as for Liv and my mother, they weren't supposed to go home until tomorrow. I was devastated when I had finally woken up, to be told by Jay about the new arrangements organised at dinner last night during my absence. Not only had I missed dinner, but I hadn't even had the opportunity to say goodbye. I didn't want to jump to conclusions without talking to either Liv or my mother first. I had questioned whether something – or someone – had upset them this weekend. Whether the events of Friday evening had caused them to leave earlier than planned or my conspicuous absence was the reason, I couldn't say.

'Joanna gave me strict instructions to leave you if you were still asleep, which you were, saying she would FaceTime you this evening when she got back home. The last thing I wanted to do was get in your mother's bad books. It's hard enough as it is living up to your family's standards without constantly being in the shadow of your perfect, rugby-playing ex-fiancé who you were with for eleven years. And you know how I know? Because they talk about him all the bloody time! So, forgive me for doing what she said. And I apologise if whatever I do isn't good enough for you. Including trying to get some semblance of a career here!'

I couldn't move past the reality that my friends and family had left without even saying goodbye to me. And to make it worse, Jay was heading out to meet up with this woman he had only known for a short time. Yet, he felt close enough to her to invite her to our wedding.

Close enough to her for Liv to take note.

I frowned at him. I couldn't understand how he could leave me on our first proper night together after getting married. However, that fact seemed irrelevant to him. I wondered if this was payback because of Ben. I was certain my family and friends didn't mention him. However, Jay complained that they had repeatedly brought Ben up in the conversation. Surely they would have gone out of their way to avoid his name? No, this was about Friday night and the text Ben had sent me, the one Jay had read. Later followed by the voicemail when I was in A&E.

Not that Jay had mentioned reading them. No. He had simply accused me of cheating with my ex-fiancé.

Nor had I brought up his accusation.

I watched as he stood up. He drained his champagne glass and walked over to the kitchen, placing it in the dishwasher.

'Is that it? You're leaving?' I spluttered, incredulous.

He looked at me. 'I don't think there's anything left to say. Do you?'

'What?' I questioned, incandescent.

'I never took you for the jealous type, Sophie. You know I don't do jealousy. That was my ex's thing.'

'Me? Jealous?' I demanded. I couldn't believe him.

I watched as he picked up the keys and his wallet.

'What about our wedding gifts and cards?' I demanded, gesturing to the dining room table behind me piled high with unopened gifts, cards and the remnants of our wedding cake.

He walked out to the hallway without saying a word.

'You're leaving? And you dare to call me jealous? Why don't we discuss you reading my texts and listening to my voicemail from my ex? And then your jealous rage afterwards?' I shouted out after him.

He continued down the hallway.

'How do you explain this?' I yelled, raising my broken wrist.

Startled, Sebastian glared at me, then jumped from my lap onto the waxed wooden floor and sauntered off, swishing his tail in objection.

The next thing I heard was the front door slamming.

I was acutely aware we still hadn't had sex. Not that I wanted to be physically intimate after what had happened. I still didn't understand how Jay could have radically changed within hours of me marrying him. My mind masochistically turned to Rachael, the singer he was meeting. The one that Liv had singled out as a problem in our new marriage. We couldn't have been more polarised in our looks if we had tried, or our personalities. She towered over me, and Jay, with her razor-sharp, bobbed black hair and angular features, enhanced with lustful full red lips and black, enticing eyeliner. She was in her mid-forties and exuded the confidence of the years of experience behind her.

It was only the second day of our marriage, and Jay had left me in pursuit of what? Another woman?

9

I heard the Transporter screech down the narrow cliff road.

'What the…?' I muttered to myself.

The first moment we had some alone time without guests or family, Jay had made arrangements to be with someone else. Some person he barely knew who suddenly mattered more to him than me. Someone that I had met just once, and that was at my wedding.

Rachael…

I went to my study for my journal and pen to document what had just happened. I returned to the couch and opened it to the last entry: the morning of my wedding.

I felt sick as I read my gushing, love-struck words bursting with happiness at what was about to happen that day.

It was supposed to be the happiest day of my life… So how could it have all gone so wrong?

How could I be here alone, without my new husband, family or best friends?

My phone suddenly started to ring. I was surprised that it wasn't Jay calling me to apologise; it was Grace.

'Hi,' I answered, trying to sound upbeat. 'Are you back home?'

'Yeah. Long drive because of horrendous traffic and being diverted, but finally here.'

'And Anna?'

'I dropped her off earlier.'

Before I had a chance to speak, she suddenly asked: 'Are you okay?'

'Of course. Why?' I lied. I was struggling with the question of whether my mother, sister and best friends would really leave without saying goodbye.

But they did, Sophie. They left.

How could they do that to you?

'Just odd that we didn't see you last night or this morning. Anna and I haven't seen you since your wedding night.'

'I know and I am devastated that I haven't seen you or Anna. I swear I slept straight through yesterday afternoon to today. I only wanted a nap as I didn't feel so great, and I woke up to find eighteen hours had passed,' I explained.

I could hear her inhaling deeply on a cigarette.

I assumed she was internally questioning why Jay didn't wake me.

Or did she suspect something?

'Why didn't you come to the cottage? You know how much I wanted to show it off?' I asked. I was gearing up to ask how she and Anna could have left without coming to see me first. It wasn't like them.

What had happened for them to leave without even a goodbye?

'Because we didn't feel welcome,' she answered.

'What?' I hadn't expected that reply. 'You know you and Anna are always welcome?'

'Are we? Seems that's not the case any more,' she stated.

'What do you mean?' I questioned, feeling my anxiety building at the unfamiliar hostility in her voice.

'I had suggested last night at dinner that we call by this morning before we left for London, so we could have a tour of your new home, but your new husband was adamant it wasn't happening. He said you wouldn't be up to it. I insisted that you wanted us to see it. But he point-blank refused. If anything, he was really off about it. I mean, you broke your wrist at your wedding reception and Anna and I haven't seen you since, which we both find weird.'

Why the hell would Jay say I wasn't up to them calling in?

I could hear the concern in her voice over Jay's behaviour.

Controlling behaviour...

My phone started to buzz: it was Liv.

Damn!

I didn't want to cut Grace off, but I had no choice. I needed to speak with Liv.

'Look, Liv's calling. I need to talk to her. I'll phone back. Okay?'

'I'm in court all week and have a pile of notes to prepare for the morning. Let's try to speak next weekend,' Grace asserted.

'Next weekend?' I questioned, hurt that she wanted to leave it that long.

I didn't know whether she heard me before she cut the call. Grace was a successful lawyer and consequently in high demand, which meant her downtime was sparse and precious. It was evident she felt put out that she had made this effort to come to my wedding for a long weekend, and I had been absent for most of it.

Or were you drugged?

I discounted the paranoid thought that kept niggling at the dark recesses of my mind.

'Hey, Liv,' I answered. 'What happened?'

'What do you mean?' Liv coolly replied.

'Why did you and Mum leave a day early?' I refrained from adding: *When I had a broken wrist and needed your support, not desertion.*

I heard Liv take an intake of breath. Then there was mumbling in the background – my mother.

'Is Mum there?'

Liv hesitated.

'I want to talk to her. Put her on,' I instructed. 'Liv? Liv?'

It suddenly went quiet. I realised that Liv had put me on mute.

How could she? And what were they saying that they didn't want me to overhear?

'Look. Mum's really tired, Soph,' Liv explained, coming back to me. 'She's got one of her horrific headaches and doesn't feel up to talking. The weekend has really taken it out of her. And she insisted on driving home from the airport.'

'She doesn't feel up to talking to me? ME?' I repeated.

'Sorry,' Liv replied.

Sorry doesn't cut it!

'What's going on, Liv?' I asked, inwardly raging at my mother's refusal to talk to me. Not to even ask how I was feeling. I hadn't seen her since I felt unwell yesterday afternoon.

Rage quickly dissipated, turning to panic.

What had happened for your mother not to want to talk to you?

I thought about what Grace had said about Jay refusing to let them come back to the cottage.

I could feel the panic unfurling inside me, rising up to catch me at the back of my throat.

'Liv?'

'Look, you really should have made an effort to come and thank Mum for coming to your wedding. You know how difficult it was for her without Daddy.'

Guilt silenced me.

'And... well, we travelled a long way to support you. You spent no time with us—'

I abruptly cut her off. 'I fractured my wrist in two places! I spent my wedding night in hospital. How could I have spent that time with you?'

'You didn't even invite us to see your new home.'

I could hear the hurt in her voice.

I knew I personally hadn't, but Jay had invited them over.

He had, hadn't he?

'Didn't Jay invite you last night at dinner to come here this evening?' I asked.

'No. He didn't say a word.'

'I promise that we planned on having you over for dinner this evening. Why do you think I was so shocked when I found out that you had left.'

'Maybe if you had come to see us off, then you would have had the opportunity to tell us?' She faltered for a moment, before continuing, 'Jay made it abundantly transparent he didn't want us there.'

'I have no idea why he wouldn't want you to call by. Of course he would want you to see the cottage. We both do.'

It made no sense.

Liv didn't say anything.

'Anyway, Jay said Mum instructed him not to wake me this morning. That if I was still feeling unwell, to let me sleep. That she would FaceTime me when you guys got home.'

'No, Mum insisted that she saw you before we left,' Liv argued. 'She wanted to talk to you in person about something. She made that quite clear to Jay.'

I was the one who was now silent. It didn't make any sense. Jay had said the opposite to me.

'What did Jay say then, when he showed up this morning without me?' I asked.

'He didn't.'

'What do you mean he didn't?'

'Exactly what I said. Jay didn't show up.'

Jay didn't show up?

I had assumed he had seen them off because he wasn't home when I woke up around midday to see the missed calls and texts alerting me to the surprising news that Liv and my mother were at Newquay Airport waiting to board.

Where was he then? Or had he even come home last night?

I had no idea...

I realised I would never have known as I was out of it.

Had he drugged you with something in the chamomile tea?

I rejected the notion as quickly as it came to me. It was a ridiculous idea. For where would he have spent the night?

Or with whom?

Rachael came to mind.

'You can see why Mum's upset with you?' Liv pointed out.

'Yes, of course I can. Look, you know Jay and I are spending this week at home together because we can't afford a honeymoon? Why don't we drive up and you guys can spend some time getting to know him and I can make it up to Mum? Instead of staying with the two of you, I'll book a hotel in the Ferry.'

'Nice idea, pity Jay's already booked your honeymoon,' Liv curtly replied.

'He what?' I asked, stunned.

We had no money left for a honeymoon.

'Oh shit!' muttered Liv. 'Sorry, it was supposed to be a surprise.'

Not that she sounded sorry.

I didn't say anything and waited for her to continue.

'Jay swore us to secrecy when he told us last night. He was worried about your broken wrist and whether the airline would let you fly, so he asked our advice. If he hadn't been worried about losing over eight grand, I doubt he would have said anything to us.

He's booked some luxury hotel in Barbados. Even said the name, but I can't recall it,' Liv answered.

Her words, 'Over eight grand', made me feel nauseous.

I was stunned into silence.

'He's waiting to see what the orthopaedic consultant says at your hospital appointment tomorrow as to whether you can or can't fly,' explained Liv in response to my lack of reply.

Again, I didn't say anything.

'Oh shit, Soph! I'm so sorry I've spoiled it for you. Just act all surprised, will you, when Jay tells you?'

If he tells you...

I didn't trust him. Nor did I know him. Not any more.

We had agreed that we couldn't afford a honeymoon.

Why would he make a unilateral decision on something so big?

'I really hope the consultant tells you that you can go. Christ! Eight grand's a lot to lose. And he didn't take out any insurance, so he can't claim the money back because you broke your wrist.'

I felt sick. I couldn't imagine where he had found the funds to pay for such a lavish honeymoon.

I swallowed, trying to dislodge the tight knot at the back of my throat.

'Are you sure he said that? I mean eight thousand pounds on a honeymoon?'

It didn't make sense. Jay said he had no money. Surely Liv must be mistaken? He was reliant on my income. We both were, and would have to wait until the submission of my next novel to release my advance. I had explained all this to Jay before we'd relocated to Cornwall, which was why I was so eager for him to get a job.

'Mum and I have noticed that Jay...' She faltered.

'What?' I questioned, not sure if I wanted to hear it.

Liv sighed. 'Just that he seems to have done everything he can to keep us from seeing you on your own.'

'No, that's not true...'

Or is it, Soph?

'Is that what Mum wanted to talk to me about before you both left?' I questioned.

Liv didn't reply.

'Liv?'

What are you scared to tell me, Liv? Did you witness something between Jay and Rachael?

Or...

Don't go there, Sophie!

'Where's Jay?' she suddenly asked.

Why would you want to know?

'Out with...' I paused.

I swallowed, trying to ignore the stabbing doubts about my sister. It was odd she was so off with Jay on our wedding night. It didn't make sense. I didn't believe she had seen him twist my wrist until it broke: simply because my mother and Liv would never have left me alone in the hands of a man who hurt me.

Never.

I tried to drown out the hornet's nest of buzzing whispers in my head, swirling in a desperate frenzy, questioning whether Liv would do the unthinkable – again. For Liv had drunkenly thrown herself at Ben at our father's funeral. I had struggled at the time to reconcile with her, feeling beyond betrayed. It didn't matter whether our relationship had turned stale: Liv should never have tried to kiss him.

Did something happen between Liv and Jay?

10

'Liv? Whatever it is, just tell me!' I demanded, getting up off the couch.

I pushed the poisonous thought away. Liv wouldn't do that to you – again. Not with Jay.

I waited for her to reply as I returned my journal to my study desk, doubting I would be in the mood to write anything after the phone call.

'Liv?'

I held my breath.

'If I tell you, promise me you won't lose it?' she warily asked as I headed back into the kitchen.

'Are you still there?' Liv asked when I failed to respond.

I now had the fridge door open, reaching for a bottle of wine, which was luckily a screw top and not a cork. My phone was on the work counter on speaker. I realised how badly I was trembling when I spilt the wine.

'Yes,' I answered, dreading whatever she was going to tell me.

The reason why they had suddenly left without even saying goodbye to you?

What had happened for them to do something so out of character? So hurtful?

'Promise me, Soph,' she repeated as the front door suddenly opened and then slammed shut.

I hurriedly picked up my phone and fumbled as I tried to take it off speaker before Jay walked through.

I hadn't expected him to return home so soon.

Unable to disguise my hostility, I ignored Jay as he came into the open-plan room, not believing he would have spent eight thousand pounds on a honeymoon.

We agreed we couldn't afford a big honeymoon.

YOU couldn't afford, Sophie. So, how did he pay for it?

'Soph?' Liv repeated.

'Is that Liv?' questioned Jay, nodding at my phone in my hand as he walked past me to the fridge.

I nodded.

'Tell her I send them my love,' Jay said as he took out a bottle of beer.

'Jay sends his love,' I numbly repeated into the phone.

'Jay's there?' Liv uneasily questioned.

'Uhuh,' I answered, the phone firmly pressed against me ear. 'He's just got back.'

I could feel his eyes watching me. Scrutinising every muscle in my face.

'Okay. Just forget everything I said. Yeah?' whispered Liv.

Jay walked around the kitchen island and looked at me.

'Everything okay?' he mouthed with a look of concern.

I nodded.

'Liv?' I questioned.

She had gone.

Jay raised his eyebrow at me. 'What was that all about?'

Despite his neutral tone, I could see the flicker of suspicion in his eyes as he watched me while taking a swig of beer.

'Nothing,' I replied. 'Why are you back so early? I thought you and Rachael had a song to work on?' I facetiously asked.

He shrugged my question off.

'Did she not turn up?' I cynically asked.

'How about you join me outside?' he suggested. 'We need to talk.'

I watched him walk over and open the bi-folding doors, then step out into the garden. The roar of the sea crashed forcefully into the room.

My mind was racing.

What had Liv been about to tell me? What could have possibly happened that caused them to unexpectedly leave? To abandon me?

Carrying my glass of wine and phone, I stepped out onto the terrace, pushing the door behind me with my foot so Sebastian couldn't escape.

The balmy evening breeze wrapped itself around my body as I took in the dramatic coastline and the random pools of cobalt blue in the Atlantic Ocean. The cliff dramatically plummeted ahead of me, giving the illusion that the ocean began where our garden ended. We had bought the cottage for the sublime views and the privacy. It was also why it had nearly bankrupted us – me.

'Sit down for a moment,' Jay said, gesturing to the wooden lounger next to him.

I hesitated, unsure of what was happening.

'Please?' Gone was the relaxed expression. He looked older, more lined and tired than usual. Even his deep tan seemed to have waned.

Maybe he's going to talk about breaking your wrist on our wedding night? Or the Caribbean honeymoon he booked despite agreeing we couldn't afford one? Or why he made your family and best friends feel so unwelcome?

I could feel the anger and resentment churning up in me like the ocean beyond.

I sat down, watching as he reached for his beer on the garden table and took a glug. The thick silver rings on his fingers glinted in the fiery rays of the setting sun.

'Do you regret marrying me?' he asked.

Maybe...

'You could have married someone your own age,' he continued. 'Someone who has similar interests as you, and has money.'

'I have money!' I countered, not needing anyone to support me.

'You *had* money,' he pointed out. 'If it wasn't for me, you would still have money. Your savings, your flat in Kensington and... Joanna and Liv's approval of the man you married.'

'Why does it always come back to Ben?' I demanded, not needing Jay to mention him by name. I could feel the irritation creeping up from my chest to my neck as my pale skin flushed red and angry.

'Because you were engaged to him before me, that's why. I got in the way of the two of you getting back together.'

Within the past year, my father had died, followed by Ben breaking off our engagement and Jay entering my life. I had then sold my flat in London and bought an outrageously priced cottage overlooking the North Atlantic Ocean in Cornwall. I was newly married, but was Jay the right man? Had I married the wrong person?

Again, maybe...

The loss of the two men I most loved in my life had somehow brought me to this place.

Had you reacted out of grief? Was Mum right? Was this a rebound?

I questioned what my father would think. But I knew the

answer. He would agree with my mother that our whirlwind wedding was a classic rebound.

And at what cost, Sophie?

'You didn't want to break off the engagement. If things had gone to plan, you'd be married to Ben now,' Jay stated, as if reading my mind.

'Where's this coming from?' This wasn't like him. He didn't do vulnerability.

'I... I just can't bear the idea of losing you,' Jay confessed.

I was caught off-guard by the emotion in his voice.

Silent, I stared at Jay, waiting for him to acknowledge the accusations I'd thrown at him as he'd stormed out earlier: that he'd read Ben's text, culminating in my husband of fewer than seven hours breaking my wrist in a violent, jealous outburst, and then listened to the voicemail Ben had left me at 1.03 p.m., resulting in him losing it and accusing me of cheating on him when we returned home from the hospital yesterday morning.

'I was a shit to you on Friday night. I lost my temper and...' He stopped and took another swig of beer before continuing, 'I was terrified that you had really hurt yourself, and it came out all wrong. I wasn't angry at you in the hospital; I was angry at the situation. That something bad had happened to you. I swear on my life that I will never behave like that again. You're the kindest, gentlest person I know, and you didn't deserve that on our wedding night. Not you, Soph. Me, yeah. But not you. I so wanted it all to be perfect for you.'

This isn't an apology, Sophie! He hasn't even acknowledged twisting your wrist so far back it snapped.

He raised his glistening, troubled eyes to meet my gaze. 'I can't stand the thought that your ex is waiting for you to admit that you made a mistake. That I'm the mistake.'

Tears spilled over from his eyes.

I watched as he roughly swiped at them.

It was the first time I'd witnessed him crying.

'Soph?'

I looked at him.

'Please, say something? Anything?'

'What do you want me to say?'

'That you forgive me?'

'For what?'

'For reading Ben's text. For losing my temper...' He faltered.

It's not enough. He needs to say it.

'If it hadn't been for me, you wouldn't have broken your wrist and...' He abruptly stopped.

I didn't break my wrist! You did!

I watched as more tears slid down his face.

He shook his head. 'I'm sorry. Oh God, I am so sorry... I'm sorry, Soph... I'll never hurt you again.'

I narrowed my eyes at him.

Was this his acknowledgement that he broke your wrist?

Before I could challenge him, he continued.

'I've tried to make it up to you. To show you how much I love you. I left you sleeping yesterday evening and this morning because I thought that's what you wanted. I collected your mother, sister and two friends and drove them to The Fish House for dinner. I then drove them back to the Driftwood at the end of the night. I didn't do that for myself. I did that for you because they're your people, and I knew you would want them looked after.'

I didn't respond. I recalled Grace telling me she had suggested to him last night that they call by the cottage this morning before heading back to London.

To check up on you...

But he had refused. Grace's troublingly words came back to me: '*If anything, he was really off about it.*'

'But they didn't want me there.'

I shook my head, 'That's not—'

He cut me off. 'I went to the Driftwood this morning to thank them for coming to our wedding. And to explain that I tried waking you, but I couldn't stir you.'

'What happened?' I asked.

I watched with surprise as pain flashed across his face as he recalled this morning's events.

'When I got there, they were nowhere to be seen. I asked reception, to be told they had checked out an hour earlier. But they asked me to meet them at that specific time at dinner last night. They knew I was supposed to be coming with you to see them off. So why would they leave without saying goodbye to us? To me?'

Incredulous, I stared at him.

It couldn't have been further from Liv's version of events.

Why would Liv lie to me?

Or was this Liv and my mother's way of sabotaging our relationship? To make me doubt the man I had married?

PART TWO

'Now hatred is by far the longest pleasure
   Men love in haste but they detest at leisure.'

— LORD BYRON, *DON JUAN*

11

'Let me get this right, they agreed a time with you?'

Jay nodded.

'Yet, when you arrived at the hotel, they had checked out an hour before without calling or texting to let you know not to come? Or even to give you – us – the option to arrive earlier?'

'Yes.'

'Did the receptionist give a reason for their early departure?'

'No.'

My mother and Liv had also failed to inform me about their new arrangements. Until Liv had called me just now, I had heard nothing from her or my mother since leaving them at the Driftwood Spars yesterday afternoon.

'I can't believe they did this!' I muttered, reaching for my phone on the table beside my wine glass.

'What are you doing?'

'I'm going to call Liv and have it out with her. This isn't on. Christ!'

'No... Please, Soph?' Jay pleaded, grabbing my good arm to stop me. 'Just leave it. They hate me enough as it is without adding more reason.'

'They have no right to hate you! You've done nothing but chauffeur them around and look after them in my absence. I need to say something. They've gone too far.'

'No. Leave it. Please?'

I hesitated.

'I don't think it would make a difference, to be honest. I'll never be good enough for them. And all it will do is cause a huge argument. I don't want to be the reason for you falling out with your family.'

'Why won't you let me tell them about your ex and how you left her your house? That you signed it over to her? Then they would understand what I see in you,' I suggested.

He shook his head. 'What difference do you think that would make? They'd still think I'm a loser because I don't have a job. Hell! I know I'm a loser.' Jay dropped his head and looked at the beer bottle cradled in his hands.

'Don't say that!'

He dragged his head up and looked at me. 'Why? It's true.'

'Losers don't protect two little boys, do they?'

'Hah! Where are they now? As soon as she got what she wanted, she refused to let them see me because they're not my biological sons, even though I raised them as if they were my own. For eight years, I was in their lives. She was pregnant with Eli when I met her, and Samuel was just one and a half. I moved her and Samuel in and turned my music room into a nursery for Eli. I turned my world upside down for her. And for what?'

The pain radiated from him. I understood from the tortured look in his eyes why he refused to talk about his past, as it stirred up too many regrets.

'I had the chance of a European tour with the band I was with at the time, and I turned it down for her. She couldn't cope without me. Begged me to stay. Said if I didn't, she would kill herself, leaving the boys all alone. So, I put my dreams and ambitions on hold for her. And you know why?'

I didn't say anything. I waited for him to continue.

'Because I didn't want to see those boys taken into care. That's why. She had no family to speak of, and who knows where or who the boys' dads were because you couldn't believe a word out of her mouth!'

I remained silent. Jay rarely talked about his ex.

'Then to find out she'd moved my mate, who I'd known since childhood, into what was once my house, that she'd been screwing him while still with me... She used to tell me she was going to the gym when she was meeting him! The gym of all places! God, Soph! I trusted her. That's what rips me apart. You know?'

'I know.' There was nothing else I could say.

'Without you, and your support, I don't know how I would have continued after her, and then the band fucking me over. You're the reason I'm still here. You know that, right?'

I held his intense gaze and nodded.

'Without you, I'm nothing. You're the only person who believed in me, unlike my ex. She was jealous of me playing gigs. She was jealous of everything and anything. But you're not like that. You get me because you know what it is to be an artist. You write fiction, and I write songs and play the guitar. I would never ask you to give it up, and I know you would never ask me to stop chasing my dreams. To quit and settle for second or third best. I'm more than that. *We*'re more than that.' He faltered. 'I couldn't cope without you by my side, Sophie. You're my best friend, my lover, my everything.' He shook his head. 'I was so scared that what happened on our wedding night would drive you away. You would think that was who I was and leave me for Ben.'

I remained silent.

'I promise it will never happen again. Please believe me? I couldn't cope without you,' he pleaded. 'Soph? Please?'

I reluctantly nodded.

'And you won't leave me?' he questioned.

As long as you don't hurt me again.

'Soph?' His voice quivered with fear.

'If you ever hurt me or call me names like that again, I will leave you, Jay. And that's a promise,' I warned him. 'No second chances.'

He nodded. 'Thank you. It's just…' He stopped himself from saying what was on his mind and ran his hand over his cropped, dark hair.

'Just what?' I asked.

He turned his gaze to meet mine. 'The fear that you'll leave me won't ever go while Ben's still very present in your life. In our lives.'

'He's not.'

'The two of you have been texting,' he fired back.

'I—'

He cut me off. 'He texted you on our wedding day to tell you he's upset you went ahead and married me. That he still loves you. He stalks your Instagram account. When something happened to you, your sister called him, regardless of the stupid o'clock hour.'

I stared at him, unable to say what I was thinking: *my mother and sister called you multiple times, frantic, and you couldn't be bothered to answer your phone to them. Or even send a text to update them. Yet, Ben immediately picked up when Liv called him.*

Neither of us spoke. I found it unsettling how quickly the conversation could turn.

'Did you speak to him?'

'No, of course not,' I answered, annoyed.

'There's no of course not!' he retaliated. 'Did you message him?'

I faltered. 'No.'

'Don't lie to me.'

'I'm not!'

I hadn't told Jay that Ben had left another voicemail message while I'd slept last night and he was at The Fish House. Ben had repeated his concerns for me: concerns about who I'd married. I'd deleted it for fear of Jay listening to it. I still hadn't called him back, terrified that I would break, when I heard Ben's gentle, comforting, soft Scottish lilt; that I would confess that Jay broke my wrist in a jealous, drunken rage.

'Sophie? If I find out you've been talking to him—'

I immediately cut him off. 'I haven't.'

'Prove it,' Jay replied.

'How?' I wasn't even sure that was possible.

'Give me your phone,' he instructed.

'What?'

'I'm not asking a lot, Sophie,' he continued. 'Imagine if my ex texted me on our wedding night, declaring she still loved me and wanted me back. Or I had a sibling who was in the habit of ringing my ex when they were worried about me. How would you like it?' He paused as he studied my mute reaction. 'Unlike you, I have no family to interfere in our relationship. You don't realise how lucky you are that I have no baggage.'

I remained silent.

'And I have only been engaged to you. You're the only person I have ever wanted to marry. I wish I could say the same about you.'

Neither of us spoke for a few painfully protracted minutes as the waves crashed against the rocks far below.

I accepted we were at stalemate. Jay had warned me he was stubborn, but I hadn't anticipated to this extent.

'Fine,' I eventually acquiesced, handing him my phone. I had nothing to hide. He had already read the text Ben had sent me and listened to the voicemail on the night of our wedding. If Jay needed this assurance, I would do it.

'Thanks,' he said, taking my phone and unlocking it.

I had shared my passcode some time back, convinced he would never access my phone without my consent. Our wedding night had proved me wrong.

I watched as he scrolled through the texts until he found Ben.

He clicked on his last message. Then started typing.

'What are you doing?' I asked, horrified.

'Jay?' I repeated with more urgency when he ignored me.

'Sending him a message telling him it's over.'

'Come on? Seriously?'

'Done,' he said.

'Don't send it until I've read it.'

I then heard the whooshing sound, which confirmed the text had gone.

What the hell?

'Jay?' I questioned, horrified.

He ignored me as he continued scrolling through my phone.

'What are you doing now?'

'Blocking him and deleting his number.'

I refrained from telling Jay that I could easily get Ben's number from Liv.

He handed me my phone back.

I looked for the text Jay had just sent Ben. I read it feeling sick:

Stop contacting me. I'm married now.

'That's all you said?' I nervously questioned.

'Yup,' he answered before taking a drink of beer. 'That's all.'

I stared at my phone, not quite sure what just happened. Or why I handed it over.

Jay suddenly got off his chair and knelt before me, placing his hands around my waist.

I looked down at him.

'Babes, I left Rachael at the bar and came home because I knew it upset you that I'd agreed to meet her. And I get it. Not that you have any reason to be jealous or insecure because I love and adore you and only you.'

I stared at him, wishing that the violence and name calling on our wedding night had never happened. That I could accept his declaration of love without the constant doubts that he would change again.

For the worse.

'And it's the same for me with Ben. I hate it knowing he can text or call you whenever he feels like it. Especially knowing he's desperate to get back with you. But he made a choice. He left you for someone else.'

I stared at him.

'And now you made a choice. You married me. Your ex has to accept that. All I've done is lay down some boundaries.' Jay sighed heavily. 'After Mum died, I found out my ex had cheated on me, and I can admit that I struggled to keep it together. Then you burst into my life and brought me back from the brink. You're everything to me. And I don't want anyone jeopardising what we have, especially your ex.'

I remained silent.

'What happened on our wedding night will never happen again. I promise you that, Sophie. Now your ex is gone, we can focus on our marriage. We own this spectacular cottage, which we'll make ours and fill with our children. I'll be making money from my music by then, and you'll have countless bestsellers and film deals.'

That was the plan.

Had been the plan...

He held my gaze, his feverish eyes burning into mine. 'I love you. I love you more than life itself. And I'll do whatever it takes for us to be together,' he said, straightening up to gently kiss my lips.

He sounded so sincere.

But can you trust him, Sophie?

12

I woke up and leisurely stretched out, forgetting for a moment about the cast on my arm.

'Damn!' I cursed at the cumbersome weight reminding me it was there.

I blinked as the sun sneakily streamed through the large window overlooking the Atlantic.

'Jay?' I mumbled, half asleep.

I felt across his side of the bed, but it was empty.

Then I heard him downstairs, whistling.

Followed by the sound of the grinder crushing coffee beans.

I thought about our conversation last night. He had apologised for his behaviour and had attempted to make me understand why he had reacted so violently to Ben's text. Not that I condoned his behaviour, but at least I could understand it. He had promised never to let his anger get out of control again, and I believed him. It was the first time I had witnessed this side of him, and I was prepared to accept it was a one-off. We had too much invested together in Eastcliff Cottage for me to call it quits.

Grace had jokingly offered to write a prenuptial agreement

protecting my income and the substantial funds I had put into Eastcliff Cottage, which had far outweighed Jay's contribution. She may have made light of it, but there was an element of her that was concerned that I'd sold my Kensington flat on a romantic whim for a significantly older man who had no income and needed me to support him, down to the level of money for attending music gigs or drinking with his friends, which was often now we'd relocated to Cornwall. She hadn't said it outright, but she'd hinted at whether Jay was attracted to me for me or the lifestyle that I could potentially offer him if *Winter's Child* became a film.

Grace had also pointed out that since Jay had invested all his inheritance into the property, I couldn't force him out if I decided it wasn't working. Not that I had any plans to throw him out. Jay's vulnerability last night had brought us closer together emotionally and physically. We had finally made love. I was starting to understand that sex was a way of connecting with Jay. It made him feel good about himself. About us.

The first time we had sex after our fourth date was awkward and bitterly disappointing. I had expected, given the sexual energy Jay exuded and the confidence that came with his age, for it to be incredible. The reality couldn't have been further from the truth. It was monotonous and lacked any depth or sensation. I was surprised at his vulnerableness and taken aback by his directness: *was he too small?*

It was a cruel rhetorical question regarding his manhood, what would medically be termed a micropenis: a condition caused by hormonal or genetic reasons.

Politeness had forced me to mumble 'no' to protect his ego. That was the first and only time he'd mentioned concerns over his atypically small penis. What Jay physically lacked in bed was compensated by his gentle, charismatic and loving nature and desire to put me first.

I now questioned whether I had fallen in love with the idea of someone coveting, even worshipping me: a love so all-consuming that I lost myself in his absolute adoration of me.

I had made my girlfriends jealous with anecdotes of how he attended to my every need and second-guessed my desires. At six o'clock, without fail, Jay would bring me an iced gin and tonic, followed later by wine, insisting I relaxed after writing all day while he waited on me. He even surprised me with clothes he bought on a whim because he thought the colour or the outfit would suit me. Effectively, Jay made me fall head over heels for him by simply loving me in a way I had never experienced before: it was intense, intoxicating and addictive.

Counterintuitively, my lack of physical connection to him had deepened and intensified my emotional attachment. So, when Grace and Anna asked about the sex, I lied, not wanting to humiliate or betray Jay, preferring the illusion that it was perfect. It was a trade I was happy to make as I knew that sexual chemistry typically waned after six months to two years. We had a much deeper connection built on trust, intimacy and loyalty, which was more important to me than a short-lived honeymoon period. We were committed to each other, and together anything was possible.

He had my back, which made me feel safe and protected. I had never craved security as much as I did when I met Jay. I assumed it was an effect of two sudden losses in my life: my father's passing and my ex's sudden decision to cancel our wedding and play the field. And Jay gave me security overload. After our fourth date, he never left me, not even for a night, and eight months later, we were married. I still couldn't believe it had all happened so quickly, so unexpectantly.

So, what happened on your wedding night, Sophie?

'Hey, gorgeous,' greeted Jay, interrupting my thoughts.

I looked up.

Here was the man I had fallen so intoxicatingly in love with and agreed to marry.

'Hey, you,' I replied, smiling, never wanting him to disappear again.

He laid a tray with warm croissants and fresh coffee on the bed and sat beside me.

'Ahh, Jay,' I said, noting the single red rose he must have picked from the garden.

'Coffee?' he questioned, smiling at me.

I hadn't seen him look so happy since the eve of our wedding.

'Of course,' I replied. I was a coffee addict and couldn't get enough of the black stuff in the morning.

I watched as he lifted the cafetière and poured me a cup of strong black coffee.

'What's that?' I asked, pointing to the tray and the small envelope with my name delicately written across it.

'Ahh,' he sheepishly grinned, 'this is my wedding gift to you.'

I sat up in bed. 'I don't need a gift.'

'I know you don't need one, but you deserve one,' he said, handing me the envelope.

I opened it and stared, transfixed at the words:

Will you do me the honour of joining me for our honeymoon in Barbados tomorrow?

'Jay?' Liv had forewarned me, but I had completely forgotten about it. 'How did you—'

'Shh,' he murmured as he leaned in and silenced me with a kiss.

'Will you?' he murmured, pulling back and gazing into my eyes. 'That is if your orthopaedic consultant agrees to it when we see him later.'

'Of course, I will,' I replied, kissing him.

I silenced the questions about how we could afford such a holiday. The moment was too perfect to ruin it with pragmatism.

* * *

I spent the afternoon in a mad panic, tying up loose ends. I wrote and posted thank you cards for our wedding gifts, emailed my agent and editor to inform them of my broken wrist which would be in a cast for six weeks, and begged for a further extension, explaining Jay had surprised me with a honeymoon in the Caribbean. I was mindful I wouldn't be paid until the manuscript was delivered, as per the terms of my contract. I then called my mother in the evening and explained that I was sorry I didn't see her before she'd left yesterday. That I had slept until midday. She accepted my explanation, asking if I had taken sleeping tablets for me to have slept so deeply for so long. Which I hadn't.

Or had you unwittingly taken them?

I noticed some odd white grainy substance at the bottom of my wine glass when Jay refilled it for me later that night. Paranoid, after my conversation with my mother, I questioned what it could be, and he suggested it was residue from the dishwasher tablet, which seemed more plausible than him drugging me with sleeping tablets.

My mother and I had ended the short, polite conversation with so much unsaid. She didn't raise whatever had concerned her about my wedding night, nor did I bring it up, mindful that Jay was within earshot. I didn't question whether they had left intentionally early to avoid seeing Jay or why Liv had lied to me about it. I assumed Liv was being dramatic and trying to cause problems between Jay and me because she couldn't accept that I hadn't married Ben. Nor did she bring Ben's name up. I had questioned whether he would reach out to Liv or my mother after Jay had blocked him, but would he know that I could no longer see his messages or take his calls? Or would he just accept the text Jay had sent from me and let me go?

It was easier to leave things as they were with my mother until I returned from our honeymoon. Perhaps by then, we both would be able to have a rational conversation, and I would have calmed down, for I was still furious that they had left early without letting Jay or myself know.

As for Liv, she didn't answer my call. She later messaged asking me to take lots of photos and to have a fabulous time. I accepted that, for whatever reason, she didn't want to continue the conversation yesterday. Hopefully, when I returned from my honeymoon, my mother would elaborate on whatever Liv was withholding from me.

If anything at all.

* * *

The following morning, much to my astonishment, we had flown to Barbados with my orthopaedic consultant's permission. We were now on day four of paradise on the south coast of Barbados in the parish of Christ Church. Our hotel was located in the Beachfront Village and Jay had booked one of the lavish Love Nest Suites, with an expansive balcony, stunning ocean views and a private soaking tub for two.

I still hadn't worked up the nerve to ask him how he – *we* – could afford such a luxurious holiday, fearing it would spoil the moment. I decided to wait until we returned home to discuss our finances.

Any doubts about Jay and his inexplicable behaviour at our wedding reception had dissipated. The tropical sunshine and glorious surroundings had banished the horrors of that night. Jay had spent the last four days worshipping me and waiting on my every whim as if attempting to make up for our lost wedding night.

I rolled over in the ridiculously expansive four-poster bed.

'Hey,' Jay said, walking out of the bathroom, ready to go out for dinner.

'Hey back,' I replied, smiling.

I couldn't remember the last time I had felt so relaxed or seen Jay so chilled. Also, he had made an effort with his appearance and rather than wearing typical jeans and T-shirts, he had dressed up for the occasion, with a white shirt and stone-coloured linen trousers.

'Are you going to get ready for dinner or do you plan on spending our entire honeymoon in bed?'

'Would that be so bad?' I asked, pouting as he walked over to me.

'Come on. We have a reservation for 8 p.m.,' he said, dragging the white throw off me.

'Spoilsport,' I grumbled, getting out of bed.

I threw my arms around his neck and kissed him.

He pulled me off. 'Come on, wife. Plenty of time for that later. I need a drink!'

'Pour yourself one,' I suggested, gesturing through to the lounge and the well-stocked bar. 'Or ring room service.'

'I want a drink at the bar, where I can show off my beautiful bride,' he replied, smiling at me.

'What? The bride with a broken wrist?' I teased.

'You'll always be beautiful to me. Even when you're a toothless, incontinent eighty-something-year-old hag, I'll still love you.'

'Hey, who says I'll wait until I'm an octogenarian before I lose all my teeth and bladder control?' I laughed.

'You know what I mean,' he said, turning serious. 'I love you, Sophie. Plaster cast and all.'

'Ditto,' I replied. 'However, let's be pragmatic here. You'll no doubt lose all your teeth before I do,' I mockingly added. 'So, I'll be spoon-feeding and wiping up after you, Mr Bradley. Rather than the other way around. You better be careful how you treat me from now on!'

A wounded look entered his eyes, reminding me that ageing and losing what looks he had left was his Achilles heel.

He broke away from my gaze.

'You've got thirty minutes, okay?' he instructed before walking through to the lounge.

The irritating drone of the TV and some sports commentary loudly drifted through to the master bedroom.

I sighed, psyching myself up to get showered and dressed. I would happily stay ensconced in the room, drinking champagne and ordering room service. All I needed was Jay's company. But, evidently, he craved more than me.

A short time later, I emerged ready to leave.

'Ready,' I announced as I walked into the lounge.

He continued watching the sports channel.

'Jay?'

He eventually turned around and looked at me, frowning. 'Oh, you're wearing that?'

I looked down at my shoulderless turquoise dress and small-heeled open-toe sandals. 'Why?' I asked, pulling my brightly coloured silk shawl around me.

'Nothing.'

'If there's something wrong with my appearance, I'd rather know,' I replied.

'It's just that colour doesn't do a lot for you, or the style.'

I stared at him.

'You asked me, babes.'

I took a step back.

'Why don't you put on that black dress I bought for you?' he suggested. 'You look beautiful in it.'

I shook my head, feeling the good mood I had emerged from the shower in evaporating.

'Why not, babes?'

'Because I wore it the other night.'

'So? No one's going to know.'

'I'll know,' I replied.

'Come on, Soph! I was just trying to help you out. You asked me, remember?'

'If I recall, you were the one who shot me a look of disapproval when you saw what I was wearing.'

He stood up and stretched. 'Look, I've already waited I don't know how long to go out for a drink with you. Please, just go and get changed, then we can enjoy the rest of the evening.'

'And if I stay in what I'm wearing?' I challenged.

He shrugged. 'Your choice. But as I said, it's not flattering on you.'

'Why have you never mentioned this before when I've worn it with you?'

'I'm telling you now.'

I held his uncompromising gaze.

'Fine, I'll change,' I conceded, not wanting this to turn into something that could ruin our evening. We only had a short time left, and I wanted to make the most of it.

'Make it quick,' he instructed, collapsing back on the couch to continue watching the TV.

I heard him turn up the volume to drown out the noise of me slamming wardrobe doors and cupboard drawers as I pulled out the dress he had requested. I was hurt by his insensitivity and didn't much feel like going out for a romantic evening any more.

'Come on, Sophie! Hurry it up!' he yelled out above the raging noise of the American sports channel.

I could feel the threat of tears and willed myself not to be so pathetic.

It's just a dress, Sophie. That's all.

But it felt much more than that.

You're losing yourself to him.

I suddenly felt a chill snake down my back. I spun around to see Jay standing, observing me in the doorway of our bedroom.

'There you go,' Jay said, looking me up and down. 'Tell me, I wasn't right?'

I didn't reply.

'You look stunning. How about I take my beautiful bride out for a glass of champagne?' he suggested.

Silent, I picked up my bag and headed to the door.

Not that Jay noticed. He was simply happy that I had followed his advice.

But are you happy following his advice, his instructions, Sophie? Are you?

13

'Did you hear what that American couple said about me?' Jay said, grabbing hold of my right hand as we walked back along the winding resort paths to our hotel bungalow.

'Huh?' I distractedly mumbled.

'Sat at the table across from us?'

I shook my head.

'They thought they'd recognised me as a guitarist from some band they like.' He laughed, revelling in their assumption. 'They couldn't believe it when I told them that my band...' He faltered for a moment, correcting himself. 'Ex-band were now touring the States, and they'd actually heard of them.'

I had switched off, not a part of the conversation. I was merely there as Jay's sidekick. I had noted with a degree of dismay that he enjoyed other people's company more than just being with me. It had never seemed as apparent back home as it was here. It was as if I wasn't enough for him any more.

Or maybe you're being hyper-sensitive?

Jay continued drunkenly talking about them, oblivious to my silence.

I was annoyed with myself that I had allowed Jay to influence me. I should have worn the turquoise dress. It was one of my favourite items of clothing. I'd bought it when I was with Ben, and he'd often said how beautiful it looked on me. So, why didn't Jay think I was beautiful in it? Rather than this clingy, low-cut black number that felt too over-the-top for the resort. But then, Ben and Jay were radically different people. Ben, like me, was more conservative with appearance, unlike Jay, who was all rock 'n' roll with an edgy vibe.

Opposites attract, my mother had wryly noted.

But do they last?

'Oh God!' I exclaimed as something scuttled sideways in front of me.

Jay laughed at my horror of the Caribbean giant land crab that shot past us.

'Seriously, Sophie, they're more scared of you!'

'I doubt it,' I answered. 'Have you seen the size of them and those huge pincers?'

'Not as big as your lobster claw though!' he joked, gesturing at my plaster cast.

Jay's conversation with the American newly-weds suddenly came back to me. He had regaled them with the tale of woe of our wedding night spent in the hospital. His version of events couldn't have been further from the truth. His erratic jealousy and violent outburst no longer existed, replaced by a romantic, arm-in-arm stroll under a star-filled sky and a singularly spectacular, low-hanging full moon. Not that he was lying. We had walked under the seductive, bejewelled night sky, but that was on the eve of our wedding. He had then embellished my fall, explaining that I had drunk too many glasses of champagne and had tripped over the silk train of my wedding dress. He had tried to save me but unfortunately failed. He had heroically carried me to a waiting car and then to the hospital, where he'd stayed by my bedside, never leaving me.

It was a great story, but not our story.

I preferred Jay's version of our wedding night. It corresponded with the man who had held my hand and kissed me repeatedly throughout dinner, mesmerised by my beauty and unable to believe I chose him. He'd told me again and again that he was the luckiest man alive.

So, why didn't I feel the same way?

* * *

'Hey, Soph! Jesus! Move over,' Jay said, pushing in beside me at the bathroom sink.

'Can't you wait?'

'Nope,' he replied as he busied himself squeezing toothpaste on his toothbrush.

I continued rinsing my face with water.

'Hey, Gringo, let me get some room!' he complained, trying to get access to the sink.

I paused rinsing my face and looked up at his reflection in the brightly lit bathroom mirror.

'What did you call me?' I questioned, confused. I recognised 'Gringo' as a derisory term in Spanish and Portuguese against a male, typically an Anglo-American foreigner. So why call me that?

Unabashed, he smirked like a child with a forbidden secret.

'Jay?' I said, unable to keep the irritation out of my voice.

'Just a joke, that's all. No harm, no foul.'

'I don't get it? Gringo? A joke?' I knew he was drunk, but I still didn't understand or appreciate the joke. 'You're saying I look like a man to you?'

His smirk deepened as he boyishly shrugged.

'Seriously?' I muttered, realising he had drunk more than I had noticed.

I resumed rinsing my face before patting it dry.

I realised he was watching me now.

'What?' I questioned, suddenly feeling self-conscious.

Gone was the slinky dress, the make-up and the wild hair sexily piled up on my head. I looked at myself, not liking my bare reflection under these intrusive surgical lights.

'What?' I repeated with an edge of annoyance.

I had never felt so exposed and vulnerable under his scrutinising gaze.

'You know your sister has the same problem as you,' he pointed out.

'What problem?' I asked, staring at myself.

'Oh, you've never noticed?'

'Noticed what?'

'Maybe it's just a hormonal condition, given that the two of you have it.'

'Have what?' I demanded, exasperated.

I could feel the apprehension flexing and tightening inside me as I waited for him to say whatever was bothering him.

'It's just, maybe it's time to get a facial wax or something?'

Open-mouthed, I stared back at his reflection unable to comprehend what he had just said to me.

'Oh fuck, babes! You must have noticed it. You've got a lot of facial hair down the side of your face and, well, on your top lip. More than the average woman who likes to be au naturel.'

'It's fine, downy blonde hair, Jay? I mea...' I faltered, unable to find the words to express myself. 'It's not noticeable like dark hair?'

'Sure, it is,' he said.

I was stunned. I hadn't given the peach fuzz on my face a second glance until now.

'So, let me get this right, you're telling me that everyone has noticed I have this problem, but no one has bothered to tell me?'

He shrugged as he caught my sceptical gaze in the mirror. 'Hey, it's not my top lip. You do as you please.'

'Thanks, Jay! Now you've made me paranoid.'

'I thought you knew and just chose not to do anything about it.'

'What?'

'Yeah.'

I watched his reflection casually walk out of the bathroom before turning back to the mirror and seeing my naked face for the first time as Jay saw it.

* * *

'What's wrong with you?' Jay asked when I finally came to bed.

I didn't answer. Instead, I turned the air-con up to make the room cooler before climbing into bed.

'Babes?'

'Nothing,' I mumbled, switching my lamp off.

I lay down with my back to him.

I felt Jay pull me in to him.

'I've upset you, haven't I?'

'No,' I lied.

'Is it the dress thing? Because I get it. You like the blue dress, and it's nice enough. But believe me when I say you look stunning in the black one; the number of men staring at you tonight was unreal.'

'Are you sure it wasn't my hormonal problem they were staring at?'

I felt Jay's body tense up behind me.

'What?' he muttered.

'You know, the one my sister and I share?'

I couldn't believe he had forgotten his devastating comment already. I had spent the last fifteen minutes scrutinising my face in the bathroom because of his throwaway remark.

'Oh, come on, Sophie! You're being overly sensitive.'

'Am I?' I questioned.

'Ahuh,' he answered, his body relaxing again against mine.

'What about your ex?'

'What about her?'

'Did she have facial hair?' I asked.

'No,' he evenly replied.

It wasn't the answer I was expecting.

'But I thought she had black hair?'

'She did.'

'So how did she not have facial hair?'

'How would I know?'

'Did she remove it?' I continued.

He didn't answer me.

'Jay?' I persisted.

'It's our honeymoon. The last person I want in our bed with us is my whore of an ex! All right?'

I didn't reply.

He sighed heavily. 'For fuck's sake, Sophie! How many times do I have to tell you that you couldn't be more different from her if you tried. You're blonde, blue-eyed, petite and stunning. I even hate thinking about that fat, ugly whore. You fit me perfectly, yeah?' he reassured me, reaching out his hand and touching my back.

'But I'm not your type,' I counterargued.

'For Christ's sake!' he muttered with exasperation.

'Well, I'm not. You're the one who said it.'

'Let it go, will you? I wish I'd never told you!'

Jay had shared with me in the early days that I was an anomaly for him, as he was typically attracted to tall, olive-skinned, dark-haired, brown-eyed women.

Like my sister, Liv.

I pushed the disconcerting thought away.

'You're different from every other woman I've been with, babes. That's what makes you so special. I never proposed to any of them.'

I held my breath, not wanting him to know I was upset.

'Don't start doubting everything. Or wishing for rain clouds when the sun's still shining. We're in paradise together, try to remember that.'

With that, he pulled his hand away.

I lay there in the dark listening to the low-level hum of the air conditioner. Soon it was accompanied by Jay's heavy, relaxed breathing.

I lifted my head to turn my damp pillow over and wiped at the persistent tears.

You're in paradise with the man you love. So, why are you crying, Sophie?

14

I watched as Jay poured himself another orange juice with a stiff shot of vodka from the drinks bar.

He returned to our breakfast table and sat down with a defiant scowl in response to my raised eyebrow. He picked up his iridescent blue Oakley sunglasses off the table and covered his puffy, bloodshot eyes.

I had no idea what had put him in such a foul disposition. He had woken up in a dark mood. Again, this was unfamiliar territory for me.

The most I had gotten out of him this morning was monosyllabic answers, if anything.

The silence that shrouded our table was awkward and palpable. Embarrassed, I enviously glanced around at the other couples laughing and intimately talking while sharing breakfast. I suddenly felt uncomfortable and out of place.

This is a honeymoon resort, Sophie.

I forced myself to resume eating my grapefruit as Jay knocked back his orange juice and vodka.

Jay never ate.

Something so obvious had only become apparent to me on our honeymoon. I realised Jay hadn't chosen the all-inclusive hotel for the restaurants but for the bars and limitless alcohol. I had asked him on our first morning here if he wanted breakfast, when he scorned me for asking such a ridiculous question. He had made it abundantly clear he found it insufferable watching me eat, particularly today, for some reason. Not that I ate a lot, self-conscious of the disgust I would sometimes catch in his eye when he thought I wasn't looking.

Why this morning? Why spoil it when we only have two days left?

He never ate until late in the evening when he was too intoxicated to resist the compulsion. He survived on a diet of coffee and alcohol, and not necessarily in that order. At least, that was what I had witnessed on our honeymoon. When we went for dinner in the evenings here, I noted he would push his food around as if contemplating eating it. It was evident now that he suffered the romantic, candlelit restaurants for my benefit.

It hadn't been so apparent back home that Jay rarely ate during the day, or perhaps I had unconsciously ignored it. But now we were in a tropical goldfish bowl, together twenty-four-seven, unable to avoid one another.

Jay nodded at the passing waiter carrying a pot of coffee, who stopped to pour him a cup.

'Anything else, sir?' he asked, smiling.

Jay shook his head.

The waiter nodded at us, then walked off.

I looked at Jay, about to strike up a conversation, but he blankly stared straight through me.

Accepting he wasn't in the mood, I picked up my phone and checked my Instagram page. I quietly smiled at how many people had liked and commented on my story yesterday, even Liv. At least she could see how happy I looked. The video of Jay and me on the beach was fabulous, accentuated by the stunning background. I congratulated myself on capturing the moment so perfectly. We were perfect together.

'Do you know how rude you are?'

Startled, I looked up.

'Sorry?' I questioned. I was unsure I had heard correctly.

'To think I paid fuck knows how much to bring you to Barbados for you to ignore me.'

'I what?' I replied, mindful to keep my voice down.

'You heard.'

'Jay, you're the one ignoring me,' I reasoned. 'I've tried talking to you, but for some reason you're in a foul temper this morning.'

'Because I'm sick of watching you on your phone. It's never out of your hand. I mean, look around you, Sophie. We're in paradise, and what do you choose to do? The first thing you do when you wake up is check your phone. Who are you messaging now? *Him?*'

'Who?' I asked, feeling hot despite the ceiling fan overhead.

'You know who,' Jay replied.

'You deleted his number and blocked him, remember?'

I was met with a stony silence.

'Take a look yourself,' I said, offering him my phone. 'I was looking at my Instagram page, that's all.'

He remained unmoved.

'See!' I held my phone up and played him the video of us on the beach, laughing and fooling around together. It felt like a lifetime ago.

He refused to look.

I waited as a couple walked past us before responding.

'What the hell's wrong with you?' I hissed, leaning across the table towards him.

He didn't answer.

Instead, he stared straight at me with a fixed, dispassionate expression.

Throwing my napkin down, I scraped my chair back.

'When you decide to act with some civility, feel free to join me,' I stated. 'Coach leaves at 9.30 a.m.,' I warned him.

I waited for a reaction. Nothing.

'You only get one honeymoon,' I stated.

'You, maybe,' he darkly muttered to himself.

'You what?'

He stared straight ahead with his arms folded across his chest.

Furious, I left him there to sulk, fully expecting him to join me later for the excursion.

* * *

I spent the day alone, isolated by adoring couples, in the most tranquil, romantic place possible, surrounded by nature in its breathtakingly brilliant glory. Hunte's Gardens, designed by the horticulturist, Anthony Hunte in the 1950s, transformed an unusual sinkhole-like gully into a botanical garden of striking beauty and international acclaim. The place had been on my bucket list for years, and when I'd got over the shock that we were honeymooning in Barbados, I was thrilled, not only to be able to visit it, but that it evidenced how well Jay knew me. He had talked enthusiastically about the trip on the flight here; his intentional absence hurt me more than I believe he even realised. Not coming with me felt spiteful and petty. As I shared photos on my social media accounts, I couldn't be more painfully aware I was on my own. I had posted about my excitement to see the botanical gardens and felt compelled to upload photos and videos as promised.

I wished the unbearably long, hot day away, anxious about Jay's absence. He hadn't called or messaged me, and I refused to reach out to him. He was patently in the wrong. I spotted the American couple that Jay had entertained with the story of our wedding catastrophe. Embarrassed, I did everything to avoid them. Inevitably, when they finally bumped into me, they were surprised that I was there without my charming husband. I lied out of humiliation and said Jay had felt unwell and had decided to stay in the room for the day. They invited me, out of politeness or pity, or perhaps both, to join them for the scheduled excursion lunch, but I desisted, feigning a loss of appetite.

Finally, the day dragged to an end, and I was back at the hotel. I always tried to avoid confrontation and suffered when caught up in it. Consequently, I had spent all day in a state of prolonged angst, not knowing what to expect when I returned.

I rushed into the bungalow and expectantly looked around. There was no sign of Jay. It was just after six and we had a reservation for dinner at the hotel's finest restaurant.

'Jay?' I tentatively called out.

Silence.

The anger that had burned inside me all day dissipated.

'Jay?' I repeated, feeling nervous.

Nothing.

The knot of unease that had taken up residency since my wedding night awakened.

I walked through to the master bedroom. The maid had been in and everything was immaculate. There was no sign that Jay had returned to the room after breakfast this morning. He knew we had a dinner reservation. One that I had been anticipating all week.

The same with Hunte's Gardens.

My sense of disquiet deepened when I checked the bathroom. Fresh towels were neatly stacked and new toiletries adorned the marble counters. If I had been hoping that Jay had returned to the room to shower for dinner, I was bitterly disappointed.

I checked my phone. Nothing.

I decided to call him. It automatically went to voicemail.

'Jay? Where are you? I'm back at the bungalow. Remember, we have a dinner reservation at the French restaurant for 8 p.m.'

I hung up and waited for him to listen to my message and call me.

Come on, Sophie! Why are you worried about him? He should be the one who's concerned about you. He spoilt your day. The one trip you have waited for years to make, and he chose not to share it with you. What the hell?

I made myself shower and dress for dinner while waiting for him to return.

I repeatedly checked my phone – nothing.

At 7.45 p.m., I'd had enough. I picked up my small bag and headed out of the bungalow. I planned to check the resort before humiliating myself and enquiring at reception if anyone had seen my husband. Or worse, if he was hurt in some way.

I soon spotted Jay, allaying my fears that something terrible had happened to him. I shouldn't have been surprised, but I was to see him sitting with his back to me at his favourite bar in the orange boardshorts, black vest top and flip-flops I had left him wearing at breakfast.

Has he been there all day?

I discounted the thought. Surely, he wouldn't have spent the entire day drinking?

A wave of adrenaline engulfed me as he intimately leaned his body into the woman sitting next to him. They both laughed about something before I heard him order another round of drinks. I knew from the way he slurred that it wasn't mauby he had spent the day drinking. It was the other Bajan drink from the island's Mount Gay Rum distillery, established in 1703 – a fact I'd learned after a tour of the world's oldest functioning rum distillery on the second day, at Jay's request.

Unable to move, I watched his darkly bronzed, bikini-clad companion, swish her thick, perfectly sleek, dark hair back off her face as she thanked him for the shot.

Jay leaned in and murmured something to her.

He'll be promising her more than rum...

I felt ridiculous and out of place with my hair pinned up, make-up on, in a backless black dress, black open-toed heels and a plaster cast on my arm. I had made an effort for Jay, wanting to put our differences aside and enjoy our second-to-last evening on the island.

As if feeling my presence, Jay glanced over his shoulder. He looked at me.

I waited, expecting him to get up and leave. He didn't.

Instead, he ignored me.

What the hell?

Humiliated, I remained standing, unsure of what to do next.

I thought of the dinner reservation I had been so looking forward to and the day I had spent alone because of him. I couldn't believe he was disrespecting me in this way.

'Jay?' I said, walking over to him.

'What?' he muttered without looking at me.

The barman caught my eye.

I shook my head. The last thing I planned on doing was joining Jay and his drinking companion.

'What?' he repeated.

'We've got a dinner reservation at 8 p.m. You've still got time to go back to the room to shower and change,' I suggested.

My voice was remarkably level, despite the tumult of emotions coursing through me.

'I'm busy,' he replied, gesturing to the bartender for another shot. 'One for her as well,' he added.

'I don't want one,' I said.

'It's not for you,' he replied, turning now to look at me.

I took a step backwards, thrown off balance by the comment and the contempt in his eyes.

'Wow!' I remarked. 'You can't be serious?'

'Try me,' he threatened.

'So, you're refusing to go to dinner with me so you can stay here with...' I faltered as I looked at the woman sitting next to him, who was suddenly scrolling through her phone. I noted that she was older than she looked at first glance, and was in her mid-fifties.

'Jamie,' he answered. 'And yeah, I'm staying put.'

'I haven't eaten all day and was looking forward to spending the evening with you,' I reasoned.

'Skipping a few meals won't do you any harm.'

He turned his back on me.

'So, I was telling you about this gig I played in Frankfurt, yeah?' Jay said to his bar companion.

'What the hell has got into you?' I demanded, grabbing his arm and yanking him around to face me.

He stared at me with such unadulterated hatred that, for a split second, I thought he would hit me.

I held his unnerving gaze, refusing to back down.

'Take your fucking hand off of me,' he lowly threatened with narrowed eyes.

I could smell the day's-worth of alcohol on his breath and sweating from his pores.

I noticed the bartender, tense and alert, about to intervene.

I released my grip and stepped back from him.

I caught the pitying eye of one of the other guests seated at the bar and felt shame radiate from me.

'You do what you want. But don't think you'll be sleeping in our bed tonight,' I warned.

'That's what you think,' he hissed. 'I paid for that fucking bungalow and for this whole shitshow! So, if anyone's sleeping elsewhere, it'll be you, sweetheart.'

He turned his back on me, ignoring the embarrassed, sideways glances from other couples within earshot.

I swallowed back tears that were threatening to overwhelm me.

Walk away, Sophie! NOW! Don't embarrass yourself further.

I willed myself not to cry. I kept my head up and turned in the direction of our hotel bungalow, accepting that we wouldn't be enjoying an intimate, candlelit dinner with champagne in a critically acclaimed French restaurant. That my new husband had publicly humiliated me by choosing instead to continue getting drunk with some older woman he barely knew. How was that even possible?

15

I returned to the hotel bungalow and pulled off the dress, replacing it with a matching vest and short PJs. Part of me wanted to go to the restaurant to spite Jay and prove to myself that I didn't need him, but I wouldn't have been able to eat because of the questioning and pitying stares from the waiting staff and the whispering glances from the other guests who had seen Jay and me together. I would have been surrounded by entranced couples murmuring their undying love and appreciation for one another, aware my husband remained at a bar drinking with some random female guest.

A stranger.

Who she had come with, if anyone at all, remained a mystery to me. Maybe her partner was alone, miserable and hurt, like me, wondering what had happened to her or their relationship.

What has happened to us? To you, Jay?

I pathetically ordered a sandwich from room service and a bottle of wine to help calm me. Not that it had worked. I picked up the glass and took another mouthful. It was a Saturday evening, and I was sitting in a hotel bedroom – alone.

On your honeymoon!

I glanced at the uneaten sandwich and potato chips on the room service tray next to me on the bed. I knew I should eat, as I hadn't eaten all day, but my appetite had disappeared along with my dinner date. And no matter how many sips of wine I took, I couldn't get rid of the dryness in my mouth.

It was now nearly 2 a.m., and there was still no sign of Jay. I had expected him to run after me and apologise profusely for being so vile.

But he hadn't.

How could he not follow you?

I knew he would have spent the evening drinking, no doubt regaling his bar companion with rock 'n' roll anecdotes from his heyday: not that he ever really had one. He had lots of tales of near misses and lost opportunities. He had a list of famous bands and singers he should have been lead guitarist with, if only...

If only he had been in the right place at the right time. And all that crap!

I surprised myself with my dark cynicism. I couldn't have been more supportive and protective of Jay's artistic ambitions. The guitarist I had watched play live and who exuded such sexual energy and charisma was the man I had fallen for – eventually. The same man that had blindsided me and made me forget who I was and why I was there that night: to forget Ben's public rejection of me. After all, my mother was the one who had to inform all our guests that there would be no wedding. My exquisite, Italian-designed wedding gown had hung on the back of my bedroom door for weeks until Grace had persuaded me to let her return it, mindful that Ben had already moved out and moved on with his life.

Very early in our relationship, Jay had confided that he was impressed I was an author and made a modest living from my writing. There was a flicker of jealousy in his eyes when he shared with me that all he had ever wanted to be was famous. That was his raison d'être.

Without that, he was nothing or no one.

I took another sip of wine as I questioned whether that was the reason why he wanted to be with me. Had Jay assumed my success would transfer to him and be a pathway to achieve his desire for fame?

No. Don't be ridiculous, Sophie. He loves you for you, not what you could offer him.

But if that were true, why was he drinking with another woman rather than with me on our honeymoon? Another, much older woman he barely knew.

I looked at my phone again for the umpteenth time, expecting a contrite apology from Jay, but nothing. I couldn't even call Grace or Anna for support, not because of the time difference, but not knowing how to explain what had happened. I still couldn't process it. We were supposed to be on our honeymoon.

So where is your husband, Sophie?

I wanted to scream at the relentless voice in my head that I didn't want to know. I was too scared to know where he was and with whom. All I wanted to do was fall asleep and wake up as if yesterday hadn't happened.

But it has happened.

I knew he was with that woman. I would have been an idiot to believe otherwise.

Subsequently, I booked a flight back to the UK for what was now today. Jay and I were due to fly back Monday evening, but I couldn't abide staying with him another day. I could have booked another room if one was available, or even another hotel, but I felt no inclination to remain in Barbados on my honeymoon on my own. I just wanted to get home.

Then it hit me. My home was now Cornwall, not my comfortable flat in Kensington, where I was close to everyone and everything.

You had a life of your own there. Independent, happy and surrounded by friends. But now?

Now wasn't the time to make rash decisions about the new property I had bought or the man I had just married. I needed time and space to recalibrate.

I glanced at my passport and my credit and debit cards on the bedside cabinet next to me. I had taken them out of the safe for the details required for booking the extortionately priced last-minute flight. I had transferred money from my savings account and used my debit card, feeling a knot of panic at the back of my throat as I could ill afford such an expense.

What choice did you have?

Whatever guilt I felt about the money I spent, along with Jay's anticipated reaction, quickly dissipated. His behaviour had left me no option.

Then I heard the door to the bungalow creak open.

It's him.

Relief coursed through me. Swiftly followed by anger.

What's taken him so long? It's been hours and hours.

I heard him stumble about the lounge, knocking into things and cursing, followed by the TV suddenly blaring.

I waited a beat, expecting him to turn the volume down.

He didn't.

Cortisone ravaged my body as I sat up in bed, rigid.

'For Christ's sake!' I cursed as I swung my bare legs out of bed and padded to the open bedroom door. I peeked into the lounge and saw him on the couch with his arms crossed over his chest, the remote clutched in one hand, watching an American sports channel.

'Jay?' I called out as I walked into the lounge area, mindful of the adjoining hotel guests.

No reply.

'Hey?' I repeated. 'Can you turn the TV down?'

Again, no reply.

I stepped around the couch to face him.

'For Christ's sake!' I muttered under my breath as I witnessed his drunken head loll forward, resting on his chest.

I waited, making certain he was definitely asleep.

I put my phone in my left hand and bent over him, attempting to pry the remote from his hands to turn the TV off.

'What the fuck are you doing?' he hissed at me as his head shot up and his eyes opened.

Startled, I jumped back, dropping my phone on the marble floor.

'What the fuck do you think you're doing creeping up on me?' he demanded.

'I thought you were asleep?' I replied.

'So, what were you about to do? Fucking photograph or video me or something twisted like that?'

'No!'

Before I had a chance to explain I was trying to turn the TV volume down, he continued: 'Were you planning on sending what you took to your fucking mother and sister to show them what a loser you've married? Or what about that moron of an ex of yours? Is that it? Or were you going to post it on your fucking Instagram page with every other trite moment you feel compelled to share?' he shouted above the blare of the TV.

'Jay? It's after 2 a.m.,' I reasoned, worried someone would complain about the noise. 'Why don't you turn the TV down?'

'Why don't you fucking stop telling me what to do? You hear me, you fucking miserable bitch!'

I stepped back from him, not recognising the man sitting before me.

I decided to go to bed. My flight home couldn't come soon enough. There was no point in attempting to talk to him. I suddenly remembered my phone. I could see that it had landed by his bare feet. He followed my gaze. Crucially, my e-ticket was in my iPhone's wallet.

I lunged forward, but seeing my panic, he grabbed it first.

'Jay? Please? Give it back to me.'

'Show me the fucking photos you took of me, you sneaky bitch!' he demanded, trying to get into my phone.

I knew he was too drunk to reason with, and the best thing to do was leave him to sleep it off on the couch. He would soon forget about my phone – and me. The more fuss I made about my phone, the more likely he was to keep it from me. I would creep back and get it later. I doubted I would sleep anyway. My bags were packed and ready for 7 a.m. when I planned to go to reception and request a taxi to the airport. My flight wasn't until 5.40 p.m., but I would rather spend the day waiting around Grantley Adams International Airport than suffer Jay's despicable behaviour. I also wanted to be gone long before he woke up and noticed I had left.

'Have you changed your passcode?' he asked, glaring up at me.

'No,' I answered.

'So, why can't I open it?'

'Maybe you're too drunk!'

He stared at me with a look of pure hatred.

'Why don't you give me my phone back and use the remote control on your lap to mute the TV so you can sleep off whatever skinful you've drunk,' I suggested.

He narrowed his eyes at me. 'That's the second time tonight you've tried to tell me what to do.'

'Go to hell!' I muttered to myself.

'Fuck you, you miserable bitch!'

Before I even had time to react, something hit my head. With some force.

'What the—'

It landed, bouncing off the marble floor.

My phone? NO!

But it was the remote control.

Stunned, I touched my forehead as the batteries rolled across the marble floor. I could feel a bump already erupting from the impact.

I checked my fingers for blood, but there wasn't any.

'You wanted the controls!' Jay slurred, enjoying my reaction.

Trembling, I dragged my head up to be met by Jay's gloating gaze.

'You threw that at me?' I questioned, finding my voice.

'Maybe you shouldn't be sharing fucking photographs of me on Instagram or whatever fucking stupid social media account you use, you sneaky bitch!'

'There were no photos of you!' I yelled back as tears of frustration started to fall. 'You're too drunk and too bloody old to even know what you're talking about!'

I realised as soon as I had said it, that I had gone too far.

Oh God, Sophie... What did you say?

16

I darted for the bedroom, but Jay surprised me with his agility. Within seconds, he was up off the sofa and behind me. I tried to slam the door closed, to lock him out, but I was too late.

The door battered my face as I stumbled backwards, thrown off balance by the force of his weight against it.

He flew into the master bedroom, and suddenly stopped.

I watched him in horror as he stared, open-mouthed, at my packed suitcase and matching holdall. My toiletry and make-up bags still had to be added to my suitcase. I had left them in the bathroom, needing them in the morning. His eyes then darted to the open closet, which hid the safe whose door was left ajar. Jay immediately noted my passport and bank cards lying on the bedside cabinet.

He frowned as he drunkenly tried to compute what it meant.

'We don't check out until Monday?' he slurred, confused as he turned to me.

I didn't reply.

I watched as the slow realisation hit him.

I could feel my heart thundering in my chest, pummelling

blood and adrenaline through my veins, as my fight-or-flight response kicked in, screaming at me, desperate for me to get out. For there was a look in his eyes that I had never seen before that flicked the genetic survival switch in me to run.

I backed away from him, unsure of what he would do.

I watched as he strode over to my packed bags and picked them up.

'What are you doing?' I asked, trying to keep the fear out of my voice.

'I can't stand any more of your whiny, pathetic moaning,' he answered, walking straight past me. 'I paid for all this,' he said, dropping my bags and throwing his arms theatrically out. 'And what do I get in return? Not one word of thanks. All you have done is dictate to me from the moment we got her. *Do this... Jay, fetch me that... No, Jay, don't do that! Don't drink! Don't have fun! Don't talk to anyone! Fucking, do this, do that! Don't fucking breath without my say-so!*' He paused for a moment as he wiped the spit from his lips before adding, 'That's all I hear from you, you selfish fucking cow!'

Stunned by his words, I simply stared at him.

'I've had enough!' he continued, walking through to the lounge area.

'Where are you going?' I asked.

'I'm going nowhere. I paid for this fucking bungalow and the whole fucking honeymoon! You're the one going somewhere,' he answered, heading to the front door.

I followed after him, as he opened the door and threw my suitcase and holdall outside. I heard them loudly roll and thump their way down the three steps leading up to our bungalow.

'What the hell? Why would you do that? That's my clothes you've thrown outside.'

He shrugged. 'Go and fetch them if you're that bothered. The maid can keep them as far as I'm concerned.'

'You're pathetic!' I muttered as I pushed past him to retrieve my suitcase and holdall.

'Let's see who's the fucking pathetic one now!' he yelled after me. 'This isn't a fucking marriage! I regret ever marrying you, you ugly, fat cow!'

I turned around, suddenly realising what he was going to do, but it was too late. He slammed the door behind me.

'Jay?'

I was barefoot in my PJs, locked outside in another country in the middle of the night.

'Are you for real? I don't have my key card!' I pointed out. It was inside, along with my phone, passport and bank cards.

He didn't reply.

'Jay?' I cried, banging with my right fist on the door.

No answer.

'I'm barefoot and in my pyjamas, for Christ's sake!' I stated.

He didn't respond.

'Please, Jay? Let me in?' I pleaded.

I stared in disbelief as the light seeping out from under the door suddenly disappeared.

What the hell?

He's gone to bed, Sophie. He's actually gone to bed!

I remained standing outside the bungalow, unsure of what to do.

He had locked me out and I had nowhere to go.

Pain now replaced the shock I felt. My forehead pounded from where the remote control had hit me, and my nose also hurt, but the throbbing pain on my bottom lip concerned me. I tentatively touched it and was surprised it felt sticky and wet. I held my fingers under the dim glow of the porch light and realised there was blood on them.

God, I'm bleeding. How?

Then it came to me. Jay had thrown himself at the bedroom door to force it open. Consequently, it had rammed into me as I'd pressed my body against it to stop him from getting in.

I gingerly felt the cut. It was still bleeding. I wondered if my top front teeth had sunk into my bottom lip when my head was knocked from the sheer force.

Remember? Your head ricocheted back from the impact of him throwing the door open?

It had all happened so quickly that I hadn't even registered it.

I touched my nose. It felt tender and swollen. I could feel the blood starting to crust on my top lip from when my nose must have bled. Tears were stinging my eyes, not from the pain but from the shame. I couldn't go to reception and ask for a new key card, claiming I had accidentally locked myself out. Not now.

'Christ!' I muttered, feeling sorry for myself.

Thoughts of my father made the tears that had been threatening start to fall. If he had still been alive, then none of this would ever have happened. I would never have met Jay. I would never have let him into my life, let alone have married him.

I felt as if my life was disintegrating around me, and all I could think of was, what if I had never walked into that bar the night Jay had been playing?

Oh God... If only...

But I knew the 'what if' game would drive me insane.

I swallowed hard, trying to dislodge the lump at the back of my throat. I then swiped at the tears that were coming hard and fast. It wasn't the time or place for a self-pity party.

I sat down on the top step and waited, hoping that Jay would back down and let me in. I counted the minutes down on my watch. When it reached 2.43 a.m., I knew that he was serious.

I debated going to reception and asking for a new key card, but pride stopped me. It was in the early hours and I couldn't think of a reason why I would find myself locked out of my hotel room in my PJs with my bottom lip split open, and a swollen and no doubt bruised nose and forehead.

I had to be pragmatic. I had a flight to catch tomorrow evening without Jay. First, I needed to survive with some modicum of dignity until dawn. Then I would access the bungalow via Alaya, the maid, when she arrived to clean it at 9 a.m. I would tell Alaya that the room didn't need cleaning to avoid waking Jay, giving me enough time to retrieve my phone, passport, bank cards and get as far away from the resort as possible. Considering Jay's extremely drunken state, I doubted he would be awake before midday.

My toiletry and make-up bags were still in the bathroom inside the bungalow, so I couldn't clean my face or even attempt to disguise whatever damage was there. I remembered that there were guest toilets in the reception area so I could at least clean the blood off.

I stood up and stepped down to pick up my suitcase and holdall. I carried them back up the steps and placed them outside the bungalow door. I then headed back down and along the winding paths, trying to remember the way to the reception area, praying that no giant crabs would cross my path tonight.

Oh God...

Terror coursed through me.

You're alone out here, Sophie. Anything could happen to you.

The place was eerily deserted. All the guests were sleeping off their indulgences, and the night staff were nowhere around.

I wandered the labyrinth of paths, aware that my sense of direction was off.

I panicked, hearing two low male voices, presumably security staff checking the grounds. I couldn't see them in the darkness, surrounded by tall, tropical, luscious vegetation that felt as if it were closing in on me. The cool night air, replenished after a quick downpour earlier, was alive with the seductive chorus of the whistling frog, drowning out the familiar cicadae.

I looked around me, disorientated. The darkness disguised the winding, lazy paths that typically led to the countless pools, bars, restaurants or the beach. Even the signposts appeared to be pointing in the wrong direction.

I held my breath and waited for the men's serious talk to fade back into the blackness of the night. My courage failed me, and I gave up on the idea of the ladies' toilets located by the reception. I was lost, exhausted and humiliated, and my bottom lip pulsated with pain. I was wearing an insect-repellent wristband and had sprayed myself when I dressed for dinner, which typically worked against mosquitoes and sandflies, but I could feel my skin breaking out in itchy spots.

I wanted to sleep. Pretend none of this had happened.

This is a familiar trope, Sophie.

I discounted the unhelpful thought, deciding to find someplace to lie down. I thought of the main pool by the breakfast dining area, but remembered that all the sun loungers were stacked away after 10 p.m.

The beach...

There might still be sun loungers left out and it would be the most private place to lie down until dawn. If spotted, I could always use the excuse that I wanted to watch the sun rise.

Anyone could be down there, Sophie.

The thought paralysed me with fear, but what choice did I have?

Ten minutes later, I was lying on a sun lounger, terrified, as I looked out at the black ocean, with hotel towels I had found layered under and over my body to protect me from the predatory sandflies. The deserted beach was blanketed in darkness, and the only noise surrounding me was the gentle lapping of the ocean waves against the sand. I had never felt so alone. So desperately isolated. So scared.

I lay there, staring into the black abyss, questioning what had happened to me. Tears fell as I was transported back to Trevaunance Cove in St Agnes, with Jay jealously raging at me as he grabbed my left wrist, twisting it so hard until the bones snapped.

Where's the man I fell in love with eight months back? How is it possible that he could change so radically into someone I don't recognise? That I don't like – worse, that I fear.

The realisation hit me with such a force it took my breath away.

You're a feminist. You're financially independent, successful, clever and attractive, so how could you have ended up with someone like him?

Maybe I was overreacting? A dangerous combination of alcohol, high expectations and being in each other's scrutinising company twenty-four-seven could account for his behaviour.

My behaviour?

I could feel myself backtracking. Not wanting to face the reality of my new marriage.

He physically hurt you, regardless of whether it was intentional or unintentional.

Then there were his cruel words, like poisonous arrows burrowed in my skin, his venomous hatred trickling through my veins, distorting my perception of myself, of the world.

I thought of my mother and how I could possibly tell her I had made the biggest mistake of my life. But I knew that she would be there for me, as would my sister. They would help me put my shattered dreams back together and get me out of the mess I had found myself in.

I considered phoning Grace when I returned to the UK and seeking her advice. Jay was a threat to my physical safety and my psychological well-being. I had more than enough evidence to implement divorce proceedings.

With adrenaline coursing through me, I threw the towels off my body and ran down into the water. Standing with it circling my calves, I stretched my arms out and stared up at the glittering heavens, and screamed as loud as I could: 'It's over! I want out, all right? I want out of whatever this is, because it isn't a marriage. Do you hear me? It isn't a marriage!'

The rage I felt inside at being cheated by him seemed to melt away.

Exhausted, I swiped at the furious tears with my right hand.

His words at our wedding suddenly came back to me: 'I'll never let you go... Never. You're mine now till death do us part.'

A terrifying thought suddenly scorched through me: would Jay let me go? Or would he prevent me somehow?

Till death do us part...

17

Too terrified to sleep, I waited until, in all her glory, the sun rose, her rays gently caressing my face. People now strolled along the beach, enjoying the promise of another beautiful day in paradise.

The spectacular golden beach, dazzling turquoise ocean, palm trees and sky so perfect were all lost on me. Despite the bright colours, the surroundings came to me in a prism of muted grey. I stood up, casting one final look at the ocean, and then headed back to my hotel bungalow.

When I reached it, the door was already open. I spotted the maid's trolley on the path by our steps.

'Hey,' I called out, before entering.

'Miss,' replied the maid.

I had expected to see Alaya.

'Hi.' I smiled, ignoring her surprised eyes as they rested on my split lip. 'It's okay, you can leave the bungalow until tomorrow. We're fine,' I assured her.

Puzzled, she nodded at me, then left.

I could feel my heart racing as I scanned the lounge area. There was no sign of Jay – or my phone.

Damn!

I crept over to the couch where he had grabbed it off the floor before I could reach it. I lifted the cushions, checking that it hadn't slid down between them. It was nowhere to be found.

I furtively glanced over at the bedroom door. It was shut.

He must have your phone with him.

I tiptoed over to the door and tried to prise it open as quietly as possible so as not to wake him.

I squeezed through the gap and then looked across at the bed. I stared in surprise.

It was empty.

Where the hell are you, Jay?

He was so drunk last night that I'd expected him to sleep it off until late morning, if not the afternoon. I turned to the bathroom, wondering if he was in there, but it was deathly quiet. I looked over to the unmade bed. I noted the room service tray discarded on the marble floor with the empty plate and bottles. Jay must have drunkenly eaten my sandwich and potato chips and finished my wine and ordered another couple of bottles.

Christ!

I hadn't realised the extent of his drinking or eating issues until we had come on our honeymoon.

I pulled the covers back, searching for my phone. Nothing. I then looked under the bed. Again, nothing. I remembered my passport and bank cards left out on the bedside cabinet. They were gone.

I ran over to the safe, hidden in the closet. The safe door was wide open and it was empty. Gone were our flight tickets home, Jay's wallet and passport.

What the—

I stared in disbelief, not understanding why it was empty.

I ran over to the bathroom. Jay's toiletries lay scattered across the marble counter. His clothes from yesterday were dumped in a pile on the bathroom floor.

Where has he gone? And crucially, where's my phone, bank cards and passport?

My gut feeling screamed at me that Jay had taken them. Why, I had no idea, aside from making certain I couldn't go anywhere. I had noted my luggage stacked in the lounge area as soon as I walked in, presumably brought in by Jay.

I switched the bathroom light on, and turned to the large mirror.

Oh God, Sophie...

I looked a mess. It was no surprise that the maid had looked at me with such alarm.

My bottom lip was split open, swollen and bloody, like my nose.

I ran hot water and carefully cleaned my nose and lip. I opened my toiletry bag, searching for antiseptic. I looked back at my bruised reflection. After a long hot shower, I would apply some make-up to disguise the worst of it and cover up the dark circles under my eyes.

I thought of my flight later, but without my passport and phone, I couldn't leave.

Damn! The last thing I wanted was to miss my flight and waste that money. I didn't want to stay a minute longer. I wanted to be gone. But the indisputable fact was that I was trapped here until Jay returned.

* * *

Showered and changed, I lay on the couch with a throw, reading a copy of Agatha Christie's *Murder on the Orient Express* that I found, waiting for Jay to return. Not that I could concentrate. I was too agitated and anxious, and every noise made me jump, making it impossible to absorb the words. It was now early afternoon, and there was no sign of him.

Where are you?

I didn't want to risk leaving the bungalow, so I ordered room service. I was famished, realising I hadn't eaten since breakfast yesterday.

I must have dozed off, because the next thing I knew, the sun had disappeared, and the bungalow was in darkness. I sat up, disorientated, not recognising where I was or why. Then it came back to me.

Where the hell is Jay? And, more importantly, my phone, passport and bank cards?

I checked my watch and was surprised to see it was 6.24 p.m. I should have been on the plane flying back to the UK.

It was then that the door opened, and Jay casually strolled in.

He flicked the lamps on, then beamed when he saw me.

'Hey, babes.' He looked at me. 'Shit!' he muttered. He took his sunglasses off. 'What happened to you?'

'Are you serious?' I asked, shocked at his surprise.

He came over to me and crouched down on the floor in front of me. 'Let me take a look?' he said, taking hold of my head and angling my face towards the light from the lamp.

'Get off me!' I said, pulling my head from his hands.

'Shh, it's okay, Soph, I'm just making sure you're all right. What happened to you?'

'Don't you remember?'

'Remember what?' he asked, frowning as if I had lost my mind.

'You! You did this to me!' I replied.

I watched as he stood up and stepped back from me as if I was crazy. 'Babes, I would never lay a hand on a woman, let alone my wife. Are you okay? I mean, I've been worried about you. You ran out of the bungalow last night, taking your luggage, telling me you were leaving. I had no idea what was going on,' he explained. 'Christ! I've been going out of my mind with worry!'

'Seriously?' I spluttered, unable to hide my incredulity.

He looked wounded by the acerbic remark.

'You threw the bedroom door into me when I was behind it,' I accused. 'And the remote control at my head,' I stated, pulling my hair back from my forehead to show him the swollen, discoloured lump.

'Did you fall over or something? I saw how much wine you drank last night.'

'I wasn't the one who was raging drunk!' I retaliated.

He didn't reply, but his expression said it all. He believed I was the one who was drunk and out of order and had hurt myself in the process.

'If you were so worried about me, did you call reception?' I asked.

'Christ, no! I know you hate people interfering and that you prefer your privacy. There was no way I would report to the hotel reception that you stormed out in the middle of the night with your bags. That you had this almighty fight with me and left. I assumed you had booked another room.'

I stared at him, struggling to comprehend what was happening here.

'And why would I have booked another room?' I demanded.

'Because you were mad with me. I had no idea what I'd done wrong. I missed the damned coach yesterday morning. I arrived as it was driving off. Didn't you see me shouting and waving?'

Taken aback, I shook my head.

'No?' he asked, surprised. He sighed. 'Christ, Sophie, you know me better than that. I would never intentionally have missed Hunte's Gardens. It's all we talked about on the flight here?'

'You could have messaged me?' I questioned, struggling to

accept that the day and evening could have turned out so differently if only I had known.

He nodded with regret. 'Yeah, I should have done, rather than being stubborn, but I swear I saw you looking at me from the coach as it pulled away. You were so pissed off yesterday at breakfast, on your phone the whole time. You got up and left me sitting there like a real chump. So, I assumed you didn't want me with you on the trip.'

I didn't reply. Jay's version of events couldn't be further from mine.

'Oh yeah,' he continued, 'your phone and the other valuables are in a safe at reception. Our safe is broken.'

'It's broken?' I slowly repeated.

'I thought you'd broken it in a rage last night,' he explained.

'Me?' I cried. 'You were the one in a rage,' I countered.

'I was fine until you showed me up,' he stated.

'How did I show you up?' I demanded. But I knew he was referring to when I found him at the bar with some random woman. The feeling of humiliation I felt when I spotted him with her resurfaced.

'Because you were so rude and off. Typically aloof. Poor Jamie! She was desperate to meet you,' he explained.

'Did you sleep with her?' I suddenly asked, unable to hold the torment in any longer.

'What? Are you serious?'

'Did you?'

'Are you crazy? All I did was rave about my gorgeous author wife to her and about how talented you are. I couldn't wait to introduce you. Jamie even downloaded two of your books!'

I didn't react.

'Babes, how could you even think I would be interested in another woman, when I have you?'

'What are you doing?' I asked as he started to lift the throw off my legs.

'Sitting down next to you,' he replied, gently grabbing my outstretched legs to place them onto his lap.

I yanked them away and protectively curled them under me.

'Come on, babes?' he said, hurt. 'I'm just trying to sit next to you.'

I turned away.

'Look, I'm sorry for all the miscommunication. I love you, Soph. All I wanted was for this to be perfect for you, and I fucked up. I'm sorry,' he apologised. 'God, I am so sorry. I was out of my mind with worry. I thought for a minute that you had flown home without me. Then I realised that you would never do that to me. You wouldn't leave me.'

I remained silent.

'Shit, Soph! I feel dreadful, yeah? Please look at me?' he begged. 'I hate you shutting me out.'

I spun my head around. 'Are you serious? You hurt me, Jay. Not just physically, but emotionally,' I stated, trying not to cry.

I felt like I was going insane.

'And I'm sorry,' he whispered, reaching out to touch my hand.

I snatched it away.

'Oh babes, I'm so sorry,' he quietly said, dropping his head.

'Where were you all day? When I turned up here this morning, you were already gone?' I asked, refusing to acknowledge his apology.

He lifted his wounded eyes to meet my cold, unflinching gaze. 'I left early so you could have some space. I was hoping you would come back. I was counting on it when I saw that you had left your luggage at the door when I came out looking for you,' he explained.

'You came looking for me?' I sceptically questioned.

'Of course I came looking for you. What kind of husband do you take me for?'

'When?'

'Shortly after you left,' he answered.

I knew he was lying. He had to be. Otherwise, he would have seen me sitting on the step.

Unless he came searching for you after you had left? After you had picked up your luggage and placed it by the bungalow door?

Nothing was making sense any more. My head felt fuzzy from lack of sleep and sheer emotional exhaustion. My mind hadn't stopped deconstructing the events of last night and piecing them back together, only to take them all apart and start over again. And again. And again.

But what really scared me was that Jay believed what he was saying. I could see it in his eyes, in his body language. He thought I was the one who had wronged him.

'I know you well enough, Soph, to know when to give you time by yourself. So, I took our passports and everything, handed them in for safekeeping at reception, then spent the day on the beach reading your latest novel.'

'You did what?' I questioned, shocked. 'You don't read?'

He smiled at me with eyes filled with pride. 'My wife's an author, how could I possibly not read her brilliant work?'

'But you told me you'd never read a book in your life?'

'Until today,' he corrected.

'Why?' I questioned.

'I felt ashamed yesterday when I was boasting about you at the bar, and someone asked me if I read all your books. How could I admit that I hadn't even read one of them? What did that say about me? So I downloaded a copy and read it on my phone.'

I stared at him in utter amazement.

'You are brilliant by the way. Not that you need me to tell you that,' he said. 'You've got enough adoring fans out there telling you that.'

I was still too shocked to say anything.

'Look, let's forget about yesterday? It's our last night here. How about I order us some champagne and their finest lobster? Let's sit out on the terrace overlooking the beach here. We can play some jazz that you like and drink champagne. Please, babes?'

I didn't respond.

'Please, Sophie? I love you with all my being. Without you, I'm nothing. I need you. Please?'

I was surprised when I looked into his glistening eyes and could tell that he meant every word. I could feel his words, his eyes, pulling me in.

Come on, Sophie! NO! He can't walk back in here and pretend nothing has happened.

'I promise, I'll make it perfect for you,' he whispered, leaning in and brushing his lips against my cheek. He pulled back and looked at me. 'God, I love you.'

I stared back at him, losing myself to him.

Come on, Sophie! Snap out of it! You can't trust him.

'Please tell me you still love me? That I haven't fucked everything up? Please, Sophie?' he begged as his desperate eyes filled with tears. 'I can change... I promise.'

I didn't speak. I couldn't. I was too fearful of what I would say.

'Please, babes? I love you,' he begged, tears trailing down his cheeks as he grabbed my right hand.

'I love you,' I found myself whispering, hating myself for being so easily won over.

How can you love him when he hurt you, Sophie? How is that even possible?

18

We flew back as scheduled and landed at London Heathrow Airport on Tuesday morning to be welcomed by bleak, grey skies and rain.

I sullenly stared out of the window as Jay drove us home.

I hadn't spoken to Anna or Grace, never mind my mother and Liv, since we left the UK for our honeymoon. I expected them to be furious with me. I was acutely aware that Grace and Anna were due to fly to Venice for a week's holiday tomorrow, so I needed to catch up with them before they left.

You're always making excuses not to talk to them because Jay gets angry, always accusing you of being on the phone with them and ignoring him. Soon, they'll stop trying to reach out to you.

And now, there's your split, swollen lip and suspicious bruises on your face; evidence that something's not right.

I thought back to the surprised, questioning looks when we checked out of the hotel, then at check-in at Grantley Adams International Airport, and on the plane. Even going through customs at Heathrow, I faced further humiliation as the customs officer narrowed his eyes suspiciously at my injuries and then turned to Jay's oblivious figure ahead of me.

I didn't want those closest to me to see me like this.

What would Mum say? Or Liv?

'Are you okay?' Jay asked in response to my silence.

'Tired. I couldn't sleep on the plane because of my arm.'

I had over four more weeks left before the plaster cast could be removed, which felt like an unbearable eternity because of the itchy skin beneath it, no doubt the grains of Barbados sand I was unwittingly bringing back with me.

'Once we get back, you go to bed, all right? I'll go pick us up some fresh ingredients for dinner along with a bottle of Sancerre.'

'You sure?' I asked, turning to look at him.

'Babes, didn't I promise to take care of you? The holiday may be over, but that doesn't mean the end of our honeymoon. At least, not for me,' he said, blowing me a kiss.

I weakly smiled, unable to quell the internal conflict I felt.

Jay's gentle, loving words on Sunday evening had soothed my raw wounds and temporarily silenced my doubts about him. But his other words, the mean and ugly ones, still cut into me like a razor, slicing at my skin until the blood ran red, discolouring everything. It was those words which relentlessly played on my mind.

How could he suddenly change and behave so erratically, so cruelly? It made no sense to me. And why now? Why, after eight months, did this dark side of Jay suddenly make an appearance? It wasn't as if we hadn't already lived together. I knew all his frustrating traits, such as leaving the toilet seat up, traces of shaven hair left in the sink and dumping his clothes inches from the laundry basket, regardless of how often I asked him not to. It irritated me to distraction, but I loved him despite it.

Perhaps those uncharacteristic toxic words were alcohol-fuelled?

Jay had drunk excessively on our honeymoon and during our wedding reception, so it was no surprise when he had no memory of what happened, struggling to believe it was even possible.

Refusing to believe it...

He had been in perfect form since returning to the hotel room on Sunday evening, adoring me in every way possible, his happy and infectious mood dispelling the darkness around me that was once a part of him. I was starting to distrust my memory and recollection of events and fall into line with his more sanitised version. It felt as if I was losing my mind.

Losing myself...

I looked at Jay. I hated to admit that he looked great, with his deep, bronzed tan, accentuating his narrow, lined blue eyes. I turned to my unrecognisable, pale reflection, miserably staring back at me in the passenger window. Unlike my husband, I looked dreadful.

What happened to you, Sophie?

I sighed heavily, willing myself not to cry – again.

'Hey? Do you want me to pull over at the next service station and get you a drink or something to eat?' Jay asked, gently rubbing my thigh.

Without looking at him, I shook my head.

'Okay,' he replied, giving me a pat before placing his hand back on the steering wheel.

I remained silent as I choked back the tears.

Why is he acting as if everything is normal between us?

It was so far from any semblance of normality I recognised. I felt dazed and numb as the world continued as if nothing had happened. I slowly breathed out, exhausted: mentally and physically. No matter how tightly I squeezed my eyelids together, a single tear still escaped, trickling down my pale cheek.

'Oh, honey,' sympathised Jay. He reached his hand out again, squeezing my knee. 'I feel it, too. I wish we were still back in Barbados.'

* * *

'Thanks,' I said as Jay handed me a large glass of wine, relieved to be home.

'For you, anything,' he murmured, bending to kiss my forehead. 'Considering how beat you are, I thought we would stay in tonight and venture out for a few drinks tomorrow evening?' he then suggested.

I nodded. Not that I thought I would be up to it tomorrow evening either, but now wasn't the time to ruin the mood.

His mood.

'Hey, Sebastian,' I cooed when he finally conceded to acknowledge our return.

Jay had asked our new neighbours if they would check in on Sebastian while we were away. Rather that, than putting him in a cattery, which Jay knew I would never do.

'See?' Jay said. 'I told you he would be fine. You worried about nothing as usual.'

'Mm...' I mumbled, unconvinced. 'He looks like he's lost some weight.'

'Nah! He looks the same overweight cat to me,' Jay stated, bending down and stroking him behind his ears. 'Hey, Sebastian? I bet you loved being fussed over by Tara? Huh? Daddy Jay would have enjoyed it as well!' He laughed.

I looked at him with a raised eyebrow.

'I'm only joking, babes. Jeez! When did you become so overly sensitive?'

Since you planted that seed of doubt in me when you shared your 'type'.

Tara, our neighbour, was tall, long-legged and deeply tanned, with long, sleek dark hair – as was Jamie, Jay's bikini-clad drinking companion on our honeymoon: both his 'type', unlike his wife.

I took a sip of wine, keeping the jealous thoughts to myself. I hated feeling insecure about my body and my looks. Until Jay, it had never crossed my mind that I wasn't attractive enough. I had never struggled with my confidence before, nor had I spent time comparing myself to other women. It was pointless, masochistic, and so unlike me. But Jay's disclosure about his preferred 'type' had infiltrated deep under my skin, slowly nibbling away at my confidence.

'Did they give you the spare key back?' I asked, shaking myself from my self-destructive thoughts.

'No, I asked them to keep it. Just in case,' Jay explained. 'They liked their Mount Gay Rum by the way.'

Before I had a chance to reply, my phone rang.

'Ahh, Soph, leave it, yeah?' Jay suggested. 'It's our first night back.'

'Liv's FaceTiming. I need to get it,' I stated.

'Oh, come on, Soph? Call her back in the morning. She'll expect you to be jet lagged, anyway.'

'I'll only be five minutes,' I assured him. 'It was the weekend before we left for Barbados when I last spoke with her.'

'Okay. But five minutes, yeah?'

'Promise,' I assured him.

He shook his head as he walked off to the kitchen area leaving me to talk.

'Hey, Liv.'

'Hi,' she answered, smiling.

I watched as her expression changed.

Damn!

It wasn't a conversation I wanted with Liv. Especially not here with Jay present. I hadn't even decided what to tell her, still struggling to process it myself. I would rather have had this conversation tomorrow, but I knew that Liv would be suspicious if I didn't talk to her as agreed this evening.

Not that she isn't already suspicious.

It was self-evident that the heavy concealer I had applied to hide the bruising and the cut on my lip hadn't succeeded.

'What happened to you? To your lip, Soph? Did you have an accident when you were out there?' she questioned, frowning at me.

'I—'

She cut me off. 'Christ! Your nose? That lump on your forehead? What the hell happened to you?'

There was a considerable age difference between Liv and me, but at times, like now, she would act ten years older, not younger than me.

'Soph?' she muttered. 'What's going on?'

I could see the suspicion in her eyes.

'It's nothing,' I replied as breezily as possible. 'Just me being stupid.'

'Don't, Sophie!'

'Don't what?' I asked, feigning ignorance.

'Don't act like that. It's not you.'

I felt Jay watching me. I didn't want to look up at him, but found myself compelled.

Oh God...

I caught his narrowed eyes.

I quickly looked back at the screen on my phone.

'Tell me he's not there?'

I swallowed. 'Of course he is,' I said with a strained smile.

Liv didn't say anything. Not that she needed to, the look in her eye was enough.

'I... I thoughtlessly walked into something. Too many cocktails and sun,' I quickly explained, feeling Jay's eyes on me. 'Lethal combination,' I half-heartedly added.

'Is that what happened on your wedding night?' she asked, taking me by surprise.

'What?' I spluttered. 'You're being ridiculous!'

I suddenly felt uneasy.

Did you see what happened on St Agnes beach?

I had questioned her abruptness with Jay the following afternoon after the wedding. I initially assumed it was because Jay hadn't answered their texts or calls when we were in hospital, citing he had no charge on his mobile. I knew it was a blatant lie as he had been using his phone while waiting with me for my X-ray results. Not that I had called him out on it.

'Am I?' Liv questioned.

'Yes. You know you are,' I replied, hearing an unmistakable quiver in my voice as I noted Jay knock back his wine before walking over.

I shook my head at him as he approached me. I didn't need – or want – his intervention, but he ignored me.

Instead of sitting next to me, he walked around the couch and leaned over me.

'Hey, Liv,' Jay greeted, coldly staring at her.

She looked up at his figure behind me but didn't reply.

'Sophie?' she demanded, her deep brown eyes ablaze. 'Did something happen to you?'

Jay suddenly took my phone from me. 'What are you implying? That I broke your sister's arm on our wedding night? That I then beat my wife up on our honeymoon? Is that the kind of shite you take me for?'

'Jay!' I pleaded, trying to reach my phone.

'IS IT?' he yelled at her, stepping back from me.

I jumped off the couch, but I was too late.

'I'll talk to Sophie when she's allowed a conversation without you policing every word!' With that, Liv hung up.

Oh Christ!

I could see from the glint in Jay's eyes that he was furious at Liv's aspersion.

'Did you say something to her?' he demanded.

'Of course, I didn't,' I answered, attempting to take my phone back.

'Nah, not so fast,' he replied, clicking on my WhatsApp messages.

'Come on, Jay! I wouldn't take your phone. Give it back to me?'

He didn't react.

'Please?' I insisted. 'I need to call Liv back and apologise.'

'For what?' he exploded. 'She should be the one apologising to me!'

'I agree,' I placated, adding, 'My phone? Please?'

He shook his head. 'Give me a minute.'

'No! What the hell do you think you're doing?' I protested as he started messaging her. I struggled with him to get him to stop, but he quickly moved out of my one-handed reach. 'Come on! You can't be serious?' I implored.

He turned his back on me.

'What are you doing?' I demanded.

I grabbed onto his black T-shirt, yanking at him to no avail.

I heard the sound of the message being sent.

I gasped.

He turned to me. 'That'll put her back in her place. You need to stand up to her more and stop letting her push you around.'

I stared at him, dry-mouthed, feeling as if I was going to throw up.

'Not that it matters now as you have me to fight your battles for you.'

'Jay? What did—'

'I promise she won't have seen that coming,' he said, cutting me off. He smiled to himself as he reread his message.

'What... What did you say?' I managed to ask. My voice was barely audible.

Ignoring me, he looked back down at my phone and waited.

'Good, she's just read it,' he said, handing my phone back to me.

My hand was visibly shaking as I took it from him.

Oh God... Oh God...

I willed myself to read what he had sent. It couldn't be that bad.

What the—?

I stared in disbelief at the words.

'Good, eh?' he simply said. 'About time someone told her some home truths.'

'What? Why didn't you tell me?' I asked, stunned by the message.

I stared at him, trying to see whether he was joking.

If he is, it's one sick joke, Sophie.

'I didn't get a chance because I had to take you to hospital. Remember?'

'But... Liv?' I mumbled, rereading what he'd sent. I was struggling to comprehend what he'd written to her and the fact that he hadn't told me. I had to find out via a WhatsApp message between them. 'Why didn't you tell me after? You've had plenty of opportunity.'

He looked at me. 'Because I, like you, foolishly thought I'd protect her.'

'But—'

'She was drunk,' he added, shrugging it off.

I didn't have time to think about what had or hadn't happened. I needed to make this all go away in case Liv told our mother.

Of course, she will. She thinks you sent it, Sophie!

'Jay! She'll think I wrote that. It's sent from my phone? I would never write anything like that. Let alone to my own sister.'

'Yeah? Well, maybe it's time you started!'

I watched as he walked back to the kitchen area to pour himself more wine.

I stared back down at the message.

Oh my God... What has he done?

19

Jay told me you hit on him, telling him he married the wrong sister. How could you? After throwing yourself at Ben at our father's funeral? What the fuck is wrong with you, you fucking slut!

Liv had read it.
Oh God...
Trembling, I quickly messaged her back on WhatsApp:

Jay sent that message. Not me. Ring me.

She read it straight away.
I waited. Nothing. No reply.
She doesn't believe you. She thinks you sent Jay's message and then panicked that you crossed a line.
'Jay?'
He took another glug of wine first before answering me. 'Uhuh?'
I slowly walked over to him. 'You need to call Liv? I mean—'

'Why?' he interrupted, putting the wine glass down.

'To tell her you sent the message,' I insisted.

'What difference will it make?' he asked.

'Christ, Jay! You know that this will destroy my relationship with her.'

'Seems to me she's been sabotaging your relationship for some time now.'

I swallowed back the panic I felt. 'Jay? Please?' I implored. 'I don't think you realise what you've done?'

'I've done nothing! Your slut of a sister tried it on with me when I went to the toilet. She followed me and started kissing me, saying I had married the wrong sister.'

'Liv?' I questioned, struggling to believe that she would even give Jay a second glance. Ben, yes. But Jay? There was no comparison.

'Yes, sweet, innocent, fucking Liv! Who else?' he fired back.

'She kissed you?' I sceptically questioned.

'Are you calling me a liar?'

I shook my head. 'No... Of course not. It's just that doesn't seem like her.'

'What? And publicly throwing herself at your ex at your father's funeral is?'

'No, but—'

'But what?'

I tried to swallow to dislodge the dryness in my mouth. 'She... she was very drunk. And, well, it hit her the hardest. She was Daddy's little girl because she was the youngest. She still lived at home while I'd moved out for uni, and—'

'And what? That's your justification for her trying to screw your ex, who you were due to marry the following month? You were still engaged! The two of you hadn't even called it off, yet! For fuck's sake, Sophie! Grow a fucking spine, will you! You let your mother and sister walk all over you!'

'I don't,' I defensively replied. 'It's just that after Daddy died—'

'I'm sick of you using his death as an excuse,' he abruptly interrupted. 'I'm sorry your dad died. It sucks. But it doesn't give your sister carte blanche to screw your fiancé, does it?'

'She didn't!' I protested, horrified.

'No! Only because you pulled her off him. Good job I'm a decent bloke because I could have fucked your sister if I wanted to!'

I stared at him, sickened by what he'd just said.

But you saw her all over Ben, Sophie.

But that was Ben, and she was the drunkest she'd ever been and inconsolable. Ben was simply a safe place to fall and she had taken his concern for her drunken state one step further than she ever would have done if she had been sober. Whereas Jay was old enough to be her father. And she had no rapport with him. Nothing.

Even more baffling, she hadn't drunk that much that night. But Jay, fuelled with alcohol, had a fatal combination of revenge and spite after seeing Tom and me dancing and reading Ben's text.

Could it be that he hit on Liv to get back at me?

I thought back to the beach when Liv came running over after I'd broken my arm. There was something off between her and Jay. But I was in too much shock to read anything into it. There was no mistaking her coolness towards Jay the following day when we met up at the Driftwood Spars.

I then remembered that she had wanted me to follow her to the toilets that afternoon to talk to me. I had ignored her, not in the mood for any more drama. Not after she had called Ben. So, what did she say to Ben that had so concerned him? What didn't she tell me? *Couldn't* tell me? I tried to recall our phone call the other

Sunday and remembered her reticence: 'If I tell you, promise me you won't lose it?'

Those were her words.

Because the day after my father's funeral, I had lost it. I had gone ballistic with her for her outrageous behaviour and threatened Liv that if it ever happened again, I would cut her out of my life. Drunk or not, Ben was my fiancé, and she was my sister.

I checked my WhatsApp. But there was still no reply.

If Jay had hit on her, was she scared to tell me, in case I didn't believe her? Fearful that I would accuse her of throwing herself at my new husband just as she did with my fiancé.

'I need to call her.'

'What? After what I've just told you? You're going to go grovelling back to her? What the fuck, Sophie!'

'She's my sister, Jay?'

'Yeah, and don't I know!'

'What's that supposed to mean?'

He ignored me and took a gulp of wine.

'I wish I'd never told you about Liv and my father's funeral,' I said, angry that he had used that information against her. 'You know I told you the next day she was mortified and begged for my forgiveness? That it's still an issue between us?'

Jay didn't immediately speak, as if weighing up how to handle the situation.

How to handle me...

'I know you're pissed off right now,' he carefully began. 'And yeah, I should have told you about Liv, but, as you say, I knew things were already on shaky ground between you two. I didn't want to make things worse. And as for her behaviour at your father's funeral, not sharing that with me wouldn't have stopped her hitting on me at our wedding.'

I just stared at him.

'I'm sorry, babes. Really, I am,' he said. 'It's so obvious that she's jealous of you.'

'Of me? Christ, no! Liv's gorgeous!'

'Maybe, but she's not you, babes. Never will be,' Jay pointed out.

I shook my head, unable to process it all. All I wanted to do was talk to Liv. To ask her what had happened on my wedding night. What it was she wanted to tell me.

Did she want to confess before Jay told me?

'Ah, babes, come here,' Jay said, walking around the kitchen island and wrapping his arms around me. 'Shh,' he murmured, brushing his lips against my hair. 'We've got this, you and me. We don't need anyone else.'

My phone started to ring. Panicking, I pulled back from Jay's embrace.

'Who is it?' demanded Jay.

'It's my mum,' I answered, unable to hide the terror I felt.

'Don't answer it,' Jay instructed.

'I can't not answer it! It's my mother, Jay.'

'So? You need to start thinking for yourself,' he suggested.

'I need to take this,' I said, stepping back from him.

Oh God...

I pressed answer.

'Hi, Mum,' I tentatively began.

'How could you say those terrible things to your sister? How? Did Jay say that to you? Because it's all lies!'

'Mum?'

'And as for Ben? Really!' she continued, not letting me speak. 'You know what a state Liv was in? Honestly, Sophie! I'm ashamed you're my daughter. I don't recognise you any more, not since you got together with him. You've changed, and not for the better!'

'I didn't write or send the message, it was—'

I stopped mid-sentence. She had cut the call.

I immediately called her back. It went straight to voicemail.

Oh my God! She declined your call.

I tried again. Again, it was declined.

'What did she say?' Jay questioned.

'Just a minute, I'm trying to call Liv.'

It went straight to voicemail as well.

What the—?

I tried again. And again.

I realised my hand was trembling.

'Oh God, Jay?' I said as I turned round to him.

'Hey, it's their loss if they don't want to talk to you,' he replied, taking hold of me.

But I didn't want him to hold me. I wanted him to make it all go away.

'You need to call them,' I said, freeing myself from his grip.

'Why?'

'To explain that you messaged Liv on my phone. That it wasn't me,' I pleaded.

'And what difference do you think that would make? You've already sent a message stating that?' he questioned, looking at me as if I had lost my mind. 'Anyway, do you think either of them will talk to me now that I've told you what your sister did? When I pushed her off me, she begged me not to tell you what she'd done, terrified you'd never forgive her again. She'll always hold that against me.'

I shook my head as tears started to fall.

'Please, Jay? Please?' I begged him.

I can't lose them as well...

'Come on, let's sit you down,' Jay suggested.

He guided me back inside and over to the couch. He then picked up my wine glass and took it over to the kitchen to refill it. I sat dazed, staring out at the ocean.

He returned and lifted the glass to my lips. 'It will help, babes,' he assured me. 'You're in shock.'

I looked at him, not understanding why he wouldn't try to make it right.

Why won't you just call them and tell them you sent that message? Not me?

20

'Lost something?' Jay asked, walking into the bedroom, as he watched me pulling apart the books and other items on my bedside cabinet.

'I can't find my phone.'

'How much did you drink last night?' he said, shaking his head at me. 'You left it on the couch.'

He handed me the steaming black coffee.

'Thanks,' I mumbled. I felt like I was going mad.

I blew on the scalding liquid before taking a small sip.

'You know, it will all work out. Just give them time,' he assured me, stroking my hair.

I flinched at his touch. I was still mad at him. I hadn't slept all night, tossing and turning, which was uncomfortable and awkward with a plaster cast. Unlike Jay, who, much to my annoyance, slept through my anxious wakefulness.

'For what it's worth, I'm sorry? Yeah?' he apologised.

I looked at him and waited.

'If I could undo it, I would. But, let's be honest here, Liv is in the wrong. She wanted me to fuck her in the toilets, for fuck's sake!'

'Jay!'

'What? If I'd been the one hitting on your sister it would be a very different story. Why, after all she has done, are you being so protective of her?'

I shrugged.

Something didn't feel right.

I heard Jay give out a frustrated sigh. I watched as he turned to Sebastian, who was curled up by my feet. 'You know I don't like him on the bed? I can't stand the hairs everywhere,' he complained as he threw a rather disgruntled Sebastian on the floor.

'Jay!'

'Don't shout at me,' he warned.

'Well, don't throw Sebastian down like that.'

'Christ! You're prickly this morning.'

'If you hadn't sent that message to Liv, then—'

'For fuck's sake, Sophie! I'm tired of you bleating on and on about that message. If you're so bloody unhappy, do something about it?'

'Like what?' I snapped. 'They're ignoring my messages and won't answer my calls.'

Jay sighed again as he ran his hand over his cropped, dark hair. 'Fuck! I don't know,' he muttered, the fight leaving him. I waited as he shook his head. 'Pointless me calling again.'

'Again?'

He looked at me. 'Yeah, I tried calling Liv and Joanna to explain while I was making you a coffee. I wanted to bring you some good news. But they both declined my call.'

'Did you leave a voicemail explaining what happened?'

He shook his head. 'No. I reckon they've blocked me, as both numbers declined my call, so they'd delete whatever message I left without listening to it.'

'Oh,' I mumbled, wondering whether they had blocked my number as well.

I had left countless voicemails and sent messages, all unread.

'Look, I've been thinking, why don't you write them a letter explaining what happened? That it was me who sent Liv that message and that I'm sorry and I'm happy to talk to them and say that.'

I looked at him, unsure.

'They'll read a letter, Sophie. Curiosity will win out. Also, you can say exactly what you want without getting drawn into a heated argument.'

'Maybe,' I said, accepting it might be a good idea.

'We okay, then?'

'Once I've heard from them, I'll feel better,' I answered.

'You get writing, and I'll drive to the post office and get it sent special delivery which guarantees to reach them by 1 p.m. tomorrow. They'll call you tomorrow as soon as they've read that it was all my fault,' he said, adding, 'I just hate that I put you in this situation in the first place.'

'When I begged you to call Liv last night, and you refused, why call her this morning?' I asked, curious.

He was so opposed to it last night that I didn't understand what had changed for him.

'My failing is my stubbornness and the fact I can't take orders from anyone. Even from someone as beautiful as my gorgeous wife,' Jay said, squeezing my hand. 'Not a good combination as you've now experienced, and I'm sorry.' He sighed before continuing, 'I saw how upset you were last night when you went to bed, and I wanted to make it right, but it was too late to call them. So, I decided I would ring and explain to them this morning.'

'Thanks for trying.'

He squeezed my hand again, giving me a sad smile. 'You've

already lost your dad. I don't want to be responsible for you losing your mum and sister as well. I'll do whatever it takes to fix this,' he promised me.

I stared into his eyes. He seemed genuine.

But I wasn't sure I believed him.

* * *

Jay had taken the letter and posted it by special delivery yesterday afternoon. I had suggested going with him, but he had other plans, assuming I would be working with my deadline for my book looming ever nearer. He returned with a receipt which evidenced my mother and sister's address, and a tracking number so I could check when they received it.

Which I had just done for the nineteenth time.

Its status had changed. It had been signed for and successfully delivered at 1.55 p.m. – fifteen minutes ago.

I slowly exhaled, feeling, instead of relief, a knot of trepidation, knowing they were about to read it. I had spent yesterday morning rewriting the letter until the words were perfect. I had apologised for Jay's behaviour and any misunderstanding between us. I had also assured Liv that I condemned what Jay had written about her. I had then asked a couple of questions: what was it that she had not been able to tell me, and what had she disclosed to Ben when I was in the hospital to make him so worried about me? I also admitted I didn't have Ben's number as it had been deleted and blocked and I couldn't ask him directly.

I had sealed the envelope with Sellotape before handing it to Jay to post. I had feared him reading it as it would have more than infuriated him and caused a huge fight. I also couldn't challenge him about wanting to post it without me, as it would show I didn't trust him to send it. However, I now had evidence to the contrary, allaying my fears.

'Jay?' I called out from the study where I was supposed to be working. Instead, I had been writing in my journal, which I now kept hidden, locked in a drawer in my desk. The last person I wanted to read it was Jay, aware he wouldn't appreciate what he would find.

'Jay?' I repeated getting up from my desk and going to find him.

I looked around the living space before spotting him outside in the back garden, looking out at the ocean. I opened the bi-folding door and headed across the lawn towards Jay. I realised when I got close enough that he was on the phone.

He didn't hear me approach him against the noisy swell of the water below.

'Yeah, I'll try. I promise. I know... I know,' he repeated.

Sensing my presence, he spun around.

'Look, I'll call you back, all right? Yeah, you too.' He gave me a quizzical look as he slid his phone into his jeans pocket. 'I thought you were busy working?'

'I was and still am. I just wanted to tell you that they received it,' I shared.

It took him a moment to register. 'The letter?'

I nodded, smiling.

He pulled me into him and gently kissed me. 'See? Everything will be fine. I bet they've called by this evening.'

'I hope so,' I answered, dreading the wait. 'Who were you talking to?'

'Oh, nothing important, just a guitar I'm interested in buying. Might make a trip back to Manchester if you don't mind?'

'Manchester?'

'Ahuh. This guitar's there and I want to have a look at it before I consider buying it,' he explained.

'Can't they just courier it to you?'

'No. I need to see how the guitar feels, how it plays first. It's a very personal thing.'

'Oh,' I mumbled, not wanting him to go.

'It'll only be one night,' he reasoned with me.

'You can't do it in a day?' I questioned.

'It's over 300 miles one way, babes. Anyway, you'll get a chance to catch up on some much-needed work with me gone.'

I sighed. 'When are you planning on going?'

'Tomorrow, I reckon.'

'Tomorrow?' I repeated, taken aback.

'Yeah. It's a friend of a friend, and he's got another potential buyer.'

'How much is it?'

Jay stepped back from me and casually shrugged.

'Seriously, Jay?'

'A lot. But it'll be worth it,' he assured me.

'And where are you going to get the money from? You know we're stretched until I get the next advance for this book,' I stated. 'Then there's the cost of the honeymoon.'

'You don't have to worry about that.'

I frowned at him. 'Of course I do. You never told me how you paid for it?'

'You never asked,' he replied.

I folded my arms and stepped back from him.

'Come on, Sophie! I have some pride!' he muttered.

I waited.

'If you must know, it's my last bit of inheritance.'

I don't know what answer I expected, but it wasn't that one. As far as I was aware, Jay had no inheritance left. When I had first met him, he had nothing. Jay was like a shipwreck survivor that I had pulled out of the dark, dangerous waters. He was a lone survivor: no family, friends, job, money – nothing.

But he had big dreams, compelling aspirations and a deep-rooted need to find love again. And that love was me.

Finally, his inheritance had come through, but he had put it all towards Eastcliff Cottage.

At least, that's what he told you.

'You've still got some inheritance left?' I questioned, unable to disguise my surprise.

'*Had*,' he pointed out. 'The honeymoon was rather expensive.'

'And this guitar?'

'It's something my mum would have wanted me to buy. Every time I play it, I'll think of her.'

I couldn't argue with him, aware of how devastated he was by his mother's death. Not that I was happy about this sudden revelation. I had no idea he had money left.

'Manchester?' I mumbled.

'Just one night, babes,' he promised, leaning in and kissing me.

I couldn't silence the sliver of doubt in my head after Jay had stayed out until after 2 a.m. drinking with another woman on our honeymoon. Despite Jay reassuring me he hadn't slept with this woman – Jamie – it had ignited an insecurity that I wasn't enough for him.

Are you really travelling to Manchester to potentially buy a guitar or is it for another reason? Another woman?

PART THREE

'There is no terror in the bang, only the anticipation of it.'

— ALFRED HITCHCOCK

21

'Jay, something's wrong. I can feel it,' I confided as I watched him getting changed after showering.

It was another glorious summer's evening, and he was getting ready to head out for a couple of drinks. I wasn't in the mood and felt too tired after my sleepless night to make small talk about our honeymoon. Or wedding. Or staring at my split, swollen lip.

But Jay was desperate to mingle with the crowds of people who would be there and share the expected spectacular Cornish sunset with a chilled pint in his hand.

'Like what?'

I shrugged.

'Soph? Come on? I haven't got time for this,' he muttered, pulling his jeans on. 'Tom will be here any minute.'

I hadn't seen Tom since our wedding night when Jay had stormed off in a jealous rage because he was dancing with me.

'I rang Mum and Liv, and neither of them answered. I've left three messages on Mum's answer machine.'

'Maybe they're busy?' Jay suggested, pulling a black T-shirt on before slipping on his favourite flip-flops.

Again, I shrugged. 'Mum signed for the letter five hours ago.'

'So? Like I said, maybe they're busy?'

I sighed as I collapsed on the bed, morosely watching him choose his rings. I couldn't shake the unease that there was no response to my letter: it didn't make sense.

He turned and looked at me. 'Why don't you come out for a couple of drinks? It'll take your mind off them.'

I shook my head. Feeling restless, I stood up and left Jay to finish getting ready. I went downstairs and poured myself a large glass of wine to help me relax. As I was taking my first sip, there was a knock at the door.

I wandered out to the hallway.

'Hey,' I said smiling when I opened the door.

'Hi.' Tom looked uneasy.

'Come in, Jay won't be long.'

'Thanks, but I'll just wait in the car.'

It was odd. Why wouldn't he come in? Had Jay said something to him?

'Are you sure?'

He nodded.

'I'm sorry about...' He faltered, gesturing towards my plaster cast, not quite able to look me in the eye.

'Yeah... well.' I shrugged.

It took him a moment to register my split lip.

'Christ! What happened?'

I held his concerned gaze for a beat too long. I wanted to ask him what he meant the night before my wedding, when he had questioned if I was certain I wanted to marry Jay. His other, troubling question came back to me: *'What do you really know about him?'*

'Sophie? Did someone do that to you?'

By 'someone', I took him to mean Jay.

My phone started to ring. It was Liv.

'Sorry, Tom, I've got to take this,' I hurriedly apologised.

'Sure. Tell Jay I'm waiting in the car.'

I nodded.

Closing the door, I answered my phone as I walked back through to the open-plan living space and the kitchen area where I had left my wine.

'God! Liv, I've been calling and messaging—'

'How could you?' she hissed with a level of anger I didn't recognise.

I could feel my face burning with the force of her words.

'How could I what?' I questioned, panicking.

'Send Mum that letter? How could you?' she raged at me.

'But I... I apologised,' I stuttered, completely thrown.

I suddenly felt nauseous. A coldness crept its way down my spine. Something was very wrong, and I didn't know what.

I numbly watched, adrenaline coursing through me as Jay, happily whistling to himself, walked down the stairs into the open-plan living space to no doubt say goodbye. He abruptly stopped and looked at me, frowning.

'Who is it?' he mouthed.

'You what? Are you for real, Sophie? You disgust me!'

'Liv?' I questioned, ignoring Jay.

'Don't you dare Liv, me! How could you? How could you write those nasty, cruel things to our mother? I don't care what you say about me, but to say that to her?'

'I... I don't know what...' I spluttered.

'You sent it! Of course, you know what you wrote! Don't act as if you don't know what you said!'

'No... Liv—'

'I hope he's worth it, Sophie!'

'Liv? Please?' I begged, frantic.

'Mum will never forgive you for this, Sophie. NEVER!'

I heard an intake of air.

Or was that a sob?

Before I had a chance to speak, she continued: 'Don't try to contact us ever again. Understand? You don't exist to us any more! YOU'RE DEAD TO US!'

'Liv? LIV?' I screamed.

But the line was disconnected.

Oh God...

I felt my legs give way beneath me as I sank down against the kitchen cabinet.

'Soph? What's wrong?' Jay cried out as he ran towards me.

I blankly stared up at him.

'Sophie? For fuck's sake? What's happened?'

I couldn't get the words out for the fear that was choking me.

You're dead to us!

Those words replayed in my head, again and again, as the tears came hard and fast.

'What the hell did she say to you?' he asked, crouching down in front of me.

I shook my head, unable to comprehend what had just happened.

You're dead to us!

I looked at him: 'What did you do?' I croaked, struggling to breathe.

Had he swapped my handwritten letter with a typed one? There was nothing in my letter that would have caused such outrage. Enough for them to... to...

'Hey! Don't turn this on me!' he snapped.

I gasped for gulps of air that I couldn't reach. I could feel myself choking, unable to breathe.

I couldn't do it without them... I needed them.

'Come on, take a slow, deep breath, Soph,' instructed Jay, holding my face.

I tried but couldn't get my breath.

'Copy me. Now slowly breathe in,' he encouraged, taking a deep breath. He waited a few beats. 'Now a longer, slower breath out. Follow me.'

I tried but failed.

I tried again, slower and steadier. Then again.

'Yeah,' he encouraged. 'That's it. Slowly letting it all out.'

A few minutes later, I'd regulated my breathing again but not my thoughts.

Jay held me as I sobbed uncontrollably.

He kissed my head when I'd finally exhausted myself.

He cracked a smile. 'You know you're one hell of an ugly crier?'

I laughed despite myself, wiping a combination of tears and mucus on the back of my hand.

'Here,' Jay said, stretching up and grabbing some kitchen towel.

'Thanks,' I mumbled, taking it and blowing my nose.

The thought hit me again, sudden and cruel: *'You're dead to us.'*

'Hey, come on, babes? You've got me now. You don't need them. Fucking pair of evil witches!'

'Don't say that about them!'

'Yeah... Okay. Sorry. But whatever she said to you just now was totally out of order.'

I nodded, choking on my tears and self-pity.

Jay gently stroked my hair. 'I'd never have posted your letter if I thought this was going to happen. I wish I'd never suggested you write to them. The pair of ungrateful—'

'Jay!' I pleaded, shaking my head at him.

'Sorry,' he said. 'It just makes me so mad to think of someone hurting you like this.'

'I know,' I mumbled. 'But they're still my mother and sister. Always will be.'

I shook my head as more tears came as the reality hit me.

You're no longer their daughter or sister. They've cut you from their lives...

As if reading my mind, Jay held my head and looked me straight in the eye. 'They'll come round. You'll see.'

I tried to shake my head, resisting his words, but he held onto me.

'No, listen, they will. But you don't need them. Understand? You have me. We have each other, Sophie. We don't need them. We don't need anyone.'

I thought back to our wedding ceremony when Jay had said he would never let me go: *'You're mine now till death do us part.'*

Had he replaced my letter with one of his own? One so outrageously vile that it cut me off from my mother and sister? So all I had was him?

Because how could your words have offended them so much that they cut you out of their lives?

22

'Don't go? Please, Jay?' I begged.

I couldn't cope being alone right now.

'I won't stay out long, I promise. Tom's waiting for me.'

My pleading eyes held his gaze.

'You'll be fine. Here,' he said, reaching for my glass of wine. 'Take a drink. I've refilled it for you.'

'I don't need a drink,' I petulantly stated, pushing it away. 'I need you!'

'You have me,' he gently replied.

But to my consternation, he stood up.

I grabbed his hand. 'Jay, please?'

He pulled away from my hold. 'Sophie! You'll be fine for a couple of hours.'

'I don't want to be alone,' I persisted.

'So come out with me?'

'What? Looking like this?'

'Change into a T-shirt and jeans. It's only Blue Bar,' he pointed out.

I shook my head. 'I look a mess from crying so much.'

I didn't add that my face was still bruised and swollen. The last thing I wanted was people staring or asking what had happened.

He didn't argue with me. I realised it was a half-hearted attempt on his part, not expecting or wanting me to join him.

'Can't we just drive up to see them?'

'Who?' Jay asked, confused.

'My mum and sister?'

He laughed. 'You can't be serious? It's roughly six hundred miles. It would take ten hours to drive there?'

'So? We can leave now and we'll be there by morning. I need to see them, Jay. To make this right. Please?'

'Babes, I'm going to Manchester tomorrow. Remember?'

'Can't you rearrange it?'

'And lose the guitar? No.'

I stared at him.

'Look, how about we discuss it when I get back? We could drive up on Sunday?'

'What about Saturday?'

He shook his head. 'That's when I'm coming back from Manchester.'

'Oh,' I mumbled.

'Definitely Sunday. I promise.'

I nodded.

'Look, I'm so late as it is, yeah? And Tom's waiting.'

I didn't reply. There was no point.

'See you later. Why don't you give Grace or Anna a call? You were complaining not so long ago that you feel that you're losing your friends.'

'I messaged them last night, but they haven't got back,' I answered.

It was odd that neither one had responded. It was hurtful. But I accepted that they were on holiday in Venice.

Or maybe they're reciprocating your treatment of them lately? All the calls you've missed. What about their messages you haven't responded to because Jay doesn't like you using your phone when he's around, which has been twenty-four-seven for the past week-and-a-half? No wonder they're not jumping now you have time for them.

'Well, try them again.'

I didn't bother explaining that they were in Venice.

Or that maybe they didn't want to talk to you? That they could be equally hurt that you have sacrificed your friendship with them for Jay.

'Look, I'll be back soon, all right?'

I watched as he headed to the front door, not waiting for a response.

If I had felt alone before, it was nothing compared to now.

A deathly silence filled the cottage. I looked around for Sebastian, but even he had abandoned me.

I picked up my phone. Not that I had anyone to call. I had prioritised Jay above and beyond everyone and had assumed it was the same with him, until the move to Cornwall had proved me wrong. When Jay had moved into my flat in London, we had spent our days and evenings together. I favoured him over my friends, believing he was doing the same. But, in reality, Jay knew no one in London. So, my assumption that he preferred to stay in with a bottle of wine couldn't have been further from the truth.

I clicked on Instagram. Then Liv's page, but nothing came up. It was the same with her other social media pages. Liv Blair Kennedy did not exist: at least not to me. Panicking, I clicked on my mother's Facebook page. It wasn't there. She had also disappeared. Liv had been serious with her threat that I didn't exist to them any more. They had erased me from their lives.

You're dead to us!

I sat back, bewildered and overcome with shock. I looked around the contemporary living space, craving my familiar, comfortable Kensington flat. My old life. The time before I met Jay. I'd sold up and left London on a romantic whim, dragged along by his dreams which he mis-sold as my dreams. Everything had changed since the day he'd walked into my life.

No, Sophie... It all changed the day you married him.
And for what?

* * *

I was in bed when Jay returned home. I didn't feel much like talking and pretended to be asleep. Not that I could sleep with my mind torturing me about all that I had lost.

He tried to wake me up. Gently at first, followed by a lot of cursing and muttering when it was apparent that I wasn't responding. I assumed he wanted sex which would rationalise his apparent annoyance. Not that I cared. I couldn't believe he'd left me when I was so upset, when it was self-evident that I needed him more than ever. I had just lost my family because of him, and he had casually gone out.

'Fuck you!' he slurred.

I inwardly gasped at his callousness.

I furtively glanced at the Alexa clock on the bedside cabinet beside me, not wanting to alert Jay to the fact I was awake. It was 11.43 p.m. In my misery, time had eluded me. Jay had disappeared just after 8 p.m. He had left me alone for nearly four hours.

Within minutes of climbing, frustrated into bed, Jay's breathing became heavy and slow. I waited until he was asleep before pulling back the throw and getting out of bed. I couldn't relax, and the last thing I wanted to do was lie next to him and listen as he snored through to the early hours. I crept out of the room, heading to the guest bedroom. It was the first time I had left our bed, and I hoped it would be the last. I didn't like being mad at Jay, but his actions were unforgivable. He hadn't gone out for a quick drink as promised; he had forgotten about me and stayed out for hours, enjoying himself.

I must have fallen asleep, because when I awoke, intrusive sunlight streamed into the curtainless room. I sat up, confused as I looked around at Jay's boxes, guitars and amps which filled the spare room. I got up and padded through to the master bedroom. The unmade bed was empty.

Damn!

I intended on returning to bed before Jay stirred, knowing he would be upset if he found out I'd left to sleep elsewhere.

I headed to the bathroom, expecting to find him there. There was no sign of him. I went downstairs and wandered through to the empty living area. He wasn't there. I noted a half-drunk coffee mug on the counter. I walked over and touched it. It was cold.

Sebastian suddenly shot out from somewhere, screeching at me to be fed.

'Where's Jay, eh?'

Sebastian looked at me, not interested in my problems, only food.

After feeding him, I looked around for a note. Nothing. I went back upstairs and checked my phone. There were no messages from Jay. I then thought to look to see if the Transporter was parked up outside. It was gone.

He was gone.

For a split second, I thought he had left me. Then I remembered his plans to go to Manchester to check out a guitar.

I was shocked that he had left without saying goodbye or even leaving a note. I realised I'd hurt him by sleeping in the spare room.

I made myself a strong black coffee before steeling myself to call him.

'Hey, where are you?'

'I told you, driving to Manchester.'

His voice was emotionless.

'Yeah, I know. But that was yesterday evening. We hadn't spoken about it since then.'

'I didn't realise I needed your permission as to when I could leave?'

I hesitated before replying. 'You don't,' I answered, 'It's just... You left without telling me.'

'Maybe if you'd slept in the same bed as me, you would have heard me get up.'

'I... I couldn't sleep again and didn't want to bother you with my tossing and turning.'

'Yeah? You were fast asleep when I looked in on you.'

'Oh... Yeah, exhaustion must have won in the end.'

'Are you sure it wasn't those two bottles of Chablis you knocked back?'

'That's not true,' I replied, trying to recall how much wine I had drunk. 'It wasn't even a bottle.'

'Well, there were two empty bottles waiting to be recycled and a third one half empty in the fridge. It's ridiculous! Our recycling bin is already overflowing.'

'Come on, Jay? You know I couldn't have possibly drunk all that?'

He was silent for a moment.

'Jay?'

'I might stay in Manchester for a couple of nights.'

'What?' I asked, taken aback by this sudden change. 'Come on, Jay! I'm your wife!'

'Are you? You see, I would expect my wife to sleep next to me. Even acknowledge me when I come to bed and cuddle her. Not ignore me.'

'I was asleep when you came to bed,' I lied.

'You keep telling yourself that.'

'Seriously, Jay? We're meant to be driving to Broughty Ferry on Sunday.'

He didn't answer me.

'How am I supposed to get there when you've got the Transporter?'

'Walk, for all I care.'

'Jay?'

'I've got to go,' he cut in. 'I need to concentrate on the traffic.'

'Which hotel are you staying at?' I quickly asked.

'I'm not,' he answered.

'Where are you sleeping? In the Transporter?'

'I'm staying with a friend.'

'Who?'

He'd told me that all his friends had cut off from him, siding with his ex, who had lied about the reason behind their breakup. When I'd asked him why he didn't tell the truth about her infidelity with one of his childhood friends, he had argued that he shouldn't have to.

'You don't know them,' he stated, adding, 'thankfully.'

'What does that mean?'

'Let's just say I don't like being interrogated because of you.'

Then it hit me.

Tom.

'Fuck knows what you said to Tom last night, but when I got in the car, he was really off with me, as if someone had given him the idea that I smacked you around on our honeymoon.'

You did... You threw a remote control at my head and smacked a door into my face.

'I don't like explaining myself to people. Especially my friends. So just watch whatever you insinuate next time. Do you think I like admitting to everyone that my wife is a drunk? That she drinks so much she can't stand up and passes out.'

'What?' I spluttered, outraged.

Jay was silent, enjoying my humiliation.

'Why would you say that?'

'Because it's true,' he said before the line went dead.

I realised Tom was right, I didn't know anything about Jay.

Christ, Sophie. Who have you married?

23

I looked at the guest bedroom and all Jay's boxes, guitars, amps and other paraphernalia. He still hadn't got around to storing most of it in the attic. I wanted the space as a guest bedroom so family and friends could visit.

I swallowed as the enormity of my sister's words hit me again like a tsunami: *'You're dead to us.'*

I pushed the thought away. I didn't have time to feel sorry for myself.

My skin suddenly felt hot and prickly. I shouldn't be here poking around his personal stuff. Jay had made it clear he didn't want me touching it.

Why, Sophie?

I noticed the case for his favourite blonde Takamine acoustic guitar. It was the guitar he used when he practised with Rachael. I assumed the song he had written for me would be inside. Curiosity compelled me to open it. I lifted the lid and stared.

There inside with his beloved guitar was a photograph.

But it wasn't of me. It was another woman.

I picked it up and stared at it – at her. It was a woman in her early to mid-forties who looked just like his 'type' – the antithesis of me. Long, tanned legs, shoulder-length black hair and brown eyes. She was wearing a bikini top and shorts with bare feet on a sandy beach.

I turned the photograph over and read the writing on the back.

To Jay x

No name. But there was a date: two years before I met him.

I suddenly felt sick.

I flipped the photograph back over.

Oh my God...

I recognised the beach and cliffs behind her.

Porthtowan Beach.

I dropped the photo as Tom's words came back to me: '*He's been coming to Porthtowan during the summer now for some years.*'

It felt as if wasps had taken up residence in my stomach, buzzing and stinging, frantically trying to find an escape. I slowly breathed out, attempting to dispel the nauseousness.

I decided to call Jay and demand to know why he had lied to me about never coming to Porthtowan. And to find out who this woman was and why he still kept a photo of her with his favourite guitar.

Was this his ex from Manchester? Was she the reason he was driving back there now?

I listened as the call went immediately to voicemail.

I hung up without leaving a message. What could I say? That I had gone snooping through his personal belongings looking for validation that he loved me?

Where is this song that you wrote for me, Jay? And when are you going to play it for me?

He hadn't mentioned any upcoming open mic sessions when he

was planning on 'surprising' me with the song he had written for me.

Was it all talk, Sophie? Just a means of impressing Liv and Mum? You?

Maybe...

I closed the guitar case and left the room. I wasn't in the mood to find out any other secrets. I knew I should look to see what other nasty surprises awaited while Jay was still in Manchester before he put everything in the attic. But I didn't have the stomach. I had seen enough for today.

I distracted myself by tidying the cottage. I wasn't in the frame of mind for writing, too agitated and restless to be able to concentrate. Again, I decided to put it off for another day, a better day.

I was surprised when I saw the bottles of wine from last night waiting in the kitchen to be recycled.

Had I really drunk that much?

I was shocked. I could see why Jay would have been equally startled.

How could you have possibly drunk so much without realising?

By the evening, I had managed to get the cottage starting to resemble something akin to home. I found photographs and prints that I hung on various walls. I needed to feel like I belonged here and wasn't just a guest. Jay's presence seemed to dominate the cottage, presumably because his guitars occupied every room, even the master bedroom. The study was the only room that Jay hadn't taken over.

I then unpacked all my books and organised them by genre, then alphabet, on the bookshelves in the study. By the time I stopped organising, it was much later than I expected.

I stepped back and was surprised to note that my desk drawer, where I kept my journal, a small box containing old letters, postcards and memorabilia from my father, our passports and legal documents was open. The key was still in the lock.

How is that possible?

I was paranoid about keeping my journal literally under lock and key. I had documented my broken wrist, the injuries to my face and the insults and slurs, all so I wouldn't forget Jay was responsible. Or be persuaded over time that Jay's violent outbursts were justified because of me, or worse, that I had injured myself, which is what he was suggesting.

Had Jay found the key and read my journal?

But how would he know where to find the key? Unless he watched you?

I kept it under the art deco, pyramid black bakelite phone on my study desk.

I shook off the unsettling paranoid thought. But the alternative was even more disconcerting.

Were you too drunk to remember coming into the study last night?

I opened the drawer. Everything was as I last remembered. I checked my journal, but there was no new drunken entry. I locked the drawer and hid the key in my hardback copy of Toni Morrison's *Beloved*. If Jay had found the key under the phone, I was sure he would never discover it in that particular book when the room was full of them.

I sat in the garden with a bottle of chilled white wine, watching the sun's glorious descent as a ball of magnificent red and orange fire into the ocean. Exhausted, I headed inside once the sun disappeared. Sebastian followed me up the stairs and took his place on the bed. Despite Jay's outrage at the cat hairs, I was happy Sebastian was settling himself on the throw beside me, grateful for the company.

I checked my phone. I shouldn't have been disappointed, but I was when I saw he hadn't bothered to call after he'd hung up on me this morning.

I attempted to read a few chapters of Jane Austen's *Sense and Sensibility*, my go-to comfort author, to help distract me. Unable to focus, I closed the book and instructed Alexa to turn the bedside lamp off. I turned over and stared at Jay's pillow, wondering where he was and with whom. A familiar wave of anxiety coursed through me as I accepted that I wouldn't hear from him tonight.

Why am I so bothered about where you are? Or who you are with?

I blinked back the self-pitying tears. I knew the reason why.

Without Jay, you have no one.

I was too chagrined to admit to Grace and Anna – to the world – what was happening. I had hoped Grace could help me, but her lack of response to my message made me reluctant to bother her again.

What would you say, anyway?

That the man you married isn't the man you fell in love with?

How could I turn to them and share these recent dark moments with Jay? Actions I hadn't anticipated or trusted him to be capable of committing. I had spent the past eight months persuading them how wonderful, kind, considerate and perfect he was, so how could I suddenly say the opposite was true?

How can you admit that you got it so wrong?

Shame and humiliation shackled me, isolating me and preventing me from messaging them again. Or calling.

I lay there in the dark, willing myself to switch off so I could fall asleep. But Tom's words the night before our wedding haunted me: '*What do you know about him?*'

Seemingly nothing. I didn't know any of Jay's friends from Manchester or even where he was sleeping tonight. The thought crossed my mind like insidious poison: had he gone back to his ex? Is that whose bed he was sharing now?

Or is he with the woman in the photograph?
Has he even gone to Manchester, Sophie?

I sighed, irritated with myself.

After the way he treats you? Why do you care?

I fractiously thumped my pillow to plump it up and turned over onto my side.

But you are jealous, aren't you?

It was paradoxical.

I stared at the trickster shapes dancing on the wall as the moonlight ebbed through the window. I didn't like being here in the house alone. I wasn't familiar with its creaks and sighs, all of which sounded ominous and foreboding, whispering of the secret terror I feared was yet to come.

24

Startled, my eyes shot open. My heart was thundering in my ribcage at some perceived threat. I lay there, breathing shallowly. I didn't dare move. I waited, trying to discern what was different. What exactly had awoken me? I could feel Sebastian's warm, purring body, unaware of my terror, next to mine.

My mind went into a tailspin at what could be awaiting me. What if it's a rapist? Or murderer?

I stopped myself from going down that rabbit hole. It was just my imagination. Or perhaps I had startled awake from a bad dream?

Trepidation scorched through me as I heard something. No, not something: *someone.*

Breathing: low, heavy, filled with malice.

I lay there, perfectly still, not wanting them to know I was awake, conscious of their presence.

Someone's here, Sophie! Oh my God...

Not daring to breathe, I slowly inched my hand towards my phone. Finding it, I wrapped my fingers around it.

'Who are you going to call?' questioned a deep, low voice from the darkest corner of the room.

I screamed and jumped simultaneously.

It took me a second to register the source of the voice.

Someone was sitting in the chair, watching me from the shadows.

'Alexa, light on!' I yelled, pulling the throw around my body as I pressed up against the antique wooden headboard.

The light automatically came on, dispelling the darkness and forcing the night shadows to retreat.

I blinked in disbelief as fear dissipated, replaced by rage.

'What the hell?' I muttered.

He didn't say a word. He continued watching me, his expression blank. It was chilling.

He was chilling.

'JAY!' I yelled at him.

He looked at me, as if surprised by my outburst.

'What are you doing here?' I somehow managed to question, fighting the adrenaline that was screaming at me to get up and hit him repeatedly for scaring me half to death.

'I live here,' he replied. 'Remember? Or have you already moved me on?'

'Don't mess with me!' I threatened.

I looked at Alexa. It was 2.03 a.m.

'You're supposed to be in Manchester,' I stated, conscious that I was trembling.

'I've been trying to call you and couldn't get through.'

'What?' I spluttered, incredulous.

'I thought something had happened to you,' he continued.

'Are you being serious?'

'I don't lie.'

'I haven't received one call from you,' I stated.

He jerked his head towards my phone. 'Check your signal.'

Sceptical, I looked at my phone. He was right. There was no signal.

'The coverage here is hit-and-miss,' he explained.

'We have Wi-Fi?' I gestured to Alexa, who was connected to our broadband.

He shrugged.

Frowning, I checked my settings. The Wi-Fi wasn't connected on my phone. How could that be possible?

'The Wi-Fi's not connected,' I said. 'But I didn't disconnect it.'

Jay shrugged. 'Whatever, you gave me a scare.'

I stared at him, surprised that he cared enough to drive back from Manchester to check on me.

As if reading my mind, he added, 'You sounded odd when we talked.'

'Me?'

He nodded, a concerned look in his eyes. 'You've been behaving oddly. Not yourself.'

I stared back at him.

You were sitting in the dark watching me sleep when you were supposed to be in Manchester.

'I was in two minds whether to leave. Then...' Jay stopped himself and shook his head. 'I thought you'd be fine without me. No doubt happier without me.'

He held my gaze.

I knew he was referring to me sleeping in the spare room.

'I love you, Sophie. More than you could ever imagine.'

I didn't reply. I couldn't. I had no words. I was still reeling from shock as my brain played catch-up despite now being more alert than ever before.

'Regardless of what you think, I couldn't live without you,' he added. 'You're the only woman I ever wanted to marry, and that will never change.'

I warily held his gaze, surprised by the sincerity in his eyes. He believed it of himself.

So, why didn't I?

I watched as he dejectedly stood up. He looked at me, waiting for affirmation I felt the same way. But I couldn't give it to him.

Not when he's just scared the hell out of you, Sophie!

He then spotted Sebastian on the bed. 'What the fuck is he doing there?'

'He's always slept with me,' I replied. 'Come on, Jay? You never used to mind?'

'I do now. I told you to keep him off the bloody bed!' he snapped as he lunged for Sebastian, throwing him out of the bedroom.

'JAY!'

'If I find him in there again, I'll fucking skin him, the little shit!'

He then headed off to the bathroom while Sebastian scarpered downstairs.

I shakily breathed out. I was going to check on Sebastian but decided against it. He would have taken refuge in my study where I kept his cat bed for when I was working there.

'Is there water by my side of the bed?' he called out from the bathroom.

I had taken his half-empty bottle downstairs when I had tidied up.

I didn't answer him.

'Could you get me a bottle if there isn't? I'm absolutely beat.'

'Alexa, light off,' I instructed as I lay down and turned onto my side to face the wall. 'Get your own water!' I muttered under my breath as I closed my eyes, willing my heart to regulate itself so I could try to fall back to sleep.

If that's possible...

* * *

I suddenly woke up to something cold and wet hitting my face with some force. I couldn't breathe as it went up my nose and filled my gasping, wide-opened mouth. I spluttered and coughed, choking. I struggled, trying to sit up, fighting for air. I wiped frantically at my eyes, terrified of what had gone into them. It took me a few moments to realise it was water.

'What the hell do you think you're doing?' I screamed when I saw Jay standing over me.

'I didn't splash you as I opened the bottle did I, babes?'

I stared at his shadowy, self-satisfied figure and the two-litre bottle of water he was holding, highlighted by the hall light streaming through the open door.

I was drenched. I stared at him, shocked.

'Why? Why would you do that to me?' I demanded, my voice trembling.

'I asked you for one simple thing. I drove over 700 miles in one day because I was concerned about you. Because you mean everything to me. And you couldn't even fucking get out of bed and fetch me a bottle of water to replace the one you'd thrown away?'

'You're crazy,' I replied.

'Am I?' he said. 'At least I'm not a selfish, fucking bitch who's only focused on herself.'

He then turned away from me in disgust, walking around to his side of the bed.

I threw the covers back and got out of bed. 'You're the one who's bloody selfish, Jay! And unhinged!' I said, furious.

'You're lucky it wasn't acid,' he muttered as he climbed into bed.

I stopped. A coldness crept down my spine.

'What did you just say?'

'Turn the hall light off on your way to the bathroom,' he instructed.

I stared at him.

Had I imagined it?

I watched as he pulled the covers over himself and closed his eyes as a flicker of a smile played at the corner of his lips.

'The light?' he repeated.

I ignored him and turned back to pick up my phone from the bedside cabinet.

'What are you going to do, babes? Cry to your mummy that Jay was being mean to you? Ah, but that's right, she and your sister couldn't give a fuck about you, you pathetic piece of shite!'

I stumbled to the bathroom in tears.

I switched on the light and stared at my reflection in the mirror.

How have you ended up here, Sophie? How?

Repulsed, I switched the light off, unable to look at myself.

I pulled off my wet T-shirt and threw it on the floor. Shivering, despite the warm evening, I somehow managed to pull a towel around myself one-handed. I collapsed to the floor and sat in the dark with my knees hugged into my chest. I stared at my phone, willing them to ring me to prove him wrong.

I swiped at my tears feeling as if I was going insane.

Who will believe me if I'm struggling to accept what he's just done?

I shakily breathed out, trying to figure out what I was going to do.

I pressed call, hoping that by some miracle my mum would pick up. It went straight to voicemail.

'Mum? It's me, Sophie. Please? Please, I need you; I need you to help me. I don't know who else to talk to...' I faltered as the hot, desperate tears choked me. 'I... I'm scared, Mum. I'm so scared...'

I broke down sobbing, unable to continue.

I cut the call. Then deleted the message.

25

I didn't know how long I sat on the floor in the bathroom. The sun eventually forced the darkness of the night from my mind. I looked at Jay, sprawled across the bed without a care in the world.

His world was peacefully perfect.

Unlike mine.

I swallowed back the rage. I wanted to rip the throw wrapped around Jay's lower body and—

I stopped myself mid-fantasy.

I turned away, pulled out some clothes and left him to sleep off his demons. The suffocating air in the bedroom was pungent with stale sweat. The bottle of water he had emptied over my face while I slept lay discarded on the floor. A chill slithered its way down my spine as I recalled his muttered words – his threat: *'You're lucky it wasn't acid.'*

I knew I hadn't imagined him saying that.

I wandered downstairs and found an empty bottle of tequila on the kitchen counter with a shot glass. Jay had finished off the two-thirds left in the bottle. I understood now that the stench in the bedroom was the alcohol sweating out of Jay's pores. Beside the empty bottle were Jay's keys, wallet and phone. I considered looking inside his wallet and checking his phone but managed to fight the compulsion. I didn't want Jay reducing me to this. I was better than that.

Better than him.

I tried to remember whether it was Friday or Saturday as I carried a black coffee and my laptop out to the garden, closing the bi-folding door behind me to prevent Sebastian from escaping. Without a routine, the days all blended together. Jay didn't work, so every day was the weekend for him. As for me, writing structured my days, but I still couldn't bring myself to work. Guilt and fear that I wouldn't complete the manuscript on time relentlessly buzzed at the back of my mind. I had lost my family; I couldn't afford to lose my career. I had already persuaded my agent to convince my editor to give me a month's extension. Something I had never resorted to before, no matter how tight the deadline.

It's Saturday, Sophie. Two weeks yesterday, you were preparing to get married.

The sudden thought brought with it a wave of anxiety at the realisation it was the weekend. It meant Jay would be going out tonight. He would expect me to go with him, to pretend to his bar friends, the world, that our life together was perfect and enviable by default.

Then I remembered he'd said he had told Tom I was a drunk.

Was it just Tom? Or was it all his bar friends? Even our neighbours?

I sat down and looked at my laptop.

Come on, Sophie! How do you think you're going to manage to meet your extension if you don't write?

But my body was still on high alert, and I couldn't shake the foreboding feeling that something terrible was going to happen. It was as if I had found myself in a warzone, surviving one day to the next, unable to plan for the future.

What future?

For, at this moment, I couldn't see one. I hadn't anticipated Jay's Jekyll and Hyde nature.

Why would you, Sophie? You trusted him to be genuine. You trusted him to love you, not terrorise you.

I swallowed back the strong, bitter coffee as I forced myself to log into my bank account, something I had been avoiding for weeks. I didn't want to face the reality of my finances post-wedding and house purchase.

All I wanted to do was pack a bag, call a cab and catch a flight to Scotland, back home to my mother, my family. To leave Jay lying in his alcohol-drenched sweat, and have no further contact. But that option was gone. Whether Jay had intentionally or unintentionally destroyed my relationship with them was a moot point; it had happened, and the question was what to do next.

Not that I could leave my marital home as I knew it would take years of wrangling through divorce lawyers to force Jay out. It was his dream house. His dream location. So, why would he willingly leave? And he had invested money into the property and was rightfully on the deeds.

But his act of terror in the early hours had been a wake-up call. We were only two weeks married, and so much had already happened. Where would I be in two months, two years from now?

God, Sophie.

I took another mouthful of coffee to sober me up, but it didn't work. I was drunk on fear.

I looked at the screen as the bank site loaded. I recalled his surprising revelation that he still had inheritance money left. So why had I been paying for his lavish lifestyle? But what funds he had were used to pay for the Caribbean honeymoon and whatever guitar he had bought yesterday in Manchester. Even that betrayal was unexpected.

Breathing in, I forced myself to look at my current account balance.

Damn it!

I was nearly two thousand pounds overdrawn.

How the hell are you so in the red?

It was a rhetorical question. An impulse purchase flight ticket home explained the worrying deficit. So much had happened since that night that it had become indistinguishable from one traumatising event to another. It was all background noise now: static, grey and bleak.

I still had my savings account which I dipped into every month to pay the bills and living expenses.

I switched accounts and stared at the dwindling balance.

Christ, Sophie! How long do you think that will last?

My financial reality hit me. I needed to get that book submitted so I could release my next advance payment.

But I still had my credit card for emergencies which could tide me over if things started to get financially tight.

I clicked on my credit card account. Wide-eyed, I numbly stared at the balance.

There shouldn't be a balance! You haven't used the card, Sophie!

But Jay had.

The balance was over the agreed twenty-thousand-pound limit by six hundred pounds.

What the hell?

I was furious with myself that I hadn't checked my statement, but the wedding and the subsequent past two weeks had distracted me.

However, you didn't expect Jay to spend the entire credit limit and more within a month.

I swallowed the bitterness of the now cold coffee, glancing at the statement. I had stupidly requested a second credit card linked to my account so Jay could have some financial independence.

How could you have been so naive? So trusting?

Then I caught sight of the most expensive charge against the card.

What the—?

I had paid for our luxury, all-inclusive bridal bungalow in Barbados. It was there in black print on my credit card statement.

Christ!

I couldn't believe he'd lied to me.

If he lied to you about this, what else has he lied about?

Another excessive transaction caught my attention.

Oh my God!

There was a four thousand, nine-hundred-pound charge to Johnny Roadhouse Music in Manchester.

Jay had paid for his new guitar with my credit card.

I looked down the list of other purchases.

Fuel and transactions at Blue Bar were regular charges. The most recent charge was for nearly two thousand pounds to a security surveillance firm.

But it was a charge for a three-thousand-pound bill for the Bristolian jeweller Diana Porter that caught my attention.

What the?

Jay hadn't given me any jewellery. A wave of unease descended over me as I questioned what he had purchased and for who.

Horrified, I slammed the laptop lid down and stared out at the tiny boats bobbing on the dazzling turquoise waters as the world continued, oblivious to my financial plight. How could my new husband have spent twenty thousand pounds in one month?

What the hell was Jay thinking? And where did he think you would find the money to pay for it all? You're already paying for everything, including the mortgage and a loan on the Transporter! What the hell, Sophie?

* * *

'Hey,' greeted Jay as he walked into the open living space.

I looked up at him from the couch.

'What's up?' he asked, surprised by my sullenness.

I watched as he scratched his head, yawned and proceeded to make himself a coffee.

'You want a cup?' he asked.

He turned around to me when I didn't reply.

'What? You're giving me the silent treatment because I accidentally spilt some water over you when I opened the bottle?'

I raised my eyebrow at his casual statement.

'Christ! I was tired, all right? I'd just driven a roundtrip of over 700 miles to get back to my wife. No wonder I spilt it.'

'You poured the entire contents over me,' I evenly stated.

He looked at me, frowning. 'Soph, it must be the writer in you because you exaggerate everything. Do you know that? Talk about being hyperbolic!'

I stared at him.

'It was a drop of water. What's the harm?'

'What about what you muttered under your breath?'

'What?' he questioned as he turned his attention back to grinding coffee beans.

I waited until the grinder finished.

'Remember?' I continued.

'I haven't a scooby,' he replied with his back to me.

I heavily sighed. What was the point?

'You also knocked back some wine last night. So maybe your perception of what happened is a bit off?' he suggested. 'When I came back from Manchester, you were dead to the world. Out cold. Anyone could have broken in.'

I didn't bother mentioning the nearly empty tequila bottle on the work counter.

'That reminds me. I booked a surveillance company to come and install CCTV cameras internally and externally. They're due mid-afternoon.'

The news wasn't a shock to me as he'd paid for their services with my credit card. But why he felt the need to without talking to me first was a surprise. I wondered what had precipitated Jay's sudden security concerns. He had extolled the low crime rate in Cornwall compared to London and yet contradicted himself by installing a state-of-the-art security system.

I watched as Jay looked at the clock on the cooker. 'Which is in less than an hour. Shit! I can't believe how much that drive yesterday wiped me out.'

'Why?'

He turned his head. 'What do you mean why?'

'Why do we need cameras around the house?'

'Duh! In case somebody tries to break in, dopey.'

I held his patronising gaze.

'What the fuck's wrong with you? Someone still got a hangover? I would have thought you'd be over the moon that I didn't stay over in Manchester. Starting to wish I hadn't bothered coming back now.'

My silence confirmed the feeling was mutual.

Moments later, he came over and sat down next to me.

'What's going on, babes?' he asked, concerned. 'It seems that I can't do right for wrong nowadays?'

I handed him the credit card printout.

'What's this?' he questioned.

'How much we owe,' I coldly replied.

'Fuck!'

'My sentiment exactly.'

'We'll pay it off when you get your next advance, so what's the problem?'

'The problem is, we've...' I hesitated, wanted to say 'I' but knew it would be inflammatory, 'run out of money.'

'There's enough to see us through until your next book payment though? And what about your royalties?'

'I don't get a royalty payment until October.'

'You'll get your advance way before then, surely? When's the book due?'

'The first of August,' I answered.

'So, what's your problem? We'll be fine until then.'

'We can't keep continuing like this, Jay. You need to get a job. I can't keep supporting both of us.'

'Where has this come from? You know I'm looking.'

'Are you?'

'What? Of course, I am. Don't start bloody guilt-tripping me!'

'I'm not! I'm just saying I'm really worried about our finances. I pay...' I faltered, unsure whether to commit, but maybe it was time for some home truths. 'I pay for everything. Food, all the household bills and your expenses.'

'What the hell? You're accusing *me* of being extravagant?'

'The honeymoon?' I threw back. 'And your new guitar?'

He narrowed his eyes at me. 'That's what this is all about? You're pissed off at me because I charged them to your credit card?'

'You said you'd used the money your mum left you,' I stated.

'Ahuh,' he said, his eyes suddenly hostile. 'I used it because of the legal cover credit cards offer in case anything went wrong with the honeymoon. As for the guitar, it was easier to pay with your card. Do you think so lowly of me that I'd lie to you and cheat you out of money?'

'No,' I found myself replying, despite myself. I couldn't silence the fear that he wouldn't pay me back. 'But I'm just worried about money.'

'Well, if it makes you feel any better, I'll transfer the money later. Okay?'

I nodded. 'Thanks.'

I then remembered the charge for the jeweller's.

'The other stuff on there, who did you buy it for?'

'Like what? Groceries, fuel? All for us. Including the multiple weekly wine purchases.'

I ignored his jibe. 'The three-thousand-pound charge to Diana Porter?'

'Shit, Sophie! Thanks! You've ruined my Christmas surprise!'

I stared at him, holding back from stating the obvious – it was only July. It was also charged to my credit card.

'What the hell's got into you? Talk about Paranoid Patsy! Who would I be buying anything for other than you?'

I shrugged.

'Sophie, babes, when will you trust that I love you more than anything? Eh? This obsessing of yours about not being my type and worrying if I'm screwing our neighbour or God knows who else, it has got to stop. It's driving me insane. I'm terrified to talk to another woman now for fear of you thinking I'm shagging her.'

'I don't think like that!'

'You do and you know it,' he stated. He gently stroked my cheek. 'I desire you and only you.'

I instinctively flinched at his touch.

'What?' He dropped his hand. 'Soph? God, I love you. I'd never hurt you. Or let anyone else hurt you. Why do you think I've been so angry?'

I shrugged.

'Because I can see the pain caused by Liv and Joanna's spiteful behaviour. It tears me up inside. I want to do something, but they hate me. Whatever I say will only make matters worse, not better,' Jay softly reasoned.

'It couldn't get any worse,' I pointed out.

'Oh, babes, come here,' he muttered, leaning in and brushing his lips against my forehead. He pulled back. 'Why don't I make you a cup of chamomile tea? Then go lie down upstairs. I'll cancel tonight with Tara and Damien.'

'Tonight?'

'Yeah, remember we were meeting them for drinks at Blue Bar to say thank you for looking after Sebastian?'

I shook my head. I had no recollection. I wondered whether I had forgotten or was it that Jay hadn't mentioned it to me.

'It's not important. We'll do it another time. What is important is you getting some rest and getting back to being the Sophie I fell in love with eight months ago.'

I couldn't tell him that version of myself no longer existed. That Sophie had disappeared, leaving me with the shadow of my former self. Much as the man I'd fallen in love with wasn't the man I married.

Who exactly did I marry?

26

Bleary-eyed and confused, I padded down the stairs annoyed it was so late. It was after 8 p.m. and Jay had left me to sleep the entire afternoon and early evening away.

'Hey, sleepyhead,' he said, looking up at me. 'I didn't expect to see you until the morning.'

He stopped whatever he was doing on his phone and got up off the couch and walked over to the kitchen area.

'Why didn't you wake me?' I groggily complained.

'Because you were out of it. You slept straight through the guys installing the security cameras. They were here for hours, drilling and whatnot.'

I shook my head, not understanding how that was possible. I was typically a light sleeper and any slight noise woke me. I assumed the chamomile tea, coupled with the past few sleepless nights, had knocked me out.

Or... Is Jay drugging you?

I could admit Jay lied and provoked me, but surely, he wouldn't drug me?

I discounted the thought as too ridiculous.

'Did they come into the bedroom?' I asked, embarrassed.

'No. I didn't think you'd want a camera in the bedroom. Wine?' he asked, opening the fridge.

'I've just woken up.'

'So? It's Saturday evening,' he replied, taking a bottle out. 'Oh yeah, I've stored all my stuff up in the attic while you slept. And I don't want you going up there.'

'Into the attic?'

Jay glanced up at me as he picked up the corkscrew. 'Yeah, I don't want you going up there. You agreed I could keep my parents' stuff in the attic. I've also shifted some of my guitars up there.'

'I don't understand?'

He avoided eye contact as he opened the wine and then poured me a glass. He handed it to me before answering.

'Since it's already boarded out with electricity and two Velux windows, we should consider paying someone to install a staircase and a door rather than those pull-down ladders. I could have it as my music room. What do you think?'

I stared at him, wondering what he was afraid I would find.

You already found a photograph of another woman taken here in Porthtowan in his precious Takamine guitar case. Two years before he allegedly ever came here. He lied to you, Sophie. What other lies are up there in the attic?

'I don't understand why you don't want me to go up there?' I questioned, unable to hold back. 'It's as if you're hiding something?'

His eyes dangerously narrowed. 'Maybe I just don't want you touching my expensive guitars!'

'I don't!' I retaliated.

'So, what do you call searching through my Takamine guitar case yesterday? As soon as I left for Manchester, there you were riffling through my belongings.'

I was about to argue, but he cut me off.

'Christ, Sophie! I didn't take you for a liar! I asked you specifically not to touch anything and as soon as my back was turned, that's exactly what you did!'

I had convinced myself that I had left everything as I'd found it, but clearly not.

He knows you found the photograph, Sophie! Of course, he does! Why do you think he's hidden everything in the attic?

Before I could challenge him, he changed tactics.

'And I told you I don't want your fucking cat sleeping on our bed!' he complained. 'I can't stand the cat hair. It's everywhere up there, including under the bed. And you say you spent the day cleaning? All it looks like to me is that you spent the day going through my personal belongings and then hanging your photographs and prints all over the walls, leaving no space for my pictures. I thought this was supposed to be our fucking house? Not solely yours?'

His phone pinged. I watched as he checked it.

'That's Tara. She and Damien are asking if we're joining them at Blue Bar?'

'I thought you said you'd cancel it?' I questioned, resisting asking why he had Tara's number and not Damien's.

I noticed that Jay hadn't poured himself a glass of wine. I looked over at the couch where he had been sitting and the empty beer bottle lying on the floor. I realised Jay was wearing his favourite skinny jeans, flip-flops and silver skull ring, which meant he was going out.

He had no intention of waking you, Sophie.

'Yeah, but you were sleeping, and I didn't want to spend a Saturday night stuck in on my own. Look out there,' he said, gesturing towards the two bi-folding walls of glass and the garden and ocean beyond. 'It's a beautiful evening. Shame to waste it. It's really annoying as well that we can't open the bi-folding doors because of your bloody cat. It's like living in a glass prison.'

I imagined he restrained himself from adding: with you!

'So, you're going out?' I questioned, ignoring his objection to keeping the doors closed so Sebastian couldn't escape.

'Well, that was the plan.'

'I see,' I muttered before taking a sip of wine.

'Why don't you get changed and join me?' he asked as the edge disappeared from his voice.

I shook my head. 'No, I'm not in the mood.'

'Come on, Soph? You're never in the mood lately. Come out. You'll enjoy yourself. You used to love going out for a couple of drinks with me.'

'With you – not with Tara and Damien,' I answered. 'And I don't know them. Not really,' I added.

'Well, now's your chance.'

I shook my head again. 'Another night. You go, I'll be fine.'

Jay raised his eyebrows, unsure whether I was trying to trick him.

'Go! I could use the time to do some writing.'

Someone has to work to pay my credit card and all the bills!

'You're sure?'

I nodded, walking over to the fridge to see what food was in there.

I noticed a couple of five-litre plastic bottles with chemical hazard signs on the work counter. I picked one up. 'What's this for?'

'To unblock the shower.'

'The shower?' I repeated.

'It's not draining as well as it should,' he explained.

I accepted that Jay spent longer in the shower than me and would know if it wasn't draining effectively.

'Hydrochloric acid, though?' I questioned. 'And two bottles?'

'Best solution for drains. Also, I have no idea how much I'll need. Leave them there,' Jay instructed as I opened the cabinet door to put them away. 'It'll remind me to do it tomorrow.'

'Sure,' I muttered, pushing away the memory of last night's threat to throw acid in my face.

I watched him pick up his keys and wallet from the counter.

He hesitated. 'You definitely don't want to come?'

'Positive,' I answered, not in the mood for watching Jay shamelessly flirt with Tara. 'I need to catch up on work. I've let it slide for long enough.'

Jay leaned in and kissed me. 'Love you, babes. Don't work too hard.'

'I won't. I just need to make some notes for tomorrow.'

'You're working tomorrow? It's Sunday? I thought we could do something together?'

'I need to hand this book in to get my advance released. We need the money, Jay. It doesn't grow on trees. What with those gigs you want to go to this month and next and…' I stopped, annoyed at our financial situation. At being the one who was holding it all together. 'I mean,' I found myself continuing, 'if you don't want me to work weekends, then you need to get a job.'

'For fuck's sake, Soph! That's all I've heard from you since I got back from Manchester. I feel shit enough that I don't have work at the moment.'

'I've never known you to have a job. Then again, why would you when you can spend my credit card instead?' I hit back.

I held his furious gaze.

'Maybe transferring me the money for the honeymoon and the guitar might help your masculinity crisis?' I fired.

I'd checked before I came downstairs to see whether he had transferred the money as promised into my bank account. But he hadn't.

For a moment, I was certain from the glint in his eye that he was going to hit me.

'Fuck you, you controlling bitch!' he muttered instead before turning and walking away. The slammed door reverberated behind him.

Slowly exhaling, I carried my wine over to the couch and sat down. I picked up my laptop and opened my manuscript and stared at it, not knowing where to start. But I had no choice as I needed that advance.

I glanced at the surveillance camera in the corner of the room, now understanding why the security firm's bill was so expensive; Jay had had them hardwire the units into the electrics. There was no way of disconnecting them.

Is he watching you?

I quickly discounted the paranoid thought.

It's crazy. Why would Jay be watching you? Also, he only has an old, prehistoric Nokia flip phone: it would be impossible.

* * *

Hours passed by without me realising it. I only became aware of the time when darkness sneakily crept in, taking over the house. I checked the time: 11.15 p.m.

I asked Alexa to turn the lamps on and got up to make myself coffee. I planned on writing a bit more, and then I'd call it quits and go to bed. I heard the front door open.

'Hey?' I uneasily called out.

'Hi,' answered Jay as he walked through from the hallway. 'I was hoping you'd still be up.' He beamed, drunkenly leaning in and brushing my lips with his own.

'Working,' I explained, trying to avoid his beery breath. 'Did you have a good night?'

'Yeah. Tara and Damien send their love,' he answered, walking around me to the fridge and taking out a bottle of wine. 'Where's your glass?' he asked.

I shook my head. 'I need to keep working. Sorry. You have one.'

'I was planning to,' he sourly answered, his cheery mood gone as quickly as he arrived.

I ground some coffee beans as he poured himself a liberal glass of wine. He then went over to the couch and sat down.

I inwardly sighed when he turned the TV on. Then turned it up.

'Jay? I was working,' I complained.

'For fuck's sake, Sophie, it's late on a Saturday night! All I want to do is come home and relax which is what you should be doing rather than working any more.'

Because you're always going to Blue Bar to be with your drinking buddies! Or driving off last minute to Manchester.

I poured my coffee into my mug keeping my thoughts to myself. It wasn't worth it when he was drunk.

'Come on, sit down next to me, babes?' he begged. 'Just for a bit, yeah?'

I walked over with my mug and sat down next to him.

'You're the best,' he said, squeezing my leg.

'Ten minutes, and then I need to get back to work.'

He didn't say a word, but I could see from the clenched jaw that he wasn't happy.

I stared straight ahead at whatever violent film he'd started watching. I had no idea who the man sitting next to me was any more.

He quickly knocked back his wine and stood up. 'You want some?'

'No thanks,' I replied, not looking at him.

'You know I was embarrassed tonight without you?'

I didn't respond.

I watched as he returned to the bottle he'd left on the counter. He filled his glass and came back over, spilling wine on the wooden floor.

'Tara and Damien and the others were asking if I'd murdered you or something. That they haven't seen you since the bloody wedding.'

I didn't want questions about my split, swollen lip and the bruising that had developed under my eyes. Nor did I have it in me to play the happily married couple.

Jay collapsed down next to me.

'You know how humiliating that is for me? The fact you can't be bothered to go out with me, or socialise with our friends? It's as if you think you're too good for them because you're a fucking author.'

'That's not true,' I replied.

'Isn't it? Seems that way to me.'

'Right,' I said, sighing heavily. 'I'm going upstairs. I need to get up early to work.'

I accepted that continuing writing with the TV blaring was impossible. I also knew asking him to turn it down would be pointless.

'Fuck work! I haven't seen you all day and night!'

'Come on, Jay? You know this book is long overdue.'

'And do you want to tell me why that is? I run around taking care of you. Buying your fucking wine, cooking your meals, waiting on you like a butler, and you're doing what? Fuck all by the sounds of it! I'm sick of being your fucking unpaid butler while you whine and moan about having no money when it's your own fucking doing! I have done everything in my power to help you get that shit book of yours together, including giving you a pity fuck because no man in their right mind could stomach touching you, and still, you can't get your shit together and fucking write whatever drivel it is that you do.'

I grabbed my laptop and stood up, willing myself not to react.

'Did I say you could go? Sit the fuck back down!' he threatened.

There was a chilling glint in his eyes that I was starting to recognise.

I shook my head as I made a move to walk away.

His hand suddenly grabbed hold of my baggy T-shirt.

'Let go,' I instructed, trying to keep the anger out of my voice.

'It's your fucking career or me! Understand? I want a wife who wants to spend time with me. Not dedicating every minute of every goddamned day writing some shite that no one will ever read.'

I pulled away from his grip, ripping my T-shirt in the process.

'Your choice! Your career or me because I'm done with you treating me like a grade-A schmuck! I'm not your fucking ex!'

I walked away, ignoring him.

He screamed after me: 'You better give it up, or I swear I'll make you! Do you hear me? You're married to me! ME! Not your fucking shite writing! I'll destroy your career if I have to!'

I threw my laptop down on the bed, angry at my tears, furious that his words could hurt me so. To cut deep under my skin with such precision, such expertise.

What happened to the man you fell in love with, who, until your wedding night, had been the kindest, most considerate man you had ever known?

How could the same man now be threatening to sabotage my career? How did he think we could afford his lifestyle, the mortgage and food if I wasn't allowed to work? It was crazy! Why would he want to sabotage my career?

The answer suddenly came to me, chilling me to my core: *he's isolating you, Sophie, until you're left totally at his mercy.*

27

I pretended to be asleep when Jay finally fell into bed, pulling me into him. His touch made my skin crawl.

Is this the man you wanted children with? Thank God you're still on the pill and didn't come off it like he insisted!

His low, deep breaths and occasional grunts strangled the air. I tried to lift his arm from around my waist, but it had the adverse effect of him gripping me even tighter. I waited before trying to release his hold on me.

'Where are you going?' he mumbled.

Damn it!

I kept silent, staring into the suffocating darkness.

'Where are you going?' he repeated, starting to wake up.

'The toilet,' I hoarsely whispered.

'I don't believe you,' he replied.

'Jay, I need the toilet?'

'You're leaving our bed to go to the spare room, aren't you?'

'I'm not. I honestly need the toilet,' I replied with an edge of frustration.

'Don't you think I'm humiliated enough as it is that you refuse to join me with our friends? Or sit with me and watch a film without you wanting to sleep in another bed two weeks into our fucking marriage? But this isn't a marriage, is it? It was just your way of publicly hurting your ex because he dumped you weeks before the wedding. Don't think I'm not onto you, you devious fucking cow!' he spat, digging his fingers into my flesh as he gripped me tighter.

I didn't reply. I held my words down and willed myself not to move or breathe. I needed to think of the long game: my exit plan because there was no way I could stay with him.

Wait it out, and then get the hell out.

I knew that if Jay didn't physically break me, being alone with him at home, twenty-four-seven would mentally break me. He was right about one thing: this wasn't a marriage. At least, not the one I'd anticipated when I'd tearfully whispered my vows to him.

'You leave, and you'll live to regret it,' he hissed.

I stayed perfectly still, despite the desperate need to pee. The thought of waking up drenched in a bottle of water like last night was enough to keep me there.

Or, to be precise, the two bottles of hydrochloric acid sitting on the kitchen counter.

An hour or so later, I still needed the bathroom. Convinced Jay was definitely asleep, I gently prised myself from his hold and gradually climbed out of bed, easing my feet to the floor. I listened as he turned over in bed, my heart thundering with anticipation.

I waited for his breathing to slow and deepen.

What the fuck are you doing, Sophie? You're pathetic!

I tiptoed across the floor as carefully as I could, not wanting to wake him.

I stopped, hearing him turn over.

Damn!

I waited.

'Soph?' he mumbled.

I suddenly dropped to the floor, lying down, not wanting him to see me and demand I come back to bed. I didn't want him touching me or trying to have sex with me.

I waited for what felt like an excruciating eternity.

I then inched my body along the wooden floor, listening for movement behind me. I didn't want to risk standing back up in case it woke him up. I didn't know Jay, not any more. Consequently, I didn't know if he would hurt me. He had threatened to, and if he did, who was there to protect me?

He has hurt you, Sophie! He broke your wrist! He threw a remote control at you and smacked a door into your face! He woke you up in the middle of the night by drenching you with water! What more do you want?

The floorboard creaked under me.

Oh God!

I stopped, held my breath. I didn't dare exhale as I waited for a reaction. But it was hard to hear anything above the rush of blood pounding in my ears.

Excruciating minutes ticked by as I lay there, paralysed by fear.

Finally, certain that he was still asleep, I inched closer to the bedroom door.

Trembling, I sat on the toilet, trying to steady my breathing, willing myself not to cry. Not to be pathetic. But the reality that it had taken me ten terrified minutes to reach the bathroom hit me hard.

What the hell has happened to you?

Now I wasn't allowed to leave our bed. Not even for the toilet.

I'd had enough. In the morning, I would figure out leaving him. I'd take Sebastian, my laptop and a holdall of clothes. I could make what money I had last for the time it would take me to complete the book. Without any distractions – without Jay – I'd finish it in no time. I just needed to get away without alerting him; because I knew he would do everything in his power to keep me here.

I could wait until Jay went to Blue Bar for a drink, which he typically would as it was the weekend, and call a taxi. There was no point in taking the Transporter as I wanted to leave with as little disruption as possible. Jay still hadn't added me to his insurance policy. The last thing I wanted was to give Jay a reason to track me down, which he would if I took his precious VW. I wanted to disappear from his life and leave everything else to lawyers.

I crept back into the bedroom and lay beside Jay's unaware body, clinging to the edge of the bed to avoid him touching me. I held onto one thought: *you'll be gone soon, and he'll never touch you again.*

28

The morning came, dispelling all my dark fears and bringing with it hope. Liberating light streamed through the large window. I lay for a moment, watching the dust particles dance in the golden rays. I'd surprised myself by managing to sleep for a few hours. I felt better than I had done for a while. I had a plan. I had a way of reclaiming my life back.

I sat up when I heard the explosive noise of the coffee grinder below.

He's already up.

I turned over. His side of the bed was cold.

I slowly breathed out.

Nothing's going to happen, Sophie.

Minutes later, I heard him walking up the stairs.

'Good morning, my beautiful wife,' he said as he came in holding out a coffee for me.

I forced a half-smile. 'Thanks, babes,' I replied, taking the coffee and acting as if everything was fine between us. I had no idea what he would do if he suspected I planned to leave him.

'You look better than I've seen you in days. See what sleeping next to your husband does for you?' He grinned, stroking my cheek.

He held my gaze, as I weakly smiled back at him.

'God, I love you!'

He leaned down and kissed me as the doorbell rang.

'Damn! I was going to get back into bed with you.'

'I'm not going anywhere,' I forced myself to murmur.

'You better not,' he replied, giving me another kiss.

I watched as he left the bedroom and waited until I heard him walking down the stairs before jumping out of bed and throwing on some clothes.

'Hey, honey,' I heard Jay greet as he opened the door. Moments later, he called up the stairs: 'Babes, Tara's here.'

I was surprised. But when I looked at the time on the Alexa alarm clock it was nearly eleven.

How had I slept so late?

But I knew how. I hadn't been able to fall asleep until well after dawn as I'd obsessed over exactly how I would execute my plan to leave Jay.

'Coming,' I yelled.

I checked myself out in the mirror first, taming my hair and applying some concealer and lip gloss before joining them in the kitchen.

'Hey,' I casually said as I walked in.

'Hi,' beamed Tara.

'You've just been surfing?' I asked, since she was sat in a black dryrobe with tangled damp hair.

'Yeah. It's amazing down there this morning. Too amazing though.'

I frowned, not sure what she meant.

'It's so busy. Holidaymakers crowding out the locals,' she explained, before adding, 'You should give it a try when your cast comes off. I'd be happy to give you some basics. Been surfing these waters since I was six.'

'I'd love that, thanks,' I appreciatively replied. If I had intended on sticking around, I might have taken Tara up on her offer.

Despite my insecurities about the fact that she looked like a Greek goddess with long, golden brown legs that reached my shoulders, I liked her. As did Sebastian, who was desperately meowing his way towards her from the couch.

She handed me the jar she was holding. 'This is for you. Honey from my parents' beehives.'

'Thanks!' I said, surprised at the gift.

'Jay said you were working so hard on your next book and how worried he was about you. So, I thought some honey might cheer you up,' she explained. 'And, to be honest, I've been desperate to have an excuse to see my new best friend,' she purred, bending down and scooping Sebastian up in her arms.

'Thanks, Tara. That's really thoughtful of you,' I said, touched.

'It's Jay you should really be thanking. He's so sweet! He just adores you! He was asking my advice last night—'

'Tara!' interrupted Jay with a faux-offended expression.

She laughed, ignoring him as she nuzzled Sebastian. 'As I was saying, he wanted to know what he could do to make your life easier. Believe me, Damien could take some pointers from your husband. Don't get me wrong, I love him, but just sometimes I wish he would do something to surprise me,' she shared.

I smiled, resisting the urge to confide that being surprised wasn't all that great.

Jay suddenly came up behind me and wrapped his arms around me. 'You had no idea about the honeymoon, did you, babes?'

'Nope, not at all,' I answered.

'God! Damien wouldn't even think to book a surprise holiday for me,' Tara complained.

'He's got his good points,' Jay reassured her.

She smiled at him. 'Mm, sometimes.'

'Now, I'm going to head out to get some supplies to cook my beautiful wife some brunch,' he said, kissing my head.

'See? That's what I mean. Damien wouldn't even think of that!'

'I've got to take care of her. Otherwise, she might leave me,' Jay replied.

Tara laughed as she gently placed Sebastian back on the floor. 'Sophie, you'd be crazy to leave him. There's a queue of women out there waiting to snap him up! If I wasn't with Damien, I might be the first in line.'

I smiled at her as I held onto Jay's arm. 'Believe me, I'm not letting him go!'

I felt Jay kiss my head again.

'Right, I need to go! The sight of you two newly-weds is making me jealous!' Tara said, smiling at us.

'Thanks for the honey,' I replied. 'It's really kind of you.'

'I just hope you like it.'

'I'm sure I will,' I replied, removing myself from Jay's arms to walk her to the door.

I watched as she headed down the drive back to her property further down the hill.

* * *

I waited for Jay to head out as promised and buy some provisions, but for whatever reason, he didn't. I ravenously ate some toast and honey before going to my study. Jay believed I was writing, whereas I was busy researching hotels in London and one-bedroom bungalows that allowed pets, followed by train times from Truro to

Paddington Station. The last train was at 22.08, changing at Plymouth before heading to London. If Jay went out this evening, which I fully expected, I would be on that train. I doubted I would make the earlier 20.08 train. I decided to purchase my ticket at the station, to avoid leaving a paper trail. There were no local Uber cars, so I looked up a taxi firm in Truro. I couldn't pre-book one, unsure when Jay would leave for Blue Bar. I would have to take a chance that they would have a car available.

The door suddenly opened, startling me. I quickly shut down my web browsers and went back to my Word document.

'I realised that I haven't installed the security surveillance on your phone,' Jay said, coming in.

I swivelled round to him. 'I can do it, can't I?' I said, reluctant to hand over my mobile.

He gave me an affectionate smile. 'Sophie, what is it you call yourself?'

'A Luddite,' I calmly replied, despite feeling anything but calm.

'Yeah. I'm surprised you still don't write with a quill and ink by candlelight!'

'I'm not that bad,' I reasoned.

'Nope. You are.' Jay laughed.

He was in a great mood. I wondered whether it was because he had seen Tara, who had affirmed what a perfect husband he was. Or that, as far as he was concerned, I'd done as he said and stayed in bed. Not that it mattered. I accepted that I would never understand his triggers; what was important was keeping the status quo so as not to alert him of my plan to leave.

'Phone,' he said, holding out his hand. 'I got this security system for you, so you would feel safe when I'm out or away at gigs overnight.'

I couldn't think of a good enough reason not to give him my phone. I found myself handing it over, hoping that he wouldn't check my search history and see that I'd been looking up train times to London and hotels.

Oh God, Sophie... What if he realises what you're planning?

'You get back to work while I add the system to your phone.'

I waited until he'd closed the door and walked off down the hallway before shakily breathing out.

I looked back at my laptop and my Word document. The panic I felt at being caught searching for a way to leave him without his knowledge coursed through me.

But he has your phone now, Sophie? He could be checking exactly what you've been up to...

Or are you being paranoid?

* * *

It was now late afternoon, and he still hadn't returned my phone. Feeling uneasy, I went looking for Jay to get it back. I found him upstairs, lying in our bed. I realised he was naked when I noted his T-shirt, jeans and boxer shorts in a heap on the floor.

'What are you doing?' I asked, realising he had my phone in his hand and was scrolling through it.

'Just finished installing this software on your phone,' he answered, looking up at me. 'Sorry, I had a nap first and slept longer than intended.'

'Can I get it back?' I asked, trying to dispel the disquiet I was feeling. I couldn't explain it, but there was something not quite right.

He held my gaze, contemplating my question. 'What's it worth?'

'Sorry?'

'What's it worth?' he repeated.

I shrugged, trying to act casual.

'Well, you've got your banking app on here, that must be worth something. Then, there's all your contacts.'

I stared at him.

'How about you take all your clothes off to avoid me wiping everything?'

'What?' I spluttered. 'Come on, Jay. This isn't funny. Give me my phone.'

'I'm serious. I'll factory reset your phone and wipe everything if you don't take your clothes off,' he repeated.

'You can't,' I objected, hoping that he was simply fooling around.

'I can and I will. And don't think that because you've got an iCloud account everything will be saved to there because I'll delete that account using your phone.'

I shook my head. 'You can't—'

'Oh, I can. You see, all your passwords are in the notes on your phone. It doesn't take Einstein to figure them out.'

I couldn't believe him.

'Or, I might just smash your phone...' He paused, gauging my response.

I silently stared at him.

'So, if you want your phone back, you need to do what I ask. Understand?'

I nodded, forcing myself not to cry. Not to tell him to go screw himself.

Play the long game, Sophie. Get your phone and get out.

'Now, take everything off.'

I didn't move.

'Now! Or I wipe your phone.'

I slowly started to remove my clothes, not once taking my contemptuous eyes off him.

Eventually, naked and humiliated, I waited.

'My phone?' I asked when he didn't say anything.

'Come and get it.'

'You disgust me, you know that?' I spat as I strode over to him to take my phone back.

When I was within reach, he smacked me hard across my cheek.

'Don't you ever talk to me like that again you vicious, fucking cow!' he hissed.

Stunned, I staggered backwards from the blow. Before I knew it, Jay threw the sheet back, jumped up and had me by my hair. Shocked, I screamed out in pain, but he ignored me, throwing me down and pinning me to the bed as he straddled my body. I struggled and fought to get him off. But he overpowered me.

'Get off me!' I screamed. 'GET OFF!'

He responded by holding my plaster cast-covered wrist and my good one down with one hand using the weight of his body while the other covered my mouth and nose. I tried to move my head to free myself from his hold.

Stop, please...

I felt his legs force my thighs apart.

God no... NO!

I fought with what strength I had to get free. But the harder I fought, the harder he became. Tears slipped from my burning eyes as I stared up at him, pleading for him to stop. But whatever compassion he might have once had was gone, overridden by a primitive desire to hurt and debase me.

He continued, his wild gaze ravaging my restrained body with every thrust, as he grunted and exerted his way to oblivion. I dropped my gaze unable to look at his chilling, black eyes as they tore the flesh from my body. Droplets of his sweat sickeningly fell onto my face, slowly trailing across my skin.

I struggled to breathe. Struggled to move. Struggled to believe that my husband of seventeen days was raping me in our marital bed.

How had it come to this?

I tried to turn my head away from him but couldn't.

I did all I could: I squeezed my eyes shut against the horror of what was happening.

29

Finished, he rolled off me and lay on his back, panting.

I didn't move. I didn't speak. I couldn't.

Whatever rage had consumed me had dissipated. I was numb. My body felt cold and heavy, as if it didn't belong to me.

Not any more.

I tried to swallow, but my mouth was too dry. Tears continued to slip silently down my neck to my ears. The wetness was uncomfortable, but still, I couldn't move.

Then something cold, hard, hit me in the stomach.

I jumped.

'There's your fucking phone!'

I turned away from him and looked at the wall.

He grabbed my head and twisted it round, his fingers pinching my flesh. His breath was sour as he hissed in my face, 'And if you ever fucking think of leaving me, I will have you killed. Make no mistake, one call is all it takes. I'll have them hunt you down, torture you and then fucking kill you, and no one will know.'

I gasped as his grip increased, shocked at his words.

Had he seen my search history?

The blackness in his eyes intensified, burning with feverish malevolence as they bore into me. I could see he meant every word.

'And if you think of telling anyone, I wouldn't bother. No one will believe you. Not the police, not our neighbours. No one. Too many people know me here. They know how well I look after you. But as for you,' he spat at me, 'they know what a drunk you are. You did this to yourself!'

I wanted to scream at him: *How? How did I do this to myself? You did it! You're the one responsible for—*

But I couldn't bring myself to admit what he had just committed against me.

He raped you! Your husband of just over two weeks raped you, Sophie! There's no getting away from that.

Disgusted, he let go of my head thrusting it back against the mattress. 'You fucking repulse me, you ugly, snivelling bitch!'

I turned over, unable to look at him.

I felt him get up off the bed and walk out the room. Minutes later, the shower went on, followed by loud whistling.

I lay there, staring at the wall, wishing I was dead.

Oh God...

I had no idea of time passing as I blankly stared ahead, willing my heart to stop beating and my lungs to stop breathing.

The overhead light flicked on as Jay walked back into the room.

'Are you getting up?' he asked.

I couldn't reply: he'd stolen all my words.

I heard him drag open drawers and the wardrobe door as he pulled out clean clothes.

'I'm heading out to meet Rachael soon. I'd arranged to see her this evening to go over some material. I reckon we could be ready to play at the open mic at The Victory next Thursday.'

His words floated down on me like burning ash.

I felt nauseous.

The reality of what had happened hit me with such force that I got out of bed, stumbling my way to the bathroom. I collapsed to my knees in front of the toilet and threw up.

'Soph?' he called out, knocking on the door minutes later.

I shook my head before retching.

'You, okay?'

I continued retching as piercing screaming filled my head.

'Look, I'll cancel Rachael?' he suggested.

The screaming intensified.

Holding my hair back, I dragged my head up.

'Soph?' he prompted.

I shook my head. 'Just go,' I croaked, unable to turn and look at him.

'Sure?'

The screaming inside my head got louder, more persistent.

'Yes,' I hoarsely replied.

'You sure?' he asked, not quite convinced.

Get the hell away from me!

I breathed in. Steadied myself, and nodded. 'Yeah.'

I could feel the hesitation in him. The resistance to believe that I was all right. That we were all right.

How the hell could we be all right? HOW?

'Go!' I assured him.

'Okay. Love you,' he said.

I could feel his eyes on me, waiting.

Swallowing back the bile, I forced myself to utter, 'Love you.'

Satisfied, he left me alone.

I shakily breathed out. Trembling, I stood up. I staggered over to the shower cubicle and turned it on full blast. I covered my broken wrist and arm with a waterproof cast protector, then stepped into the shower. Hot, scalding water stabbed my skin as my body convulsed with deep, wrenching sobs. I scrubbed at my flesh, tearing at every inch touched by him. But no matter how much I washed the raw skin, I couldn't rid myself of him. For his hatred had penetrated so deep as to defile my soul. I would carry his act of debasement, betrayal and misogyny until the day I died.

Come on, Sophie! You need to move!

But I couldn't. My body was paralysed.

MOVE! YOU NEED TO LEAVE!

I swallowed back the despair as tears merged with the hot pummelling water.

GET OUT!

Sobbing, I turned the shower off and willed myself to walk out the bathroom and out of his life.

I called a taxi before grabbing Sebastian and locking him in his cat carrier downstairs. I then threw clothes in a leather holdall, not really noticing what I was packing, blinded by tears and panic. Next, I chucked in toiletries and make-up. I looked up from the bed and caught sight of myself in the large antique mirror leaning against the wall.

I turned away; I looked a mess.

Worse, you look deranged!

I decided it didn't matter. All that concerned me was getting away from here before Jay realised.

I had five minutes before the taxi arrived.

I checked the bedroom. There was nothing else I needed or wanted. Most importantly, Sebastian was secure, but not happy about it, in the hallway. I ran down the stairs with the holdall. I picked up my large brown leather shoulder tote containing my laptop and wallet and passport and slung it over my shoulder.

My phone pinged.

My taxi was arriving.

I looked over my shoulder at the expansive living space and two breathtaking glass walls of bi-folding doors with the Atlantic Ocean as the backdrop. It was beautiful. I couldn't believe how much I had invested in this place, both financially and emotionally. But I couldn't stay here a minute longer. Not after what he had done to me.

I opened the front door as the grey sedan taxi pulled up at the bottom of the drive.

'Hey, Sophie?' called out Tara as she jogged past.

Oh God! Why now of all times?

I picked up Sebastian's cat carrier and my holdall, pulled the front door behind me and walked towards the waiting taxi.

I watched as Tara stopped, and ran back down.

Oh God, no!

She ran up to me and then bent over, panting. 'That hill's a killer!'

I didn't answer her.

'You off somewhere?' she asked, looking up at me, surprised.

'Vet's,' I lied. 'Sebastian's eaten something and I'm worried it could be poisonous. He's been sick and lethargic all afternoon.'

'He doesn't seem lethargic,' she pointed out as Sebastian continued to wail in protest at his imprisonment.

'Ahuh,' I muttered, trying to get past her to the taxi, willing the driver not to get out and ask if he was picking me up for the train station.

I could feel beads of sweat rolling down my forehead and back, making my linen shirt cling to me.

'Are you all right, Sophie? You don't look so well, yourself?' she asked.

'I'm great. Just worried about Sebastian. The vet said to bring him straight in. They might have to keep him overnight.'

Tara held my gaze. 'Are you taking him to the vet hospital in Truro?'

I nodded.

I could see that she didn't believe me. Her questioning brown eyes had already noted my bulging holdall.

'Where's Jay?'

Oh God!

'He's down at Blue Bar going over some material with his new singer, Rachael. I didn't want to bother him. And he couldn't drive us anyway, as he'll have had a few pints.'

Tara simply looked at me. 'He's taken the VW.'

'Yeah, well...' I awkwardly shrugged.

'Hey, Mr Sebastian, you take care?' Tara bent down and murmured to him. She straightened up and looked at me. 'I hope he's okay. Text me, will you? That little guy has really got under my skin.'

'Yeah, of course,' I distractedly agreed, my attention now on the taxi driver as he got out of the car.

'Truro train station?' he asked.

I ignored Tara's surprised expression and nodded at the taxi driver as he opened the boot.

I heard the screech of brakes first.

Oh God!

I hurriedly handed my holdall to the taxi driver and opened the back passenger door. I forced Sebastian's cat carrier inside, not daring to turn around when I heard his low, deep voice.

'Hey, honey,' Jay casually said.

'Hi, Jay,' replied Tara.

I detected the discomfort in her voice.

'Right, let me know he's all right?' Tara uncomfortably said to no one in particular. I could feel the discomfort radiating from her as she left us – me – and started jogging up along the cliff, heading for the coastal trail that led to St Agnes Beach.

I wanted to ask her for help. But she was gone before I had the chance. Embarrassed, I assumed, at whatever was going on between Jay and me. It was obvious I wasn't going to the vets, the taxi to Truro train station and my holdall a giveaway. As was the fury in Jay's stabbing eyes that he couldn't mask.

'Soph?' Jay demanded. 'What's going on?'

'I think Sebastian's been poisoned. I'm taking him to the vets,' I lied, willing my voice not to betray me.

'Well, I'll take you,' he said.

I could feel everything slipping away from me.

'Move out the way and I'll grab the poor guy.'

'No! Leave him,' I replied. 'I'm taking him myself.'

Before I could get in the taxi, Jay grabbed my arm.

'I said, I would take you,' he growled, keeping his voice down.

I struggled, trying to pull away from him, but he had a tight hold of me.

'Get the cat. Now!' he hissed, digging his fingers even deeper into my flesh.

I looked over at the taxi driver for help, but he turned away, embarrassed by whatever domestic he thought was unfolding.

Numb, I picked up Sebastian's cat carrier, not knowing what else to do.

Jay grabbed it from me.

'Sorry about that, bud,' Jay apologised to the driver. He took his wallet out. 'Where were you going?'

I felt my mouth suddenly dry up as a coldness descended me.

'Truro train station.'

'Is that right?' Jay muttered, handing him more than enough cash to cover the wasted journey.

'Thanks,' said the taxi driver, handing me my holdall, unaware of what was happening.

Or what was about to happen.

'He's ill, is he, Soph?' Jay questioned, looking at Sebastian.

Paralysed with fear, I watched as the taxi drove off.

Jay took hold of my arm and dragged me back up the drive with him as his words replayed in my head: '*If you ever fucking think of leaving me, I will have you killed. Make no mistake, one call is all it takes. I'll have them hunt you down, torture you and then fucking kill you, and no one will know.*'

30

I tried to pull my arm away, but Jay held firm. There was no way he was going to let me go – or leave.

'Please?' I begged, trying to get him to release me.

'Get in the house,' he ordered, keeping his voice down.

'No!' I protested, struggling with him to release me.

'If you don't get in the house, I swear he will need a fucking vet!' he lowly threatened.

'You wouldn't?' I questioned.

'Try me!'

There was a look in his eyes which scared me.

Oh God, Sophie. He's serious.

He shoved me off balance as he released my arm, hissing, 'Leave then! Just leave if that's what you want!'

I stumbled backwards, unsure.

I looked at the cat carrier and then at him. Waited. Jay didn't react.

'Sebastian? Can I have him?' I asked.

'You go. He stays.'

'Please, Jay?'

'Your choice. But if you're leaving me, you're leaving him,' he flatly answered.

I could see the hatred in his narrowed, small dark blue eyes.

Hatred for who? You or Sebastian? Or both?

I discounted the idea. Jay wouldn't hurt an animal.

Sophie, this is the man who—

I stopped myself, still unable to acknowledge the unspeakable act he had committed against me earlier. The question was, did I believe him capable of hurting Sebastian?

Yes. Without hesitation.

More so, since Sebastian's presence had always rankled Jay: his association with my ex, Ben, who had bought him for me the reason.

But he knew I would never leave Sebastian.

I dropped my eyes to my left hand still covered in the plaster cast.

Think, Sophie! You follow him into that house and you're dead!
And Sebastian?

I slowly inhaled in and held my breath.

I questioned whether I was being hyperbolic. Catastrophising when he had every right to be mad at me.

He caught you with Sebastian and your bags packed, getting into a taxi: a taxi booked for Truro train station. Not a word of warning that you were disappearing. No surprise he's mad with you.

'Let's get inside and talk about this?' he reasonably suggested.

Gone was any anger.

I watched as he walked up to the front door, pushing it open. He didn't even reach in his pocket for his keys.

How did he know I hadn't locked it?

Tara had distracted me, and I'd forgot about locking the door.

How could he have possibly known?

I looked up at the security camera.

It's impossible. Jay only has his old Nokia flip phone.

Was it simply a coincidence he arrived at break-neck speed just as you were about to get in the taxi?

Jay looked back at me, his brow furrowed. 'Babes? Come on, let's talk about this. Yeah?' he offered, his voice gentler, inviting. 'If you're unhappy, then I'll change. I'll do whatever it takes to make you stay.'

I didn't move.

He smiled at me.

'Come on, babes?'

Don't trust him. Listen to your gut feeling, Sophie. You know he'll hurt you as soon as he gets you on your own.

I repeated his words over in my head: *'I'll do whatever it takes to make you stay.'*

He's going to hurt you so bad that you won't ever be able to run from him again.

My eyes dropped to Sebastian's meowing, desperate face staring out at me from the cat carrier. It was then I knew I had no option. Sebastian meant everything to me.

I gripped my phone, contemplating what to do. My finger found the power button and nervously started rapidly pressing it: once, twice, again, a fourth and finally, a fifth time. I let it slip from my desperate grip and watched as it landed on the gravelled drive.

I hurriedly bent down to retrieve it. I looked at the screen, checking it had worked.

'What the fuck are you doing?' he hissed across at me.

'Checking that I haven't broken the screen,' I lied, turning the volume down before sliding the SOS Emergency slider on my screen to make the call.

While waiting for the taxi, I had turned the siren off in settings, making sure the 'Play countdown sound' was toggled off if – *when* –

I implemented the Emergency SOS to call the police, not wanting to alert Jay and allowing him to cancel the call.

I had gone through the 'what if' scenarios in case leaving him didn't go to plan.

Not that you had expected him to catch you leaving.

I was convinced I would be gone before he got back.

'For fuck's sake, stop pissing around!' he muttered.

I clicked the speaker before straightening up, satisfied the call had gone through. I wouldn't hear the emergency call handler, but they could listen to the situation without Jay being aware. Now it was a case of waiting it out until the police arrived.

Are you sure about this, Sophie? What if nothing happens and you make a fool of yourself?

I ignored the doubting voice. My gut feeling was screaming at me that once I was inside the cottage alone with him, I was in serious trouble.

I casually dropped the phone in my tote bag and walked towards him.

He yanked the bag from my shoulder and shoved me inside the door. 'Don't think you'll be needing your phone or the other contents of this bag,' he stated.

I stumbled in, not knowing how long it would take the police to get here.

Or will it even work? What happens if they think it's a prank call? Or worse, they don't arrive in time?

Jay came in behind me and dumped the cat carrier on the floor along with my bag.

He slammed the front door, then locked it.

'Jay?' I nervously began as I dropped my holdall.

He didn't respond as he put the keys in his jeans pocket.

'Jay?' I repeated.

I could feel the anger emanating from him as he turned to me.

'I'm—'

'You're what? Sorry? Too fucking late for that!'

'Jay? Please?'

'I told you! Didn't I? I told you what I would do if you left me!' he shouted in my face.

I backed up against the hallway wall, terrified of what he would do to me.

To Sebastian.

'Give me your keys,' he demanded.

'What?' I questioned, startled.

'Your keys. I want them.'

'Why?'

'Why do you think?' he fired back.

So, you can't get out, Sophie. He's going to hurt you – kill you – and you're not going to be able to run from him.

Panic filled every atom of my body, screaming at me to run.

I looked at the bi-folding doors wondering if I could make it carrying Sebastian in the cat carrier with a broken arm.

'They're both locked. Even if you get out there, where are you going to run to? Over the cliff?' he mocked, reading my mind.

Numb, I shook my head.

'Now give me your keys.'

'They're in my bag,' I whispered, my voice betraying the fear I felt.

'Well, fucking get them!'

I crouched down for my bag. I looked at poor Sebastian next to it. I couldn't bear the thought of him left locked inside the carrier, which he detested, if something happened to me. I reached over and released the catches. Sebastian shot out past me and up the stairs without a second glance.

'What the fuck are you doing?' Jay demanded. 'Did I tell you to let him out?'

'No, but he was distressed,' I answered.

'He's a fucking cat!' he snapped.

I tried to swallow back the dry knot of fear lodged at the back of my throat.

I opened my bag and started searching.

'What the hell's taking so long?'

'I... I can't find my keys,' I replied, aware my voice was quivering.

One-handed, I fumbled around in my tote bag.

'For fuck's sake! Give me your bloody keys!'

I grasped them in my fingers, feeling the ridge of the cold metal. I hesitated.

'I mean it! Give me your keys! And your phone!' he added. 'I don't trust you, you conniving, miserable bitch!'

Stab him with the keys, Sophie. NOW!

'Phone!' he demanded.

I faltered, not wanting him to have my phone in case he realised that I had the emergency services on the line, listening to us.

To him.

But before I had the chance to act, I felt an explosion of pain in my side. Winded, I gasped as momentarily everything went black, and I collapsed onto the floor.

'You stupid, fucking cow! Why can't you follow one simple instruction?' he yelled. 'One simple fucking instruction!'

I felt another blinding explosion in my side. Followed by another.

I couldn't breathe. Tears streamed from my eyes. I lay there, my cheek resting on the cool waxed floorboard, spit drooling from my open mouth as I tried to find my breath through the excruciating pain.

I heard him walk down the hallway to the kitchen. Then the fridge door opening, followed by the clinking of bottles.

Move, Sophie! Move before he comes back!

Wheezing, I dragged my body, crawling towards the door, my keys still clutched in the palm of my hand.

Now get up! GET THE HELL UP!

I struggled to get up onto all fours, puffing from the exertion. I willed myself not to throw up as the pain intensified with each movement.

Focus! Focus on getting out!

Breathing shallowly, I somehow managed to force myself up.

I didn't hear Jay come up behind me. All I felt was his hand grab my hair, twisting it tightly in his fist.

I screamed.

'Shut the fuck up!' he ordered as he tightened his grip, pulling my hair from its roots.

I screamed again. Louder, more desperate.

He pulled my head back, then smashed it into the door.

I felt the keys falling from my grasp with the shock of the impact.

'I mean it! Shut the fuck up!'

He spun me around and wedged his arm under my throat, pinning me against the door.

I tried to prise his arm away with my fingers, clawing and tearing, but he didn't feel it.

He got into my face, breathing beer fumes over me. 'Why do you piss me off? Why not do as I fucking ask you?'

There was a sudden tentative knock at the door, followed by: 'Sophie?'

Jay's expression darkened. 'Don't fucking dare!' he threatened as he shoved his elbow deeper into my windpipe so I couldn't breathe.

When she didn't get a response, she hammered on the door.

I gasped and choked, fighting to get air.

'Sophie? Jay?' Tara repeated on the other side of the door, a tremor of fear in her voice.

I started kicking the door with my heel. Again, and again. To let her know that—

Blinding pain exploded in my head as everything became distorted.

I blinked as my eyes watered from the sudden impact.

Oh God...

I stared at Jay's clenched right fist as he pulled it back from my face.

'Sophie?' Tara shouted, banging with her fist on the other side.

I stared in horror at Jay's maniacal expression, questioning whether he had even registered Tara's presence.

I then heard her talking hurriedly to someone. Begging for help.

The police. She's calling the police.

I collapsed to the floor as Jay suddenly released me. I waited for something to happen. But he didn't move. Instead, he contemptuously watched me as I scrambled on the floor towards the stairs.

If you can get to the bathroom, you can lock yourself inside until the police arrive.

Then I heard the door handle being tried. Tara was trying to get in. Then the key in the lock.

How does she have a key?

Then I remembered that Jay had left the spare key with her in case of an emergency.

Oh God... What if he hurts her?

'Sophie?' she tentatively called out again before opening the door.

Then I felt Jay behind me, grabbing me by my ankle and yanking me back down as my chin ricocheted off the wooden steps.

I screamed and kicked like a wild animal as he twisted my long, curly hair around his fist.

A few moments later, Tara tremulously shouted out: 'Let her go!'

He stopped, turned and seemed surprised to see Tara. I felt his grip slacken.

Run, Sophie. Get up and run!

I pulled away from him and turned and ran as fast as I could, stumbling towards Tara, who grabbed me and yanked me out the door as Jay followed.

Ignoring Tara with her arm around my trembling, sobbing body, he looked straight at me. The cold, intelligent blackness in his beady, piercing eyes paralysed me with abject terror. The malevolence was beyond my comprehension, beyond human, akin to pure evil. I felt as if I couldn't breathe.

'One call is all it takes,' he promised in a guttural voice before slamming the door and locking it.

Tara put her arm around me, guiding my trembling body down the drive away from him. 'Come on. Let's get you to my house until the police arrive.'

'Sebastian?' I somehow managed to say through the sobs.

'Shhh, you're safe now. He can't hurt you any more, Sophie.'

I shook my head.

'Sebastian?' I repeated. 'He's inside with Jay. Please? We need to get him?'

I saw the flicker of fear cross Tara's face. I realised she was too scared to go back for Sebastian.

And why wouldn't she be after what she heard, what she saw?

'Let's wait for the police. They'll go in there and get Sebastian for you,' she assured me.

Then a terrifying thought hit me: the police would arrest Jay.

This was only the beginning...

I knew now that I would never be safe. Not once the police were involved. I had outed Jay as the sick, sadistic abuser that he was in *his* village, amongst *his* friends. He had lost everything.

Because of you, Sophie.

And now... His parting promise to me: *'One call is all it takes.'*

I turned around and looked back at Eastcliff Cottage.

What have you done, Sophie?

PART FOUR

'I have learned over the years that when one's mind is made up, this diminishes fear; knowing what must be done does away with fear.'

— ROSA PARKS

31

I couldn't stop trembling.

'Sophie?' the older male police officer gently prompted.

Hours had faded into the night since their very public arrival, with sirens and lights flashing as Tara brought me to her house. They interviewed me, then Tara. When questioned about my broken arm, I dismissed it with the story Jay had so often cited: too much champagne and a dangerously long wedding dress train. I didn't show the police officers the injuries to my body where Jay had kicked and stomped on me, not wanting to make it worse than it already was, terrified of the repercussions; of what Jay would do to me.

Fear made me minimise everything that had happened. I didn't want to give Jay more reason to come after me. I just wanted to get Sebastian and go as I'd planned. To disappear so he could never find me and let Grace or one of her colleagues start divorce proceedings. I didn't dare to go ahead with criminal charges. I would be publicly outing Jay as a wife-beater. That scenario had only one outcome: *'I'll... torture you... then fucking kill you...'*

But the police already had the 999 calls from Tara and me. Also, our witness statements and the physical evidence on my face, which they photographed. They had enough to arrest him.

'Sophie?' the officer repeated. 'I appreciate it's really late and you gave us a statement earlier. But there's one more thing I need from you.'

I blankly looked at him.

I couldn't remember his name. Or his colleague's. Nor could I differentiate between their faces as both looked the same to me, aside from one had flecks of silver in his neatly trimmed hair.

I shook my head, more tears slipping down my face.

Tara had discreetly left me with the two specially trained domestic violence officers. Both were male, which surprised me.

Silenced me.

I rejected the thought. I had silenced myself for fear of the repercussions from my husband.

I had publicly betrayed him.

And now what?

The thought filled me with dread, stirring up the buzzing hornet's nest that had taken residence in the pit of my stomach.

But shame and humiliation had also silenced me. I was humiliated to be sitting in my neighbour's house for the first time, disclosing excruciatingly personal information to the police. Humiliated that I had ended up in this position, that it was my fault somehow that all this had occurred to me. Subsequently, I minimised everything that had happened, downplaying Jay's abusive, coercive behaviour and omitting the brutal fact he had raped me earlier that day.

It's your word against his. And who would believe that you – a successful professional – are capable of being controlled and physically ill-treated by a man you *chose to marry?*

I felt scorching chagrin that I had let this happen.

How was that possible? How could you, Sophie? How?

I had opened myself up to a man who, in reality, I knew nothing about.

I swallowed the bitter taste of self-hatred. I was an author of a series of standalone romance novels. Yet, I had found myself living the antithesis of the fiction I created, a life that no one could have imagined, let alone would struggle to accept even as fiction. It wasn't supposed to have turned out this way.

'Sophie? You said you have a journal? That you documented the abuse? That tonight wasn't the first time?'

I nodded, not recalling mentioning it.

Nor did I recall crying hysterically as I fled down the stairs away from Jay.

Tara's statement to the police replayed over and over in my head. Her shocked words as she'd tried to make sense of what she'd witnessed: *'He's so lovely, a really caring guy who would do anything for anyone. I thought he adored her, the way he talked. Even the way he acted. I just saw them this morning when I called in with a jar of my parents' honey, and Jay was all over her and she was with him. You know? The perfect couple. They were married just over two weeks ago. God! Damien and I were at their wedding. It was beautiful. They're still in their honeymoon period and... Christ! I just can't believe it...'*

I wiped at the snot and tears with the ball of tissues the officer had handed me. For some reason, I couldn't stop crying or shaking, despite the warmth of the evening.

'Right, as I explained, we've processed him, and he's being detained in a cell overnight, followed by questioning tomorrow.'

I nodded, but none of it made any sense. I didn't understand what would happen tomorrow. Or the next day. Or the next. Or what would happen to me now? I felt like my world had imploded, and all I could see was grey ash falling, obscuring and deadening everything around me. I didn't know how to navigate my way through this unfamiliar world: one not of my choosing.

The officer gave me a reassuring look and paternalistically reiterated, 'We've arrested him, but tomorrow he'll be interviewed, and a decision made as to whether to charge him. The main thing is that you are safe now.'

Am I?

He didn't know Jay the way I did, for my husband believed he was above the law and reproach. Consequently, adrenaline coursed through me, preparing me for the fallout from my actions.

You should never have called 999, Sophie. And Tara should never have got involved.

But if you hadn't, if Tara hadn't, you'd be dead!

I swallowed at the stark realisation that at least death would be final, bringing with it peace. For now, I had to live with the terror of waiting for it to happen.

Because he will kill you for this. He'll make you suffer, slowly and sadistically.

I noted the other, younger officer glance at my leg as he stood up. I followed his gaze and realised I was anxiously jiggling it. I rested my hand on it, but the nervous energy rampaging through me was too great to override the twitching.

It was time for them to accompany me home with the assurance that they would make sure the front door was secure after forcing it open.

When they had attempted to enter Eastcliff Cottage earlier, no one had answered. They had kicked open the resisting wooden front door to discover Jay's key left in the lock. He was found drunk, naked and asleep in our bed. He had knocked back considerable shots of tequila after I'd left. When they'd arrested him and placed him in the rear of the police car, he had effusively told them what a great job they did, without irony or shame at being removed from his home – his bed – for beating his wife. He had also added in the patrol car: '*She's not getting that fucking house!*'

As the younger officer had said in disgust to me when recounting the scene: '*Angry small man syndrome.*'

Not that it helped ease my fears.

I knew this was only the beginning. It was going to get a lot worse.

Now the police and our neighbours are involved.

32

The police brought me back to the cottage after 4 a.m., and then left me with Sebastian and the terror of what would unfold. I could have stayed at Tara's, but Damien was due back from his night shift in a couple of hours, and I didn't want to be there when he returned. Tara had offered to stay with me, but I just wanted to be alone to reflect on what had happened and what would happen next. Not answering questions about Jay, her good neighbour and friend, or so she had believed. Tara had looked quietly relieved when I refused her offer, presumably feeling awkward and unsure of what to say. Not that there was anything she could say that would make a difference.

All I wanted was my mother and sister, but that wasn't an option. Nor did I want to end Anna and Grace's holiday with the news that Jay had assaulted me. I knew they would both be on the first flight back from Venice. I didn't want that. It could wait. And at this point, I didn't know what would happen. I had never felt so alone.

Ben came to mind. Jay had deleted his number and blocked him on my phone. I was sure I had a copy of his number in my study somewhere, or I could reach out through one of his social media accounts. Ben would come to my rescue as soon as I contacted him. But I didn't want my ex charging into my life with the satisfaction that he had been proven right and that the man I had married, instead of him, was even worse than he could ever have imagined from what my mother and Liv would have told him.

The burning ochre ball of fire rose as always at the front of the cottage. I sat in the shade at the back of the cottage in the open-plan room, staring out at the endless expanse of azure ocean, transfixed by the despair of its vastness.

A knock at the front door startled me. Startled Sebastian, who bolted from my lap, taking sanctuary somewhere else. I ignored it, protectively pulling my cashmere throw around myself as the fear awoke again.

Is it Jay? Have they released him?

A second knock followed. Then a third, harder, more intrusive this time.

A woman's voice called through the letter box to me: 'Sophie? It's PC Jess Kimbrell. Can you let me in?'

I forced myself to get up.

'I've just started the day shift and I'm taking over your case,' she explained at the door.

I didn't reply.

'Can I come in for a minute, Sophie?'

I shrugged, unable to look her in the eye, and walked back into the lounge area, leaving her to follow.

I didn't want strangers coming into my home and investigating my life.

Speculating about your bad decisions that culminated in Jay assaulting you in front of a neighbour.

'I imagine this has been quite a shock for you,' she sympathetically stated. 'The officers who attended last night said you kept a journal detailing some historical abuse?'

I nodded.

'Can I take it just to have a look?'

'Why?'

'Because the more we have against him makes it easier to charge him.'

I must have looked surprised.

'He hasn't any priors,' she explained.

'But the 999 call I made?'

'Yes, it's difficult to make out exactly what's happening above...' She faltered, noting Sebastian strolling out from behind the couch. 'Your cat whose distress drowned out a lot.'

'Oh,' I mumbled. 'My phone was in my bag on the floor next to his cat carrier.'

She nodded. 'Don't get me wrong, we have your neighbour's witness statement and yours of course. And I can see from the trauma on your cheek and forehead that you were injured. But I just need evidence to substantiate that this isn't a one-off drunken argument.'

I was about to state that I was sober. I had never been more sober in my life.

'On his part,' she clarified.

I nodded.

'Obviously, your journal is your word against his, but it could be a useful insight.'

I noted the way she looked at my plaster cast. But she didn't say anything.

'Why don't you fetch me that journal and I'll be on my way.'

Embarrassed, I went to the study. I reluctantly handed over my diary. I had lost complete control of my life.

'I'll bring it back,' she assured me. 'Do you have anyone to call who can stay with you today?'

I shook my head.

She gave me another sympathetic smile. 'Well, I'll call you to keep you updated as to whether your husband's going to be charged or cautioned.' She noted my confusion. 'If he's charged, he'll be on police bail until his court hearing. It means he's not allowed near you or your home. He's not even allowed to drive up your road. But if he's cautioned, then, effectively, he has every legal right to return here.'

'What?'

'Don't worry, he's being detained at the station for now. If he is released, you'll get plenty of prior warning.'

Fear of the consequences if released silenced me.

I watched as she left me with the stupefying news that he could return.

* * *

I sat on the couch, clutching my phone, waiting for her call as the white sailboats bobbed carefree on the unattainable horizon. The late-afternoon sun streaming into the room chastising me for still being there.

I forced my legs to move and headed upstairs into the bedroom and stared at the crumpled bedding. I noted Jay's phone charging by the side of his bed. Curious, I picked it up and looked at the most recent text.

I felt a twist of jealousy tighten in my stomach.

Hey, hope all's okay after you had to dash off last night. Hope you're still on for later. Rachael x

It had been sent this morning.

I thought of Tom's question on the eve of our wedding: '*What do you really know about him?*'

My phone suddenly rang, startling me. It was an unknown number. I hesitated.

'Hi.'

'Sophie? It's Jess. PC Jess Kimbrell,' she greeted. 'Good news. I've charged him. I'll explain everything to you when I return your journal later. First, a police escort will bring him back to your home to collect some belongings and his car. When the police arrive, give them access to your property, then wait in another room. So, you don't see him. Okay?'

I didn't want him charged. I wanted him cautioned so I could have left for London as planned. I wanted it all to go away. To move on with my life without his threat hanging over me. But the roll of the dice had changed everything – for the worse. Now he had nothing to lose.

'I'm not sure—'

'Sophie?' she interrupted. 'I read your journal entries. I know what he did to you. I copied and sent them to the CPS. We have enough evidence to charge him, with or without your consent, and the fact he confessed—'

'He admitted it?' I questioned, shocked.

'Only because he thought he was getting off with a caution. The duty solicitor advised him to do that, unaware I was waiting to hear back from the CPS as to whether we had enough to charge him.'

'Oh,' I mumbled, feeling nothing but terror.

* * *

I watched from the guest-bedroom window as Jay sat in the Transporter with the window down, joking around with the two male police officers who had escorted him back. I couldn't understand why they hadn't left. He had taken what he wanted, so why hang around?

But I knew why.

He's intimidating you, demonstrating that he's done nothing wrong. Ergo, he has no reason to hide, unlike me.

I had stayed skulking in the shadows of my study as he had freely walked around the property. His deep, low voice boomed off the walls, under the door, seeking me out, amiably chatting with the officers, proving his point: he wasn't responsible for his actions – I was. How could he possibly have terrorised and assaulted me when the two male police officers were conversing with him as if nothing had happened?

Did they know what he'd done? Did they even care?

I watched as the officers laughed at some anecdote Jay was telling them.

If they didn't see my husband as a threat, how could they protect me from him?

33

When they finally drove off, I noted that Jay had taken his phone and charger from his bedside cabinet and various clothes. It was odd he had left his phone when arrested as he had the wherewithal to take his house and Transporter keys and wallet. The fact he had access to the property terrified me, regardless of the police's assurance that he was under bail conditions and restricted from coming near me or entering the property without a police escort. I seriously doubted that would stop him.

I had heard the attic ladders being pulled down and assumed he had taken a couple of guitars and whatever it was up there that he didn't want me to find.

Bracing myself, I opened the hatch and pulled out the ladders, deciding to go up and check out the forbidden space. It was dusty, claustrophobic and hot. Piles of boxes and paraphernalia covered the boarded-out space. I looked around, not knowing where to start. I noted that all his guitar cases were gone, as were a couple of the smaller cardboard boxes with his documents and photographs, the sealed contents detailed on the sides in his spidery writing. I regretted not taking the opportunity to look through them the day he had been in Manchester.

I decided to search through what he had left behind, but fear of reprisals if Jay figured out that I had been up here suddenly caught me off guard.

Come on, Sophie! You're being pathetic.

I realised Jay's unpredictability and the uncertainty of what he would do to me once he was released had me policing myself. Jay had instilled within me something akin to the eighteenth-century panopticon prison, designed in such a way that one guard could survey all the inmates at one time, so they never knew whether the guard was watching them or not, and ended up self-monitoring.

Acknowledging this observation didn't make me feel any more in control. I felt uneasy, as if he were watching me. I instinctively looked up at the rafters.

What the hell?

There was a security surveillance camera there. Jay must have installed it to see if I disobeyed him and went into the attic. He had no means of viewing the security footage on his old Nokia phone, and the system was faulty as all the cameras had been off since yesterday evening. I had handed my phone over to the police so they could access the footage, but the system had crashed just as I left the cottage when the taxi arrived. Consequently, there was no recording of Jay assaulting me last night.

I caught sight of a strip of tablets on the floor. Curious, I picked the small foil packet up. I assumed Jay had dropped them when he was in the attic retrieving his guitars and whatever else he took.

It was a half-used packet of nitrazepam 5 mg tablets. It was a type of benzodiazepine and a powerful sedative. I knew this because when my father unexpectedly died, my mother had been prescribed them by her GP to help with her severe anxiety and insomnia.

It's a sleeping tablet...

Why would Jay have these? To my knowledge, I had never known him take sedatives or sleeping tablets.

Oh my God... He's been drugging you, Sophie!

No surprise you slept straight through for eighteen hours that Saturday when he took your family and friends to Newquay for dinner.

I realised he must have crushed them up and added them to the chamomile tea he encouraged me to drink. And my wine.

The grainy substance on the bottom of my wine glass wasn't dishwasher tablet residue, as he'd said: it was powdered nitrazepam.

I jumped when I heard someone knock at the front door. I climbed down and pushed the ladders back up, hastily shutting the attic hatch. I checked my watch: it was 4.43 p.m. I ran down the stairs and answered the door to find PC Jess Kimbrell.

'Here you go,' she said, handing me my journal.

'Thanks,' I answered, embarrassed that she had read it.

Other people had read it as well.

'Can I come in for a minute?' she asked.

'Of course,' I said, holding the door open for her. 'Just go through to the back room.'

I closed the door and followed.

Jess was standing by the kitchen island looking out through the bi-folding doors at the view of Porthtowan Beach.

'It's stunning,' she appreciatively said, turning to me.

'It is,' I agreed, even though the allure had gone. I had one of the most breathtakingly beautiful, unadulterated ocean views, but fear of who I shared that aspect with blighted it for me.

'So,' she began, 'as I said on the phone, Jay's on police bail. If he breaks it, he'll be arrested and remanded in police custody until his court hearing.'

I uneasily nodded.

'Are you okay?' she gently questioned.

Again, I nodded, trying to dispel the growing anxiety I felt.

God, Sophie! Within twenty-four hours, your life has radically changed.

For better or worse?

I pushed the disconcerting thought away.

'Where is he?' I asked.

'He's staying at a hotel in Truro.'

'Which one?'

'I'm sorry, I can't disclose that information.'

I didn't reply.

'I did everything in my power to stop him from coming back here,' Jess assured me. She paused before continuing, 'When I interviewed him, he had no remorse, nothing. What concerned me was the look in his eye. I knew that if he was released with a caution and the recommendation that he stayed in a hotel for a few days to let things cool down, he would ignore the advice. Instead, he would let himself into your home in the middle of the night and...' she hesitated.

But I already knew what she was going to say. It was what I had been living, breathing from the moment the police arrested him.

'He would kill you,' she quietly confided.

I silently stared at her as her words fell like ashes around me.

He would kill you.

I swallowed, overcome with nausea, for this was a police officer who had interviewed him telling me she believed he would kill me.

Oh God...

It suddenly made it all real.

You're not catastrophising, Sophie. He will kill you. Maybe not today or tomorrow, but he will. That's a fact. The question is, what are you going to do about it?

'I've witnessed that look in the eyes of other men who go on to kill their victims, and I didn't want to take that risk with you.'

To end up another statistic, Sophie. Another number on a spreadsheet. To become one of the three women killed every week by a man in the UK.

'Can I change the locks?'

'Unfortunately, not. While on bail, he needs a police escort to gain entry. In the meantime, you can apply for an Occupation Order in advance of his court hearing this Thursday in case he doesn't get a prison sentence.'

'An Occupation Order?' I repeated.

'It's a court order that grants you the right to change the locks because he wouldn't be allowed back into the property. To my knowledge, they're six to twelve months. But at least it would give you peace of mind. If he doesn't go to prison, your husband has every right to return home.'

Numb, I shook my head. 'After everything he's done?'

'I know,' she sympathised.

'So, I would have to leave this house, and he gets to stay here, and I'm the victim?'

'If you co-own it, I'm afraid so,' she answered.

I was stunned.

How could that be possible? He had assaulted me and yet—

'I've done all I can,' Jess said, making a move to leave. 'It's in the hands of the courts to decide what happens to him. He'll appear at the magistrates' court in Truro this Thursday, and they'll decide whether it goes to trial at the Crown Court, or if he's released with a fine, community service or a suspended sentence.'

I mutely nodded, only hearing the words: *'if he's released…'*

'We've got an excellent victim support officer. Tina's a retired detective inspector. She'll be in touch with you to keep you up to date regarding the court hearing.'

I remained silent. I trusted and liked Jess and consequently didn't want someone else taking over from her. She understood what Jay was like. She had seen that abhorrent blackness lurking in his eyes, stirring deep in his soul.

'After what I read in your journal,' Jess began as she glanced at the cuts and bruising on my face, then my broken wrist, 'the beatings are nothing compared to what he did to you psychologically. I can't even begin to imagine what you went through on your wedding night.'

I didn't reply.

She gestured to my plaster cast. 'Why didn't you tell the attending officers he broke your wrist? Or that he assaulted you on your honeymoon?'

I shrugged, ashamed at myself for allowing fear to silence me. 'I was scared of what he would do to me if I reported it.'

'You're safe now, Sophie. I promise you,' she assured me.

'Am I?'

'A patrol car will be driving by your house while he's on bail. He can't hurt you.'

He can... And he will... For what good is one patrol car every couple of hours? Who protects me when they've gone?

'He's not stupid, Sophie. He won't incriminate himself while he's on bail,' she added in response to my silence.

Would he care? I seriously doubted it. Not now. Not after losing the image of the perfect husband, friend and neighbour.

* * *

After Jess left, I poured myself a glass of wine and made a cheese sandwich. I forced myself to eat half, but that was all I could manage. Exhausted and numb, I sat on the couch, staring around the large, white, minimalistic room. I didn't want to be here any more. But I couldn't run. Not yet. And where could I go to where Jay wouldn't find me? He had threatened that all it would take was one call. Would that call be made to some nefarious characters from his past in Manchester? There had to be a reason why I'd never met them and why he had cut all ties.

But had he really left his past behind?

I had to trust in the police and the legal system that they would protect me from Jay. Until his court hearing, I had no choice but to wait it out.

Unsettled, Sebastian jumped onto my lap and wailed at me, sensing my unease.

'We'll get through this, Sebastian. You and me. You'll see,' I murmured as I stroked him until he began purring profusely. 'We just need to wait it out.'

And trust in others to keep us safe. To keep us alive.

I was surprised when my phone rang. I answered the unknown number. It was another police officer: Jay had requested a second police escort.

'Now?' I objected. 'It's after six? He was here less than two hours ago.'

'He needs something,' the male officer flatly replied.

What else do you want, Jay?

But I also knew this was about terrorising me – exerting his control.

Over the law. Over me.

'Do I have a choice?'

'Not really,' he replied. 'He has a right to his possessions.'

'Fine,' I reluctantly conceded.

'He'll be there with a police escort before 7 p.m.'

'Does it have to be this evening? Can't he wait until tomorrow?'

'He's here in the police station now. He's heading to Manchester this evening for the remainder of his bail.'

'Manchester?' I mumbled.

The word filled me with dread. Why would he be going to Manchester when his court hearing was on Thursday?

'How do you know he'll definitely go to Manchester?'

'Because he has to report to a police station tomorrow at 8 a.m. and the following morning as per his bail conditions.'

'And he isn't tagged?' I asked.

'No.'

'Why is he going to Manchester?' I found myself asking.

'He has a friend there he can stay with until his court hearing.'

'A friend?' I repeated.

Jay's threatening words returned filling me with disquiet: *'If you ever fucking think of leaving me, I will have you killed. Make no mistake, one call is all it takes. I'll have them hunt you down, torture you and then fucking kill you, and no one will know.'*

I cut the call.

Oh God... Was this why he was going to Manchester, to pay someone in advance of his court hearing? Just in case he received a prison sentence and couldn't carry out his threat himself?

34

What the—

I couldn't breathe.

My heart was frantically fluttering like a trapped butterfly in a specimen jar. I thought it would rupture as I tried to make sense of the view outside the guest-bedroom window at the front of the cottage. Exactly where I had watched Jay cavorting with the two police officers who escorted him back for his belongings and to collect the Transporter.

Here he now was, brazenly sitting in the vehicle, window down, wearing a pair of blue iridescent Oakleys and staring straight up at me.

I jumped back from the window. But it was too late, as he had seen me.

I thought back to PC Jess Kimbrell. She had said that his bail conditions forbade him from coming anywhere near the road leading up the hill, let alone Eastcliff Cottage. Yet, Jay was flagrantly parked at the bottom of the driveway.

Staring at the cottage.

Staring at me!

I tried to breathe, gasping for oxygen that repeatedly eluded me.

He can't do anything to you, Sophie. The police will be here any minute now.

I looked at my watch. It was 6.46 p.m.

I thought about calling 999 and telling them he had broken his bail conditions. I decided to wait, rather than waste their time, and report it to the officers when they arrived to escort him into the house.

I sneaked another look out the window, making sure he couldn't see me. He was still there, staring straight up at the window.

At you, Sophie. He knows you're here hiding from him. He can smell your fear like an animal stalking their prey.

And you're his prey.

Oh God... Oh God...

I could sense his chilling anger as he continued to look up at the window, willing me to step out of the shadows so he could see me.

Terrorise me.

I sank to the floor, pulling my knees up to my chest and waited, too terrified to move. I clutched my phone, prepared to call the police if Jay entered the house.

Prepared to tell them I was going to die.

He was fifteen minutes early and had boldly broken his bail conditions.

Why? Why would he do that?

But I knew the answer: because he could.

He believes he's above the law.

Sometime later, there was a hard knock at the front door.

Oh God...

Another loud, insistent knock this time.

I reminded myself Jay wouldn't knock. He would surprise me when I least expected it.

My phone rang, startling me. It was an unknown number. I shakily stood up, pressed my body against the wall and peeked out the window. Jay had moved the Transporter further up, and a police van had taken its place.

I answered the call.

'Mrs Bradley? PC Penrose. I'm at the door of your property as arranged.'

'Give me a minute,' I replied.

I hung up the call, taking some deep breaths to prepare myself.

You can do this, Sophie. He won't be back after tonight.

I swallowed back the familiar knot of fear at the back of my throat.

Maybe not him... But someone will.

I hid again in my study with a disgruntled Sebastian, waiting for Jay to take what he urgently needed. I nervously paced up and down, holding Jay's passport, waiting to hand it to PC Penrose. His passport typically remained locked in my study desk for safekeeping. Since I was in the study, and he wasn't allowed near me, he couldn't access it. I didn't want Jay to have another reason to return with a third police escort.

I glanced at my passport that I'd left out on the study desk. It was my backup plan. I intended to take Sebastian to the vet in the morning to get him vaccinated against rabies so he could travel to Europe. If everything went catastrophically wrong, I knew where we would go; someplace Jay or his friends could never find us. I had gone through my limited options, discounting my family home in Scotland and my friends in London. Even if I were welcome, they would be the first places Jay would look for me.

You don't think you're being hyperbolic, Sophie? Running from him isn't the answer.

But if my worst nightmare came true on Thursday, I would have no choice. If the court released Jay with the right to return to what the police termed the 'family home', I had no option other than to leave.

After what felt like in perpetuity, PC Penrose knocked at the door.

'Your husband's got everything he wants,' he concluded.

'His passport,' I said, handing it over.

He nodded, taking it, and turned to leave, striding towards the front door. He swung it wide open and walked out without another word.

'Can I check something with you?' I questioned, unsure of whether I should mention it. To him.

He stopped and turned around with an edge of irritation.

I stepped back, immediately intimidated by his hostile six-foot-six body, which dominated the doorway; seemed to dominate me. His commanding presence eclipsed the golden warmth of the evening sun behind him.

'I... I...' I faltered as I noted him clench his clean-shaven, square jaw.

He stared at me, hostility radiating from him as he waited for me to say whatever I had to say to him.

I assumed it was the end of his shift, and this was his last job and one that was evidently a waste of his time.

'My husband arrived here fifteen minutes before you did and

parked up directly outside the house and...' I hesitated, not wanting to tell him his job.

Or my rights.

The disdain in his gold-flecked hazel eyes informed me that my question – my words – were irrelevant to him. I held his glare, willing myself not to be cowed into silence by a man who looked ten years my junior.

'And?'

'I... I thought that was a violation of his bail conditions?' I challenged.

He sighed. 'He's leaving for Manchester. He couldn't get further away from you if he tried.' With that, he turned and headed in the direction of Jay.

I stood, blinded by the evening sun, shocked by his candid derision.

Jay broke his bail. He sat in the Transporter staring straight up at the house – at you. Intimidating you. How could the officer not take that seriously?

I waited as PC Penrose strolled up to the Transporter and handed Jay his passport. He said a few words, glancing back in my direction before heading back to the police van. Ignoring me, he climbed in, performed a three-point-turn and pulled off, leaving me alone and bewildered.

I watched as the black-tinted VW Transporter slowly rolled back down the hill, window down, 'Creep' by Radiohead blasting. Jay braked, turned his head in my direction, and glared at me. I could feel the malignant intent behind his Oakley sunglasses as his small, narrowed eyes bore into me. He then turned his head and drove on as 'Creep' continued blaring.

I slammed the door shut, then locked it. I turned and rested my trembling body against the wood as I tried to make sense of what had just happened.

I thought about whether to call 999 and report the officer. But what good would that do? Jay would deny it. It was his word against mine. But surely Officer Penrose must have noted that the Transporter was already parked when he arrived?

How could the police not take the violation of bail conditions in a domestic violence case seriously? How was that even possible?

35

I had gone around the house checking that all the doors and windows were locked, but I still couldn't relax.

It was only just after 8 p.m. I imagined it would be a long night.

A light tap at the front door startled me.

I got up and tiptoed to the front room and peeked out, expecting Tara.

She had asked again if I wanted to stay the night at her place now that Jay had been released on police bail. But I didn't want to leave Sebastian on his own. Tara had then suggested that she spend the night at mine, to keep me company. But her awkwardness around me now made me feel like a social pariah. I managed to persuade her that I would be fine and that I would call if there was a problem.

Like what? Jay turning up?

I discounted the terrifying thought and went to open the door.

Tom's smile faded as he stared at the cuts and bruises on my face.

'It's worse than it looks,' I stated, surprised but pleased to see him.

He didn't look convinced.

'Do you want to come in?'

'Sure. But I've only got a few minutes. I just wanted to check in on you,' Tom explained, adding, 'Tara told me what happened...'

I nodded. It was evident he felt embarrassed. I imagined he didn't know what to say. Or maybe it was me that now made him uneasy?

He followed me through to the open-plan living space.

'Sit down,' I offered.

'It's okay. Can't stay long.' I had never seen him look so uncomfortable.

'Of course,' I replied.

'I'm sorry, Soph. I had no idea that Jay was capable of...' He faltered as his eyes rested on my injuries.

I remained silent. There was nothing I could say.

'If I had known...' He shrugged.

'Can I ask you something?'

'Sure,' he replied, but there was resistance in his eyes. It was clear he just wanted to appease his conscience and get away.

'You said something to me the night before our wedding?'

He looked down at me and waited.

'That was I sure I wanted to marry Jay, and what did I really know about him?'

Tom nervously ran a large hand through his messy curly blonde hair. 'Yeah... I'd had a skinful. Sorry. I should never have said that to you.'

But you did say it... Why backtrack now?

'But you also said that he'd been coming to Porthtowan for a couple of years?'

'Yeah, that's true.'

'With another woman?' I asked, thinking of the photograph I'd found in Jay's Takamine guitar case.

'*Women*,' he answered.

'What? I thought he was in a long-term relationship for eight years before he and I got together?'

Tom didn't say anything.

'How many? One or two?'

He shrugged. 'I lost count.'

I must have looked horrified as he continued: 'He sometimes came with a woman, always a different one, or he would come alone and hook up with someone here.'

What the—?

'What about now?' I asked.

Tom looked uneasy.

'Rachael?' I questioned.

'Maybe. I'm not sure,' he replied. 'I'm sorry, Sophie. I...' He shook his head. 'As I said, I had no idea he would hurt you.'

'Neither did I, or I wouldn't have married him.'

'Look, rather than staying here on your own, why don't you stay at Tara and Damien's?'

I shook my head. 'I'm fine.'

He raised his eyebrows.

'Honestly.'

He nodded, then turned and headed into the hallway.

'Tom?' I called as he opened the door.

He looked at me.

'If he gets in touch, will you let me know?'

'He already has,' he replied.

'When?' I asked, surprised.

'This morning from the police station. He called to ask if he could stay with me while he was on bail.'

I must have looked stunned because he then added: 'I said no, of course.'

'But his old Nokia flip phone was left charging here?'

'Didn't he have a new iPhone? I saw him with it the other night when I picked him up.'

Oh my God... That was how he knew you were leaving. He must have been watching the security cameras on his new iPhone.

It suddenly all made sense.

* * *

I lay in the double bed in the guest room, unable to bring myself to sleep in the master bedroom. Not after the events yesterday afternoon.

He raped you, Sophie!

It was 9.30 p.m.; Monday was coming to an end. I was exhausted as I hadn't slept since Saturday evening. Before retiring upstairs, I'd triple-checked all the locks and left my key in the front door. It was the words before PC Kimbrell's deathly statement that clung to my feverish skin: '*He would let himself into your home in the middle of the night.*'

I shakily breathed out, trying to quell the nausea I felt. Sebastian jumped onto the bed and warily looked at me as if I was going crazy. I smiled at him affectionately. He purred in response, hypnotically holding my gaze.

'I guess you're right. The police do know what they're doing.' I leaned over and kissed him on the head. 'You'll keep me sane, won't you?'

I looked at my phone, questioning whether to call Grace or Anna. I dismissed the thought, deciding that now wasn't the time. I didn't want to disrupt their holiday.

Or is it you don't want to tell them? Too ashamed to admit what's happened to you? That your perfect relationship no longer exists – if it ever did – and now the police are involved.

I couldn't silence the prescient feeling that something terrible would happen.

He's gone, Sophie. Back to Manchester. You need to trust the police.

But the problem was I knew Jay. I knew what he was capable of, and that was terrifying.

* * *

Exhaustion won over fear in the end, and sleep took hold. I was surprised to be woken by my phone ringing and the morning sun streaming through the guest bedroom window. I blearily blinked as I reached for my phone.

'Hi.'

'Sophie?'

'Damien?' I questioned.

'I don't know how to say this, but whatever you do, don't look out the front bedroom window,' Damien firmly advised.

I did the exact opposite and threw the covers back and rushed to the window.

I didn't understand why Damien was holding onto a sobbing Tara at the bottom of my driveway, dressed in her running clothes. Nor did my brain quite register what was lying on the gravel right in front of my window.

Or who.

Oh my God... OH MY GOD! NO!

My phone slipped from my hand as Damien turned and looked up at me aghast.

I didn't realise I was screaming like a wounded animal, unable to hear anything other than Damien's warning: '*Whatever you do, don't look out the front bedroom window.*'

36

I wailed as I knelt on the gravel, cradling Sebastian's cold body.

'How?' I mumbled as I stared at him. 'How could this have happened to you?'

I looked up, tears streaming down my cheeks, searching Damien's embarrassed face for answers.

He turned away, not wanting to speak his mind.

'Damien?'

He shook his head. 'Come on, you need to get up,' he suggested, moving the conversation on.

'I can't,' I said, trying but failing to hold back a strangled sob.

I felt an arm around my shoulder. 'Sophie, come on, let's take him inside. Yeah?'

Tara was now crouching down beside me. Her tear-filled eyes glanced at Sebastian, secure in my arms. It looked as if he was asleep, oblivious to the drama ensuing around him. She nodded up at Damien. He approached me and awkwardly helped me up to my feet.

Between them, they walked me back into the cottage as I carefully carried Sebastian.

I sat on the couch and held him, unable to process that the rigid body, its life extinguished, was really Sebastian: this wasn't some cruel joke. It made no sense.

Tara sat down next to me. 'Can I get you something to drink?'

I shook my head unable to speak as my body convulsed with sobs.

Oh God... Sebastian...

The raw, agonising pain I felt blinded me to everything other than the fact Sebastian was dead.

He's all you have, Sophie...

I didn't notice Damien disappear to check the windows and doors. Or Tara get up and make a cup of tea with honey for me.

'Sophie? You must have left this bi-folding door open just enough for Sebastian to slip out,' Damien stated, looking across at me.

'No, it can't have been. That door is always locked. I checked every door last night before going to bed,' I hoarsely stated.

'It's open,' he assured me.

It was the door we never used, favouring the one that opened out onto views of Porthtowan Beach and the opposite cliff and the Atlantic. The key was kept in the kitchen drawer. I had left the key for the other bi-folding door in the lock as I did with the front door key.

'That door was locked before I went to bed. I am sure of it.'

I noticed a look pass between him and Tara.

'What?' I questioned.

Tara shook her head at Damien.

'Tell me.'

Damien shrugged at Tara's furious glare, before turning to me. 'You won't want to hear this, but when Tara said she had found Sebastian lying on your drive, my first thought was that Jay had killed him to get back at you.'

His words chilled me.

'How?' I mumbled.

Damien looked first at Tara, then back to me. 'Poison.'

'Poison?' I repeated.

'There's froth around his mouth,' Damien explained when I looked up at him in confusion.

Oh, my poor baby...

I shook my head as more desperate tears fell.

'But Jay's in Manchester. He came back last night with another police escort to collect some things he'd forgotten earlier,' I stated.

'He definitely left last night?'

I could hear the doubt in Damien's voice. He didn't say any more.

I looked down at Sebastian.

Could he have done this? Could Jay hate you so much he would kill the one thing you love more than anything else?

You know the answer, Sophie.

Something struck me.

'Can you pass me that blanket, Tara?'

She nodded and picked up the mohair cover from the other end of the couch. She placed it next to me.

'Thanks,' I mumbled.

I laid Sebastian carefully down on it. I then shakily stood up, forcing myself to look at the foam coming from Sebastian's tiny open mouth as he lay on his favourite blanket.

I turned and headed to the kitchen. First, I checked the drawer. The key wasn't there. Then I saw it lying on the counter.

How is that possible?

Jay could have placed it there last night before he took Sebastian and... poisoned him?

I then pulled open the kitchen cupboards under the sink and frantically started throwing everything across the floor.

'Hey, Sophie? What are you looking for?' Tara asked, worried as she stood behind me.

'Hydrochloric acid for unblocking the shower. Jay bought two bottles the other day and...' I stopped.

They were missing.

I stared in horror at the space where they should have still been.

He took them yesterday evening, Sophie. That's why he came back. He wanted the two five-litre bottles of hydrochloric acid.

'Sophie, look, forget I said anything,' Damien said, coming over to the kitchen area.

I turned to him, my expression wild. 'He took the bottles. He came back last night and he took them.'

'Are you certain?' he asked.

'I put them at the back of this cupboard on Friday night,' I explained. 'And now they've vanished.'

Damien didn't say a word. Neither did Tara.

'Can I get a toxicology test to prove that he poisoned Sebastian?' I questioned.

'Maybe call the police?' Tara proposed.

Damien cleared his throat.

We both turned to him. 'The bi-folding door was left open, Sophie. Sebastian could have got out and walked around to the front of the cottage.'

'So?'

'You have lilies there. Close to where Sebastian was found. Lilies are poisonous to cats.'

'But...' I faltered as tears of anger and frustration fell. 'The door was locked last night. I checked,' I insisted.

But had I checked? I never used that door. I was now starting to doubt myself. I was so exhausted and traumatised by the past few days' occurrences that it wouldn't be unusual to have missed something.

It isn't 'something', Sophie. It's a door, and you checked them all last night.

Also, Jay had calculatedly told the police he was going to Manchester, so there would be no need to send a patrol car around to drive past the cottage.

I thought back to PC Penrose's callous, contemptuous words: '*He couldn't get further away from you if he tried!*'

What had Jay said to convince him that I was somehow in the wrong? That I didn't deserve protecting? That Jay was above breaking the law, exempting him from his bail conditions?

What gave that police officer the right to put your life in jeopardy? Yours and Sebastian's lives. All because his shift was finishing, and he saw you as a waste of his time? Not worthy of having the law implemented on your behalf. To protect you against a man – your husband – already charged with assaulting you.

WHAT RIGHT DID HE HAVE?

More so when his colleague, PC Jess Kimbrell, went all out to have Jay charged, to prevent him from letting himself into your home in the middle of the night because he would kill you.

I felt a hand delicately squeeze my shoulder.

I glanced up at Tara.

'Come on, let me tidy all this up. Yeah? You sit down and drink the tea I made you. It will help with the shock,' she suggested.

I resisted telling her that nothing would ever take the shock away. It would always follow me, be with me, haunt me. Instead, I nodded, accepting her kindness.

I sat at the kitchen island, sipping sweetened tea while choking on tears every time the tsunami of wrenching pain hit me.

Tara had found an unopened box of tissues, most of which I'd reduced to scattered, soggy clumps of scrunched-up grief.

'Do I call the police?' I asked them when there were no tears left in me.

Tara looked to Damien.

'I don't know what they can do, to be honest. If the police say he left for Manchester, then...' He shrugged.

But did Jay leave for Manchester?

I shivered as if icy cold fingers trailed down my spine.

Jay did this to Sebastian as a warning.

I swallowed as my grief was overshadowed by fear.

He let himself in to the cottage in the dead of night. Did he watch you? Did he think about pouring the acid that's missing over your face as you slept?

Oh God...

'If it makes you feel better, call the police. But without any evidence, I doubt they'll do anything. Especially if Jay is in Manchester now,' Damien reasoned.

'Sophie, I need to go as I have to get ready for work,' Tara apologised, 'but Damien will bury Sebastian if you want?'

I swivelled the bar stool to face the bi-folding doors that opened out onto the back garden and the Atlantic Ocean beyond. I questioned whether Sebastian would want to remain here forever.

Without you.

At that moment, I knew I would never stay here. I would sell the cottage and leave Jay's dreams, Jay's promises and Jay's deadly threats behind me.

I shook my head. 'No,' I mumbled. 'He's coming with me when I leave.'

Tara gazed at me as if I had lost my mind.

'I want him cremated,' I explained.

She nodded, giving me a sympathetic smile. 'That makes perfect sense.'

Damien cleared his throat. 'Look, my shift doesn't start until 2 p.m. Why don't I take Sebastian to the vet for you?'

'No, I'll do it,' I replied.

He raised his eyebrow at me.

It was then I realised I must look deranged. I was an ugly crier at the best of times, but Jay's assault on Sunday had left bruising, now compounded by swollen, puffy, bloodshot eyes and a raw, red nose from repeatedly blowing it.

'I think you might be better staying here and getting some rest,' he persisted. 'I think it will just traumatise you even more. If you want, I can ask the vet to see if they can determine what happened?'

'Okay,' I reluctantly conceded, fighting the compulsion not to let Sebastian go. 'Thank you,' I added, looking first at Damien, then Tara.

I gently wrapped Sebastian in the mohair blanket and, kissing him, forced myself to release him into Damien's arms. Jay had robbed me of my family and now he had taken Sebastian from me. What would be next?

* * *

A few agonising hours later, I was still awaiting a return call from the police. I had called them when Tara and Damien left to report Sebastian's suspicious death.

My phone finally rang. It was an unknown number.

'Hello,' I hurriedly answered.

'Hi, Sophie?'

'Yes,' I replied.

'Hi, this is PC Gareth Davidson, calling about your cat's sudden death?'

'Yes, thank you,' I answered, breathing a sigh of relief.

'From the notes here, you believe someone poisoned him?'

'Yes. My husband, Jay Bradley.'

'Ahuh,' he replied. 'I checked the records, and he's in Manchester? He went there last night after the police escort back to the family home,' he evenly stated. I could hear the scepticism in his voice.

'Yes, I know that, but he has keys to our home.'

'He signed in at the agreed police station in Manchester at 8 a.m. He also provided an address where he's residing until tomorrow when he returns for his court hearing on Thursday morning.'

'Yes, and he could have poisoned Sebastian—'

'Sebastian's the cat?' he interrupted.

'Yes,' I replied, frustrated that he wasn't taking me seriously. 'Jay could have poisoned him and then driven up to Manchester?'

I heard him sigh. 'I'll come out and look around if that makes you feel better?'

'Please,' I immediately answered.

'But it won't be for a few hours,' he advised.

'No, that's fine.'

I disconnected the call and turned to the CCTV camera in the corner of the lounge.

I walked over to it and stared up at the black round orb. The surveillance system was disconnected on my phone. However, as the admin password holder, Jay could have disabled my iPhone, while his was still operational.

Are you watching me, Jay?

The initial fear I felt at this thought evaporated as anger coursed through me.

Did you watch me sobbing hysterically as I held Sebastian's body? DID YOU?

I stared into the camera, willing him to be watching me. To see not fear, but pure, unadulterated rage in my eyes.

You haven't succeeded, Jay. I'm not dropping the charges.

You've taken Sebastian from me. So now, I have nothing left to lose.

37

Consumed by grief, I didn't notice the hours fade away. Even the midday sun and unblemished blue sky eluded me, obscured by the grey shadows, surrounding me like ravenous spirits devouring all light.

A knock at the door by the police dragged me out from the darkness that consumed me.

I followed PC Davidson around the cottage as he diligently checked the doors and windows, realising that he was only here to reassure me. He suggested that the second bi-folding door was left open by accident. As he pointed out, the key was on the kitchen counter. As for Sebastian's death, he had refuted my suggestion that Jay was in any way involved because of logistics: he was in Manchester. PC Davidson also agreed with Damien's suggestion that the lilies could have poisoned him.

'The vet is performing a toxicology test you say?' he questioned, as he stepped out of the front door.

'Yes,' I answered as he turned to face me. 'To determine whether Sebastian was poisoned and if he was, whether it was a natural toxin, such as the lilies, or if it was a household chemical.'

'How long before the results?'

'By the end of tomorrow or Thursday.'

He nodded. 'I'm sure you'll find it was the lilies. They are toxic to cats, and if he wasn't used to coming outdoors, well...' He paused, giving me a sympathetic look. 'Or you might find he digested a poisoned mouse or ant bait. I've come across that before.'

I didn't reply. My gut feeling was that Jay was instrumental in Sebastian's death.

PC Davidson looked across at the lilies. 'You can see they've been disturbed,' he pointed out.

I could see for myself that something had been digging around them. But it could have been foxes or other cats, not necessarily Sebastian.

What were the odds that the first time Sebastian escaped, he died from poisoning?

'Look, I think it was just coincidence that your cat managed to get out,' he reassured me. 'You have nothing to worry about regarding your husband, he's in Manchester until tomorrow evening, and will be checking in at the police station in Truro when he returns.'

I stared at him, feeling anything but reassured.

'Can I ask you something?'

'Go on,' he warily invited.

'If I wanted to protect myself from an intruder, or...' I faltered. 'My husband?'

He nodded.

'Can I keep a knife on me or something like a baseball bat under my bed?'

I was fearful if I defended myself against him, I would end up in prison, like other female victims who tried to protect themselves from their abusive partners. Instead of being buried by the state, which would have been their outcome if they hadn't killed their abuser, they ended up incarcerated. If I didn't have some weapon at hand, I would be powerless to fight him off, ending up another statistic. I couldn't stop thinking about the missing hydrochloric acid.

How do you defend yourself if someone throws acid over you?

He raised his eyebrow at me as he rubbed his hand over his sandy-coloured receding hair, not liking the implication of my question. 'Look, I wouldn't be thinking like that. Anything that's premeditated will get you arrested.'

'So, I can't keep a knife under my pillow in case he lets himself into my home with the intention of killing me?'

He cleared his throat as he broke away from my gaze. 'To be clear, you can protect yourself using an object as a weapon in the "heat of the moment", but I am advising you not to have a weapon on you that you wouldn't ordinarily have in that situation to avoid it becoming pre-planned.'

I frowned at this statement.

'Such as a knife on your person or in the bedroom. Or a baseball bat under your bed. Now, if you were in the kitchen and grabbed a knife to defend yourself, that's different. It's not premeditated.'

I remained silent.

How was I supposed to protect myself without being seen as the assailant?

'If someone enters your property without your consent, you can protect yourself without waiting for them to attack you first. But...' He faltered as he held my confused gaze. 'You must stop attacking the intruder once you are no longer in danger. And whatever you do, do not pre-plan an attack. If you believe someone is intending to enter your home without permission and hurt you, you need to involve the police.'

Someone? Not someone, my husband... And I have involved the police.

'Do not take matters into your own hands,' he insisted.

I nodded. 'Thanks for clarifying that for me.'

'Right, well, if you have any other concerns, call us,' he concluded.

'Actually, I do. The security cameras in the cottage,' I began. 'I can't access the account and I'm scared he's watching me.'

The look in his eye was enough for me to know he thought I was completely paranoid. 'When I read the case notes, it said that the surveillance cameras are down?'

'Yes, but maybe Jay shut it down, so there was no footage of him assaulting me, and he has now turned the cameras back on? I can't tell if he has blocked me from the account, or if it is genuinely down. He's the account administrator,' I explained.

PC Davidson sighed. 'You could ring the company that installed it?'

'I did and left a voicemail. They haven't come back to me.'

'All right, when I get a chance, I'll call your husband and check it out.'

'Thank you,' I said, relieved. 'When?'

'If not today, then tomorrow,' he said.

'Where will my husband be staying on Wednesday evening?' I asked as he started to walk away.

He stopped and looked back at me. 'He said a hotel in Truro.'

'You spoke to him?'

He nodded. 'He was adamant that he never returned here last night after the police escort. That he understands his bail restrictions.'

I felt sick. I was certain Jay would have been the model citizen when he talked to him.

Why wouldn't he be?

And if he understood his bail conditions so well, why did he flagrantly break them when he parked outside for fifteen minutes glaring up at the cottage? At me?

'He also made it quite clear that he has no intentions of coming near you or the property again. That whatever the outcome of his court hearing, he's staying in Manchester.'

I remained silent.

Unconvinced.

'I'm telling you this to reassure you. Rather than you living in constant fear, looking over your shoulder, while your husband moves on,' he explained. 'Or thinking about carrying a knife, which carries with it a four-year prison sentence or an unlimited fine, or both.' He shook his head at me. 'Whatever you are thinking, don't! That's my advice. He's moved on, you need to as well before you injure yourself or someone else.'

I wanted to scream at him: *How? How do you move on when your husband has threatened to kill you? When your husband is biding his time, assuring the police that you're not at risk from him? He's the good guy in all of this, and you're just the irritating, hysterical woman spitefully making a drama out of a minor domestic.*

'When I talked to him, he sounded genuine. He wants the hearing over with to put it all behind him,' he added to appease me.

Of course, he would say that to you... I would have said exactly the same thing.

Another thought came to me.

Maybe he has moved on romantically.

I recalled the text I'd read on his old Nokia phone from Rachael while he was held overnight by the police. Did that mean he would let go of his hatred of me? I doubted that very much. Not when my actions had blown our relationship up, exposing it for everyone to see.

'Look, Sophie, think on about what I've said,' PC Davidson advised.

I looked at him, itching to leave and get on with some genuine policing. He was in his late thirties, five foot eleven, slim but muscular and exuding self-assurance.

'Have you ever been terrified? Not just scared, but I mean terrified?' I found myself asking him.

His expression confirmed my suspicion.

'No, I didn't think so. Well, I am, and my husband, who you say has moved on, did that to me. He's left me feeling like this. I'm not acting irrationally or crazy when I ask you if I can protect myself, I'm terrified he'll come back and kill me and there's nothing I can do about it.'

'As I said, he's in Manchester at the moment, he'll be back here for the court hearing and then he'll return to Manchester. He won't be coming near you,' he said, repeating his assurance.

I wanted to ask him if I could hold him to that but realised it was pointless.

I watched as he drove off, convinced he thought I was deranged and delusional.

Maybe I was?

* * *

After PC Davidson had left, I took his advice and rather than sitting, waiting for my world to end, I decided to take some defensive measures. I called a solicitor's firm in Truro and explained my situation. The receptionist booked me for an urgent telephone consultation with their domestic violence specialist, Karen Hodgson, to start the legal process. She calmly explained that I would appear before the Truro County Court and Family Court to apply for an Occupation Order and a Non-Molestation Order to protect me from Jay coming near me or entering our home. The law firm would also deal with my divorce as the marriage had irretrievably broken down, which was an understatement. I felt relieved that I had someone on my side. She had listened with compassion but primarily with professionalism. She was the reassuring antithesis of my emotional, knee-jerk state of mind.

When the call ended, I felt reasonably reassured. Karen had all the details she required and would update me as soon as she had confirmation of the court hearing date for the Occupation Order.

I realised I had a voicemail from an unknown number while I was talking to my solicitor. I pressed play. It was from Tina, the victim support officer. She would visit me at 10 a.m. tomorrow.

I shakily breathed out. It was all happening. I couldn't believe I wasn't even three weeks married, and yet, I was instructing a solicitor to proceed with a divorce against my husband.

Nor did you expect him to be on police bail after assaulting you, Sophie.

I tried to push all thoughts of Sebastian away, knowing it would disempower me. Jay knew Sebastian was my weakness, which was why he'd killed him. I had no doubts at all where he was concerned. Regardless of the fact, the police didn't believe me.

Or want to believe me?

* * *

Neither the police nor the security company came back to me about whether Jay had activated the security cameras, so I'd booked into a hotel in St Ives for the night, not prepared to risk Jay watching me or, worse, letting himself in – again. To prove that the police were wrong and that I wasn't mad.

It was now 9.47 a.m. I was in my hotel room at the Boskerris, waiting for Tina. Not that I wanted to see anyone. Or have someone else elicit an opinion on my life – my failings. I just needed to get to tomorrow and the outcome of Jay's court hearing. That was all that concerned me – and the necropsy results. However, my solicitor had called to inform me that she had scheduled a hearing at Truro County Court and Family Court at 3 p.m. I was to meet her at the court fifteen minutes beforehand.

* * *

'I'll be staying here tonight as well. It's just after what happened to...' I stopped myself.

Tina nodded. She was sitting across from me in my hotel room.

Starting to feel myself get upset, I dropped my gaze to the coffee and biscuits on the small table between us.

Neither of us spoke for a moment.

'I'll be at Jay's hearing tomorrow, so I'll ring you to let you know what happens.'

I looked at her, not quite understanding why.

'If he is released, then he has every legal right to return to the family home.'

'Oh...' I mumbled.

'You can't be there,' she added. 'You will have to leave. That's why I'm here to help you find somewhere to go.'

I shook my head. 'No, I'm fine.'

She looked surprised. 'Do you have alternative accommodation?'

'An officer spoke to Jay yesterday and said he would be going back to Manchester.'

'Maybe he will, or maybe he'll change his mind tomorrow dependent on the hearing?'

Her suggestion made sense.

'My solicitor is applying for a temporary Occupation Order at court this afternoon to prevent him coming back to our home.'

'Yes, that's wise,' she said. 'And you're not thinking of dropping the charges after what happened to your cat?'

'No. Why do you ask?' I questioned, surprised.

'Because most of the victims I deal with drop the charges at the eleventh hour.'

'Why?'

'Because they believe that their partners will change, or they haven't got the strength like you to stand up to them, fearful of reprisals.'

I shook my head, refuting her assertion. 'Believe me, I'm not strong.'

'He killed your cat as a warning to intimidate you into dropping the charges, and you're not. You're still going ahead.'

'You really think he killed Sebastian?' I asked, shocked at her clinical statement.

She held my startled gaze. 'One hundred per cent.'

I could feel tears threatening to humiliate me. Aside from Damien and Tara, she was the first person to suspect that Jay had killed Sebastian to scare me.

I swallowed, willing myself not to cry. 'Thank you, Tina... For believing me and supporting me. I feel like I've got someone on my side now. The officer who came out to my home yesterday completely dismissed the notion. He didn't even take me seriously when I suggested Jay might be watching me on our security camera system that he had set up.'

Tina raised her eyebrows at my comment.

'That's another reason why I booked in here,' I explained.

She nodded. 'I can't answer for that officer, and he might not be versed in the full details of your case like me. I've dealt with too many situations similar to yours, and killing your cat to intimidate you is textbook.'

I nodded, as I swallowed back the pain of her statement. Her affirmation that I hadn't imagined that Jay killed Sebastian terrified me.

If he could kill Sebastian, then he could kill you. And he's coming back tonight...

38

When Tina left, I showered and changed into a black skirt suit and low open-toe heels that I had brought with me for the hearing at Truro County Court and Family Court. I was meeting my solicitor, Karen, there at 2.45. The hearing was for a temporary Occupation Order on the property.

She advised me not to speak to Judge Bane unless addressed before entering the small courtroom. The entire process took less than ten minutes. I silently watched as he glanced over some paperwork. Only once did he look at me over his reading glasses, then he resumed flicking through the notes. Karen had disclosed that he would have a copy of the police report and statements. I tried to contain my anxiety and appear as impassive as possible. I didn't want to seem irrational or unreasonable. I was asking for the law to protect me as best it could against my husband. I willed myself not to move as I nervously waited on this late fifty-something, grey-haired, middle-class man to decide my fate. It felt surreal that I could so suddenly lose agency over my own life.

He swiftly granted a Non-Molestation Order for a year, preventing Jay from coming near me, and a twenty-four-hour

Occupation Order. A hearing was scheduled for the following afternoon to discuss an extended Occupation Order. My solicitor said she would have both court orders and the summons for the court hearing served when Jay returned from Manchester by a retired detective they employed for such matters.

The rest of the late afternoon and evening passed in a blur. After collecting more clothes from the cottage, I returned to the hotel and stayed in my hotel room, not wanting people staring at my face. No amount of make-up could completely hide the trauma from the assault.

I should have felt reassured that I had a temporary twenty-four-hour Occupation Order until the second hearing tomorrow afternoon. But I found myself unsettled by Tina's words. That she believed Jay was likely responsible for Sebastian's death, but that he could potentially walk back into my life without repercussions and I, the victim, had to hide somewhere. He could resume his life as if nothing had happened and I had to leave: as if I was the guilty party. She shared that she had recently separately rehoused two women and their children after their abusive partners walked from court with a police restraint order and occupation rights to the family home.

Dawn brought with it fear of the unknown. I hadn't slept, too anxious about the day ahead and terrified of the prospect of seeing Jay.

Jay's hearing in the magistrate's court was scheduled for 9 a.m.

He and I were both to appear before a judge in Truro County Court and Family Court at 12 p.m. I was horrified, knowing I would be in the same room as Jay. It seemed cruelly sadistic to me that I would be in such proximity to the man who had assaulted me – threatened to kill me. Karen had assured me that he wouldn't be able to intimidate me in the courtroom.

But what about outside the building or as you enter?

The fear of him approaching me, speaking to me and maiming me had me terrified. I was meeting my solicitor in the waiting room, which meant I would be entering and leaving alone as Karen had other court hearings.

I forced myself to eat breakfast in preparation for the day ahead. Unsurprisingly, I had no appetite, nor had I had one for the past few days, surviving on adrenaline and fear. Food had lost its pleasure, as had life, and the toast and honey I slowly chewed could have been gruel for all I cared. I simply ate to stop myself from disappearing.

Agitated and nervous, I paced up and down in my hotel room, glancing out at the glorious day beyond my reach, until Tina called me as promised to update me on the outcome of Jay's hearing. I hesitated before answering, acutely aware of the impact the court's decision would have on my life.

'Hi,' I tentatively answered.

'Hi, Sophie?' she questioned.

'Yes, it's me,' I replied.

'Well, Jay's court hearing has now concluded, and they released him with a fine—'

'A fine?' I interrupted.

'It was a first-time offence and he pleaded guilty,' Tina explained.

Her heavy words crashed around me.

'The police insisted on a Police Restraining Order, which they granted for a year,' she continued, pushing through my stunned silence. 'You said you have a twenty-four-hour Occupation Order which ends this afternoon?'

'Yes, at the end of the day. But I'm back in court at 12 to apply for an extended order.'

'Okay. And, if you don't get it extended, what will you do?

Because without one, he has the right to walk back into the family home this evening.'

I was too stunned to reply.

'You do have somewhere to go if that does happen?'

I could hear the genuine concern in her voice.

'Sophie? Tell me that if you don't get an Occupation Order this afternoon, you will leave if he decides to continue living in the property rather than return to Manchester?'

'Yes,' I answered.

Regardless of an extended Occupation Order, if the vet's report evidenced Sebastian's death was intentional, I wasn't going to wait around for Jay to break the order: I would be gone.

What good is a piece of paper to you? He will have killed or physically harmed you before it hits the police's radar.

His threat that I was lucky it was just water and not acid he poured over my face tormented me, making me terrified to walk outside. Jay didn't have to throw it: he could pay someone. In as much as he didn't have to be the one who killed me. His caustic words came to mind: *'Make no mistake, one call is all it takes. I'll have them hunt you down, torture you and then fucking kill you, and no one will know.'*

'I hope you don't mind me saying this,' Tina began, interrupting my turmoil, 'but I was shocked when I saw him as he didn't seem your type. I couldn't match the two of you together. And...' Tina faltered, unsure whether to continue.

'Go on, you can say it,' I said. I had already had a feeling about what Tina was reluctant to share.

'Well, he's an odd-looking little man, isn't he? Clearly, from his dyed blue-black hair and clothing, he has serious issues with growing old.'

I found myself smiling at her observation. She was an ex-detective inspector who would have dealt with enough people in her line of work to see someone for who they were and not who they pretended to be.

Why couldn't you have seen through him at the beginning, Sophie? Why?

* * *

I sat in a small room off the waiting room with my solicitor rather than risk being intimidated by Jay before the court hearing. I felt numb with terror at the prospect of sharing the small courtroom with him and whether he would abide by the Police Restraint and the Non-Molestation Orders after the hearing. Or if he would follow me as I left the court building and—

I stopped myself going down the rabbit hole – again.

Perhaps PC Davidson was right, and I was simply torturing myself while Jay had accepted his actions and moved on. When he'd called me earlier, he'd told me that Jay claimed he hadn't even checked the security system to know whether it was still down. Again, he'd suggested I talk to the security firm. But that wasn't the point. It was evident he believed Jay.

'Are you all right?' Karen asked.

I nodded.

'Not long now,' she reassured me. 'And we've been listed with Judge Bane again, which is good.'

I looked at her. My mouth felt too dry to speak, and the suffocating, windowless room added to my anxiety that I couldn't breathe.

'He's already familiar with your case. And he's a more liberal judge than some of the others here.'

I must have frowned as she went on to explain.

'Meaning not as adverse to restricting a man's right to access his home.'

I didn't answer. It was a world I didn't recognise or understand how to navigate. I had never been in a courtroom until yesterday, nor had I ever had any cause to deal with the police.

Karen stood up and went to the door, and checked the corridor.

'Right, Sophie. Time,' she said as she opened the door fully.

I shakily pushed my chair back and stood up. With trembling legs, I willed myself to follow Karen.

We waited, seated in the courtroom with Judge Bane in attendance, for Jay to make an appearance. Five minutes in, and he was still a no-show.

Twenty minutes later, and Judge Bane addressed me: 'I see that Mr Bradley has had two police escorts back to the family home to collect his possessions. Is that correct?'

'Yes,' I answered.

He nodded as he looked back down at the paperwork before him.

'I will grant you an Indefinite Occupation Order until the sale of the property.'

'Thank you,' I replied.

My solicitor thanked the judge and stood up to leave.

I followed Karen, not quite sure what had happened.

Once outside, she turned to me. 'I have never known a judge hand out an Indefinite Occupation Order,' she confided.

'No?'

'No,' she answered. 'Typically, it is six months or, if you are lucky, a year.'

'So why has he granted such a generous order?'

'Because your husband had complete disregard of the law and for Judge Bane. He flagrantly ignored the court summons, which the judge looked upon unfavourably. He didn't even have the respect for the court to send legal representation in his place.'

He's above the law, that's why.

'I recommend you change your locks ASAP,' she advised.

'I'll book an emergency locksmith,' I said.

'Good,' she replied.

Whatever euphoria I first felt at the unprecedented judgement had dissipated with the knowledge that Jay was out there, somewhere, a free man. I knew that an Indefinite Occupation Order wouldn't protect me from him. Nor would changing the locks.

'He's disappeared, hasn't he?' I questioned.

Karen sighed. 'Seems that way. He's not on police bail, which means he doesn't have to report his whereabouts to the authorities. He's free to go wherever he wants, as long as he doesn't go near the family home, or you.'

'But he doesn't know about the Indefinite Occupation Order, so how would he know he's not allowed back there?'

'And that's why you're changing the locks. You needed this court order first to be allowed to legally prevent him from entering the family home.'

We walked along the corridor towards the waiting room in silence.

I assumed Karen was already thinking about her next client. She proved me wrong: 'Do you have any idea where Jay could be? So I can get this order served on him?'

I looked at her as I thought about the answer to that question.

I shook my head. 'I have no idea,' I said, trying to keep my voice level. But inside, I was petrified.

He knows exactly where you are, Sophie. But as for him, he's disappeared. You'll always be watching your back, wondering where he is and if he's coming for you to finish what he started.

You have no choice now. You need to go ahead with your plan.

39

I leaned back on the bed against the plump, starched cotton pillows in my room at the Radisson Blu Hotel at London Stansted Airport and slowly exhaled, closing my eyes. I couldn't believe I had made it after nearly missing the flight from Newquay Airport at 5 p.m. to Gatwick Airport. When I landed at Gatwick, I transferred to Stansted Airport by taxi for my direct flight the following day.

I had executed my plan after I'd disconnected the confirmation call outside the court building from the vet that Sebastian had died of poisoning from a chemical found in certain fertilisers and drain cleaners. I had questioned whether to call the police but accepted it would be futile. Jay had convinced them he had driven straight to Manchester, despite evidence to the contrary on my credit card statement, which detailed a transaction for a hotel in Truro for the Monday evening of Sebastian's death. I was annoyed at myself that I hadn't cancelled his card when I'd discovered his reckless spending. Or when he'd failed to transfer me the funds for the Caribbean honeymoon and guitar bought in Manchester. I subsequently reported the card as stolen to prevent further transactions. However, if I had cancelled it earlier, I would never have known Jay had stayed overnight in Truro when Sebastian was poisoned. Even with this proof, I suspected the police would dismiss it.

What difference would it make? It wasn't as if they could bring him in for questioning: he had disappeared.

Instead of reporting the vet's findings to the police, I had immediately booked my flights, airport hotel room and car hire during the taxi journey back to Eastcliff Cottage, where I'd waited for an emergency locksmith to arrive. The locksmith was late and consequently threw me off my tight schedule, but I couldn't leave without the locks changed, as I was fearful Jay would return and potentially damage my possessions while I was out of the country.

My direct flight from Stansted to Poitiers-Biard Airport was tomorrow at 12.40 p.m., where I would collect a hire car. My plan was simplicity, in essence. I would stay at the two-hundred-year-old property owned now by my mother, once headquarters for the French Resistance, remaining for as long as it took to guarantee my safety. The only people who would know my whereabouts were the elderly couple who had looked after the property for over forty years. Camile and Francois resided in the nearby picturesque village of Saint-Loup-Lamairé, where bullet holes from Nazis remained in the walls of some of the houses, a stark reminder of the past.

Camile and Francois knew nothing of my breakup with Ben, let alone my marriage to Jay. They were only aware of our absence caused by my father's untimely death. They had agreed to continue maintaining the property until my mother decided whether to sell or keep it. Francois tended to the one-and-a-half acres of land, and the buildings, while Camile kept the main house clean and aired. While I'd waited at the cottage for the locksmith, I had rung Camile, explaining I would be arriving the following afternoon, much to her surprise and delight. I was confident that Camile wouldn't think to contact my mother, taking me at my word that I needed someplace isolated, away from distractions in the UK, to finish my current manuscript.

The French house had been my father's love, his retirement project, not my mother's. There was a small vineyard and a cellar with antiquated wine-making equipment, which he had intended to utilise, and a gite. The property, named 'Winter's Retreat', was situated high up on the riverbanks of the river Thouet, which continued a mile or so down through the idyllic village of Saint-Loup-Lamairé, and for my father, who was a keen fishing man, it was perfect. My mother had reluctantly conceded, preferring someplace further south. The property my father had bought was too isolated, too far west, hidden away in the Deux-Sèvres department and Nouvelle-Aquitaine region, and over four and a half hours north by car to Paris for my mother's tastes.

It was over a year since I'd been there – with Ben. We'd visited my parents for a long weekend, which was when my father gave me the key. I didn't understand the significance at the time but questioned now whether he had some prescient feeling that I would need to run and hide there. The following week he had died.

But thank God Mum didn't sell it. Otherwise, where else would you go?

I swallowed back the pain, still raw, from his sudden death. I didn't know whether I dared to face the ghosts of my past. I had never planned to return.

Until now...

* * *

It was a glorious late afternoon. Everything had gone to plan. I landed at Poitiers-Biard Airport, collected the hire car and left behind the western city of Poitiers, known for Notre-Dame la Grande, its medieval Romanesque church, with its intricately carved facade that was lit up late at night during the summer months with a spectacular light show which was breathtakingly beautiful. I pushed the memories of summer evenings spent with my parents and Ben in awe of the magical light show to the back of my mind as I drove away.

I took the N149, turning off for the ancient fortified town of Parthenay, surrounded on two sides by the river, where I picked up provisions from the supermarket and stopped for a coffee at the cafe I frequented when here with my parents. I sat outside, alone, in the late-afternoon sunshine marvelling at the fact I was here. That I had managed to get away from Jay.

I still hadn't told Grace and Anna what had happened or that I was no longer in Cornwall. I couldn't bring myself to speak about it until I knew I was safe from reprisals from Jay. Or his friends. There would be plenty of time in the future when it was all over to tell them. But, for now, I didn't want them talking me out of being here all alone. I needed to see this through by myself.

I left Parthenay and continued on the D938 towards the village of Saint-Loup-Lamairé, too caught up in memories of time spent here to appreciate the glorious yellow fields bursting with sunflowers or the tall, tree-lined, shaded roads or the quaint, old houses and shops in the flower-filled pavements and town squares of the villages of Viennay and Lageon.

Thirty minutes later, I crawled through the hamlet of Crémille, smiling at an elderly, wispy, white-haired woman sitting in her small garden shelling peas on her lap who paused to stare at me as I attempted to inch around the dangerously tight bend, trying to avoid the centuries-old stone-built corner house. I left the hamlet with the car intact, turning off onto the mile or so dirt track that led to 'Winter's Retreat' with a mixture of unease and excitement. It was bittersweet: I was thankful for the bolthole, but I didn't know whether I wanted to be back here so soon – if ever.

I caught sight of my plaster cast as I swung the car around the steep bend that dropped down, leading to my parents' isolated property. The cast was due to be removed in three weeks. It made no difference if I attended a hospital here in France, or back in Cornwall.

I pulled into the drive and parked the car in the double-open garage. Attached to the garage, overlooking the river, was a large workshop containing gardening equipment, bikes and other items stored by my parents. I melancholically noted the four yellow and blue kayaks suspended from the garage ceiling.

I got out and deeply breathed in the heavily scented air. The river Thouet seemed to roar at my arrival. I walked over and looked down the grass embankment to the fast-flowing water where I had enjoyed summers swimming and kayaking. I had once loved spending time here. Now, without my dad, I wasn't so sure that would ever be the case.

I walked back up and paused to look at the orchard off to my right, filled with pear and apple trees and the sound of bees blissfully buzzing in the lazy late-afternoon sun.

I knew I was procrastinating, putting off the inevitable.

I gathered my groceries and bags and walked up the worn stone steps to the wrought-iron gate at the top. I pushed open the creaking gate and walked into the mature garden, stopping at the gite. I tried the handle, but the door didn't open. My father kept the key to the gite in the reading room in the main house. He had chosen to use the gite as his study rather than the reading room, with its French doors opening out onto the garden and view of the dense trees on the opposite side of the river.

The gite was a work in progress. The electricity and water were connected, but the small kitchen and bathroom still had to be fitted. My father's imposing, burgundy leather inset desk sat in front of the two large windows overlooking the river. It was perhaps the best view from the property, his reason for claiming it as his space. He had a separate landline connected to the gite, so he could take business calls rather than bothering my mother in the main house. The mobile signal at the property was non-existent, and there was no Wi-Fi to connect to as my parents didn't feel the need for it, so a landline was critical for contact with the outside world. Not that I expected to use it, as I had no one to call aside from Camile in an emergency.

I glanced over at the large wood store on the opposite side of the gite, stacked full of logs in preparation for the cooler months.

Will you still be here to use the wood-burning stove? Maybe...

I headed across the well-maintained garden to the large, four-double-bedroomed house. I glanced at the living-room French doors that led out onto the patio as I walked around to the front of the house. I looked over at the stone wall that separated the garden from the steep embankment feeling a stab of sadness. Francois had put the wooden garden furniture under the decorative grapevine arch by the circular stone wall that jutted out like a castle turret so I could sit and watch the river fiercely thunder below. I knew it would be Camile who had instructed him to place it there as that was where my parents spent their summer evenings. I had such happy memories here with them, Liv and Ben. Of us all sat outside drinking wine, eating dinner, laughing, arguing and just enjoying being together. We would sit, enthralled by the bejewelled night sky, the constellations glittering like a diamond map above us. I never failed to be in awe when the space station passed so clearly in the night sky overhead.

They were happy times, Sophie... And now?

My hand trembled as I unlocked the door straight into the kitchen. I was grateful for the cool air that greeted me. The property had an external heat pump which kept it cool in the summer and warm in the winter. I looked around the room. Nothing had changed. I waited, expecting to hear someone. But there was nothing but silence.

I dumped my bags and picked up the note left by Camile on the kitchen table. There was also a fresh baguette and a bowl of seductive cherries beside it. She detailed that she had left some supplies in the fridge. She also suspected from the scraping noise this morning while she was here that there might be *fouines* living in the attic. *Fouines*, also known as beech martens, were widespread in most regions of France, preferring cover in attics, old barns and outbuildings. They reminded me of a ferret with a long body and tail, short legs and black eyes with an inquisitive face. However, the *fouines* had a distinctive white patch under the chin and chest. Camile suggested Francois investigate the attic next Saturday when he came to cut the grass. I had postponed his coming tomorrow as I knew he would already have sorted the garden earlier today.

Relieved, I slowly breathed out. I was safe now.

* * *

That evening, I sat outside watching the river below as I drank wine and absorbed my surroundings. My father's possessions were still here. My parents hadn't officially moved to France, but they had shipped over a considerable amount of furniture and personal belongings. I had to compartmentalise and push all sentimentality to one side.

If I didn't, I suspected I would drown in the sadness I felt at being alone here, in the place my father so loved, and where he died. I needed to focus and use the house as intended. There would be plenty of time later to grieve my father's loss and reminisce.

I watched as a turquoise kingfisher with an ochre chest swiftly descended, dived into the Thouet and ascended with whatever it had caught. I marvelled at the beautiful bird as it flew off with its catch. I recalled my father telling me the first summer they had purchased the property that the kingfisher was allegedly the first bird to fly from Noah's ark after the flood and that its breast is the orange setting sun and its blue back the sky. I smiled as I thought of how much he loved this place. It was his piece of heaven, and if he could have chosen anywhere to die, it would have been here.

I automatically turned and looked back at the house. The upstairs windows were all shuttered. I glanced at what we called the 'French room' because of the interior design. The previous Parisian owner had handsomely paid for the room to be decorated in a traditional design; the walls padded and covered in predominately blue flower-patterned material. It was the largest room in the house, with two aspects: one overlooking the vineyard to the side of the property and a view of the gardens and river to the front. It was my parents' bedroom.

It *had been* their bedroom. I doubted my mother would ever come back. With my father gone, she had no reason to.

My bedroom was at the front of the property, next door to the French room. I had checked all the other bedrooms, aside from my parents, unable to bring myself to enter where my mother had found my father. The access to the attic was through a door in their room, which led upstairs to the overhead space.

I turned from the house and looked across at the dense woods on the opposite hill. I couldn't be more isolated if I tried, hidden from everyone and everything. I closed my eyes and let the abundant noises of the river and the excited chitter-chatter of the birds as dusk descended drive away all thoughts concerning my mercurial missing husband.

For the first time in weeks, I was at peace. I could relax and relish in the fact I had escaped.

I've defeated you, Jay. You can't hurt me now.

40

The long, hot days blended into one another, and before I knew it, the weekend had passed, and it was Tuesday evening. I had arrived last Friday and filled my days without opening my laptop and working on my manuscript. The house felt too much like a mausoleum with my father's possessions everywhere, his presence in every shadowy corner, for me to be relaxed enough to write. It was as if he was still here, waiting for me to find him. The book he was reading was left open in the living room with his reading glasses.

I questioned whether I had drunk too much the last few nights, noticing that items weren't where my parents had last left them. It was as if someone had picked them up to inspect and then discarded them. Even my father's book had been disturbed: the last page he read was lost now to me.

Is that you, Sophie? Drunkenly and morbidly looking at Dad's possessions in the dark because they are too much to handle during the sober, sun-filled days?

The loneliness was starting to get to me. I doubted every noise and creak of what had once been a silent house that now seemed to have sensed my presence. It groaned as if its wooden bones ached from age – or loss.

Doors I thought I had closed suddenly sprang ajar as if the house was teasing me, tormenting me, trying to terrify me. I would find windows open, the shutters banging in the wind that whistled down the valley on the tail of the roaring river. Now even the *fouines* had started to stir at night, creeping across the attic floor, assuring me I wasn't alone.

I stared up at the bedroom ceiling above me. The house was silent – for now. I sighed, rolled over and closed my eyes and waited.

* * *

I woke up with my heart thundering like a cornered wild animal. Blood deafeningly pummelled through my rigid body to my ears, eclipsing any other sound. My damp vest top clung to my sweating, cold skin.

Where are you? Christ! Where the hell are you?

It was pitch black.

Too black.

Petrified to breathe, let alone move, I stared into the impenetrable blackness trying to make sense of my unfamiliar surroundings. It took another moment for my brain to catch up with my body's location.

You're in the French house, Sophie. In the bedroom next to the French room? Your parents' room. Remember?

I shallowly breathed out as my heart refused to decelerate.

So why is it so dark?

I reached out for the light switch to flick the bedside lamp on. I clicked, but there was nothing. I clicked it a couple of times. It was dead.

Damn!

I fumbled for my phone and found it on the bedside drawers next to the lamp. It was 3.03 a.m.

The haunting hour.

I swallowed, attempting to dislodge the fear that had a stranglehold over me.

Stop being ridiculous, Sophie! There is no such thing as ghosts.

I could hear myself challenging that assumption.

Isn't there? So, who switched off the hall lamp then?

I stared in the direction of the open door leading out to the landing. I had left the lamp on the hall table switched on in case I needed to get up and go to the bathroom.

So why isn't it on?

I blinked, straining my eyes to see. But with the wooden shutters closed, the suffocating, blinding room was like a sealed coffin.

Christ, Sophie! Stop it! You'll kill yourself from fear.

I then thought of my father. He had died from a 'silent heart attack' in the epitome of health. Had something terrified him to death here?

I shuddered at the thought.

So much death in this house, Sophie.

I felt icy terror take my breath from me.

Before my father, the Parisian owner who had decorated the French room had died here after falling down the stairs and breaking his neck.

Annoyed with myself and my foolish thoughts, I clicked the torch app on my phone and swung my bare legs out of bed, forcing my feet on the cool wooden floor.

There has to be an explanation for the hall light.

I padded over to the open door, stabbing the beam of light towards the hall table, intentionally avoiding the treacherous wooden stairs leading down to the yawning black abyss. I walked over to the lamp and clicked the switch. Nothing happened.

Damn it!

I knew the electrics were outdated; my father had planned to have the entire house rewired with the circuit board replaced, but death had beat him to it.

I forced myself to walk downstairs into the lurking shadows to inspect the circuit board in the utility room. I stared at it, not understanding the outdated system. I conceded that Francois would have to check it out, and worst-case scenario, an electrician.

I turned and left, the torchlight guiding me back through to the kitchen. I caught sight of the illuminated kitchen table and noticed the half baguette I had left was gone.

How the—?

I glanced at the empty bottle of wine.

What the hell, Sophie?

I shook my head at myself and made my way back upstairs to bed, and plugged my phone into its charger.

Damn it!

It wasn't charging. The electricity was off which meant a power cut or—

I stopped myself going there.

I switched the torch app off. I didn't want to waste the remaining charge left on the phone.

I slowly exhaled, willing my overactive imagination at bay. Every moan from the two-hundred-year-old house conjured up ghosts from the past. I thumped my pillow in frustration, then turned over.

I suddenly jumped.

Something was above me, moving around.

Someone!

Cortisol flooded my body as I grabbed my phone, not that it

would do any good as there was no signal. The landline phone was downstairs in the living room. I needed to get to the phone.

Holding my breath, I waited.

There it was again.

Oh God... Is that footsteps above me?

Terrified, I shut my eyes, not wanting to see what was lurking in the blackness.

My mind had gone into a tailspin of 'what ifs' because it felt like someone was watching me from the densest corner of the room.

Get it together! No one's in your room!

Trembling, I breathed out. But the acknowledgement failed to reassure me, lying in the dark, alone, in the middle of nowhere in a foreign country, with something moving around above me: stalking me, for it felt predatory.

What have you done, Sophie?

I strained to hear. Then I wished I hadn't heard it: a noise, but not from overhead. It was coming from the French room next door. There was another squeak, this time louder, like a door opening.

The attic door? Was someone hiding in the attic?

It was followed by a floorboard creaking. My mind went into overdrive, as did my heart, which thundered in anticipation of what would follow.

Silence ensued. Heavy, pregnant and malevolent.

I knew then that someone was there. I could feel it with every inch of my body screaming at me. Someone was waiting in the blackness for me to fall asleep.

And then what do you think will happen?

Not prepared to find out, I slowly sat up to avoid the mattress squeaking and swung my legs over the double bed, holding my phone in the palm of my plaster cast with my fingers wrapped around it, and made my way towards the open door.

I then blindly felt my way down the stairs with my one good

hand. I quietly stepped into the kitchen and headed to the living room. Moonlight streamed in through the French doors, guiding me to the telephone on the small table. Hand trembling, I picked it up, but a deathly silence greeted me. It was dead.

Then I heard it again. Another creak from above me.

Oh God. Is he here?

Or maybe someone has been living here while it has been left empty?

It was a possibility.

Oh God, Sophie... What have you done? You're in the middle of nowhere. No one will hear you scream. Not this time...

My heart thundered in my chest like a trapped animal, trying to burst out.

Trembling, I retraced my steps back into the kitchen. I fumbled to open the drawer of the handmade wooden dresser, fear making me clumsy. I needed the key to the gite.

Then something caught my attention. It was a distinctive smell: petrol.

What the...

Desperately, I scrabbled around in the drawer.

Oh God...

I noticed my car keys weren't in the bowl on the wooden dresser where I had left them. Someone had taken my car keys. Someone had disconnected the phone line. That someone had brought petrol into the house. Why?

You know why!

Jay's words came back to me, reminding me of his promise: '*Make no mistake, one call is all it takes. I'll have them hunt you down, torture you and then fucking kill you, and no one will know.*'

I was paralysed with terror. I could feel myself struggling to breathe.

What have you done, Sophie?

I inwardly screamed at myself to stop catastrophising and to take control.

This is what Jay wants, for fear of him to paralyse you.

Spurred on, I scattered everything in the drawer until my hand felt a key. It was the key to the gite. My father had a second phone line in there. I could call the police.

I paused, hearing another movement. Closer this time.

I lurched to the front door to unlock it. My good hand blindly searching for the front door key, but it wasn't there in the lock where I had left it.

Someone has removed the key.

Oh God, Sophie! Oh God...

Then I remembered the key to the French doors in the reading room. My parents kept it on one of the bookcases in there. Whoever was here wouldn't necessarily know that.

That is if the key is still there.

I ran down the hallway to the reading room at the other end of the house, knocking my left shoulder and plaster cast against the wall. The blow forced my phone out of my hand.

'Damn! Damn! Damn!' I cursed as I scrambled around on the wooden floor for it.

I could hear the objectionable creak of the top stair step as someone's weight descended on it.

Hurry up, Sophie!

I grabbed my phone, clasped tight, with my fingers pressing it against the palm of the plaster cast, and then bolted into the reading room for the bookcase I remembered the key to be on. My right hand felt along the fourth bookshelf until cold metal connected with flesh. Snatching it, I ran to the French doors and groped for the lock before trying to jab the key in place.

Come on! Please...

Another step descended on the wooden staircase. Followed by another.

SOPHIE!

I struggled to get the key in place.

Come on! COME ON!

Finally, I secured it. I held my breath as I twisted it, desperate to hear the click of the lock as it released me.

I threw the doors open.

I didn't dare look behind me.

I didn't want to see who was coming for me, for I knew it wasn't my imagination: I could hear their heavy, ominous footsteps walking down the hallway towards the reading room.

RUN! Run, Sophie!

I ran barefoot, in knickers and a vest top, across the grass to the gite. The bright moonlight illuminated the grounds as the roar of the river rushing by filled the night air. I reached the door, panting. I somehow lodged the key into the lock, twisted it and pulled it open.

Oh my God... Thank you... Thank you!

Beams of light from the large windows overlooking the river seeped into the room. I stumbled over to my father's desk. It was covered in unfinished paperwork. On top of some writing paper lay my father's antique letter opener. The blade glinted under the shimmering, silvery moonlight. I reached for the phone, not wanting to turn around. To see who had followed me.

The line was connected.

Thank God!

I pressed 17, which was the emergency police number to report a crime requiring immediate response.

'Put the phone down,' a voice behind me commanded.

I froze as my blood turned icy cold.

It's him, Sophie! He found you.

'I said, put the fucking phone down. NOW!' he shouted.

I dropped the phone and turned to him, keeping my back against my father's desk.

A French voice was now speaking with some urgency on the other line.

'Cut the fucking call!' he hissed.

'How did you know?' I whispered, unable to hide the fear in my voice. 'I told no one.'

He didn't answer me.

But I already knew. I'd figured it out days ago.

'When you took my phone to add the CCTV surveillance camera app, you installed mSpy to monitor my texts, phone calls and GPS. You tracked every movement I made, didn't you?' I accused. 'But you also watched me on the security cameras? Even though you told the police the system was down and that you wouldn't even think to watch me. But you lied, of course. When I rang Camile from the cottage with my plans to come here, you recorded every word. Didn't you?

He ignored my question.

'Disconnect the phone,' he repeated, not taking his burning black eyes off me as he blocked the doorway. He was holding a metal fuel can and was clutching something in the other hand.

A lighter?

Or a knife?

I couldn't see. Not that it mattered. Not now. No one could help me. Not out here in the middle of nowhere. By the time the police arrived, if at all, it would be over.

Is he planning on burning the house down with your body inside? To get rid of any incriminating DNA evidence that could tie him to you? To here?

But then his passport and phone would place him in France, surely?

He dropped the fuel can and suddenly rushed at me, throwing

me hard against the desk as he reached for the phone. He disconnected it and then threw it out of my reach.

'You kill me, and the police will know it was you,' I challenged. 'The police will trace you by your passport and phone.'

I protectively pressed my left hand with the plaster cast across my body, while my right one surreptitiously reached behind my back to the desk.

He laughed at me with cold eyes. 'You think I'm as fucking stupid as you?'

'They'll know you're here,' I argued. I was stalling for time. I was only interested in how I would make it out: alive.

He shook his head. 'As I said, I'm not as fucking stupid as you! I paid someone to sail me from Falmouth to just off La Rochelle. When I landed, it was two hours by cab. I arrived at Airvault late Saturday night and walked the hour and a quarter here, making sure no one saw me. I waited in the tool room next to the garage until you woke up and unlocked the front door to the main house. Then I sneaked in and hid in the attic.'

'You paid someone to get you into France illegally?' I questioned, shocked.

No one would know he was here.

Oh God...

'Look at all the illegal immigrants making their way by boat to the UK. Surprising what money can buy you, in particular anonymity. Pay-as-you-go phone, so no one traces me. My phone and passport are back in the UK.'

'You mean your new iPhone?'

He simply stared at me.

My fingers touched what I had been feeling for and grabbed it.

'You're one dumb bitch. Do you know that? You really believed you could hide from me?'

I didn't respond as I gripped it tight in the palm of my hand, ready for him.

'You played straight into my hands coming here where it's so remote. Who's going to come and save you now?'

I didn't react. I suddenly felt very calm, as if everything was as it should be. It was always supposed to conclude this way. There was no other possible ending. Not with him. He would hunt me down until the day he finally killed me.

'You always underestimated me, making me feel intellectually inferior. You're right, I have been watching your every move. Did you actually think you could outwit me? I've been waiting for this moment, imagining what it would feel like to finally fucking make you suffer!'

I remained silent as time seemed to slow down.

'Well, who's the dumb fucking bitch now, eh?'

He suddenly grabbed my hair and yanked my face close to his, leering at me.

Startled, I screamed.

'I said, who's the dumb fucking bitch, now!' he snarled as he pulled back his other hand.

I glanced down and realised it was a knife he had been holding. I felt the blade, paradoxically ice hot, separate my skin as it seamlessly slid into my abdomen.

I gasped with shock.

It wasn't supposed to be like this... This wasn't the plan.

'Stupid fucking bitch! You thought you could win! That you could take everything from me? ME? I fucking did everything for you! And that's how you repay me?' he yelled as he pulled the blade out.

I couldn't breathe as white exploding pain erupted, spreading out from my stomach like a virulent poison.

I looked down at my white vest top at the blood seeping across the material.

He readied himself to strike again as he tightened his grip on my hair, making me groan out in pain as he pulled the knife back.

Sophie? You're going to die... SOPHIE!

I screamed a guttural, primal sound as I brought my hand around from my back and raised it, stabbing him in the neck exactly where I had visualised over and over as he'd raped me. I felt the long, sharp blade of my father's letter opener sink deep into the flesh. I twisted it with the force of every insult, injury and pain he had ever caused me. For the suffering he caused Sebastian. *For his death.*

He grunted, shocked.

Teeth gritted, lips bared, I pulled the blade out with all the strength in my body. Blood immediately spurted from the wound. His eyes filled with horror as he realised what had just happened.

He hadn't expected it.

Of me.

I repeated the action, cutting into his left internal jugular vein again. Exactly as I had imagined.

He let go of my hair, collapsing to his knees as blood sprayed everywhere. His hands grabbed at my legs, scrambling, frantic.

'I lured you here!' I spat. 'I knew you would follow me. Didn't you question why I handed your passport to the police to give to you? You thought you were in control, hunting me down, whereas I baited you. I brought you out of hiding to finish it. Why do you think I didn't cover the cameras or get the company to remove you as the account administrator once I had the Occupation Order? Why?' I repeated as I stared down at his pathetic, shocked face. 'I wanted you to know everything I was planning. Down to my phone call with Camile about coming here. But you knew about this place anyway. Didn't you? Because you had gone through my drawer in my study desk. You had found the key to the property and the letters and postcards my father used to send me when he was over here in the box I kept.'

He stared in disbelief as he tried but failed to stop the blood that ran like the rushing river Thouet outside through his fingers.

'How does it feel?' I questioned as I forcefully kicked him away from me. 'To be powerless?'

He fell backwards and lay, surprised and helpless, staring up at me, fingers pointlessly pressed against the gaping wound.

I watched, numb, as life, ugly and messy, ebbed from him.

Then overwhelming relief came.

It's over, Sophie.

My plan had worked. I had lured him out with the perfect location to commit murder and get away with it. And he took the bait. Otherwise, I would have been watching over my shoulder for the rest of my life.

Until... Until he finally chose to come for me and end it.

I dropped the antique paper knife. I had executed PC Davidson's advice that the crime should not look premeditated. I had killed an intruder – my husband – in self-defence with a makeshift weapon I had picked up from the desk to protect myself. Not that Jay, or the police would ever know that I knew it would be on my father's desk as I ran to the gite instead of running out into the woods to hide. I had spent eighteen long summers here and knew this land, knew the river. I could easily have hidden from him.

I heard the sirens in the distant night air. Shivering, I sank to the ground with my fingers pressed against my bleeding abdomen as shock took hold.

You've survived, Sophie... You survived.

Raw, I stared at his body as his pulse faded to nothing. I swallowed back the tears.

It could have been me lying there. Dead.

'Freeing yourself was one thing, claiming ownership of that freed self was another.'

— TONI MORRISON, *BELOVED*

EPILOGUE

'So,' Dominic concluded, 'how do you feel that we're coming to the end of our last appointment?'

'Okay,' I replied. I was better than, okay. I was happy. Something I had never thought possible.

He nodded.

'I don't have to spend my life looking over my shoulder, waiting for him to—' I stopped myself. We had spent nearly a year dealing with the past. There was nothing left to say.

I had started seeing Dominic as my therapist shortly after I'd returned to the UK with my mother and sister. They had flown to France as soon as the police had contacted them and were by my hospital bed when I came around from surgery. I had returned to Broughty Ferry with them, grateful for their support while I'd processed the horrors of what happened to me.

Both of them had felt guilty for what they had seen as their abandonment of me. But Jay had played his hand well. It was classic abuser behaviour, isolating me from them. He had hit on Liv on my wedding night, suggesting he'd married the wrong sister.

Terrified to tell me, for fear I wouldn't believe her after drunkenly throwing herself at Ben at our father's funeral, she'd kept silent.

Divide et impera had been Jay's tactic, dividing us to conquer me by twisting what I had confided in him about my family. He had destroyed my letter and sent a typed one filled with abhorrent lies and unforgivable accusations: cruelly, that my mother was responsible for my father's death. As for the eye-watering language he'd used to describe my hatred for Liv – blaming her for ending my relationship with Ben and trying to sabotage my marriage – it was no surprise they had cut me off. I had shared with Liv and my mother some of the trauma I had suffered at Jay's hands, but not everything. I wanted to protect them from the worst parts, not wanting to add to the guilt they already felt at cutting me off. So, I chose to see a therapist to talk about the darker aspects of Jay's abuse that I couldn't bring myself to disclose to them.

I had struggled with whether to see Dominic, but decided that maybe a male perspective would help me understand how I had got it so wrong. Our sessions over the weeks, followed by months, had helped me understand that I was in no way responsible for Jay's actions or behaviour towards me. All I was guilty of was reeling from my father's unexpected death, followed by Ben's sudden abandonment of me weeks before the altar. That chink in my armour left by grief and abandonment had allowed that man – that psychopath – into my life.

It was that simple. That unfortunate. That unfair.

But PC Davidson's advice had paid off. When the paramedics had arrived, Jay was pronounced dead at the scene. The subsequent French police investigation found no evidence that what had happened that night was premeditated – on my part. The only person who knew the truth about that night was dead. I felt no guilt at what had happened and consequently didn't feel the compulsion to tell anyone, not Dominic or my mother and sister. It was simple, either Jay lived, and I died at his hands, or I survived by — I stopped myself and touched the silver memorial ring I always wore with Sebastian's cremation ashes suspended within it, reminding myself I had no choice.

But as for Jay, the evidence against him was damning. He had followed me, precisely as he'd said, illegally by boat to France. His passport, Nokia flip phone and new iPhone were locked up in his Transporter, parked up in Falmouth. The police had traced its location by its registration details.

There was no obvious answer as to why he became so abusive towards me. Jay was hardwired that way long before I met him. Testified by his long-term ex in Manchester, who I had tracked down with the help of a private detective. Everything Jay had told me about her was a lie, and the converse was true: he was the cheat, not her. He had inveigled his way into her life, her children's, iceberg hopping from one relationship to another, leaving behind another shell-shocked, battered woman for his new victim.

She had somehow endured eight years of Jay's abusive behaviour until he met me that night in The Slaughtered Lamb in Clerkenwell. It was a sliding doors moment for both of us. She was terrified to kick him out for fear of reprisals. I had saved her life, she'd said, when he'd upped and left her for me. When he'd returned to Manchester to buy the guitar, he'd visited her in an attempt to rekindle their relationship, telling her his marriage was over. That I had cheated on him, and he had left me, and that he regretted ever leaving her, and was returning to Manchester to live. This news horrified her, unlike her reaction to his death, which was pure relief. She knew she was safe now for the first time in years.

As for the band touring the States, it was all a lie. They had never heard of him. His ex had said he had been in a local band but later found out that he'd slept with the singer's girlfriend just before he'd met me, and they'd kicked him out.

'It must have been cathartic selling all his guitars and the Transporter?' questioned Dominic.

I looked at him and nodded. 'I admit it felt good.' I had donated all the proceeds and the fifty thousand pounds left of his inheritance that I had discovered, to a women's shelter in Truro. As for the belongings he didn't want me to see in the attic; there was nothing there but junk. It was all about control.

'And Eastcliff Cottage?'

'Sold for an astronomical price.'

'What do you plan to do?'

'Buy someplace by the beach in Broughty Ferry close to Mum and Liv. As for my second home, I'm thinking Connecticut or New Hampshire in New England.'

He raised his eyebrow at this news.

'Mum sold the French property, and so we need someplace to go. And now that *Winter's Child* has gone to production...' I shrugged, feeling embarrassed by my sudden good fortune.

Dominic smiled.

I watched as he picked up my latest book from the table between us.

I had submitted the overdue romance book first before writing my next book in six weeks: a psychological thriller – *The Perfect Husband*. It had gone to a bidding war, and the foreign rights had been sold to twenty-two countries, along with the film rights.

'Relationships?' he asked.

'No. Not yet,' I answered. 'Remember you said at our first session, I had to wait a year before I began dating again?'

'Yes, that's right.'

'I have someone in mind, though,' I replied with a faint smile.

'But first, my mother, Liv, Grace, Anna and I are taking a two-week road trip along the west coast of the States to celebrate.'

'The success of your new book?'

'Something like that,' I answered as he handed my new book over for me to sign.

ACKNOWLEDGMENTS

Thanks especially to my mother and sister for their amazing support and for coming back into my life. I am truly indebted to you both. Thanks to Francesca, Charlotte, Gabriel-Myles and Ruby. Thanks to Peter Dempsey for all your invaluable support.

Thanks to Tom Avitabile, without whom I would never have contemplated writing this book. Particular thanks to Pamela Letham, Gill Richards, Tina Stapleton and Suzanne Forsten for being there at the time when I needed them most.

Thanks to Michelle Lumsden, Lynn Baillie, Karen Knox, Kim Robinson and Vicki Smith.

Thank you to Kirstie Long, Victoria Damrell, Ayo Onatade and Caroline Raeburn for all your support.

Thanks also to Clare Usher, Amir Assadi, Daniel Ruddick and Seth Kitson for all your legal expertise and support.

Thanks to Michael Proudlock and the domestic violence charity, SomeOne Cares. Thanks to Northumbria Police.

Thank you to my fantastic literary agent, Annette Crossland.

Thanks also, to all at Boldwood Books, for your brilliance and being such an amazing team. And in particular, Caroline Ridding for being such a fabulous person to work with and an exceptional editor – thank you.

MORE FROM DANIELLE RAMSAY

We hope you enjoyed reading *The Perfect Husband*. If you did, please leave a review.

If you'd like to gift a copy, this book is also available as an ebook, large print, hardback, digital audio download and audiobook CD.

Sign up to Danielle Ramsay's mailing list for news, competitions and updates on future books.

https://bit.ly/DanielleRamsayNews

ABOUT THE AUTHOR

Danielle Ramsay is the author of the DI Jack Brady crime novels and other dark thrillers. She is a Scot living in the North-East of England and was previously published by Hodder & Stoughton and Avon.

Visit Danielle Ramsay's Website:

https://www.danielle-ramsay.com

Follow Danielle Ramsay on social media:

 twitter.com/danielleramsay2
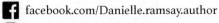 facebook.com/Danielle.ramsay.author
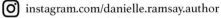 instagram.com/danielle.ramsay.author

THE *Murder* LIST

THE MURDER LIST IS A NEWSLETTER DEDICATED TO SPINE-CHILLING FICTION AND GRIPPING PAGE-TURNERS!

SIGN UP TO MAKE SURE YOU'RE ON OUR HIT LIST FOR EXCLUSIVE DEALS, AUTHOR CONTENT, AND COMPETITIONS.

SIGN UP TO OUR NEWSLETTER

BIT.LY/THEMURDERLISTNEWS

Boldwood

Boldwood Books is an award-winning fiction publishing company seeking out the best stories from around the world.

Find out more at www.boldwoodbooks.com

Join our reader community for brilliant books, competitions and offers!

Follow us
@BoldwoodBooks
@BookandTonic

Sign up to our weekly deals newsletter

https://bit.ly/BoldwoodBNewsletter

Printed in Great Britain
by Amazon